Danger from the Woods

Count von Wolfram trudged into the great hall, the sound of his hobnailed boots echoing off the vaulted ceiling. Spotting Adele in the gallery, he called, "Something terrible has happened. Young Magda Brandt, Wilhelm Brandt's daughter . . . they found her on the edge of von Wolfram property, attacked by wolves . . . they don't know if she will live."

He heard a gasp, but it was not from his imperturbable sister. A figure moved from behind Adele, and he saw Elizabeth Stanwycke appear at the high carved railing.

"A wolf attack?" she said. "How terrible!"

Her face in the gloom of the gallery was pallid, her expression concerned, but she didn't swoon, or in any way demand attention for her own shocked sensibilities. He headed for the stairs and strode up them two at a time, forgetting his weariness.

"I am so sorry, Miss Stanwycke," he said. "I should not have spoken so abruptly, but I thought Adele was alone, and—"

"No need for an explanation, Count," she said, the whole line of her body stiffening. "I was shocked but I will not wilt, I promise you."

They stared at each other for a moment, and he remembered coming upon her in the night in the library, where she had no right to be. The proud tilt of her chin was familiar to him already from the encounter, and the determined set of her lips. He supposed he should be happy she was no swooning lily, but he was not sure so much strength and resolution was best suited to his own purposes, or whether a more timid sort who would stay in her room and hide would have been better. Too late now, anyway. They would have to see.

Awaiting the Moon

Donna Lea Simpson

BERKLEY SENSATION, NEW YORK

THE BERKLEY PUBLISHING GROUP
Published by the Penguin Group
Penguin Group (USA) Inc.
375 Hudson Street, New York, New York 10014, USA
Penguin Group (Canada), 90 Eglinton Avenue East, Suite 700, Toronto, Ontario M4P 2Y3, Canada
(a division of Pearson Penguin Canada Inc.)
Penguin Books Ltd., 80 Strand, London WC2R 0RL, England
Penguin Group Ireland, 25 St. Stephen's Green, Dublin 2, Ireland (a division of Penguin Books Ltd.)
Penguin Group (Australia), 250 Camberwell Road, Camberwell, Victoria 3124, Australia
(a division of Pearson Australia Group Pty. Ltd.)
Penguin Books India Pvt. Ltd., 11 Community Centre, Panchsheel Park, New Delhi—110 017, India
Penguin Group (NZ), Cnr. Airborne and Rosedale Roads, Albany, Auckland 1310, New Zealand
(a division of Pearson New Zealand Ltd.)
Penguin Books (South Africa) (Pty.) Ltd., 24 Sturdee Avenue, Rosebank, Johannesburg 2196, South Africa

Penguin Books Ltd., Registered Offices: 80 Strand, London WC2R 0RL, England

This is a work of fiction. Names, characters, places, and incidents either are the product of the author's imagination or are used fictitiously, and any resemblance to actual persons, living or dead, business establishments, events, or locales is entirely coincidental. The publisher does not have any control over and does not assume any responsibility for author or third-party websites or their content.

AWAITING THE MOON

A Berkley Sensation Book / published by arrangement with the author

PRINTING HISTORY
Berkley Sensation edition / February 2006

Copyright © 2006 by Donna Lea Simpson.
Excerpt from *Awaiting the Night* copyright © 2006 by Donna Lea Simpson.
Cover art by Vittorio Dangelico.
Cover design by George Long.
Interior text design by Stacy Irwin.

ISBN: 0-425-20849-4

BERKLEY SENSATION®
Berkley Sensation Books are published by The Berkley Publishing Group,
a division of Penguin Group (USA) Inc.
375 Hudson Street, New York, New York 10014.
BERKLEY SENSATION is a registered trademark of Penguin Group (USA) Inc.
The "B" design is a trademark belonging to Penguin Group (USA) Inc.

PRINTED IN THE UNITED STATES OF AMERICA

10 9 8 7 6 5 4 3 2 1

For my mom, who made sure I learned to read early and always had books.
For Michael, whose steadfast encouragement carried me through many doubts.
For Cindy, whose enthusiasm is inspiring.
For my friends—you know who you are!—who were there for me always.

But most of all, this is for Mick, who believed in me before there was any reason to, and who gave me the courage to dream, when the world says dreams are for fools. I don't know what I would have done without so much faith and support in good times, but more importantly, in difficult times, when having someone to lean on is all that kept me from losing hope.

Chapter 1

"I'VE HEARD that werewolves roam the woods of Germany," Elizabeth Stanwycke said, peering out of the carriage window into the dark wintry woods, the snow on the ground gleaming in the moonlight.

The swift intake of a breath was her companion's only response, and she glanced over at Frau Katrina Liebner. The elderly woman glared at Elizabeth and let out that breath; it crystallized in the air, as frigid as the woman's expression.

"You will please not say such foolish things when we arrive at Wolfram Castle," she said, her tone gruff and her lightly accented voice holding anger. "Ever!" She huddled in her black cloak and frowned over at Elizabeth in the dim light cast by a carriage lamp, her dark eyes snapping with annoyance.

"I . . . I was speaking in jest," Elizabeth said, weakly. She shoved her gloved hands together deep in her muff to warm them—with no success—as she tried to decide in this instance if silence or an explanation would be better. As kind as Frau Liebner usually was, her occasional descents into anger mystified Elizabeth. "All thinking people," she said, carefully, steadying herself as best she could against the jolting of the carriage along the deeply rutted road, "know that werewolves do not exist. Those tales are merely folklore, bedtime stories told to frighten little children." When she received no response, she continued, "We are in the year 1795, not 1595!"

"The year does not matter," the woman replied. "Do you think because we live in this modern time that the eternal has ceased to exist? That is blasphemy. There are in this world, Elizabeth, phenomena that we do not understand, and more that we will never comprehend. Their invisibility to our mortal selves does not negate their existence, and they are not a matter for jest."

Elizabeth sighed. She sat back in a shadowed corner of the carriage, out of the pale yellow gleam of the lamplight. "I was not denying the presence of the deity, Frau Liebner, nor was I postulating a worldly view denying all that is preternatural. All those old horror tales, though—ghosts and witches and werewolves—those are just myths."

But the woman had turned her face away, effectively ending the conversation, so Elizabeth was left to direct her thoughts elsewhere, to her destination, Wolfram Castle, and her new position as tutor to Charlotte von Wolfram. It was a wrenching and difficult decision she had had to make, to leave England and travel all the way to Germany, but the opportunity had presented itself just when life in England had become insupportable for her. If not for the friendship of Frau Liebner and her miraculous offer of such a valuable position, Elizabeth didn't know what she would have done. Her reputation in tatters, her life turned upside down and with nowhere else to go, it had been a godsend.

But she rejected such morose reflections on past mistakes and past pain as a shivering excitement rose in her. They were close, Frau Liebner had told her an hour or so ago, as the sun began to descend and the moon to rise; though it was only late afternoon, the sun set early in January. If not for the full moon they would have had to stop for the night, but the shimmering orb made travel possible, so they had continued the last several miles toward Wolfram Castle.

The woods had closed in on either side of them a half hour ago as they moved past a village and toward the castle, and though it would seem to be monotonous, miles of unbroken forest on either side of them, Elizabeth found the mysterious timberland strangely compelling. It was so very different from what she was accustomed to, and what she had grown up with.

Her home in Dover, the misty seaside, the fishing boats . . . all had receded into the hazy past and lived only in her memory now. She might not return for years, or even decades. Or ever. That part of her life was over, and she must be brave in her new adventure.

Though she felt that she should be composing her thoughts for the evening ahead when she would meet her employer, Frau Liebner's nephew-by-marriage Graf Nikolas von Wolfram, the scene outside the carriage window tugged her attention away from those serious thoughts. Optimistic by nature, she hoped this journey would take her to a better life, and she was determined to achieve peace, at the very least, and respect if she could earn it.

And yet since they had started on this lonely highway a few hours before, she had been feeling, along with the increasing excitement, uneasy. Perhaps it was just how towering the pine trees were, how deep the glittering snow, how bright the full moon. That luminous disk, following them with a wise gaze, was behind her sudden unfortunate mention of werewolves, for every bit of folklore she had ever read had mentioned the full of the moon as the time humans transformed into the beasts and roamed, looking for prey.

Ridiculous, she supposed, but still there was some vestigial fear that haunted even the most pragmatic of people. Who in their life had not experienced the fear of the unknown?

In her case her whole future life was unknown to her at that moment, and she was poised on the lip of a precipice, the yawning chasm before her, black and unexplored. But fear would not defeat her. Friendship was proven in moments of great need, and Frau Liebner, for all her idiosyncrasies, had been a fast friend. This position was a boon, a treasure; it was the promise of a new life far away from those who had hurt her. As they crossed the channel and began their land journey at Ostend in Belgium, she and Frau Liebner had often spoken of that immediate past and the deception she had suffered, but in recent days the subject had paled in comparison to the future, and that was how it should be. The journey—difficult and dangerous as it was at times—had become a symbol to her as she turned away from old torment and betrayal toward her new life.

"I still don't think I understand everything about the

household yet," she said, breaking the enveloping silence. "Your nephew, Graf Nikolas von Wolfram ... should I address him as 'my lord,' or 'Graf,' or ... ?" Elizabeth trailed off.

Frau Liebner shrugged her heavy shoulders and huddled back into her cape. "In my brother-in-law's time, the head of the household was addressed by the English who visited as Graf von Wolfram, but Nikolas ... he has been educated in many other places—Italy, France, Greece—and so has other ideas. His title is 'count' in your language, you know, and so I presume he will be known to you, but I have no doubt Adele will tell you how to address them, for she is very correct."

"Adele ..." Elizabeth searched her memory, for she and Frau Liebner had spoken about the entire household on the journey, though not in depth. "That is Graf von Wolfram's eldest sister, Gräfin Adele von Wolfram. I suppose I would call her 'countess' in English, though I think I will stay with German titles until I am told otherwise."

"She is the keeper of the house, also. She was accounted the beauty, you know, of the sisters, but it was her younger sister Gerta who married."

"Gerta ... uh ... von Holtzen? Am I right? That is her married name." Frau Liebner nodded and Elizabeth continued. "She lives at Wolfram Castle, too, and ... has two children."

Frau Liebner was silent for a long moment, and Elizabeth thought perhaps she had drifted to sleep, but then she spoke again. "Eva and Jakob are her children, twins, you know, but they are at school, and have been so for some time. Nikolas is their guardian, as well as of Charlotte, your charge. Christoph—Charlotte's brother—has reached his adulthood, though I would say he acts still the boy in his refusal of any career. And yes, Gerta is a widow now; her husband has been gone fifteen years, almost. Very fragile, she is, frail." Her tone was full of sadness.

"How did her husband die?"

"It was a very bad time. We do not speak of such things," the woman said, harshly, biting off each word.

Silence reverberated in the dim carriage. It was not the first time Frau Liebner had roughly ended a conversation by simply saying, "We don't speak of such things," and Elizabeth wondered if she would be continually putting her foot wrong in conversation at Wolfram Castle. She would try to be retiring, though it was not in her nature, as it was vital to her comfort not to offend in her new position. Natural curiosity, a good imagination, and enthusiasm, all traits she had thought worth cultivating, were her enemies in this instance. They were not suitable qualities for a tutor, nor for a governess, as she had discovered in her last position.

"This road is getting worse," Elizabeth said to change the subject, having to toss her muff aside and hold on as the carriage bumped and jostled.

"Yes, it is this weather. It has likely thawed and now the road has frozen again into these ruts." Frau Liebner was holding on grimly, too, but then her expression softened, her wrinkled face in the lamplight wreathed in a broad smile. "When the snow is new we use a sleigh. I remember Viktor, when we were young and first married; how proud he was of his new sleigh! It was painted red and was very beautiful, with brass lanterns and silver fittings on the horses. He would take me driving for hours with the fur robes piled high in the sleigh, and then we would come back and he would warm me in front of the fire."

Elizabeth was silent, for Frau Liebner rarely spoke of her husband, now gone for many years. But as always the woman didn't say any more, lapsing into abstracted silence.

They went on for another ten minutes, and then the carriage slowed and the incline became more pronounced. It was the signal Frau Liebner had said would mean they were approaching Wolfram Castle.

"We must be getting close," Elizabeth said, as the carriage jolted and jounced.

"Yes, we are . . ."

Frau Liebner's comment was interrupted as the carriage jerked and skidded sideways, the lamp spilling oil as the wick went out and the body of the carriage creaking with an ominous shudder as it came to a halt at an angle. Frau Liebner shouted a guttural expletive in the sudden blackness, and the door popped open at that moment, the faulty latch Elizabeth had noticed earlier giving way.

"I'll find out what's wrong," Elizabeth cried and crept from the relative darkness of the carriage to the moonlit road.

The vehicle shuddered and creaked as the team of horses kicked and pawed in their traces and the driver shouted at them in unintelligible German. The carriage tilted precariously, having slid too close to the embankment that edged the road.

"What's wrong?" Elizabeth shouted, staggering sideways on the slippery hump of frozen snow and mud. "What happened?"

She attempted to regain her footing, but the driver ignored her as he tried to bring his team into control. The horses were wild, stamping and bellowing, rolling their eyes, steam puffing from their nostrils. Elizabeth, who had been trying to approach the driver, was forced back by fear of the giant beasts, and as she stepped back she slipped and fell, her skirts and cloak wrapping securely around her legs until she was bound as tightly as a babe in swaddling clothes.

As if she were separated from her body, she could hear her own voice whimpering in fear, and the snort and whinny of the horses. Peril, as close as the slashing hooves of the horses, loomed above her and she rolled out of the way, crusty ice tearing at her gloved hands. But then she saw, crossing the road in front of the pawing horses, a woman, as slim and lithe as a young girl but most definitely an adult woman. Silvery hair unbound and streaming, her body naked, gleaming pale in the moonlight like a ghost, she bounded down the embankment and raced into the dark woods on the other side.

Elizabeth only had the chance for a brief glimpse of the spectral vision before a horseman on a black steed, his cloak billowing and a hood concealing his face, galloped across the snow-coated road. She struggled to right herself as he skidded down the other side and crashed into the woods after the woman.

"Help her!" Elizabeth screamed, unwinding her skirt and struggling to her feet. "Help that poor woman," she cried again, striding to the side of the carriage near the driver, who was finally succeeding in getting his team under control.

He glared at her with dark eyes, his pouchy face a mask of incomprehension.

"Help her!" Elizabeth shrieked, pointing into the forest, but he just stared at her and then shouted a string of unintelligible syllables. "Oh, for pity's sake *I'll* do it, then." She found the path in the moonlight and crunched down the embankment, her feet breaking through the crust of icy snow. Her bonnet obscured her view, and she pushed it back impatiently.

"Elizabeth!"

She turned and gazed up the hill; Frau Liebner sat in the doorway of the carriage, moonlight illuminating her pale face in stark contrast to the gaping maw of the dim vehicle.

"I have to go," Elizabeth cried, pointing into the forest. "There's a woman, a girl . . . she seems to be in trouble . . ." It was useless to try to shout out the case from such a distance, and she gave a cry of exasperation and turned and stared back into the woods; could she see movement in the black depths? Or was it her imagination?

Hands grasped her from behind and she gasped, struggling as the driver tried to haul her back up the hill toward the carriage.

"No," she shouted, twisting away from him. "No, there is a woman . . . *eine frau ist in die* . . . oh, what is the word for forest?" she cried out in frustration, speaking to herself, for there was no one else to understand. "How do I say she needs help?"

Her world abruptly turned upside down as the stolid driver hoisted her over his shoulder and carried her toward the hill.

"No!" she yelled and twisted in his grasp. "Let me go!"

But he was strong and determined and urged on by Frau Liebner, who sat in the doorway of the carriage screeching commands in German. As much as Elizabeth struggled, she could not break free until he had scaled the embankment and deposited her at Frau Liebner's feet.

Elizabeth, gasping and out of breath from her ordeal, rose and dusted the snow off her dress hem as best she could and with what dignity she could muster. "What was the meaning . . ."

"Do not *ever* go into the forest alone!" Frau Liebner said. She had her ebony cane, the knob a silver wolf's head, and she banged it on the ground for emphasis with each word. "Never!"

Shaken, Elizabeth gazed at her friend as she peeled her saturated and torn gloves off her cold, scraped hands. "You don't understand. I saw a woman running across the road and a man on a horse behind her, chasing her. She may be in danger, and I wanted—"

"If what you say is true," Frau Liebner interrupted, glaring up at her, "what could you do to a man on horseback?"

"It's true, I saw her!" Elizabeth cried, latching on to the doubt in Frau Liebner's remark. "Do you think I'm fabricating this? She was . . . she was . . . running." She turned back to gaze at the fringe of deep green conifers at the bottom of the steep decline and gesticulated, trying to illustrate, frustrated by Frau Liebner's lack of action. "The horseman, he was mounted on a black steed and had a cloak on, and he rode down the side of the embankment into the forest," she said, pointing to the trail left in the pristine snow, "and galloped into the woods after her."

"And what would you do if you were so fortunate as to find them in the dark of the forest? It is likely a matter between husband and wife, and so not our affair."

"But—"

"No!" Frau Liebner held up one hand. The driver stood to one side and watched their exchange. When Frau Liebner spoke to him again, waving her cane, he nodded and mounted the driver's seat. "Help me get in, Elizabeth. I have hurt my head and need your aid."

"But that poor woman, she wasn't even properly dressed—she'll freeze to death."

"We cannot help her," she said.

Her tone was grim, and Elizabeth stared at her, the wrinkles on the woman's face pronounced in the moonlight, shadows concealing her eyes. Clouds had gathered around the moon like a shawl drawn around a dowager, but instead of concealing the moon they radiated a clearer light, casting a more even, diffused glow. By that blue-white light Elizabeth could see that there was indeed a trickle of blood on her friend's forehead; she tossed her spoiled gloves into the carriage and drew a kerchief out of the small purse she had tied to her waist. She dabbed at the wound, stanching the flow.

"I don't understand," she said in a low tone, shivering with the cold. "How can we ignore what just happened? That woman clearly needed our help."

Frau Liebner pulled herself to her feet and began to climb back into the carriage, grunting with the effort. "Help me, Elizabeth!"

Elizabeth offered her arm, and they managed to get back into the black interior of the carriage, the faint smell of lamp oil all around them. No sooner were they settled—the faulty door latched as securely as possible—when the team started and the carriage bumped and jounced, eventually finding the rutted path on the highway again and moving on.

"I don't understand," Elizabeth repeated, unable to leave the subject alone. She tried to right her bonnet as best she could, tying it under her chin again and tucking in a stray wisp of hair. "Why can't we help that poor woman? Who knows what that man intends? Who knows—"

"Enough, Elizabeth." Frau Liebner's tone was weary. "I have heard enough. I would ask that you not mention this when we arrive at the castle, please. If I feel it is necessary, I will tell of what you saw."

In silence they moved on through the night; Elizabeth no longer gazed out the window but let the darkness of the carriage envelop her. Her subordinate position had never irked her more than at that moment, when she truly felt how helpless she was to do what she wanted, what she felt was right. Would she ever learn not to strain at the traces? Her fate was to do others' bidding, but how hard a fate it seemed when one had an independent spirit.

"Elizabeth," Frau Liebner said. "You are beginning a new life here. Do not begin it badly. Do not make trouble for yourself."

"I won't," Elizabeth said and was surprised to feel Frau Liebner's gloved hand take hers in the dark. "I won't," she repeated, warmed by the old woman's concern. "I promise."

"I would not have you make an unfavorable impression on my nephew. Things at the castle are not always easy. There are many personalities, many people, and some may not have your best interest at heart. I have been away many years, but this I know. Be wary."

With that warning ringing in her ears, Elizabeth settled herself, as hard as it was, to forget the slender, pale figure and her pursuer. There was truly nothing more she could do without the cooperation of Frau Liebner and the driver. It infuriated her and she worried about the woman who would surely freeze to death in hours if she was not helped, but there was not another thing she could do.

The carriage made a final turn and Wolfram Castle came into view, an imposing structure of stone and wood, with two wings stretching back from a central tower. It hugged a flat outcropping on the hillside like a giant predatory bird ready to take flight into the moonlit sky. Elizabeth shuddered and Frau Liebner squeezed her hand.

"I will not desert you, child. This I promise. Always, you can rely on me."

What should have been a comforting reassurance left Elizabeth feeling uneasy. But as they drew close to the porte cochere, and the brooding entirety of Wolfram Castle was not before her, replaced as it was by the view of an open door and lamplight streaming out yellow into the night, her worries eased.

I am not faint of heart, I am strong, brave, and have survived much in my life. This will be no exception, Elizabeth promised herself. *I am not a child, but a woman of intelligence.* She would try to find a way to get help to the woman in the forest, if it was at all possible. But it might not be possible, and she would have to accept that fact.

With the aid of a liveried footman, she descended from the carriage and stood by while two others helped Frau Liebner step out. The elderly woman leaned on her cane and gazed up at the structure, murmuring something in German; she then held out her arm to Elizabeth.

Elizabeth took her friend's arm, but as she began toward the steps up into the castle, a sound in the distance made her skin raise in bumps and the hair at the nape of her neck bristle. She looked over her shoulder. Somewhere in the nearby woods a wolf howled, and even the stolid footman cast a fearful glance into the dark edge of the forest.

"Never mind that," Frau Liebner commanded. "Let us go in together."

They started up the steps, Elizabeth suppressing the urge to accelerate her pace. She would not look foolish, nor superstitious; she was neither and wouldn't give in to mere nerves. At that moment, from the great hall, a woman stepped out onto the landing at the top of the steps. "Tante Katrina," she called out, as Elizabeth and Frau Liebner ascended.

Frau Liebner advanced on the other woman, a slim lady of perhaps forty years with a coiled braid of silvery blond hair worn high on her head. "Adele, how many years it has been?" she said, speaking in her flawless, but accented English. "And still you are slim as a girl."

"Ah, how good that you have come home," Gräfin Adele von Wolfram replied, she too using English.

Elizabeth expected that a familial greeting would follow and the two would embrace, but instead they shook hands, as strangers would on first meeting.

"And this is Miss Elizabeth Stanwycke," Frau Liebner said, drawing Elizabeth forward with a hand at her elbow.

"Welcome, Miss Stanwycke, to Wolfram Castle." She inclined her head, her only form of greeting.

Elizabeth curtseyed but was at a loss for words.

"But your head, Tante Katrina!" the woman exclaimed, reaching out but not quite touching the wound. "What has happened?"

Though Frau Liebner's cut had stopped bleeding, the mark

was still evident on her pale forehead. "It is nothing, Adele, nothing. Please do not mention it again."

Gräfin von Wolfram inclined her head once more, in answer, and then said, "What am I thinking, keeping you standing out here on this cold night? Come in, come in!" She turned and led the way into the great hall. "I trust," she said over her shoulder, "that you had a good journey. The roads are better than they were just a week ago when we had an unexpected thaw."

"You would trust wrongly, Adele," Frau Liebner said. "The roads are terrible! What is Nikolas thinking, not to send out some men to make them better?"

"Nikolas has other concerns," the other woman retorted, her tone sharp.

Elizabeth halted, awed by the cavernous great hall that the Gräfin led them into. Vaulted ceilings soared fifty, or maybe even sixty, feet receding into dimness; gothic arched windows lined the front, the brilliant moon glistening through, making them silver. Along the side of the hall opposite the wall of windows, stone pillars supported an upper gallery, and blood red pennants on posts mounted on the pillars fluttered in the breeze from the open door. Flambeaux lit the chamber, the wavering flames casting ghost shadows across the floors and walls; liveried servants scuttled back and forth, their footsteps echoing.

Though she had been in great houses in England, never had Elizabeth seen anything like this, and she felt as though she had been transported back in time to medieval days. Any moment a knight in armor would stride into the hall claiming it in his own name. When she stopped gaping, Elizabeth met her new acquaintance's gray eyes and unsmiling expression. With all that had gone on, she felt raw and preternaturally aware of everything, every nuance, every voice, every gesture.

The Gräfin, though welcoming, appeared distracted. *"Willkommen,"* she said, opening her arms wide and gesturing to the hall. "Welcome to Wolfram Castle. I hope you will be happy here, Miss Stanwycke. My brother is otherwise occupied at the moment, but I will see to your comfort."

A door slammed somewhere and a susurration of voices echoed in the upper heights of the hall, perhaps from somewhere along the gallery. But Elizabeth's attention was caught by another door opening closer, the light streaming out chasing away the shadows under the second floor gallery and showing her that there were clearly rooms off the main hall, formal reception rooms perhaps, with gothic arched doors of heavy, deeply carved oak.

One of these was the door that had opened and two men came from the room beyond—one of the gentleman older, with a paunch and a gray, balding pate, and the other tall and of middle years, distinguished and immaculately dressed.

"Ah, what a pleasure," one of the men, the older, balding fellow, said in heavily accented English as he approached them. "This must be our new little teacher, and of course my dear sister, Katrina. How long it has been!"

He put out his arms to embrace her, but Frau Liebner merely stuck out one gloved hand and gruffly said, *"Tag,* Bartol. *Wie geht es ihnen?"*

"Ah, you have not changed," he said with a comical look of dismay on his round face. "Always, you are most cool," he continued, waggling a finger at her. "But English, my sister, English, for I have been practicing; I had no English when you last saw me, but now . . . I speak so very well. We have a new little friend in our midst, and I would not exclude her." He shook his sister-in-law's hand and turned to Elizabeth. "Unless you speak German, my dear?"

"A very little," Elizabeth said, taking his offered hand.

He tilted his head to one side and peered nearsightedly at her, as he cradled her hand in his large, knobby one. "So, you are the little teacher. How delightful you are, so pretty. We are fortunate indeed to have you in our midst." He patted her hand and released it.

Such a gracious welcome warmed Elizabeth, and she relaxed.

Gräfin von Wolfram said, "This is Miss Elizabeth Stanwycke, Charlotte's new tutor. Elizabeth, this is Herr Bartol Liebner, my uncle." With a softening expression, she turned then to the taller of the two men, a distinguished and courtly looking gentleman of middle years. He had a mane of silvery white hair drawn back from a high forehead, and he was clad in a powder blue velvet jacket and silver knee breeches. "And this is Count Delacroix, our honored guest."

The gentleman cast her a fond look and turned to Elizabeth, taking her hand and bowing low over it. "Mademoiselle. I am only a poor émigré from the terrible revolt in my land." He kissed the air an inch above her hand. "My lady, the Countess Adele is too kind, for it is I, an exile from my suffering land, who treasures my time in this gallant and stalwart place."

Elizabeth noticed a quickly concealed expression of concern on Gräfin von Wolfram's gaunt face.

"As I said, my brother is this minute busy," the woman said, interrupting the Frenchman's courtly gesture of welcome. "But he will presently greet you properly. Come, and I will see you settled in your rooms, Miss Stanwycke, Tante Katrina."

Her body trembling with exhaustion, her mind reeling from the last hour of strange happenings and this overwhelming welcome, Elizabeth wearily mounted the stairs, the stone steps worn in the center from centuries of feet, following Gräfin von Wolfram and Frau Liebner. They made it to the gallery floor, slowed by the oldest lady's deliberate progress and the heaviness of their winter cloaks, but as they were about to mount the steps to the third-floor bedchambers—the lady of the house explaining that the second floor was taken up with family living areas since the main floor was formal reception rooms—a dark figure slammed out of a room and strode down the hall toward them.

Elizabeth, her nerves jangled by a difficult day, gasped, the sighing sound echoing up through the staircase.

"It is merely my brother, Nikolas," Gräfin von Wolfram said, a tone of reproof in her hard voice. She cast Elizabeth an assessing look. "Nikolas," she said, raising her voice, "we have here our Tante Katrina and new tutor arrived."

The man, dressed in black breeches, black boots, and with a white silk shirt stretched taut over muscular shoulders and arms, looked up and stopped in front of them. His unsmiling face was ruddy, his lips compressed into a single hard line. His eyes were the dark gray of an angry autumn sky, and Elizabeth thought she had never seen such a handsome man in her life.

But it was more than mere good looks that made him attractive. He charged the air about them as a storm does, with electricity, and she felt the same exhilaration, the same anxiety mixed with excitement as she had as a child on the beach, watching a storm approach from sea.

This man was her new employer, the one she would have to impress with her skill and awe with her erudition. And she would have to do all that while ignoring the way he made her heart pound and palms sweat.

How awful.

Chapter 2

FRAU LIEBNER, during their journey to Germany, had described Nikolas von Wolfram as slim and studious, retiring, diffident. Unless the lady's memory was faulty, he had transformed in the years his aunt had been away from a boy into a man of unusual force of character and presence.

His steady gaze locked with Elizabeth's and she could not stop staring, aware that her expression could be seen as unbecoming and forward, but unable to look elsewhere. She could feel the confusion mantling her cheeks with pink, the heat spreading through her body.

Tall and broad shouldered, a lock of raven black hair falling over his high forehead, he was casually dressed, his white shirt loose at the neck, exposing a shocking V of dark hair on a bare chest, the skin pale as alabaster. All of this she had taken in before their eyes met. She had the odd feeling that he had made a rapid assessment of her, too, his gaze traveling her body in the few seconds it took to meet in the hall. He was the first to break their connection, though, as he heeded his sister's abrupt repetition of his name and turned to his aunt. "Tante Katrina, welcome home."

"You have changed, Nikolas," Frau Liebner said with a wry twist to her lips. "I left and you were a boy, but now . . . I would not have known you."

He took her hand and squeezed. "Circumstances have made me who I am." He then turned his attention back to Elizabeth and held out his hand.

She offered her own, but instead of shaking it he bowed and brought it to his lips. It was the merest whisper of a moment, but she felt the warmth of his breath on her naked skin and sighed. He stood, still holding her hand, and their gazes locked again; she saw confusion in his gray eyes, or was that just the mirror of her own emotions? Moments passed.

The Gräfin cleared her throat, breaking the silence. "I was about to show Miss Stanwycke to her chamber, brother, as she is undoubtedly exhausted after such a journey, and Tante Katrina, too, of course."

He released Elizabeth's hand and bowed. "Of course. Excuse me, and excuse my attire, ladies," he said, mopping his damp brow with a cloth he had tucked in his waistband. "Cesare and I—Cesare Vitali is my secretary, Miss Stanwycke— have just been fencing. It is a habit of ours this time of day, for exercise in this frigid season is vital for the spirit and body."

Gräfin von Wolfram, Elizabeth noted, gazed at him and raised her eyebrows. There was some silent communication between brother and sister, but it ended abruptly when the Graf bowed once more and excused himself, heading up the stairs ahead of them, bounding two steps at a time, muscles flexing and bunching under the tight breeches he wore for exercise.

Elizabeth would have sunk down to sit on the step if she were alone, for she felt light-headed and ill. He was nothing she had expected, and her stomach twisted with combating sensations of attraction and repulsion. He was very handsome, but it was in an alarming way; he had dark eyes and hair, a sensuous full mouth, broad forehead, and muscular physique only too evident under his breeches and damp, clinging shirt, and the overt masculinity of him was not reassuring to someone who depended on his kindness for her living. In her experience, such vigorously vital men were not gentle, nor were they forgiving of even the slightest errors.

And yet, his dark good looks and charismatic mien had enkindled a glow within her that she must conquer, for her own benefit. The last thing she needed was to be so attracted to her employer, for that could only mean trouble if he were a man like other men, willing to take advantage of a position of power. But she was stronger than such a weak feminine reaction to an attractive man, and she would maintain a distance. She had learned from the past and would never let herself be vulnerable again.

Stiffening her backbone, she took a long, deep breath. "Shall we go on?" she said and mounted the step, placing her foot in the damp footprint left by her new employer.

Her room, second from the stairs, was lovely, much more than she ever expected in such a large and ancient castle and for a woman in her position—tutor to a young lady of the house. Left alone by Gräfin von Wolfram and Frau Liebner, Elizabeth sank down on the partially canopied bed and gazed around her as she undid the ties of her bonnet and loosened her cloak, welcoming the warmth of the blaze in the hearth.

It was a big room, but not so high ceilinged and fearfully tomblike as she had feared. The walls were covered in ivory fabric, and the bed was draped in the same material. A Turkish carpet covered part of the floor, though the rest was wood, and near the fire were two chairs with a table between them. By the high window, the curtains of which were closed against the darkening night outside, was a table and chair suitable for use as a desk.

On the far wall, barely perceptible in the gloom, was a large carved garderobe, and her trunk had already been placed near it.

How had the trunk arrived upstairs before her? Of course there must be another staircase used by serving staff, she reasoned. In such a large castle there were likely more than just two staircases, in fact, for it was clear from her brief view of it in the twilight that there was a central part to Wolfram Castle, the old stone portion of the castle, but then jutting additions built later, likely, flanked it, spreading like a raven's outspread wings on either side of the main body.

She tossed her bonnet aside and lay back on the bed, closing her eyes. What had Frau Liebner once said about Wolfram Castle, that once you entered, it entered you, too, and never left, always to be a part of your soul? At the time it had sounded like superstitious nonsense, but now she thought she understood. The castle seemed to possess a spirit of its own, a powerful personality much like that of its master.

She blinked and sat up abruptly. It was best to face the truth at once and be done with it; she was powerfully attracted to the master of Wolfram Castle, but it was surely just the fleeting, transitory attraction of purely physical response, enhanced by exhaustion. It was imperative that she eradicate such wayward thoughts from her mind forever if she was to blot out the misdeeds in her past. Giving in to a physical impulse was dangerous for a woman, as she had learned to her everlasting regret. This opportunity, presented to her by the kindness of Frau Liebner, was a chance to cleanse herself of her indiscretions and she would not make the same mistakes over. Only a fool did that, and though she was impulsive and headstrong at times, she was no fool.

She heard an outcry and a scuffle and crossed swiftly to her door, wondering what was happening. But when she glanced out, she only saw a door close down the hall toward the end. Her overactive and weary imagination was making something out of nothing, she thought, closing the door and returning to the bed. If only she had time for a nap, just to cleanse her mind as a mint leaf cleanses the palate, for the jumbled impressions of a long journey, finished by the odd sight of that poor woman in the forest, had left her nerves jangled and raw.

However, she was expected downstairs for dinner, perhaps to meet her student, so she would have no time to calm her frayed nerves. She would, however, try to find peace in establishing herself in her new home and in changing out of travel-soiled clothes. Fighting fatigue, she shrugged out of her heavy traveling cloak and unpacked her trunk, shaking the wrinkles out of her modest wardrobe. She then unpacked her traveling desk, removing her quills, ink, sand, and sealing wax and then her most precious traveling companion, her journal.

She set the journal down on the desk and touched the engraved leather binding, tracing her name in gilt letters on the cover. Had she done the right thing coming all the way to this foreign land? Her English upbringing seemed so far away now, and there was a desolation in wondering if she would ever return. This land was interesting, and she had been welcomed with some warmth, but it wasn't England.

A maid tapped at her door and entered with a pitcher of steaming water. When thanked in English she looked uncomprehending, and so Elizabeth repeated the thanks in her limited German. The maid curtseyed then and answered with a string of words of which Elizabeth only caught a fraction. How she wished she had spent more time with Frau Liebner on the journey learning more than her sparse smattering of German words! She had learned French as a girl, but no other language had been deemed important by her frivolous and flighty mother. It was a failure she vowed she would correct now that she was settled. As she taught English manners, so would she try to be the student, learning German.

Elizabeth stripped to her chemise and washed quickly, shivering in the chill away from the fire. Her pale face, framed by her dark crown of hair, looked ghostly in the mirror, and she was stopped by her own expression reflected there.

"You look," she said sternly to herself, "as if you have been frightened by an apparition. You must calm yourself, for as you know from past troubles you are too imaginative by nature. Frau Liebner was likely right about that poor woman in the woods." She folded a cloth and patted at her neck and cheeks. "It was merely a domestic matter, and as much as you abhor physical correction of a wife by her husband, it is an unfortunate fact of life. Men are brutes." She nodded sharply, happier at the returning color in her cheeks. Talking to herself occasionally had such a salutary effect, for she rarely heard so much sense as she heard from herself.

Men are brutes. Elizabeth rinsed the cloth in the warm water and scrubbed her face, blotting her eyes, trying to rid them of the sleepiness and grime of a long, tedious day. That bitter refrain—*men are brutes*—was the philosophy of Elizabeth's mother, passed on to the daughter, not believed at first but sadly confirmed by unfortunate experiences in the past year. Men, her mother had told her, preferring scandal and gossip over bedtime stories as fit conversation for her daughter, had the upper hand in all of life and cared little for women. They all went on their own way, she had said, taking what they wanted and discarding that which no longer suited them.

Elizabeth, as a child, had understood little of what her mother was talking about, but as she grew and saw the fights between her mother and father, the tears and tantrums, the anger and cold silence, she had begun to see. Though they claimed to be extravagantly fond of one another, still they tortured each other with petty quibbling and bitter acrimony. That was what marriage became, clearly, even when one began the lifelong bond as in love as her mother and father said they were. Later experience gave her little reason to think differently as she witnessed much the same in other homes after her parents' death.

Elizabeth wrung out the cloth and laid it over the edge of the plain porcelain bowl, then she turned to the wardrobe and selected one of her favorite dresses, a pale blue gown of simple cut. Though not in the modern style, which was following the French pattern of higher waists, she had altered it so that it was flattering, if a little worn at the cuffs.

Perhaps it was good that life, for her, seemed destined to be lived as a spinster, she thought, as she slipped the gown on over her head, for she had no good opinion of a woman's role in marriage. Spinsterhood would require overcoming a shamefully acute physical appreciation of masculine company, but she was stronger than her impulses, and those unfeminine sensations would dwindle with time and self-mastery. She had vowed to put her own good ahead of any urgings of her impulsive nature this time. She would not waste this opportunity to start fresh.

She buttoned her dress, made sure she was neat and tidy, and went to sit by the fire for a while, just to warm her feet and hands. The chair was comfortable and the blaze cheery; she stared into the flickering flames and felt her inner turmoil calm. This was good. This was what she would learn to trust in herself, this strength of character, this coolness, this resolution. No one would ever disturb her peace and convince her against her conscience again.

Just as she was beginning to get sleepy, a rap at the door startled her out of her drowsy state. She rapidly rose, crossed the room, and opened the door.

A young girl, garbed in a simple but well-made gown that denoted her status as an upper servant, stood in the doorway. She curtseyed and said, "Dinner is about to be served, Miss Stanwycke. I am to escort you."

Elizabeth was extremely hungry, she realized, retrieving her shawl and joining the girl in the hallway. This was a different maid from earlier, and she spoke perfect English, though it was oddly accented. Someone had thought to send this girl instead of the German-speaking one from earlier, and she blessed the kindness.

"Your English is very good," she said, closing the door behind her. "What is your name?"

"Thank you, Miss Stanwycke," she said with another graceful curtsey. She was a pale, plump girl, very pretty, but solemn. "My name is Fanny, miss. My father was English, valet of the previous Graf; because I speak English, Gräfin von Wolfram told me to escort you. I will attend you, also, in the future, and act as your maid when necessary."

Elizabeth appreciated the gesture from the lady; it indicated a kindness not readily apparent in her bearing, but likely there beneath the surface. She followed Fanny, grateful for the guide, for the castle was daunting in its size. They moved to the stone staircase, descended two flights of stairs, during which she only had the fleeting impression of other halls branching off, and reached the huge great hall, where a cold draft fluttered the pennants. In Fanny's wake Elizabeth drifted across the cold stone floor until they reached the overhanging gallery, beyond which she could dimly see the large gothic arched doorways, their heavily carved oak covered in a riot of symbols and shields.

Fanny then curtseyed and melted away, leaving Elizabeth to enter alone, past liveried footmen who held open the door for her. It was not the dining room she entered, though, but a large hall with two fireplaces, one on each side, each big enough to walk into if one was so inclined. But only one had a fire in it and she approached, for that was where the group of people was gathered.

Looking around nervously for someone she recognized, she saw Gräfin von Wolfram standing alone and moved toward her, welcoming the beckoning heat of the fire. "Thank you so much for sending Fanny to me, ma'am. I will make the attempt to learn German so I can communicate with the rest of the staff." The woman inclined her head. Elizabeth glanced around. "Is Frau Liebner not coming down for dinner?"

"No, my aunt has taken a tray in her room. She is exhausted, I believe."

"Miss Elizabeth Stanwycke," Bartol Liebner cried, approaching with a smile. "How lovely you look, my dear. So beautiful . . . and how becoming that dress. The color is just the shade of your eyes, so pretty a sky blue, yes?"

Smiling, Elizabeth curtseyed and thanked him. It was reassuring to be welcomed so effusively.

"Enough, Bartol," the Gräfin said sharply. She turned back to Elizabeth. "I was concerned earlier of whether I should take you immediately to see Charlotte, but I think we decided rightly to give you time. I know how tired you must have been when you arrived, and you will see Charlotte now. Come, I will introduce you."

With an apologetic smile for Herr Liebner, Elizabeth followed her hostess to the tight knot by the hearth. The French count was there and he bowed and smiled and murmured a greeting to her as she passed. Adele singled out a lovely young woman, pale with blonde hair, who stood by an equally blond young man of startling beauty.

"Charlotte, this is Miss Elizabeth Stanwycke, come all the way from England this day to be your tutor."

The girl, her face a pale oval and her lips plump and perfect above a cleft chin of molded perfection, curtseyed and opened her mouth to speak, but as she was murmuring a hello, she was interrupted.

"Adele, you should have introduced me first, as the eldest lady present," a peevish, thin, nervous-looking woman said.

"I thought, Gerta, that since Charlotte is her student—"

"Never mind, I am accustomed to being last always," the woman said.

"Miss Stanwycke," Adele said, with restraint evident in her voice, "this is my sister, Gerta von Holtzen." She gestured with her bony hand at a woman smaller than she and somewhat younger.

"Gräfin von Holtzen," Elizabeth said, offering her hand and hoping she had addressed her correctly. "So pleased to make your acquaintance."

The lady, as blonde as her older sister but not as distinguished looking, nodded, but seemed not a bit mollified. She ignored Elizabeth's outstretched hand and turned away pettishly. She drifted to the French count's side and took his arm, clinging to him possessively.

"And this is my nephew, Christoph von Wolfram, Charlotte's brother."

The young man merely bowed and said nothing. His beauty was almost ethereal, his skin pale, and his hair glittering golden in the firelight, but the luminous affect was spoiled by his peevish expression. A pulse throbbed in his neck, and his lips were pursed in an unattractive pout.

Elizabeth smiled, but he didn't return the expression. "You will have to excuse me," she said, taking in everyone with her gaze, "if in the next few days I address anyone wrong. Frau Liebner most kindly has told me much of German ways, so if I misstep in my address or manner it is my own misunderstanding only, and I would appreciate being corrected."

"Nicely said, Miss Stanwycke," the Gräfin said, her tone cool. "But on the morrow I will sit down with you and tell you anything you wish to know. We do not stand on ceremony when it is just this family group."

"No, we don't stand on ceremony," the lord of the castle said as he strode toward the group from the doorway.

Among the gathered family and guests he seemed even larger, Elizabeth thought, watching as the others greeted him, each in their own way, and then parted before him. The French count, who, she noted, had shaken off Gräfin von Holtzen's steely grasp and was standing apart from her, was as tall as he, but slender comparatively, and neither Christoph von Wolfram nor Bartol Liebner were as tall. Far from his disarray earlier, Graf von Wolfram was very correctly dressed in a gray sateen frock jacket, velvet knee breeches, and clocked stockings, but she could not forget how he appeared before, though she would try to erase that image from her mind. It was disturbing to her peace, for some unfathomable reason, the memory of that open-necked shirt and thatch of dark chest hair. Perhaps it was worse for her because unlike the pure and chaste young woman she must pretend to be, she had a too-vivid idea of what taut musculature filled the perfect jacket and formal knee breeches.

"Miss Stanwycke," the Graf said as he approached. He bowed formally. Glancing around and gathering his family group within his gaze, he said, "I would like you all to make this young lady welcome here. It is a great sacrifice to leave your homeland, as she has done, and it behooves us to show her we appreciate that." He directed his look especially at his nephew. "And in her presence, please speak English, as I am sure you have been, all. To do otherwise would be discourteous. For those of you not comfortable in that language," he continued, eyeing Herr Liebner, "it is an opportunity to practice."

"Yes, nephew, for I have already said so, have I not?" The older man beamed a smile, glancing around.

Elizabeth, her gaze riveted on her employer, felt that she was missing something and glanced around, but most of those gathered had neutral expressions. Charlotte was quiet, and her gaze was directed to the floor. That seemed odd, for if Elizabeth was in her place she would be examining her new tutor, at least covertly. But for the rest of them, Graf von Wolfram's arrival seemed to have revivified the gathering, that electricity Elizabeth had noticed earlier in his presence sparking the others to a livelier expression.

"Shall we dine?" he said, glancing around at his family and guests.

He turned and was moving toward her, but his eldest sister, Adele, grasped his sleeve and drew him away from the others for one moment, and Count Delacroix offered Elizabeth his arm in his courtly manner. She gladly accepted and they all strolled to the dining room, which proved to be a large hall adjoining; her escort murmured to her that this was the family dining room. There was another in the new wing—new only in that it was under three hundred years old—that was larger, an even more formal dining hall. Gerta von Holtzen directed the seating, which Elizabeth found odd considering this was supposed to be an informal family dinner according to the Graf, and she ended up last, on the left of the French count, quite a ways down the table from her new employer and across from her pupil. She didn't mind, because it gave her the opportunity, partially obscured by shadow, to observe this group. She still felt awkward and drained, but she trusted in a night's sleep to give her more confidence.

When Graf von Wolfram entered with his sister there were only two places left, with him at the head, of course, and his sister on his right. He paused, glanced down the table at Elizabeth, and seemed about to make some remark, but she smiled and spoke to her dining companion, Count Delacroix, and the Graf sat down.

Conversation was desultory at first, as appetites were sated. Elizabeth feared that the Graf's injunction that they all speak only English in her company had stilted things badly, though most seemed to have an excellent grasp of the language. Some, as time went on, slipped back into their native tongue as they conversed with each other.

The Frenchman, though, offering her wine and taking some with her, said, after sipping, "I admire your bravery, mademoiselle, in crossing the continent so, surely a feat for a gently born English lady?"

They chatted about her trip for a few minutes as they ate, he questioning her closely about the situation of the French armies and their attitudes, gathered as the forces were in the southern and western portion of Germany. The count's soothing voice was perfectly suited to putting her at ease, and she was grateful to Gerta von Holtzen for her firmness in seating people.

Though the food was delicious and served on the most exquisite of china, and even as hungry as she was, weariness blunted her appetite. She ached all over, but she did her best to stiffen her back and appear engaged and calm. This family's first notion of her was vitally important, especially so with the absence of her champion, Frau Liebner. It was up to her to fit in seamlessly and make a good impression. She took small bites and chewed thoroughly, leaving much untouched as the footmen removed plates. It was unlike her to eat so little and strange considering her hunger, but she was sure she would make up for it the next day once sleep had revived her.

"Have you formed any opinion of your student yet?" the count said, as a footman placed before him a plate of fish and another refilled their wineglasses.

"Not at all, sir. I will leave my mind open and make her acquaintance on the morrow, I'm sure."

"She is a lovely young lady, but very shy, I fear. And depressed of spirits."

"It may just be that she is not sure how we will deal together."

"I would say shyness is her natural manner. I have long known the family. Was this your type of position before, Miss Stanwycke?"

"I was . . . more of a governess," she replied, measuring her words carefully as she picked up her silver fish fork. "The girls were younger. But if you are asking about my tutoring the young lady in manners, my mother was a lady-in-waiting to Her Majesty, Queen Charlotte, for a time, and so I am well acquainted with court ways. My mother spoke of it often."

The count glanced over at her, his eyebrows knit tightly. "Pardon, but I fear I do not understand. If your mother was lady-in-waiting, that means she was of elevated . . . pardon my English, I'm not sure I am expressing right."

But she understood him perfectly. She frowned down at

her food and chose her words, as there was much in her life she had decided to conceal forevermore. "Yes, my mother was daughter of a viscount. I . . . both my parents died many years ago leaving little money, and a position as governess seemed my best chance at life. I lived with some distant family members and taught their daughters."

"Do you have no close family to take care of you?"

Elizabeth was silent, slowly chewing a mouthful of food. How to answer that?

The count glanced at her as he cut his turbot and said, "I must apologize, Miss Stanwycke, for my intrusive and unbecoming question. A thousand pardons. It was unforgivable and mere concern on my part that such a gently bred lady as yourself should be left to fend in the world without someone to look after her."

Elizabeth, hysteria bubbling up within her, laughed out loud at the notion of a family member being required to care for her, but she felt an awkward tear rise in one eye. She dashed it away, impatiently, and said, "Family does not always have one's best interests at heart, sir." Her voice sounded unnaturally loud in the sudden silence, and when she looked up it was to see many pairs of eyes upon her. "Excuse me," she said, her voice echoing. "I—"

"We were merely having an amusing exchange," the count said with a flourish of one hand. "And Miss Stanwycke was so polite as to laugh for my benefit." His smooth manner sent everyone back to their meals and conversations, but there was still one pair of eyes locked on her. Elizabeth met them. Graf Nikolas von Wolfram was not persuaded.

She glanced away again and stared at her plate. Her position in the castle depended on concealing her past, and on the very first night she had been so foolish as to reveal that her relationship with her family was not all that it should be. She didn't want to raise questions that she was not willing to answer, and she must learn to be circumspect. Timidity and reserve must be her subjects of study, for she was unnaturally bold and forthright, she had been told lately. It was unwomanly to be so independent.

Taking a deep breath, she finally dared to look up. She was still the object of scrutiny, but this time the one studying her was Charlotte, her future pupil, and Elizabeth couldn't help but think that the expression on the girl's face was one of profound resentment.

Chapter 3

DINNER FINALLY drew to a close.

Servants, on some unspoken command from the hard-featured Gräfin, Adele, moved to take away the last remove. As Graf von Wolfram rose, the count stood, too, and murmured to Elizabeth, "Come, mademoiselle, we do not stand on English manners here. The gentlemen do not stay at the table to drink. Here, the company moves together into the hall once more for conversation. Unless you wish to excuse yourself? I will make your apologies to the rest."

As the others rose, too, with a rumble of talking and the sound of many chairs being pulled back across the floor by footmen, Elizabeth stood and said, "No, thank you. I'm fine, really. I will go with the group, if that's what is expected of me."

She was answered as her employer approached her and bowed. "We now will remove to the drawing room, upstairs, Miss Stanwycke. It is customary for us to sit together after dinner; some play cards, some talk, the ladies embroider or read aloud."

"She is weary after her journey," Count Delacroix began.

But Elizabeth held up one hand as the Graf frowned. "No, thank you for your concern, sir, but I would be delighted to join the group."

The Graf bowed gravely and said, "You must excuse yourself when you feel weary and wish to retire."

He straightened and offered her his arm. Elizabeth took it, and he guided her from the dining room to the great hall. Together they crossed the broad expanse, then mounted the stone steps up to the gallery, and then to the drawing room, the rest falling in behind them. It was a long walk, and cold, but he said not a word on the way, and it seemed an awkward procession that the family made. She was relieved that it was not likely that she would be expected to dine with the family every night. As a tutor, she was employed by the Graf and would take her meals with others of her station or in her own room.

The drawing room was another large chamber warmed by two fireplaces, as the formal reception room had been, but this room was wood paneled and adorned with lavish carpets, comfortable furnishings, and thick, vivid tapestries of hunting scenes in crimson and gold and sapphire.

"How beautiful," Elizabeth exclaimed and then glanced up at her companion.

His expression, habitually grave, softened with a faint smile. "It is by my sister's account the most comfortable room in the whole of the castle. It is unchanged since my mother's time. Much of this place is ancient, as you have no doubt seen, so this room, though part of the old castle, appears very modern in contrast."

He guided her to a chair by the fireplace and sat down near her in the matching armchair. She wished she could match his ease, but her exhaustion after a long and bewildering day left her full of tension.

"My sister, Adele, will speak to you of many things," the Graf said, sitting back in his chair and crossing one long leg over the other, "but please ask me any questions for your immediate information."

Elizabeth summoned her wits and clasped her hands in front of her. The others were clustered in tight knots, and conversation, mostly in German, buzzed, but she tried to shut out the distraction in this first important conversation with the master of the household. "Is your niece conversant with the reason I have been hired, and does she approve?"

"I am her guardian, and have decided for her best interest."

Not the answer she had hoped to hear. And yet there was something daunting about the Graf that made her loath to contradict him or question him too closely; it was a hard tone in his voice that intimidated one, the expectation of instant and unquestioning obedience. But still . . . she could not resist. "Is it in her best interest," Elizabeth said, choosing her words carefully and frowning down at the burgundy figured carpet, "if she goes to marriage unhappy?" She glanced up at him to judge his expression. Perhaps it was foolish to venture even so much, but she had made the journey all the way there; he would surely not let her go for a mere question.

"Miss Stanwycke, my niece's happiness is not your concern. You are merely to tutor her in all the finer points of life at court in your country, to improve her English—which is sadly lacking, I fear—and to teach her the etiquette of your people."

His face, partially obscured by shadow, was hard to tear her glance from. His eyes were dark, a charcoal gray, and his hair, almost black, was flecked with silver at the temples, even though Elizabeth knew he was not above thirty-four or thirty-five.

"An unwilling pupil is unteachable."

His expression calm but unyielding, a muscle flexing in his square jaw, he said, "Then you will have to make her willing."

So, it was that clear cut. Elizabeth stared over at Charlotte, who sat with her brother Christoph, Gerta von Holtzen, and Bartol Liebner at a small card table several feet away. They appeared to be playing Silver Loo or Commerce, or some other simple game. Adele von Wolfram and Count Delacroix were sitting playing piquet at a table on the other side of the fireplace. Charlotte's gaze was still down, and she fiddled nervously with the fringe of her shawl.

Tomorrow. She would meet her pupil on her own terms the next day and come to an understanding of the girl. That one hostile glance during dinner had left her worried, but she would not let that one impression taint her relationship with the young lady.

"Graf von Wolfram—"

"I would have you use English words, Miss Stanwycke," he said, abruptly, tapping the arm of his chair. "Adele will speak to you of our decision, but we may as well start now. I am styled 'Count' in your language, and so it will be."

"Yes, Count von Wolfram," Elizabeth said. She stared at the paneling, tracing the odd pattern, while she tried to think of a way to introduce the subject she wanted to raise. "I would like to ask you . . . that is," she hesitated, but could not keep quiet. It was impossible to stifle every natural urge within her, and this she had to say. She glanced sideways at the count but then returned her gaze to the paneling again. "I saw something on the way here, to the castle . . ."

"Yes?" he said when she stopped.

She braced herself, took a deep breath, and said, turning in her chair to stare into his face, "I saw a woman running across the road, and then a rider, a man on a horse ran after her." She could not bring herself to mention the woman's nakedness. She gazed up into his eyes.

He knit his dark brows. "Did you ask the driver to stop, Miss Stanwycke?"

"I . . . no, you see the carriage had already stopped, for the horses were shying at something and the driver was trying to regain control. I was on the road, having gotten out of the carriage to find out what was the matter."

"And once he regained control, did you then say something of what you had seen?"

"Yes . . . er, no, I mean. I had followed, down the embankment . . . I was going to go into the forest to try to help the woman, but Frau Liebner shouted after me and told me there was danger in the woods. I tried to say something, to get the driver to help me follow the lady, but he didn't understand my English and I couldn't think of the German words. And then . . . the driver, he . . . he came after me," she explained, gesturing with her hands to indicate the driver's shocking behavior. "He hefted me over his shoulder and carried me like a sack of kindling back up to the road. Frau Liebner had been hurt when the carriage stopped abruptly, and so I . . . I felt it my duty to help her." It sounded like a jumble, a fantastical confusion, but she had decided that she could not just let the incident go without saying something. It would tug at her conscience until she had done all she could.

The count twisted his lips and stared at the fire. "Where did this happen?"

"We had just begun the hill toward the castle," Elizabeth eagerly explained, taking a deep breath, relieved to have told the story. "They crossed the road from our right to our left. There should still be visible marks in the snow from the horse galloping down the embankment."

He called a footman over and spewed a string of German, then dismissed the man. Turning to Elizabeth, he said, "I have told him to send someone out to see if there is anything or anyone."

"Frau Liebner said perhaps it was a . . . a domestic dispute . . . villagers."

The count, his eyes narrowed, said, "It is too far from the village for a woman on foot, I think. And I would allow no man in my village to treat his wife with such cruelty as you indicate. No man should chase after his wife like an animal. I will find out, though, who it was."

His autocratic manner and definite statement soothed Elizabeth, and she sighed, sitting back more comfortably in her chair. It was off her conscience, for she had done all she could. "Thank you, sir. I've been worried."

"But not worried enough to mention it earlier? I will quite possibly find nothing out at this late hour. If they are outsiders they will be long gone."

"I . . . I'm a stranger in a foreign land, sir, and it behooves me to go carefully," she answered, sitting up more correctly again. "I don't understand the ways of your land, yet."

"We are civilized, I assure you," he said, stiffly, grinding out the words. "The English do not have a patent on good manners and gentility. We do not beat our wives daily."

Silence was her only answer. As exhausted as she was, she could easily make a wrong answer or say something she would later wish she hadn't. The count's attention was taken by some question asked by his sister, Gerta, and Elizabeth appreciated his focus being taken away from her. Sitting by the warmth of the fire, with the murmur of conversation around her, Elizabeth felt an odd drifting sensation as she again relaxed back in the chair. It was pleasant, thoughtless, like being in a rowboat and letting the waves carry her. Quite, quite lovely.

"Miss Stanwycke. Miss Stanwycke!"

She looked up. Count von Wolfram was standing before her gazing down at her and it was so delightful, his eyes so lovely a gray, that she smiled up at him. The oddest urge to reach up and touch his face overwhelmed her, and if she could have moved she would have done it.

"Miss Stanwycke," he said, gently. "You should retire, for you have been sleeping for a while now."

Elizabeth shook herself awake and, mortified with embarrassment, sat bolt upright, clutching the arms of her chair. Sleeping in public, and on her first night there! "Oh, Count, I beg your pardon for such an impoliteness! It's just the warmth of the fire and the wine from dinner and . . ."

He held out his hand to help her stand and offered just the faintest hint of a smile. The twist of his lips hinted that there could be a lighter side to his character than she had yet seen. "*Schoen traeumer,* Miss Stanwycke. That means, I wish you beautiful dreams. Retire, and no apologies. We will speak on the morrow."

The others were watching with great curiosity. Her cheeks burning with embarrassment, Elizabeth stood with his aid and summoned what dignity she could. She nodded to the company. "My apologies, everyone," she said, her voice echoing off the high ceilings and long expanse of dark paneled wall. "I'm very weary, and will retire now. Thank you for such a wonderful welcome. Good night."

Nikolas watched Miss Stanwycke go, the smile still lingering on his lips. She was a lovely young woman, perhaps too pretty to be a tutor. Her face in repose had revealed a sweetness of expression she must purposely conceal when awake, for she had appeared, before that, only cold and reserved. He wondered if she was as anxious as she seemed, and if it was only a desire to make a good impression or some other tension.

Fanny met her at the door with a candle to light their way through the dim corridors of Wolfram Castle and the two young women disappeared into the dimness beyond the doors. He sobered as he thought of the tale she had told, troubled by the impression it had made on her. He had had English visitors before and always they had a notion that his country was less civilized than theirs. He hadn't meant to be abrupt with her, but it disturbed him and he had reacted rudely.

When he was certain she would have begun the ascent to her bedchamber, he vaulted out of his chair and strode toward the door.

"Nikolas!"

He turned, his hand on the door handle.

"Nikolas," Adele repeated, striding toward him. "I have something to ask."

"Not now, Adele. Later. Tomorrow. I have things to take care of right now." He slipped easily back into German from the English he had been using all evening.

"This cannot wait," she said and told him of her concerns.

It was a long diatribe, and he glanced uneasily toward the group by the fire. A couple cast him side-glances, in particular Charlotte, who had appeared unhappy at the dinner table, he had noticed. He was gravely concerned about her state of mind, of late. And Christoph seemed brooding and wretched, his gaze flicking anxiously around the room. Gerta, as usual, was oblivious to the rest, only her flighty movements and agitation betraying her state of mind.

"So what should I do?" Adele finally said, after expressing her worries.

"Use your best judgment, as always. What else can I counsel?"

"I thought you would want to be consulted," Adele said, resentment in her tone.

He glanced down at his sister and studied her expression. She had grown gaunt and bleak with the weight of their joint responsibility. For fifteen years the family had been primarily his duty, but Adele had always shouldered more than her share of the burden. She should have married and left the castle, but she had stayed and shared the obligation. Now that Christoph was fully grown and Charlotte was being prepared for marriage, one would think the responsibilities would ease.

But it was not so. There were always new worries. And there were Eva and Jakob, Gerta's children, to think of, their future happiness.

"Nikolas!" Adele said, tugging his sleeve to remind him she was still awaiting an answer.

"Ask for Uta's help," he said in response to her primary worry; he spoke of Uta von Wolfram, his ancient aunt. "And let Mina watch if you are concerned." Mina, his aunt's personal servant, was mute, but her value was more in her absolute unswerving loyalty to the family she had served her whole life than in her silence. She could always be counted on to provide a taciturn, watchful presence when the need arose. "But I think all will be well this night."

"I am not so sure," Adele fretted.

Charlotte met Nikolas's gaze across the room and he saw hostility in her blue eyes, even from such a distance. Perhaps he had given the new tutor an impossible task.

"I haven't time for this," he said gruffly, turning back to his sister. "Do whatever is necessary."

"As always," Adele said. "I'll take care of things, as always," she repeated and turned away.

"Adele," he said. She turned back and stared at him, waiting. What could he say? She should have been living her own life, finding her own happiness, but instead she had devoted herself to their family. It had made her sharp and resentful, and increasingly she took that resentment out on him. But he hadn't lived for himself either; he had sacrificed much more than anyone would ever know. He was doing his best and would continue.

"What is it?" she said, compressing her thin lips together, waiting for him to say whatever he had been about to say.

But what was there? "Nothing. It is nothing." He tried instead to find that peace between them, the unspoken agreement as they worked in tandem, like a team of strong oxen. He pushed down on the door handle. "What think you of Miss Stanwycke?"

"I think she is very intelligent," Adele said. "Perhaps even too intelligent. And very beautiful." Unconsciously, she ran her hand down her gaunt frame and plucked at the expensive material of her fashionable, high-waisted gown as she gazed back at the group. Gerta was trying to sit on Count Delacroix's lap, and he was laughing as he denied her. Adele sighed and looked back at her younger brother. "Do you not think so, Nikolas? That Miss Stanwycke is very beautiful?"

How could he deny it? No man could. "She is. But that is not what I was asking about."

"Ah, but it is what you have noticed." Adele glanced over at the group again. The French count had stood and moved away from Gerta; he was leaning over, speaking to Bartol Liebner. "And Maximillian, too. Even he is foolish for her. I could see it in his eyes when they met, and at dinner, making her laugh . . ." Adele stopped and compressed her lips in a thin line, faint wrinkles creasing and puckering the edge of her mouth.

"Miss Stanwycke is here to work," he reminded his sister, pushing open the door.

"Yes. To work. And I . . . I must get back to the others," she said.

"And I must go to my task."

They parted ways.

EXHAUSTION claimed Elizabeth immediately as she reached her chamber. She said good night to Fanny, disrobed, slipped on her nightgown and into bed, and remembered nothing more until awakening with the room still dark and the house silent.

What time was it? How she wished she knew, but there was no clock in the room, and no way to find out. That she would need to remedy, for she must have a clock so she would never be late in a house that appeared to be strictly run.

It was quite possibly still the middle of the night, for she had retired so early and never slept more than six hours, no matter how tired she was. So it could be only three or four in the morning, hours before she could expect others to awaken. She wished she could speak to Frau Liebner, but she couldn't even think about that for several hours at least. Her friend was not an early riser and did not like to speak before eating breakfast.

Elizabeth sighed and turned over, but sleep eluded her.

Finally she slipped from the bed, gasping as her feet hit the cold floor where the rug did not cover. It was no use; she was just not sleepy. She padded over to the fire with her candle in hand, lit a taper from the banked embers, and held the tiny flame to the wick.

Then she opened the curtains, hoping for a little predawn light—there was none, but by the waning moonlight she could see silvery flakes of snow dancing against the panes—and dressed, thinking she might as well explore her new home. Even if it was temporary, it was exciting to live in a castle. She had agreed to the position knowing it would only take a few months or a year at most to adequately prepare Charlotte von Wolfram for marriage to an Englishman, but desperation forced one to either give up and be defeated, or become optimistic. Faith in the future was her choice; once her duty to Charlotte von Wolfram was done, she felt sure she could find another employer in Germany, Prussia, or Austria with a similar situation. With the count's good recommendation, and if she could manage to learn German in the time she was there, she would be sure to find other work. Determination would drive her to discharge her duty beyond their expectations.

She dressed in the chilly darkness—donning extra petticoats and wool stockings again to ward off the frigidity—and took the candle, exiting her room quietly, her soft shoes making no sound on the hall floor. It took a moment to orient herself in the dark hall. A dim lantern burned, casting a faint glow, and she looked to the right and then to the left. The hallway to her right stretched off into the darkness, but to her left she could dimly make out the stone staircase that led down to the second floor and the gallery that overlooked the great hall. Hesitating for a moment, she wondered if she was wise to set out to explore alone, but who would ever know? And what harm could it do? She was restless and couldn't just sit alone in her bedchamber for hours waiting for light. She set off toward the oldest part of the castle, the public rooms on the second floor.

The air was dank and cold and the familiar numbness set into her fingers and toes. But the excitement of exploration made her forget how icy the air seemed, and a pleasant trickle of anticipation fluttered her stomach. The stone staircase that signaled she was in the central old portion of the castle—the staircases in the newer portion were all of wood, she had noticed—took her down to the second floor, and she found her way along the gallery. She found the drawing room she had been in the night before. It seemed almost warm, with the embers of the previous night's fire still banked in the hearth. She held her candle up high and examined the tapestries that lined the paneled walls. A hunt scene, with mastiffs attacking a beleaguered wolf, was the first tapestry. On second viewing the tapestry didn't seem so beautiful; much of the scarlet wool was used to indicate blood, as the wolf was downed. But the next tapestry carried on the scene; two more wolves had joined the fray and were now defeating the terrified and cringing mastiffs while a huge black bird—a crow or a raven, Elizabeth supposed—wheeled in the cloudy sky above the scene.

Interesting, Elizabeth thought, given the family name, which meant, according to Frau Liebner, "Wolf Raven."

She exited the room and moved on, finding next a music room with an array of instruments, including a beautiful harpsichord she looked forward to playing. Thus ended that part of the castle, and so she doubled back, staying away from the railing that overlooked the great hall. The room in the newer section—it would be directly under her own room, she calculated—appeared to be some sort of exercise room, with a variety of swords and weapons lining the walls. That made sense, she thought, remembering that the evening before this was the direction the count had come from when she first met him, and he said he had been fencing. The candlelight glinted off the weapons hung on the paneled wall—silver-bladed swords, wickedly long and sharp, and rapiers, their tips blunted with guards. The floor was marble and there were chairs set against the opposite wall, perhaps for spectators to view the practice. She shivered at how the flicker of her weak light glinted off the blades. She exited the room, held her candle up high, and peered down the hall. It was dark, but there didn't appear to be any other doors along the hall. Perhaps, being so long, the exercise or sword room was the only room on that branch of the castle. She returned to the gallery and slipped along the wall to the other side, the matching half of the castle, as it were.

It appeared that there was one room occupying the old portion of the castle on this side; she approached, then pushed open the big arched door and entered what turned out to be a library. This was what she had been hoping for! Thick carpeting made the room seem warm, even though there was no fire at this time of night. She held her candle up and gazed in awe at the dark wood bookcases soaring to twenty or thirty feet, the faint light of her candle gleaming off rich gold trim. She reverently approached and ran her fingers along the leather bindings; though the majority of the books were in German, there were many titles in French and English, Latin and Greek, and other languages she could not begin to decipher.

She would ask for permission, as her German got better, to read from selected works. It was an opportunity to better herself, and she must find the courage to push herself to take it, no matter how difficult. Turning in a circle, her candle held high, she noticed glass cases containing ancient parchment scrolls and geological specimens set against the far wall, folio tables in the middle of the room with gilt-edged maps spread out on them, and deep chairs placed nearby, with modern lamps set at a good space for reading. An enormous desk took up one end of the room, with more bookcases soaring above, on the wall behind it. It was truly a magnificent room, the library of a family that valued learning.

A lectern in the far corner near some more bookcases drew her attention, and she circled it, setting her candle on a high shelf behind her. It appeared to be a family bible on the lectern, and she opened the massive tome, marveling at the lovely illuminations in red and gold and purple, and the dozens of names written, with corresponding dates of birth, marriage, and death. The count's lineage was indeed ancient and well-documented; the names went back three hundred years or more. But she was only interested in the modern generations, so she ran her finger down the page until she found names she recognized.

Nikolas, Gerta, and Adele's dates of birth were all recorded, as well as Johannes, Charlotte and Christoph's father. He had died fifteen years ago, she noticed, just three weeks after their mother, Anna Lindsay von Wolfram. How tragic! The children would have been four and six years old at the time, and to lose both parents within weeks of each other was terrible.

Gerta's marriage and her husband's name were also recorded close by, with his date of death, and then the date of the birth of her twins, Eva and Jakob, just weeks later. Elizabeth stared at it for a moment, and then went back to the dates of Johannes and Anna's deaths. Hans von Holtzen, Gerta's husband, had died on the same day as Anna von Wolfram.

What had Frau Liebner said? That it was a very bad time and that they did not speak of such things. Bad indeed, in that three family members had died in such a short time—two in one day? There was no indication how they died, but certainly two unrelated people were unlikely to have died of natural causes on the same day, given that she had never heard word of any kind of plague or fever. Elizabeth bit her lip and stared down at the page, but her attention was drawn by a creaking noise and she gasped, the sound like a whisper in the cavernous library.

Another creak and a loud click echoed. Where had it come from? The castle was old but sturdy, and she had not heard such a noise since she had been in the library. Her heart thumping heavily, she stood still and listened, gazing into the dim reaches of the cavernous room, but there was no further sound. Deeply breathing in and out, calming her racing heart, she returned to her perusal of the bible, but another echoing click, sounding closer but muffled, interrupted her, and she started, swallowing past a lump in her throat. She turned to retrieve her candle, intent on returning to her room. She hadn't considered it before, but it could be seen as prying, perhaps, to be looking at the family bible, and she would not be caught at such a thing. If the servants were stirring then she should ready herself for the day.

"What are you doing in here?"

She whirled, almost dropping the candle, to find the count standing by the desk in the far corner, a black cloak on and snow sparkling on his broad shoulders. "What . . . how did you get in here?" she cried.

He pulled off his gloves as he circled the desk and crossed the floor toward her. He seemed larger in black boots and cloak, she thought, larger and more forbidding. Her wavering candle showed dark circles under his eyes, and she had the feeling he had not slept at all that night.

Instead of answering, he asked, "What are you reading so intently, Miss Stanwycke?" He circled behind her and gazed down at the bible, still open to the recent family history.

Unnerved by his looming presence and the crisp scent of the outdoors that he carried, she moved to the other side of the lectern, feeling more comfortable with it between them. She held up the candle and the golden light played shadows over his face as the flame wavered. "I was just trying to get a sense of your family. Frau Liebner would not speak much of it."

"And is that knowledge of my family history vital to teaching my niece the finer points of English etiquette?" His hard jaw flexed as if he was restraining some powerful emotion, and he slapped his black gloves against his thigh.

"Perhaps. Perhaps not." Her voice quavered with disquietude. She took a deep, calming breath, gazed at him steadily, and said, "How am I to know yet?"

"Indeed. But then, how are you to know anything?" His expression remained grave. "You are an early riser. And curious."

He made both attributes seem like infractions of some unwritten rule, and she supposed she should have stayed in her room until beckoned. That was no doubt what a proper lady, one with the correct instincts of decorum, would have done. It struck her that he may begin to doubt her ability to teach etiquette to his niece if she was devoid of it in his eyes. She shrugged and glanced toward the door. It was closed, still, and she wondered again where he had come from. The snow on his cape was melting and trickling in rivulets down the black wool of his cloak. One drop caught in the bristle of black hairs on the back of his broad hand, and she stared at it, her mind working feverishly.

He couldn't have come through the door and made it all the way across the room and behind the desk before she noticed, because although her head was down and her attention was focused on the bible, she was facing in the general direction of the door to the hall. And why would he creep in, waiting to say anything until he was in the far corner of the room? If he was coming into the library from the gallery he should have noticed her right away and confronted her immediately.

But where else could he have come from?

Closing the book with a soft thump, he circled the lectern and stood in front of her. She met his gaze, trying, but failing she feared, to quell the hint of defiance she was feeling and that no doubt emanated from her. It was her downfall, that sense she had and radiated, apparently, that she was just as good as her employers, and perhaps better. It had gotten her in trouble before and would again if she didn't subdue it. She looked down at her feet, hoping the gesture would pass as an appropriate submission. He chuckled, and she met his gaze again to find his lips twisted in a mocking smile.

"Let me say, Miss Stanwycke, that I hope to bend Charlotte to my will because it is what is best for her, but I fear very much that I have brought into my home a less than ideal tutor, if I wish my niece to learn meekness and surrender." He flung his cloak off, sending a shower of silvery drops spraying.

She pointedly wiped one droplet from her cheek and said, proud that her voice was steady now, "In my experience, Count, meekness and surrender are not always the best attributes for a woman to cultivate."

"I think in this case you should at least pretend to possess them if you want to stay well and happy here at the castle." He whirled and strode to the door but stopped before exiting and gazed back at her, his face shadowed. "I will see you later today, Miss Stanwycke, and if you have any questions or concerns, I will address them then. I would return to your room now, if I were you. And please leave your tour of the house until we can provide for you a guide."

And then he was gone and Elizabeth let out the breath she had not known she was holding. A dire warning indeed, and from the master of the house. She should pretend to be meek if she wanted to stay well and happy? What did that mean?

How *had* he entered the library? She was now certain it wasn't through the door that let out to the gallery. He had come directly from outside, he hadn't slept yet that night, and he had not come through the normal egress, the doorway to the gallery. She glanced around the library but no longer felt the urge to explore. As much as she disliked it, his warning had unnerved her, and she crossed the carpeted floor in the count's damp footsteps, leaving the library to return to her own room.

Chapter 4

". . . SO I will introduce you today to the other members of the household, and leave you, later, to become familiar with your pupil," Countess Adele said, briskly, as she guided Elizabeth along the gallery.

Fanny had arrived as light began to fill Elizabeth's room, little knowing that the tutor had already been up some hours; the girl guided her to breakfast, which she ate alone with the countess. They were now on a promised tour of the house, though they were, much to Elizabeth's chagrin, in the same corridor she had traversed just hours before. Already she had seen, briefly, the two tower rooms at the front of the castle. The east tower room was a conservatory filled with plants, some exotic, some more homely, for, the countess told her, some of the household members liked to dabble in gardening. It passed the long winter hours. The west tower room was a chapel, but Elizabeth had the distinct impression that religious observance was not emphasized to any degree in the house, though Countess Adele made sure the chapel was cared for reverently. As the sun rose, stained glass windows that soared high in the tower colored it blue, green, and red, with a brilliant overlay of gold.

They had gone, from there, up the stone steps to the gallery, and now were in the corridor where the drawing room was located. Elizabeth guessed, as she half-listened to the count's elder sister relate the history of the house, that she had sat alone in her room by her faintly glowing fire for three hours or more, which meant her meeting with the count occurred at about four in the morning, as she had suspected.

"It is interesting, is it not? This house and how it came to belong to the von Wolfram family?"

"Very interesting. Thank you, Countess, for the explanation," Elizabeth said meekly. She should have been listening, but the puzzle of the count's appearance in the library still tugged at her brain. She didn't like any of the possible explanations.

"This is the music room," the woman said, throwing open the door beyond which Elizabeth had already been. "Do you play a musical instrument?"

"Of course," Elizabeth said, strolling in as though it were the first time she had seen it. "I play the piano and harpsichord."

"Good," the countess said, the *d* on the end of the word sounding more like a *t*, virtually the only inflection of her native tongue Elizabeth had so far noticed. "You will play for us one evening," the woman continued, straightening a woven tapestry runner on a table under a grim painting of the castle. "Nikolas adores to hear music well played."

"I didn't say I was proficient, Countess, merely that I play."

The older woman stopped and glanced sharply back at Elizabeth. There was silence for a long minute as Elizabeth realized her mistake; she did not hasten to fill the quiet, though. Rushing to soften her impertinence would only emphasize it. Instead she dropped her gaze and waited.

"We will go on now," the countess finally said. She followed Elizabeth out of the room and closed the door behind her. They passed the drawing room on their way back to the gallery, since she had seen that the previous evening, and the countess ignored the branch of the hall that held, Elizabeth knew, the exercise room. As they hustled along the gallery, the countess briskly pointed out the soaring leaded-glass windows that fronted the castle, and then, leading the way down the hall, she paused by the library door, putting one blue-veined hand on it, and said, "This is Nikolas's room, the library."

"Does no one else use it?"

In the dimness of the hallway, Countess Adele's feature were in harsh relief. "No. The ladies have a smaller room with books, one of the parlors down on the first floor near the breakfast room. Why do you ask?"

"I . . . I hope to learn your language while I'm here, and if you have any books in German . . ."

"We have many novels in German, and many books o travel, too, in the ladies' library. I will show you later."

Routed in her plan to examine the library in the light o day, she determined to let the subject lapse. She had promise herself to curb her unsuitable curiosity, and this would be a useful exercise for that determination. "I hope," Elizabeth said hesitantly, "that I will be able to see Frau Liebner thi morning?"

"Certainly today. But not before luncheon, I think. M aunt is a late riser."

Elizabeth bit back the retort she would have made, tha having spent a couple of months with the lady, she certainly knew her habits better than the niece the good Frau hadn' seen in ten years. She merely nodded and followed the count ess back down the hallway to the new section. The layout o the castle was beginning to become clear to Elizabeth; it wa like a large U, with the old section of the castle representing the bottom of the letter and the newer sections the upper arms

"These are my rooms," she said, touching a door but no opening it. "There is no need for you to see them, as I wil only ever meet with you in my office, which is next down thi corridor." She led the way, her stride brisk. "This is my of fice," she said, throwing open a door to a smallish room.

Elizabeth stepped in, expecting it would be like a monk' cell, but found it was the most luxurious and opulent room yet. It was papered in wine and draped in burgundy. The fur nishings were heavy but excellently made of dark, carved oak A large desk, masculine in size and style, dominated one en of the room, and near the fire was a seating area, with a cou ple of tables and several chairs finishing the room's accou trements.

"It's . . . l-lovely," Elizabeth stuttered, not sure exactly what was expected of her.

Countess Adele's countenance warmed just briefly and then shuttered again, as if a window had been slammed shut on a warm summer day. "Yes, it does me well. Let us move on. We have much to cover today, for I expect you will wish to commence work with Charlotte on the morrow, will you not?"

"Of course," Elizabeth murmured.

The countess closed and locked her office, using a key from the bunch that hung on her waist ribbon, and led the way down the corridor. "These," she said, when she reached the end finally, "are Maximillian's rooms . . . the Count Delacroix . . . and those of his niece, Melisande."

"His niece?"

"Ah, yes, you have not met Melisande yet. She . . ." The countess twisted her lips, stared at the door, and then continued. "She lives here with her uncle; she lost her parents in the Terror, you see . . . or at least she lost her mother, Maximillian's sister. Her full name is Alexandra Melisande Davidovich. Her father is a Russian. We do not know where he is."

The way she said the word *Russian* was condemning, and Elizabeth didn't ask any questions.

"They have a full suite, with a parlor and dressing rooms, and their bedrooms, of course. It takes up the rest of this floor in this wing. Follow me."

Elizabeth followed the countess up the stairs at the end of the corridor. They were now on the same floor but at the opposite end of the house from her own room, she thought. It was getting a little confusing, but she thought it wouldn't take her long to sort it out, since she had an excellent sense of direction.

"This," Countess Adele said, touching a door opposite the stairs, "is Christoph's suite of rooms." She led the way farther down the corridor. "And this is Charlotte's suite," Countess Adele said. She rapped sharply on the door and then pushed it open.

Charlotte von Wolfram was seated by the window with her

brother, and they were speaking together rapidly in German. Both stopped abruptly as the countess led Elizabeth in. Christoph rose, bowed sharply, and exited, his boot heel echoing in the hall.

"Charlotte, say hello to Miss Stanwycke."

Charlotte rose, curtseyed, and said, "Hello, Miss Stanwycke."

It was a chilly little speech, and the young lady's gaze was directed, the whole time, at the door behind them, where her brother had just exited. It was awkward. Very awkward.

"What a pretty room you have," Elizabeth said, trying to find a topic of interest. The room, Charlotte's sitting room, was modern, with light papered walls, dreamy paintings hung at intervals, and white-painted furnishings gilded in the French style. The carpeting was thick and patterned with roses and vines.

"Thank you, Miss Stanwycke."

"Charlotte, please meet us down in the yellow morning parlor in one hour. I wish to speak to you both about how Nikolas and I expect things to proceed."

At such a cold command, Elizabeth was not surprised at all to see a resentful glare from the girl, though the countess did not seem to notice her niece's hostility. She would have to soften the command by making the lessons enjoyable for them both. Perhaps at first she would not even try to inculcate much, using the first few days to learn what she could about the girl and her family. If she could befriend her, find out her own feelings on matters, it might go a long way to making their work easier.

When her niece didn't respond, Adele merely nodded. "Good. Miss Stanwycke and I are seeing the house right now." She led the way out of the room, her brisk pace leaving Elizabeth no time to say anything more to the girl or do aught but smile and wave.

"The other wing, as you know, holds your room, but also the room of Cesare Vitali . . . that is my brother's secretary. He is Italian."

Again that censure, Elizabeth thought. The countess

seemed to censure everyone who was not German. Perhaps she felt the same way about Elizabeth's nationality. "Is that all in my section?"

"No. Gerta and her children's suite of rooms takes up the rest of that end of the house. Above you is . . . well, let us go and see the others."

Rapidly, the countess traversed the main section and up a set of stairs to the new section above Elizabeth's rooms. It seemed there was no old section; the fourth floor was new section only. "Aunt Katrina's rooms are here," she said, passing a door. "And then there is Uta."

"Uta?"

Adele's face cracked in an odd expression, and Elizabeth realized it was the first time she had seen a smile on the woman's hard face.

"Uta. Come."

She rapped loudly on the door but didn't pause as she pushed it open. The room was gloomy, but as her vision adjusted Elizabeth saw that despite the early hour there were several people there. Charlotte must have made her way there by another passage, because she sat by another girl. Frau Liebner was there, and Elizabeth thought she had never been so happy to see another person in her life as she was to see that dear, familiar, obstinate face. But in pride of place by the fire, in an enormous, shabby old chair, was a woman . . . or what was likely a woman. She was wrapped in voluminous blankets and her white hair was topped by a lace cap. Her face was like that of a wrinkled apple doll, with eyes set deep in folds of skin and wrinkles creasing her cheeks.

"Wer ist da?" she said, her voice surprisingly hale for such a tiny apple-doll character.

"It is Elizabeth Stanwycke, of whom I was just speaking," Frau Liebner said, getting up with difficulty and making her way across the room to her protégé. "Come, Elizabeth," she said, taking her hand and leading her over to the old woman. "Kneel!"

Surprised, Elizabeth knelt where Frau Liebner indicated, finding that a stream of light from the one window in the room touched her face. The old woman in the chair leaned forward and peered closely at her. She took Elizabeth's face in her hands and stared, turning it this way and that, her crooked fingers feeling Elizabeth's skin and the contours of her cheeks. The old woman's eyes were milky and her sight clearly very poor, but there was a stubborn and proud look in her expression that Elizabeth was riveted by. "*Ja*, a beauty. Too bad. We vill haf to see, Katrina, how dis all turns out."

Her English was good though her accent was strong, most words affected by it, and yet her diction was clear. The *w*'s sounded like *v*'s and the *d*'s a little like *t*'s. But what did she mean, that it was too bad she was pretty and they would have to see how it turned out? Elizabeth scrambled back onto her feet and met Frau Liebner's gaze, but her friend merely shrugged.

"This is Miss Melisande Davidovich," the Countess Adele said, indicating the girl sitting beside Charlotte.

The girl rose and shook Elizabeth's hand. "Bonjour, Mademoiselle Stanwycke. I am pleased to make your acquaintance."

"And I, yours, mademoiselle," Elizabeth said, taking her hand. The young woman's politeness was a pleasant contrast to Charlotte's sulky behavior so far. Mademoiselle Davidovich was a very pretty girl; her dark blond hair was streaked with gold and was as fine as cobweb, and she had a pale, lightly freckled complexion, blue eyes, and a pink bow mouth. And yet, with so much beauty around her—for Charlotte was lovely, Melisande pretty, and Countess Adele striking—it was to the oldest woman's face that Elizabeth's gaze returned. If her life was represented on that face, then it had been hard, but had had its rewards.

"Uta is my great aunt," the countess said. "She is my grandfather's youngest sister. She—"

The countess's explanation was interrupted when a serving woman came into the room and gestured. Adele moved toward her, watched her gestures, and nodded.

"I must go for one moment, so please remain here, Miss Stanwycke."

"She will have tea with us," Frau Liebner said. "Mina," she continued, addressing the woman who had just approached the countess, "bring another cup." She turned back to Elizabeth. "Sit with us. I was just catching up with Uta, for we are old friends."

Bewildered, Elizabeth took a chair, which happened to be near the old woman who sat listening and catching the movement around her. Should she speak to her? Should she address only the others?

Her dilemma was solved by Uta herself.

"*Elizabeth*; dat is good name. Is it family name?"

"No. My mother thought it pretty, and she liked pretty things."

They spoke on innocuous subjects for a few moments, but then Uta, with a sly expression, said, "I hear, girl, dat you had frightening time on the road. *Ja?* Woman ran out, overturned carriage?"

Elizabeth glanced at Frau Liebner in surprise, but she just shrugged and smiled, as if to say no one kept anything from Uta.

"Well, it didn't exactly happen like that; we had our little accident first, and then I saw the woman . . . or girl. But it was upsetting," Elizabeth said with an uneasy look at the two girls, who whispered to each other on some intense topic. They spoke in German; Melisande seemed fluent in it, as did her uncle Maximillian, Elizabeth remembered, from the night before. She would have to learn, too. "I told the count about it, and he said he would look into it for me."

"But you . . ." the old woman said, poking at her with one crooked finger. "You were going into forest after the woman?"

"I didn't like to see her chased," Elizabeth said sternly, perturbed by the hint of laughter in Uta's voice and irked by the poke in the ribs. "The poor lady! What if the brute was going to hurt her? What if—"

"What if she was going to enjoy it, eh?" the old women erupted in gales of laughter, her blankets shivering and her lace cap falling askew.

Both girls were now watching and listening, and Elizabeth had to assume they had heard some of the story of her journey to the castle the previous night. As her dour maid, Mina, brought Elizabeth a cup of tea, Uta settled herself and straightened her cap.

"You must excuse," she said, "an old woman's laughter. I haf not much to laugh about. Your coachman was right to pull you back from going in woods. Danger is dere." She dropped her voice and leaned forward. "Danger. Bad things. I who haf lived here my whole life through tell you dis."

The two girls were still listening.

"What kind of things, Countess Uta?" Melisande asked in English.

"Terrible things. I will tell you story dat happened to me. Once, when I was young, I was walking in forest."

"You said the forest was dangerous and one should never go in," Elizabeth interjected, setting her cup aside on a table.

"But I was foolish maiden, you see. *Toericht* . . . most foolish, dat means, Miss Stanwycke. I walked in the light of the full moon to meet a lover, you know."

Charlotte giggled, but then covered her mouth.

Uta was good-humored even at her great-niece's rudeness. "*Ach*, I know, so old as I am now, who would want me? But I was pretty den, prettier dan you, Charlotte," she said, waggling a bony finger. "And with better breasts, ja? Bigger ones dan yours. *Sei still, maedchen.* So, I was going to meet my lover. He was not good enough for me, my father said, and he was right, but the fellow was a strong lad, and I liked him. So I was going to meet him. I thought if I got with child my father would let me marry Siegfried, so I was going to get with child."

Both girls gasped, but Elizabeth watched, noting that their shocked reaction was just what Uta was hoping for. Frau Liebner was silent, watching, too.

"It was dark, near midnight, and cold. I was wrapped in cape and walked quickly, trying to get warm. When out of nowhere big, big wolf leaped into the path!"

Both girls jumped and shrieked. Uta laughed.

"He was big, gray . . . a handsome, shaggy beast," she continued. "But terrible to see," she said, dropping her voice to a hoarse whisper, "for his mouth was dripping with blood, fangs three inches long and red blood dropping onto fresh snow from dem!" The sunlight touched Uta's wrinkled face and she turned toward it and continued her tale. "I backed one step and he followed. I backed, and still he followed, just one step at a time."

Elizabeth stole a look at Charlotte and Melisande; both girls were listening openmouthed, their expressions fearful.

"And den he leapt!" Uta cried, flinging her hands up, shaping them like claws.

The girls shrieked again and clung to each other.

"I turned and ran, tripping; I was thinking, you see, every step I took would be last, dat I would fall and wolf would be on me and do awful things, rip into my—"

"What absolute rubbish," Elizabeth said, her voice deliberately loud, not liking how Uta was relishing frightening the two girls. "I don't believe that ever happened to you."

Frau Liebner cried out in horror, "Elizabeth! You should not—"

"No, Katrina, no. Let her speak," Uta shouted, her hoarse old voice crackling with either laughter or anger.

Again, her impertinence was about to get her in trouble, Elizabeth thought, scanning the room. Well, better here than in front of the count or countess, she supposed. But still she hesitated.

"Speak, Fraulein Stanwycke," the old woman commanded.

Charlotte and Melisande watched, wide-eyed, their gazes flicking between Uta and Elizabeth. Folding her hands in her lap, Elizabeth said, "I do not believe that any girl, no matter how foolish, would go into the woods at night in winter for . . . for the purpose you described."

"Ah, but Siegfried and I were to meet and go to cottage he knew of in woods."

"Then I think he would have come closer to the castle to accompany you. You said he was of a lower station than you.

You would have made him meet you, not waded through the snowy forest on a cold night. You would have met him nearer the castle."

"I was very young, and my father—"

"Then you would have arranged something else, but I still will never believe you went calmly walking through the forest in the middle of a snowy night to meet a man."

Uta's rheumy eyes sparkled with humor. "Katrina," she said, reaching out for Frau Liebner's hand. "You did not tell me dis one was so quick . . . and so bold. *Was kann Ich sehe, aber Ich war zehr jung und toericht?* Dat means, young miss, what can I say, but dat I was very young and foolish?"

"Then a girl so foolish would have been caught by the wolf and devoured, I think," Elizabeth said. She glanced over at the two girls and both were calmer; Charlotte was gazing at her with a measure of speculation.

A nice-looking, very proper gentleman wearing spectacles entered the room just then and glanced around the gathering. "Good day, ladies. I have come to find Miss Stanwycke." His gaze settled on Elizabeth and he moved in front of her and bowed, taking her hand. "Miss Stanwycke; I am Cesare Vitali, the count's secretary. Countess Adele sent me to retrieve, you, miss, for she wishes to continue your tour of the castle."

Elizabeth rose, curtseyed to the gathering, and said to Frau Liebner, "May I visit you later?"

Frau Liebner nodded.

Uta, still grinning, said, "Come back and see me. I miss speaking to dose with any brain, for dey are few in dis dull house."

NIKOLAS trudged through the huge double doors of the castle and knocked snow from his boots. His vision was blurred and his whole body ached with weariness. If he did not find his bed soon, he would drop where he was.

Two servants approached and he gave them his snow-covered cloak and gloves and related his desire for something hot to drink once he reached his own rooms. There were things he should have been doing, plans he should have been making, but he had to sleep before he did anything else.

He trudged into the great hall, the sound of his hobnailed boots echoing off the vaulted ceiling.

"Nikolas!"

He looked up. Adele gazed down at him from the gallery, her gaunt face pale in the dim upper reaches of the hall above him. Glancing swiftly around and seeing several servants, he decided it was too risky to impart his awful news in German, for they would understand him and he didn't wish to alarm them a second before he needed to, so in English he said, "Adele, something terrible has happened. Young Magda Brandt, Wilhelm Brandt's daughter . . . they found her on the edge of von Wolfram property, attacked by wolves . . . they don't know if she will live."

He heard a gasp, but it was not from his imperturbable sister. A figure moved from behind Adele, and he saw Miss Stanwycke appear at the high carved railing.

"You should have warned me that she was there," he said to Adele in German, his stomach clenched as though by a fearsome fist.

"A wolf attack?" Elizabeth Stanwycke said. "How terrible!"

Her face in the gloom of the gallery was pallid, her expression concerned, but she didn't swoon, nor did she cry out, scream, or in any other way demand attention for her own shocked sensibilities. He headed for the stairs and strode up them two at a time, forgetting his weariness.

"I am sorry, Miss Stanwycke," he said when he stood before the two ladies. "I should not have spoken so abruptly, but I thought Adele was alone, and—"

"No need for an explanation, Count," she said, the whole line of her body stiffening. "I was shocked but I will not wilt, I promise you."

They stared at each other for a moment, and he remembered coming upon her in the night in the library, where she had no real right to be. The proud tilt of her chin was familiar to him already from that encounter, and the determined set of her lips. He supposed he should be happy she was no swooning lily overcome by every shock, but he was not sure so much strength and resolution was best suited to his own purposes, or whether a more timid sort who would stay in her room and hide would have been better. Too late now, anyway. They would have to see.

Adele said, "We were just on our way to meet Charlotte in the yellow parlor. Is Magda Brandt really so bad? What can we do?"

He struggled with what to say, in the company of his niece's new tutor. There was much going on that he would need to keep from her. In fact, there was much that he kept from everyone, and even some from Adele. "I have not seen her, but her father says—"

"What was she doing in the woods?" Elizabeth Stanwycke said, her brow furrowed, blue eyes narrowed in thought.

He frowned. What *was* Magda Brandt doing in the woods at night . . . alone? He had not questioned when he heard the awful news that a village girl had been attacked by wolves on the edge of his property, but why was she out at night, and why would she be in the woods on his property at all? It was a distance from the village, and in such weather! The snow had not let up all evening and they were likely to have several feet before the drifting was done.

"I do not know."

"It is immaterial," Adele said, her tone harsh as she glanced between him and Elizabeth. "She will recover, or she will not. We need to decide . . ." She cast a quick glance at the tutor, and then said in German, "I will speak to you later, Nikolas."

"Yes," he returned in English. "We will speak later. I will not keep you ladies from your day's plan. Please, Miss Stanwycke, do not mention the unfortunate village girl to anyone."

"Of course not. I would have no reason."

He watched her eyes, but beyond the truthfulness he saw in them, there was some hint of something else, whether it was evasion or merely the vestiges of awareness left between them from their meeting in the middle of the night, he could not tell. Perhaps as he knew her better he would be able to read those fleeting expressions. He looked forward to that, he thought, taking in her simple gown and how it fit her lovely body. He most definitely looked forward to getting to know Miss Elizabeth Stanwycke.

Chapter 5

NIKOLAS COLLAPSED on his bed as his valet bustled in. "Heinrich, send for Cesare."

Heinrich did his bidding, then silently turned down his master's bed and provided the appropriate night attire, disappearing afterwards, swiftly and silently. He knew what was needed of him and did no more, nor any less, than was expected and wanted. For that reason alone he was the perfect servant for Nikolas.

As Cesare entered, Nikolas struggled to sit up again. He pulled off his boots and tossed them in the corner. "Have you heard about the girl, Magda Brandt?"

"Countess Adele just told me," Cesare said, picking the boots up and placing them outside the door. He returned and stood by Nikolas. His brown eyes held worry and something more.

"What do you want to say?" Nikolas asked, his weariness making him abrupt.

Cesare handed him the nightshirt as he stripped his clothes off swiftly in the chilly room. His secretary then went and closed the deep blue drapes against the muted light of the snowy day. He turned toward his employer and said, "You were gone all night."

"I had something to attend to." Nikolas pulled the nightshirt over his head. "And now I need sleep, or I shall drop. Tell me, have you seen Charlotte's English tutor yet?"

Obeying the hint that no further conversation on the subject of the night's activities was welcome, Cesare answered, "I saw her briefly; she met your great-aunt, Countess Uta."

Nikolas grinned. "I wonder what she made of the old dame. What think you of Miss Stanwycke?"

"She is very beautiful."

Nikolas gave him a sharp look as he crawled under his covers. "I do not care about that. My only care is if she can teach Charlotte what she needs to be a suitable bride for an English earl."

"That remains to be seen. She certainly appears well-bred and well-mannered." Cesare laid the count's discarded clothes over a chair and turned back to his employer. "But Nikolas . . . what if Charlotte doesn't want to be a suitable bride for an English earl? What if she would prefer—"

"Enough. I have decided."

Bartol Liebner then appeared, glancing in and motioning to Cesare to join him at the door. Nikolas could hear their conversation even with his face buried in a pillow.

"Tell the count that we have heard more from the village. We were misled as to the gravity of the girl's condition; Magda Brandt will recover completely, but she was badly frightened. Wilhelm is now spreading it around town, telling people that the wolf leaped at Magda from the von Wolfram property," Bartol said, his gruff voice laced with anxiety. "She is saying that the wolf appeared to be waiting for her, that he stalked her. What should we do?"

"Nothing!" Nikolas yelled, punching the pillow. "Do nothing until I tell you what to do. But now I must sleep, and the first person who awakens me before twilight will suffer the consequences."

Bartol gabbled, "Yes, my nephew, I hear you. Certainly. I just wondered . . . about the girl . . ."

"It will wait," Nikolas said again, his tone calmer. "Cesare, leave me, and close my door. And Bartol," he called out, "I do not want you discussing this with anyone. Am I understood?"

"Yes, of course, Nikolas," the older man said, peering into the dim room and bowing. "Sleep well."

THE yellow parlor turned out to be a lovely room next to the breakfast room on the main floor. It derived its name from the yellow papered walls and gilt furnishings, French in style but German, Elizabeth thought, in manufacture. Pastoral paintings were crowded on the walls, giving the room a warmer, more homely look than any she had yet seen. Magnificent it was, but still . . . there was a warmth present. Elizabeth perused it, while Adele and Charlotte stood silently awaiting her verdict. It had been agreed that since the lessons Elizabeth was going to impart to Charlotte were concerned more with deportment, public behavior, and court behavior than any formal teaching—other than a goodly dose of proper English—a parlor was the best setting. The paper was oriental patterned, and the furnishings were ornate but beautifully crafted, a yellow silk-upholstered sofa and two chairs and a mahogany writing desk in the corner.

Countess Adele had already shown Elizabeth a supply of paper and quills, for letter writing was to be covered, too, since every London hostess needed to be conversant with good letter style, Elizabeth believed. Certainly many English women were close to illiterate, but Elizabeth intended to set a higher standard, and at the end of her time at Wolfram Castle, Charlotte von Wolfram would be a credit to her teacher, able to write a proper letter of invitation, regret, or sympathy in French or English. She would sound, behave, and look like a lady should, even if few around her rose to those standards.

"Is it good, Miss Stanwycke?" the countess asked, clasping her hands in front of her.

Elizabeth, standing by one of the windows and looking out over the snowy landscape, said, "Yes, it's very good." She took in a deep breath and let it out slowly, turning in a full circle and gazing at the room, touching the white silk-embroidered draperies with one hand. "Perfect, in fact." And it was. The castle was far more beautiful than she had imagined it would be. She had pictured an austere life in a dirty, ill-kept, dank castle; the only two friends she had left behind had lamented with her over how hard her life would be from now on. Germany, they told her, was an uncivilized, rude country of half-tamed barbarians. Instead she had found that at Wolfram Castle there was warmth and elegance, and the household was run with a precise, determined rigidity that though harsh was well-ordered and luxurious. But most important of all, above considerations of physical comfort, she was safe and she was employed and she was far away from London, where the tongues could now wag with no ill effect upon her. Perhaps even now John was getting married. *Good for him,* she thought, hardening her heart, *and pity on his wife-to-be, a silly little girl just done her first season.* She turned back to the countess. "May I have a few minutes here alone with Charlotte?"

The woman hesitated, but then braced herself, sighed, and said, "Yes, I suppose. But you will not be starting today?"

"No. But Charlotte and I haven't had a chance to get to know each other yet, and I thought we would begin to at least make each others' acquaintance."

The countess hesitantly glanced from Charlotte to Elizabeth. Withstanding the urge to retreat from her request, Elizabeth wondered why the woman seemed so uncertain. Did she not trust her? Or was it her niece she was worried about?

She finally nodded sharply. "If you would like to have tea here, I will send someone. Later, with Nikolas, we will discuss what we expect you to cover with Charlotte." She turned and strode to the door. Stopping to stare back at Charlotte, she said something in German and the girl responded in an insolent tone. The countess said something else and then departed.

"This is a beautiful room," Elizabeth said to open the conversation. She strolled over to one of the sofas and sat down, hoping Charlotte would join her.

"I am not leaving here and I will not marry some old English . . . dodderer," the girl said flatly, her expression sullen and her tone harsh.

That would be among their lessons: how to speak English with a mellifluous tone and without using rude words. Elizabeth observed the girl for a long moment, noting the ugly grimace and slatternly posture. She did not have an easy task before her. "I cannot imagine your uncle would want you to marry anyone you had conceived a dislike for."

"Do not be sure! He would marry me to the devil himself if it would get me away from Wolfram Castle."

"Why is that?" Elizabeth watched the girl pace agitatedly, her swift movements betraying her nervousness.

She shrugged in reply.

"You must have a theory. You cannot have come so far in your belief without some idea of why it is so."

"He . . . wants me to marry good." The girl was not meeting her gaze.

"But I'm sure if that is his only purpose, to see you marry well—not *good*, Countess, but *well*—there must be some young man of your own country and class . . . perhaps someone you have already met?" Elizabeth watched her charge. Was it that Charlotte had conceived some ill-founded love for someone entirely unsuitable? That would explain her uncle's determination to send her away. And yet, if that were the case, he would likely have sent Charlotte to England to be schooled.

"I have not met any man," Charlotte said dully. "Not any man who could ever care for me." She plunked down on a low stool by the fireplace, picked up a poker, and jabbed ferociously at the embers burning in the grate. One popped and some burning coals fell to the hearth. "And I never will."

Baffled by the girl's behavior, Elizabeth was silent. So far at this troubled place there were far more questions than answers, an uneasy state for someone as curious as she was.

"You cannot predict that," Elizabeth said. "Even if you don't wish to do what your uncle commands, you can appeal to your aunt. Surely Countess Adele—"

"She and my uncle are together in this."

"What do *you* want to do?" Elizabeth asked, watching the girl jab again at the fire, wondering if she would burn the house down in her agitation.

Charlotte stilled and frowned, as if that question was a new one. And perhaps it was, for she repeated it. "What do *I* want to do?"

The door to the parlor swung open and Countess Gerta and Melisande Davidovich walked in. The countess was smiling, but the younger woman had the grace to appear abashed and lagged behind her companion.

A footman followed them with a tray of cups and plates.

"We heard you were having tea here, and Melisande wanted to join you so very badly," the countess said with a sly smile for her companion, who appeared startled. "I demurred, but she is so headstrong! And so we came and are interrupting your lesson. What have you learned, Charlotte?"

"She has learned how best to get one's own way," Elizabeth said with a significant look at the woman. She was not pleased at the interruption, nor at the countess's manner, which was impertinent and familiar. The woman had a hectic flush on her cheeks, almost a rash, and her movements were quick and jerky. Elizabeth watched her for a moment, thinking that if she was to do her job, she must determine how best to forestall such unwanted interference in future.

"Oh, I think she already knows how to do that," the woman said, her pale eyebrows arched and her blue eyes wide. "Don't all women?"

"I don't think so. If that were so, all women would be happy," Elizabeth replied acerbically.

"Getting one's own way does not always make one happy," the countess said, wandering the room as another footman came in with the tea and a plate of sweet cakes.

Wondering if that were really true, Elizabeth reflected that in her own case, perhaps the countess was right. Would she have been happy if a certain gentleman had lived up to his promises? Married and respectable she would be, and yet married to a man she now knew to have little or no moral quality in his soul. Would that have led to happiness?

Charlotte had been silent since her aunt came into the room. Elizabeth observed for a moment and noticed how the countess took over, serving the tea and offering cakes, as if it were a party in her own parlor. She smiled and preened and gesticulated, talking rapidly as she poured, spilling almost as much as she got in the cups. Countess Gerta von Holtzen,

Elizabeth reflected, was clearly accustomed to and relished being the center of attention. Melisande Davidovich, on the other hand, appeared to be trying to shrink away.

"Mademoiselle Davidovich," Elizabeth said, turning to her and speaking over the countess's rapid chatter. "Do you enjoy living here?"

Eyes widening, the young woman first looked to Charlotte, but her friend was bemusedly staring at her cup of tea as if it were a foreign object. Then she glanced at the countess, who had stopped talking and was glaring resentfully at her. "I-I suppose I do. The von Wolfram family has been very kind to myself and to my uncle. We both—"

The countess made a faint noise and the younger woman fell silent again.

"I am wondering," the countess said, her voice loud, "if that poor village girl will live . . . the one attacked and savaged by a pack of wolves?"

The two younger women were silent, but both had similar expressions of frozen incomprehension, their eyes wide and full of fear.

Elizabeth felt the first twinges of dislike for the countess, though she made an attempt to stifle those feelings. She was going to be resident in Wolfram Castle for quite a while, and she wished to get along with all of its inhabitants. She set aside the tea she did not want and cleared her throat. "Herr Liebner had some news that he imparted to Countess Adele and me as we approached the parlor; the girl's injuries were sorely overstated in first reports. She sustained a wound to her arm, but she got away without further harm," she said, "and is now convalescing at her father's home. She is going to be fine." In that moment it occurred to Elizabeth to wonder if the young woman was the same one she saw on von Wolfram property being chased by the cloaked man; if she made it a habit to be on the castle property, she may very well have been attacked by the wolves Elizabeth heard howling as she entered the castle. It was far more than likely, in fact. To believe otherwise would mean that *two* young women were wandering that night, and how likely was that in the middle of January?

"What a wonderful piece of news!" the countess said, clapping her hands.

Watching her, Elizabeth was struck by the impression that the countess could not have cared less if the girl recovered; her sole reason for imparting the appalling news seemed to be for its terrible import.

Charlotte hesitantly asked about the incident, and Elizabeth delivered a brief explanation, making it seem the merest fright on the village girl's part, not willing to dramatize things as the countess had. Countess von Holtzen snorted impolitely but had lost interest in the story and hummed under her breath.

"Could that have been who you saw on the road last night, Miss Stanwycke?" Charlotte asked.

"You saw a woman on the road on the way here last night?" the countess asked, her attention reclaimed.

Reluctantly, Elizabeth again told the abbreviated and expurgated version of the story. Feeling the weariness of her early rising and busy morning descend upon her, she made it brief and as uninteresting as possible, thinking there was entirely too much relish in horrible tales in this place.

"How odd," the woman said, frowning. "Did Tante Katrina see this woman?"

"I . . . I don't think so. But the driver must have."

"Terribly troubling," the countess said. "You must have been frightened."

"I was . . . upset," Elizabeth said, watching the other woman's expression. Countess Gerta was clearly troubled by the story; at least it was a human and appropriate reaction, and Elizabeth's early dislike was tempered by some sympathy. This was a woman who had lived a difficult life, it seemed, having lost her husband and borne twins so quickly after, albeit fifteen years had passed. Some people never recovered from such a tragedy. "But let's not speak of such terrible things!"

She glanced around at the three women. She had not been

in the household twenty-four hours yet, but already she had a sense there were undercurrents it would take her many months to fathom. Was that not true of every great household, though, where many people lived together? She had some experience of that and had no intention of being swirled into the eddy of controversy in this position.

It was her job to make this moment lighter, calmer. "What a diverse group of ladies we are!" she exclaimed. "I am from England, the Devon coast, and Miss Davidovich . . . you are from France. What part of France, pray?" It was a risky subject, but the girl smiled.

"I am from the Artois region, mademoiselle . . . near Lille, and the Belgian border. Do you know it?"

"No. I know of it from geography books, but when we traveled we went directly to Ostend, in Belgium. We could not, of course, travel through France; our journey was perilous as we traversed Belgium, and we saw French forces even in the south of Germany. What is the countryside like in the Artois region?" Elizabeth guided the conversation through such innocuous subjects for some time as they sipped their tea. The countess was silent and lost in thought for some time. Elizabeth was pleased to see Charlotte drawn out by her friend's conversation. She observed that Miss Davidovich was by far the more naturally poised of the two young ladies, and her goal would be to make Charlotte not appear so gauche when in company with young ladies of Miss Davidovich's innate grace. Charlotte von Wolfram seemed a pleasant enough girl when engaged in a subject that interested her, and she was very pretty, but she too often sank into abstracted musing or sullen brooding. Whether her nature was to be depressed or if circumstances only had made her thus remained to be seen.

As the conversation lagged, Elizabeth said brightly to Charlotte, "What is your brother interested in, if I may ask?"

When Charlotte merely shrugged, Miss Davidovich said, "He is very talented at playing the violin, mademoiselle. He even writes music."

"Is that so? And do you young ladies play any instruments?"

"Of course," the young woman replied. "We both play piano."

"You play, Meli; I stumble through," Charlotte amended. "My music master, Herr Dortmunder, called me an ignorant girl and said he could teach me no more. Then he left and went back to Vienna."

"Do you like music?" Elizabeth asked, touched by the woeful tone of her voice.

"I do, but I do not understand it."

"Perhaps Herr Dortmunder was right to give up on you," Countess von Holtzen said.

Melisande Davidovich gasped and Elizabeth was momentarily stunned by the casual cruelty of that statement, but the countess looked from one to the other of them. "What is wrong? Can she not enjoy music without having to play it? That is all I meant; perhaps she is not meant to be a great musician, but simply to listen well. Do musicians not require an audience of people who love to listen, though they do not play?"

Charlotte had sunk back into her sullen pout, and Elizabeth couldn't help but think that the countess knew exactly what she was doing. She didn't want to believe that though, for it would imply a mean-spiritedness that she would not lightly attribute to anyone. "I think that to play at all is a marvelous thing, and Countess Charlotte is to be congratulated for any musical learning she has attained." Elizabeth watched the older woman carefully and then took a chance she was afraid she might regret; she did not want to alienate any of the members of the household, but Charlotte was the most important person to win over. "Tell me, Countess von Holtzen, do you play any instrument?"

The woman bridled visibly and her lips thinned. "I did not have time for such learning, for I . . . I married young. I was a much sought-after beauty, you know."

Though the woman had rallied, it was clear she was nettled by Elizabeth's implication, that those who did not play at all should not criticize those who could play a little. When she glanced over, Elizabeth was surprised by the look of relieved gratitude on Charlotte's face. It seemed such a small thing, to defend the girl to her aunt, and yet it had won some small victory. Elizabeth was under no illusion that the way was now clear; Charlotte clearly objected to the purported purpose of Elizabeth's mission, so it would not be the end of resistance, but it was the beginning, she hoped, of some mutual regard.

Chapter 6

AWOKEN JUST in time to have dinner, Nikolas was in as foul a mood as he had ever experienced. But at least he would be able to arrange things at the dinner table differently that night. He would make sure the lovely Miss Stanwycke was placed by him at dinner so he could have a chance to talk to her and get to know her a little. He had already spoken to his Aunt Katrina, and she said the young woman was everything she should be, but he preferred always his own evaluation of people.

His family and household members had already gathered and were seated at the table, though, and there was no room for Miss Stanwycke at his side. Nor had she arrived at the table yet.

He sat in his accustomed spot at the end of the table and gazed at the gathering, examining faces, as he always did, noting expressions, evaluating the general humor. At his arrival the signal had been given, and footmen brought dishes and began to serve.

"Where is Miss Stanwycke?" he asked Adele, who sat to his left.

"In her room, I suppose," she said, darting him a swift glance.

He watched her face. It had not escaped his notice that his elder sister harbored a swiftly burgeoning jealousy for their niece's tutor. That emotion was solely inspired by Count Delacroix's gentle treatment and kindness toward the newest inhabitant of their household, and it must be just as swiftly defeated somehow, though he was certainly not the one to know how to deal with feminine intrigues and emotional turmoil.

"Did you not tell her she is to dine with us?"

"No. I thought she would be most happy eating alone. She appeared uncomfortable last night."

He turned to his sister and said, his tone low and gruff, "She had just arrived! She was exhausted and had a frightening experience on the road. She did not know anyone. Of course she was uncomfortable. From now on she will eat with the family."

"Nikolas, I will not—"

"No! Do not cross me in this, my sister." He met her gaze calmly. Though intelligent, rational, and determined, he knew his sister to be far more emotional than she ever would have confessed. Only her duty to her family kept her from melancholy, he sometimes felt, for she exerted herself every day to take care of the household, when she would rather have been doing other things, pursuing other interests. He supposed if he had ever married, his wife would have assumed her burden of management of the castle, but it was not to be. He would never marry.

He seldom contradicted her decisions, but in this case he knew himself to be right, and he also felt she would sooner get over her irrational distaste for Miss Stanwycke if she was forced to interact socially with the young lady. Adele did not reply. Her face was set in a grim and angry expression that made her appear harsher than she even was.

"I will tell her tonight," Nikolas said as a footman served him his soup. "I wish her to behave as a part of the family. How else is Charlotte supposed to learn, Adele?" He appealed to her rationality. "I wish our niece to be at ease at the table in an English household, and who here knows how that is? I have never been to England, nor have any of the rest but our Tante Katrina, and I will not place such an onerous burden on her, of teaching Charlotte."

Tacitly admitting his point, Adele did not respond directly. Instead she mused, "I had pictured from Tante Katrina's letters a rather frivolous society lady who would teach Charlotte to net a purse and sit up straight but . . ." She looked down at her lap and then at her brother. "Nikolas, she is far more intelligent than I expected."

Responding to the worry in her tone and her gray eyes, Nikolas put one hand over hers on the table. "Do not concern yourself, sister. Soon we will be able to relax our vigilance for a few weeks and then we will plan for the immediate future."

She nodded.

"I will find Miss Stanwycke after dinner and speak to her. She must come to dinner from now on, and to our family time after dinner."

Adele nodded again, but there was distress in her expression, and her particular concern he could not calm. If Miss Stanwycke was on the lookout for a husband or lover, and if Maximillian was susceptible to her beauty—and who could blame him if he was—then there was nothing anyone could do.

As Nikolas caught the subject of conversation among the rest of the family and guests, he was displeased. They were chattering nonsense about wolves and the attack the previous night. "Enough," he growled, and all paused and gazed down the long table at him. He caught each person's glance as he pushed his chair back and stood, using his physical presence as he sometimes had to, to command their attention and submission. In English he said, "There was, last night, as you all know, an unfortunate wolf attack on a village girl. But she will recover very well, I am told. Let it be a reminder to all that the woods are dangerous. Wolves are a part of our life, but if one is sensible one need not worry. Magda Brandt must have been foolish indeed to walk in the forest in the middle of the night, if that is what truly happened to her. No further discussion."

He sat back down. "Now," he said, in a more normal tone and his native tongue, "let us speak of something else. Christoph . . . how was your fencing lesson with Cesare this morning?"

With his nephew's sulky reply, and his niece's spirited defense of her brother's sulkiness, talk assumed a more normal course. No one would speak of the wolf attack again in his presence, but Nikolas had no doubt the talk would continue outside of his sphere of influence. That he could not control.

When the company adjourned, he sent a footman to ask Fanny, the maid assigned to aid Miss Stanwycke, where the tutor might be, and he was pleased to hear that she was in the yellow parlor. So, she was making it ready, perhaps. And it was the perfect opportunity to speak to her of what he expected and wished.

Nikolas paused outside the room and heard her voice as she tried to make herself understood to a footman; the hair on the back of his neck and on his arms stood at the soft, clear tones and lilting accent. He could feel it like fingers stroking his neck, and he took a deep breath, quelling the physical urges that coursed through him. Familiarity would rid him of his unsuitable infatuation with the lovely young Englishwoman, he trusted.

As he entered, she was sighing in exasperation.

"No, I don't want the table there, I want it over there, near the window! Oh, why did I not learn German on my way here?"

Nikolas chuckled and she whirled. He was pleased to see the pink rise to her cheeks. "What do you wish from the fellows?" he asked.

She told him how she wanted the furniture arranged for her purposes. He directed the men, giving her a few words to use as he did so. Elizabeth learned them quickly and practiced, though she fractured the grammar badly. Clearly she was trying to apply rules from English grammar to German, and since the two were so very different, it gave her sentence structure an odd and endearing backwardness. Perhaps she would like private lessons in his language . . . but no. He did not think it a good idea to be with her too often, nor in private. He could afford no distractions and she could most definitely be a distraction for any man denied for too long the pleasure of a woman's company.

When it was all arranged to her satisfaction, Nikolas dismissed the harried footmen. "I missed you at dinner tonight, Miss Stanwycke," he said, circling the room and examining her furniture arrangement, trying to imagine her purpose for each grouping.

"I beg your pardon, Count?"

"I missed you at dinner. Must I clarify that sentence? Is my English so bad? I expected to see you, and did not, thus I missed your presence at dinner."

"I . . . but . . ." Elizabeth clasped her hands in front of her and gazed at him. "I am merely Charlotte's tutor."

"Still, I think you should be there."

"But . . . Signor Vitali does not dine with the family."

"Cesare is my secretary. Though in some households your positions would be roughly analogous, in this particular instance I think that Charlotte needs your presence to teach her how a true English lady behaves at the table."

"This is what I have set up the table by the window for, sir." She indicated an oval mahogany table and chairs set as for a small dinner party.

Nikolas shrugged. "Why a pale imitation when night by night she can see your behavior and emulate it?" He circled behind her and inhaled her scent, reveling in it, letting it bathe his nostrils. She was sweet as honey and yet her scent carried the faint tinge of alarm that was more clearly delineated in her stiff posture. He moved away from her. "You will dine with us, beginning tomorrow night. I will expect you to be there."

Elizabeth nodded. "May I be excused for this evening from joining the family?"

"Since we have already had our dinner," he said, with humor in his voice, "of course. And I will not expect you to join the rest in the drawing room."

"Thank you."

He glanced at her sharply, noting the tartness in her tone. For a lady wholly dependent upon his continued goodwill for her employment, she was daring indeed. And he liked her the better for it, though he supposed he oughtn't.

She took in a deep breath and let it out, then turned to face him. "Count," she said. "I have been told by your sister that I am not to use your library."

Instantly Nikolas remembered their early morning encounter there. He had entered to find her standing by the lectern that held the family bible and had been startled into giving away his presence, when he would rather have entered unobserved. He saw the memory in her blue eyes, too, and wondered what she had made of his appearance in the middle of the night, snow flaking his cloak and his hair. He felt the memory physically, how as he got close to her, her warmth melted the snow and how it dripped down his hands and onto the carpet. "No one else uses it," he confirmed.

"But may I?" Elizabeth said, staring directly up into his eyes. "There are many books there, and I wish to learn German while I am here."

While she was in his home, the time limited by Charlotte's needs, she meant; she was preparing for a future in Germany, then, or perhaps just saw it as an opportunity to make herself more invaluable in any circumstance. Silence. The clock on the mantel struck the hour—nine o'clock—and chimed. Nikolas stared down at her while the clock chimed, taking in her pearly skin and oval-shaped face, the slope of her shoulders and how a single chestnut curl caressed her pale neck. A pulse throbbed at the base of her throat, life coursing through her, warm, rich blood feeding healthy pink flesh. Eager and vital, she challenged him with her direct gaze.

"You will take dinner with the family on the morrow. Tomorrow evening I will expect a private report on what you think Charlotte needs most in the way of tutelage." He bowed, keeping his expression remote. "Good night, Miss Stanwycke," he said and strode from the room.

SHIVERING from the frigidity of the great hall after the warmth of the yellow parlor, Elizabeth hastened up the stairs and toward the upper rooms.

Fanny met her in an upper hallway and curtseyed. "Miss, would you like to retire now? I have your room prepared."

"Thank you. No, I think I will find Frau Liebner first and say good night. Is she in her room?"

"I believe she is up with the Countess Uta."

Elizabeth took a deep breath. "Do you think I should join them? Would it be impertinent?" She felt like she was still feeling her way through the labyrinthine formalities of life in Wolfram Castle.

"Countess Uta adores visitors, Miss Stanwycke, and she rarely sleeps. I think she would enjoy your company," the girl said shyly.

"Then I will go up," Elizabeth said. She made her way up to the old dame's chambers and knocked on the door, then entered. But the room was empty except for the old woman, snoring in her chair by the window, and the mute servant. Elizabeth turned and was about to creep out, but before she could came a command.

"Kommen sie hier, Fraulein." The old woman sat up straighter with an effort as her servant rushed to help her.

"I . . . I thought Frau Liebner was here," Elizabeth stuttered, approaching and standing before the elderly countess.

"No, she was sleepy, and so to bed did go. But you I would speak to."

"Certainly, madam."

"Sit!"

Elizabeth, with as much grace as she could muster, sat down on the low stool the woman had indicated.

"What think you of my great-nephew?"

Elizabeth paused and thought, then said, "Christoph? He is—"

"Not him, and do not deliberately misunderstand, Fraulein. Of course I mean Nikolas."

With the memory of their encounter in the yellow room so fresh, Elizabeth, exasperated, said, "He is very . . . imperious."

Uta shrugged. "He is man. Dey so often think it necessary. But else . . . what do you think of his looks? Lusty he is, ja? And handsome? Do you think him handsome?"

It was an impertinent question as far as Elizabeth was concerned, and she had no wish to answer. She shook her head. There was nothing she could say that could not be misinterpreted.

The old woman squinted. She motioned to her servant, and Mina, a large, strong woman with dark hair well-threaded with gray, approached and turned up the lamp.

"Does she not speak?" Elizabeth said, watching the woman retreat.

"No. Never. She can hear, but has never spoken."

"You say she can hear, but you communicate with her by gesture. Why is that?"

"It is habit only. Now, tell me why you will not say what you think, dat Nikolas is the handsomest man you haf ever seen?" Her pale eyes glinted in the light.

Elizabeth gazed at her steadily. This was a woman hungry for information. Alone in her rooms all day with a mute servant, she must revel in the gossip and chatter she picked up from relatives, Elizabeth thought. "I will answer your questions, if you will first give me some answers."

It was a daring gambit. If the old woman became offended, she would say nothing and their burgeoning friendship would die aborning.

Uta nodded slowly. "I cannot promise to answer everything, but you may ask three questions. Beware: what you ask may reveal as much about you as what you tell."

"All right." Elizabeth rested her forearms on her knees and thought. "First, before we start, do you ever see Count Nikolas?"

"Dat is one question."

"No, I meant . . . oh, all right. That is one question."

Uta cackled. "Yes. He visits me every Sunday morning instead of going to church. I am his penance."

"Penance? For wh . . . oh, no, that will not be another question," Elizabeth said, catching the old woman's sly grin. "Why does the whole family live at Wolfram Castle? I can understand Countess Adele, since she never married, but my understanding is that Countess von Holtzen and her husband lived here, and Bartol Liebner does, too."

"Nikolas, and Johannes before him—his elder brother, you know—haf strong need to take care of family and also to control dem. It is ingrained, you know, like . . . like family pride and the hard demeanor. Gerta's husband, he was . . . weak. Ineffectual, I think English word is. Dey did live elsewhere, but she was with child, the twins, you know, and wished to come home. And den Hans died."

The same day as Anna Lindsay von Wolfram. Elizabeth opened her mouth to ask what happened, but Uta spoke again.

"Bartol, he is not blood relation, but he was dere mother's brother, and Nikolas swore to his mother as she lay dying that he would never expel him. He has no other home now."

She had only one more question left. The room was dim beyond the reaches of the lamplight, the curtains drawn, the fire banked but throwing off heat. "Am I keeping you from your bed, madam? And no, that is not one of my questions."

Uta cackled, and that laughter became a coughing fit. Mina came and attended to her mistress, holding a glass of water for her to sip, then faded back just as quickly as the old woman recovered. "No, I seldom sleep, apart from napping here in my chair. It is one of the penalties of old age, you know, dat dose of us with little to occupy our time haf the most time to keep occupied."

Elizabeth nodded. "Why are Charlotte and Christoph kept here at the castle, but Countess Gerta's children are sent away to school?"

"Christoph *was* sent to school. He was to join the military, you see, become an officer, but he was rejected. Dey said his health was not good enough." Uta frowned and shook her head slowly. "I do not believe dem. His health is good. But what else? I do not know. Eva and Jakob, Gerta's twins, dey are away at school, and dat is the natural way. Do not people in your country do so?"

"Yes, but it just seemed odd to me that the cousins were treated so differently, one set kept here at the castle, the other set sent away. It would make more sense if both boys were sent away and both girls kept here. That is often the way, that the ladies are tutored at home."

"Dat is merely way it is. Now, I haf answered. Your turn it is to answer questions."

"Ah, but just two," Elizabeth replied with a smile. "For

you tricked me, madam, and I truly only asked two proper questions."

"You are clever," Uta said, poking at her with one crooked finger. "And bold. Two questions den."

Elizabeth waited, but the questions, when they came, were not what she expected, for the countess did not go back to the dangerous ground of how attractive her nephew was.

"Why did you come all the way here when you could haf stayed in your own country to work?"

How to answer honestly without giving away too much? "I am without family, madam, and . . . and Frau Liebner was very kind to me. I was not needed anymore in my last position, and so when she mentioned that she might know of a job—your great nephew had written to her asking if she could find a tutor for Charlotte—I decided to take it. I have no ties to my country, and it was an opportunity to travel."

Uta stared at her intently. "I think dat is only part of truth," she grumbled.

"But it *is* truth," Elizabeth said.

"Ja, I can see dat."

There was silence for a long moment, and Elizabeth began to think the old woman had slipped into a nap, but her eyes were open.

Finally, she spoke. "Fraulein Elizabeth, if you had opportunity, would you marry?"

It was not what she had expected, and she wondered how to answer that honestly. She bit her lip, thought for a long minute, and then said, "It would depend upon a number of circumstances, to be quite honest; I am not completely opposed to the notion. But if you are truly asking another question, I did not come here to find a husband."

Uta's mouth cracked in a grin. Her teeth were stained and crooked, but her smile was merry and her eyes twinkled with laughter. "*Ach, gut!* Dat is much more dan I asked, for you answered two questions at once. Tells me great deal about you, you know. To bed now, you go. For much you have to do on morrow, no?"

"Yes," Elizabeth said, standing. On impulse she leaned

"Ten years she has been in England, to my understanding
I am so fortunate she was able to accompany me here, for th
voyage would have been fearful indeed without her company
We encountered French forces along the way—I spent muc
time pretending to be mute so I would not reveal my Englis
origin—but Frau Liebner defeated every obstacle placed i
our path. It is kind of you, from what I understand, to spen
much of your time with Countess Uta."

"She is good-hearted beneath her gruff exterior. When
first came here, even though I knew no German and she litt
French, I felt how sympathetic she was."

"How long have you lived here?"

"Two years." The girl's voice broke and she bowed h
head.

Two years. Elizabeth shivered as a footman brought her
plate with her requested breakfast. Just a little over two yea
had passed since the awful news of the execution of t
French king had shuddered through English society, and he
was a girl who had suffered from the awful consequences, f
her mother had perished in the madness. It was an awful r
minder of how dangerous the times were, and how fortuna
she had been to pass safely through to Wolfram Castle.

"This is a good place to be safe," Elizabeth said gently.

Charlotte's gaze swiveled to regard her solemnly. "You s
so now. We shall see."

Bartol Liebner, frowning, said, "I heard some noise l
night. Did anyone else hear it?"

Countess Adele cleared her throat and folded her lett
laying it aside. "My apologies, everyone, for being so rude
to read my letter at the table, but it could not wait. Of wh
were we speaking?"

There was silence, and Elizabeth noticed that the cou
ess's kinsman ducked his head and did not repeat his questi
The young Count Christoph pushed back his chair and stro
from the room without a single word, and Countess Ad
paled visibly at his rudeness.

"I apologize for my nephew," she said. "That was unf

over and kissed the old woman's soft, wrinkled cheek, then
was horrified she had done so.

But the old woman smiled complacently. "To bed," she repeated sternly, pointing at the door.

To bed, but not to sleep. She was so far beyond tired that
she could not, no matter how much she tried to fill her mind
with mundane thoughts, rid herself of the notion that there
was something she had forgotten to do or say. Fitfully she
slept, for how long she had no notion.

But once she awoke, sleep abandoned her, and so she lay
awake staring into the darkness. Had she done the right thing
in coming so far? There had been other possible avenues, she
supposed, if she had explored them. She had a maiden aunt in
Yorkshire, and she would have taken Elizabeth in out of family loyalty, perhaps, but that woman had long abjured the frivolous abandon of her brother and sister-in-law and would no
doubt censure the offspring of that union. Elizabeth had visited her once when a child and had found the woman's life
bleak and her disposition grim.

She had come so far in her contemplation when a noise
outside her chamber caught her breath in her throat. It was the
sound of footsteps, which paused at her door and then continued. A servant, no doubt, she thought as she turned over and
closed her eyes, up late and pausing only incidentally by her
door. She was merely anxious and unnerved by the state of the
house since she had arrived, the melancholy she sensed. That
had to be the explanation for her nervousness.

A shriek and moan ripped her from such a comfortable reflection. She bolted from her bed. Perhaps that same servant
had fallen and lay at the bottom of the stone steps in pain. Perhaps . . .

She slipped on a robe, tied it loosely at the waist, and exited
the room, looking to the right and left. No one in her passage,
which meant the awful sound had to come from the gallery or
the great hall. She flitted down the hall and toward the gallery,
her slippers slapping softly on the luxurious carpet.

Flambeaux lit the gallery, throwing the wafting pennants
into eerie relief, their fluttering patterned into batlike shad-

ows. She approached the ornate oaken railing with trepidation, crouching in the shadows, not certain why she hid but
following what eons of instinct taught her was right.

A scuffle below! She peered through the spindles but could
not see from that angle and so stood, staring down to the great
hall below. Two men supported another figure, the moaning
wafting up in uncanny drifts of sound.

Then another scuffle. The figure twisted and turned, and
the larger of the two men bound the smaller figure in his arms,
wrapping it, containing it with his strength. Elizabeth gasped
and the tableaux froze. Then, in the dim light of the flaming
torches, she saw a face turn up to her.

"Miss Stanwycke," Count von Wolfram said, his voice
hoarse. "What are you doing there?"

"I . . . I awoke at the sound. Can I . . . can I do something
to aid you, sir?"

The figure had collapsed between the two who held it up.

"No, it is merely an ill servant. Go back to bed."

Every nerve in her body, every instinct, screamed at her to
listen, to obey, to heed the subtle warning in his voice. But
some lingering stubbornness prodded her. "Are you sure I can
do nothing?"

"I am sure, " he said, his voice gruff, his tone grating. "Go
to bed."

She retreated, but then tiptoed back to the gallery when she
heard them scuffle off. But all she could see was the trailing
remnant of a cloak, and a door closed behind them as they retreated into the servant's quarters.

Slowly she made her way back to her room and to her bed.
Slipping off her robe, she lay it over a chair but started back,
trembling. Her curtain was open, and it had been closed when
she left the room.

Or had it?

Chapter 7

THE BREAKFAST table was well populated but silent
when Elizabeth made her way there. The breakfast room itself
was much smaller than the dining room, of course, and less
formal, with cheerful papered walls and a long oval table.

"Good morning, everyone. I've forgotten; how does one
say that in German?" she asked, scanning the company.

"Guten morgen," Bartol Liebner said, rising and bowing.
"And how lovely a morning it will be, now that you have arrived, Miss Stanwycke."

The French count and his niece were at the table, too, and
he rose and bowed. Count Christoph von Wolfram, sulkily
piling food into his mouth, did not rise. He appeared ill and
tired, with dark circles under his pale eyes and his blond hair
straggling over his forehead in choppy locks. Elizabeth took a
seat by Melisande Davidovich and Charlotte. The only other
person at the table was Countess Adele, but she was silent, her
attention absorbed by a letter she was reading.

"I have been up to see Frau Liebner already this morning,"
Elizabeth said to the two girls, trying to ignore the mood of
grim silence that infused every person present—with the exception of the smiling Herr Liebner—with gloom. Charlotte
did not reply. She was watching her brother, her lips set in a
severe line. She too ate rapidly, scooping her food, her fork
scraping the plate.

"She seems a very . . . kind lady," Melisande replied, her
hesitant gaze darting from face to face, finally flitting to and
resting on Elizabeth with a sigh of relief. "And Countess Uta
is pleased to have her back. She has been gone a great while,
I understand, and the countess has missed her sorely."

givably rude but . . ." She seemed about to excuse him, but then shook her head.

Bartol Liebner, ever the conciliator, it seemed to Elizabeth, said, "Ach, youth! Who would be young again, with so much pain and strife, eh, Maximillian?"

The French count smiled faintly but seemed perturbed mostly to be considered a contemporary by the older German. "Please, Countess," he said, his cultured voice pacific in tone, "do not distress yourself unduly, for we all know Christoph to be occasionally thoughtless."

"He is not thoughtless," Charlotte cried, tossing down her fork and rising. "You do not understand him. No one does."

"Charlotte," Elizabeth said, putting out one hand, "I don't think anyone meant he was thoughtless in the way of deliberately rude, but in the sense that he does things occasionally without thinking. Am I correct in that?" She glanced around, and the Frenchman at least nodded, as did Melisande.

Trembling, Charlotte collapsed back in her chair, and Elizabeth thought that everyone had had enough emotion for one morning. Whoever had told her the German people were stoic and unemotional certainly had never met this troubled and overwrought family. Whatever was distressing this household, it was not her affair, and she would have to sternly remind herself of that, for her curiosity was tugging at her like an impatient two-year-old. This morning was distinctly different from the morning before, with a thread of anxiety wending its way through the group and reeling them all in. Why was everyone so on edge? Had others heard the scuffle with the master of the house, as she had? She hadn't seen anyone else from her gallery observation post, but it didn't mean there wasn't someone else in the shadows. An uneasiness prickled in her spine, but she shrugged it off. She must be resolute and not allow the gloom of this odd family to draw her in.

The French count seemed to be following her train of thought; changing the subject, he said, "Miss Stanwycke, what do you think of the castle so far? Is it not magnificent? A gothic masterpiece."

"I have been trying to take it all in, but it is difficult. I look forward to many more opportunities. I think there is much of the castle I have not yet seen."

"There are some marvelous paintings you should see; Holbein, Tintoretto, Raphael. The gallery and art treasure room is a trove of wonders. That is the large room beyond the ballroom. Perhaps you have not yet seen it. I would be delighted to accompany you on any necessary exploration, mademoiselle," the Frenchman said, bowing his head.

Countess Adele said harshly, "I have begun the tour, and I will finish it. Let me know what you wish to see, Miss Stanwycke, and I will show it to you."

"Ah, but I was about to offer the same," Bartol Liebner said, smiling. "I who have so little to do can at least offer my services for that."

Elizabeth looked from one to the other and noted the expression of concern on the countess's face as she glanced over at Count Delacroix. "Thank you, Countess Adele," she said, choosing her words carefully. "I will be pleased to accept your offer."

Nikolas strode in just then, and Elizabeth happened to be looking in his direction. His expression was grim, but as he entered he assumed a mask of coolness, the harsh lines next to his mouth smoothing. There, at least, the overt emotionality of the family was ruthlessly subjugated to his strict self-discipline.

He greeted his family and guests and then approached Elizabeth. "Miss Stanwycke," he said, bowing and taking her hand. He raised it to his lips.

Elizabeth heard a gasp from someone but could not tell from the various expressions around her where it had come from, nor why.

The gasp had not gone unnoticed, and Nikolas wished that he could take back the gallant gesture. It was out of character for him, though he couldn't honestly regret it, nor the enthralling sensation of her cool, soft skin against his lips. Straightening, he glanced around the gathering, but still could not guess who was so surprised by the unconventional—for him—act. The English tutor had colored a faint pink, which only made her more beautiful.

"Nephew, how gallant this morning!" Bartol said, a broad grin on his smooth, placid face.

Nikolas shrugged, took a seat, and waited for the footman to pile his plate with his customary breakfast. He had not, as usual, had nearly enough sleep, but he would snatch an hour later. It would have to do. He stole a glance at Elizabeth, but her gaze was fixed firmly on her plate as she finished her meal. How to explain to her what she saw the night before? There was no way, and he wouldn't even try. She would have to learn not to be so inquisitive.

Elizabeth rose. "Excuse me, everyone." She turned to Charlotte. "Shall we meet in the parlor in one hour?"

"Pardon, Miss Stanwycke," Nikolas said, watching her. "I would like to see you first, briefly, in my library."

Slowly, she turned to gaze at him. "Did we not establish what your wishes were last evening, Count?"

Charlotte snickered, and his sister cast her a quelling glance. Elizabeth colored, as she perhaps realized how challenging her tone sounded.

"Not at all. I became . . . distracted and did not express myself thoroughly. Come to me in my library in one half hour. Then you may meet Charlotte in the parlor."

"Yes, Count," she said, ducking her head in deference, though her eyes glittered with challenge.

That she was restraining herself from retort he could tell. Though he did not know her at all, there was much he could surmise, and part of that was that her very nature must make it difficult to retain her position as a subservient employee of a household.

"Nikolas," Adele said. "I am perfectly capable of telling Miss Stanwycke—"

"I know you are," he said to his sister in German. "But I have something in particular I wish to say to her."

The tutor's gaze slewed back and forth between them.

"One half hour. In my library. You wished to see it again," he said with challenge in his own tone. "So meet me there."

He finished his breakfast quickly and left the breakfast table, not one to linger when there was much to be done. When she rapped at the library door exactly half an hour later he called out a sharp, "Come in, Miss Stanwycke."

She entered and he saw her examine the walls in as covert a fashion as she could manage. "This is a beautiful room, sir," she said.

"Sit, Miss Stanwycke."

She took the seat in front of his desk and crossed her hands in her lap. That was what he wished for his niece. This young woman before him was out of her element, out, even, of her home country and dependent upon others for her comfort. She was mired in a very odd situation and with unexplained things going on around her, and yet there was an indefinable air of calm about her. She appeared to belong, even if she didn't feel she did.

"We have not truly spoken of what I wish from you."

"I suppose that's true. But you did mention that we would speak after I have an opportunity to evaluate Charlotte today."

"Yes, but there is another topic of some importance to settle between us. I have the sense that you do not agree with my objectives."

"Is that important? I am not her guardian, Count, nor is it my affair to decide on the merit of your plan for Countess Charlotte."

"I am relieved you admit that, Miss Stanwycke."

She raised her well-shaped eyebrows. "I would never say otherwise. I may disagree with your plan, or I may even abhor it, but it is not my place to contradict you."

"But I would have you agree with me."

"I wish that were as easy to command as my actions, but I'm afraid I cannot bend my opinion as easily as my will."

"So you still think I am doing wrong in planning an English husband for my niece."

"Perhaps if I understood better your reasoning . . ." She let her words trail and raised those elegant brows again.

He clasped his hands before him on the desk. "Your country . . . I think it a very civilized place."

She nodded. "Is Germany not so as well?"

"These are tumultuous and confusing times; nothing is very settled, but yes, Germany is civilized. Are we not allied? Have we not provided for you your last three kings, and your queens, too?"

"Well, the first King George, anyway, and the queens. I would count the succession of Georges English. Certainly the Hanover line has been . . . er . . . productive and relatively stable."

He grinned at her as she colored delicately. She had approached in as circular a fashion as possible the stupendous reproductive capacity of Queen Charlotte. "Yes. Productive indeed. I am related to them in some fashion; we are quite near Hanover, you know. They are just thirty miles or so north of us. Your crown prince is about to marry my cousin, Caroline, who is from Brunswick. That state, too, is nearby, about the same distance as Hanover, but to the east."

He sat back in his chair and steepled his fingers. "Enough of the geography lesson. After your journey here you must be aware of the state of affairs in my land. Though the Rhine is some ways away, it is said that all of the German states to the south and west of that river are now in French hands. Civilized or not, our country is not at peace. I fear the effects of the French problem, you know, and I hear that which concerns me gravely of their plans to push beyond the Rhine and toward us. My plan is to marry both Charlotte and Eva, her younger cousin, to English gentlemen, thereby ensuring their safety."

He gazed steadily at her, and it was clear from her skeptical gaze that she did not believe him. However, there was an element of truth in what he said. Their safety was most important, and that could best be secured by marrying them to Englishmen. Any other reasons were immaterial and not necessary for her to know.

"What I want from you, Miss Stanwycke," he said, sitting forward once again, "is to give to Charlotte your grace, your elegance, your charm. I see it in the way you walk, and in how you talk. I do not know why even my sisters do not quite have that, but it is so."

She colored again, prettily, and he thought he should be bewitched if he stared too long, so he looked away and stared at the door. But her voice, when she spoke, was cool and betrayed not an iota of her embarrassment, if that was what had caused her blush. His thudding heart would have told him it was the attraction he felt for her answered from herself, and yet he dared not allow his thoughts to travel down that path.

"I will do what I can. It seems to me that what you wish me to teach her will benefit her no matter whom she marries or where she is to go in life."

He looked back up at her as she stood. "I am pleased that you see it that way." Tamping down the sweet and heady rush of pleasure just the sight of her invoked, his voice, when he spoke, was harsh and gruff. "Make it so and you will be well rewarded."

She stiffened, nodded her head, and began toward the door.

"Miss Stanwycke!" he called out.

She turned and waited.

"Are you . . . comfortable here? I would have you be happy and comfortable while you live in my home."

She smiled. "Everyone has been most kind."

It wasn't what he asked, but it would have to satisfy him. For now. "Good. Good."

CHARLOTTE was sitting at the small oval table staring out the window when Elizabeth entered the parlor. There was that in her posture which would need to be corrected, for she slouched and lounged. That would never do.

"Good morning, once again, Countess." Elizabeth took a seat opposite her pupil. When Charlotte did not respond, Elizabeth continued. "You seem very close to your brother. I find that admirable."

She shrugged. Elizabeth let the silence lengthen, studying the girl. Charlotte was rounded and childish looking still, even though she was nineteen, past the age when many English girls were already married and mothers. Why she was so untutored in deportment when she had two aunts living with her constantly was impossible to guess, so Elizabeth didn't even try. They would begin now and see what could be accomplished. Though no teaching masters lived in the castle now, both Charlotte and Christoph had had the benefit of music and dancing lessons and art tutelage, but with no system of learning, Charlotte, at least, did not seem to have benefited all she could.

And yet before her was an example of all that could be learned in the embodiment of Melisande Davidovich, who was as graceful and well-bred as could be imagined, and the girls appeared to be fast friends. It was her task now to instill in Charlotte the desire to learn and become more ladylike.

"Charlotte," Elizabeth finally said. "I suppose you love your home as much as anyone, but have you ever thought of traveling? There is so much to see in the world, so many places and people. If you were to leave home for that purpose, to travel and see the world, would you not enjoy it?"

"Miss Stanwycke, I am never leaving here. My uncle only wants me to leave here and go to England to marry some old man. He has a list, a *long* list, of suitable gentlemen. I've seen it, and I know who they are. The men are old and horrible . . . one is even over forty. That is close to dead!"

Elizabeth bit her lip to keep from laughing out loud, for it wasn't funny, truly, not in her pupil's eyes. "Is that your only objection to your uncle's plan? The age of the suitors?"

"No. I don't want to leave. Why should I?"

Elizabeth sighed and clasped her hands on her lap. It was clear she couldn't even begin to teach Charlotte anything if the girl had no wish to learn. Staring out at the crisp blanket of snow and the clear blue of the sky beyond the frosted panes, Elizabeth was stymied as to how to do so, how to revive any desire Charlotte had to learn how to deport herself in a manner befitting her status. Perhaps if she got to know the girl, she would better understand how to teach her.

"It looks so lovely out," she mused. "Tell me, do the groundskeepers clear a way around the house?"

Charlotte nodded. "The stable boys will be out to clear around the house and the stable yard, and the way down to the village will be made better by using a sledge to pack the snow. We use a cutter, of course, to travel down to the village most times, but still, they will clear near the house."

"The sun is shining and it looks lovely. I haven't even seen the outside of the house yet. Would you go with me for a walk? You could be my guide."

With a shrug, Charlotte murmured her assent, and Elizabeth made a plan to meet near the front door in one half hour.

Chapter 8

CHARLOTTE'S OUTDOOR attire was a charming cloak in palest blue velvet lined in blue silk, the hood drawn up against the cold. Within it, her blond hair sparkled like spun sugar nestled in pale blue tissue. If she would only smile, and if she had a more graceful air, she would be a very pretty young lady, Elizabeth thought, as the footmen held open the huge oaken doors for them.

It was the first time she had been outside since arriving two nights before, and the atmosphere was wholly different in the light of day. She breathed in deeply and coughed, the air was so fresh and crisp. All around them, as Charlotte led her down the front steps, a blanket of fresh snow piled like chipped sugar, coating bushes and shrubberies, stone walls and pillars, sparkling in the brilliant morning sun.

"How beautiful," Elizabeth breathed, standing in one place and turning in a full circle. The front portion of the castle, the older section, was of gray stone, but the turrets on either corner had unusually enormous glass windows, stained glass for the chapel and clear glass for the conservatory. "How absolutely breathtaking is Wolfram Castle!"

Charlotte frowned and gazed up at the castle walls. "It is?" she said, her breath puffing out in steamy clouds.

"It is. Have you never noticed?"

"It is just my home. I have never thought of it any other way."

"If you were once away from it, you would see it differently when you came back. How large the castle is!" Elizabeth gazed up at the stone battlements of the main section and then at the timbered wings, stretching off on either side, the geometric puzzle of timbers filled between with pale cream plasterwork. Farmland belonging to the family was to the east of the castle, Charlotte said when asked, pointing out the blanket of snow stretching out in undulating waves. Behind the castle beyond the stables and other outbuildings was a steep hill that rose above, climbing toward the sky; blanketed in thick forests laden with crystalline snow; in fact, the forest hemmed them in on three sides—west, north, and south. In front, which was the north face of the castle, the lane descended toward the village of Wolfbeck through the dense forest, the impenetrable wall of conifers almost black where they lined the road. She glanced around and saw that there had been some attempt to shove snow away from the route to the front door and beyond, along the base of the castle. "May we walk the perimeter of the castle, at least? I badly need some exercise."

Charlotte shrugged and began to lead the way. But as they rounded the first corner of the older section of the castle, three huge beasts loped toward them, gaining speed, mouths open as they howled in excitement.

"Wolves!" Elizabeth cried and stumbled backward. A rut in the cursed snow caught her heel and she felt herself falling backwards down to the ground, and the beasts, their fanged mouths open and slavering, leaped on her. She closed her eyes at the sight but could feel their hot breath and dripping saliva as she beat at them with closed fists, trying to roll away.

"Heinz, Margrit, Reinhardt, halt!" Count von Wolfram shouted.

He strode toward them from the stable area behind the castle and kicked at the animals as he shouted. The beasts instantly slunk away and lay down in the snow a few feet distant.

Shaking, her whole body quivering with fear, Elizabeth felt herself being hauled unceremoniously to her feet by the count. Gazing around, bewildered, she could see Charlotte, convulsed and shaking, holding her arms over her stomach. Count Nikolas gazed down at Elizabeth, his mouth split in a grin, his own white, strong teeth far too like the awful creatures' for comfort.

"But . . th-those are w-wolves!" Elizabeth sheltered behind him, though the creatures seemed pacific enough now, she could see, as she peeked from behind the safe wall of the count's body.

"No, they are dogs only," he said, turning and sheltering her with his black cloak. "Or at least . . . they are mostly dog. And though I know you cannot fathom it in this moment, they were only trying to greet you. They would have licked your face if you had not been flailing at them. I kicked them away as much for their own good as yours, you know, for you are very fierce."

He chuckled indulgently, and she felt like kicking him.

"Did Charlotte not warn you about my pack?" Nikolas's voice was gentle as he pulled Elizabeth around to face the dogs; he put his arm around her shoulder and pointed to the animals, which were whining and crawling toward their master on their bellies.

"Dogs?" she repeated, stupidly. She swiveled her gaze toward Charlotte, who was unsuccessfully trying to stifle what Elizabeth now knew was laughter. Shaking with anger, now that her fear was gone, Elizabeth did her best to stifle the fiery temper that threatened to turn her into a shrieking fishwife in that moment. She would deal with Charlotte in her own way, but to react in anger now would be to allow the girl to set the tone of their association. "No, she must have forgotten," she said through gritted teeth.

Nikolas gazed down at her and then over at his niece, who was straightening and staring at them both with a challenging look. He gently dusted the snow from Elizabeth's cloak, his hands lightly patting at her waist and down over her bottom. She shifted away, but he put his arm over her shoulders again.

"Look," Nikolas said, crouching and pulling her down by him. The dogs bolted to him and groveled at his feet. He was clearly their master; their subservient behavior in his presence would have told Elizabeth that even if he hadn't. They rolled on their backs, presenting their pale bellies trustingly to him.

"They look like wolves," Elizabeth said, noting the brindled charcoal gray and white fur. Their winter coat was thick, with ruffs around their large heads and thick shoulder muscles. She crouched at Nikolas's side and held out one hand. The smallest of the animals rolled back onto her belly and sniffed Elizabeth's gloved hand curiously, the expression on her face oddly like a smile.

"That is Margrit, the lead bitch. They are part wolf," Nikolas admitted. "Wolf and dog are so close together that they can breed, though in nature it would never happen, for the wolf would kill the dog as a competitor for food. My game master took pity and rescued a lame wolf once, several years ago. When it recovered, it would not leave his side, so devoted it had become. He bred the wolf with our female dogs, and this is the result. They are good hunters and like to be together, but also, unlike the wolves, they like humans. Wolves you will never see, for they shun mankind."

"Except for the girl in the village," Elizabeth pointed out, watching his face as he caressed one of the male dog's muzzles. It licked the count's hand and whined.

"There I am going now, to find out the truth." He stood and gave his hand to Elizabeth, pulling her up. He threw a severe look at his niece, who was doing her best to appear innocent. He turned back to Elizabeth and gazed steadily down into her eyes. "I hope you were not hurt by this foolishness."

"Only my pride," she said, staring up into his dark eyes, shadowed though they were by thick black brows. His high pale forehead had one lock of hair carelessly drooped over it, the result of a prominent V of dark hair, a widow's peak.

He touched her shoulder. "Charlotte should have warned you."

"I think she was playing a trick," Elizabeth admitted, glancing over at the girl, who was cavorting with one of the wolf dogs, which dashed about in the snow in a frenzy of joyousness, yipping and yodeling and leaping at her outstretched hand. "But she may just have forgotten."

"You are very kind. I must go now, but shall we talk later?" She nodded, and he strode away back toward the stables, his step energetic and powerful, the set of his shoulders straight and wide. The dogs followed him, bounding at his side.

"You like my uncle."

Elizabeth turned at Charlotte's words, finding that the girl was approaching her. She ignored her statement, though. "That was a clever trick, not telling me about the dogs. You must have known they would be out and that after Uta's talk of wolves I would jump to the conclusion that that is what they were."

The girl, her blue eyes wide, stared at her, neither admitting nor denying the charge.

Elizabeth thought for a moment, her gaze turned to where Nikolas had disappeared. Could the girl in the village have been attacked by these dogs? Though they were friendly enough in the light of day with Charlotte and Nikolas around, they were big and looked like wolves and with that blood in them were no doubt capable of attacking if provoked or threatened. And who knew what an animal would perceive as threatening?

How close was the girl to the castle when attacked? Supposedly, she was merely on the edge of von Wolfram property and had been stalked by the beast—or beasts—that attacked her, but Nikolas indicated that real wolves avoided humans, not hunted them. Could the girl have been on her way up to the castle, or near it, to meet someone when she was attacked? Could the wolf dogs have been responsible?

And was she the same girl, perhaps, that Elizabeth saw on the road? As she had already pondered, it was surely too great a coincidence that two women were out that same cold, moonlit night. But then, who was the man following her, and why did she not complain of that when she spoke of the wolf attack, if that was the case?

"Let's walk," Elizabeth said, starting off and not waiting to see if Charlotte would follow. *Let her follow or not.*

The path led around the castle toward the back, between the castle wall and a lane. Along the stone walls of the older part of the castle, Elizabeth noticed a couple of wooden doors at the base. "What do those lead to?" she asked, looking back at her pupil, who trailed a few feet behind her.

Charlotte merely shrugged.

"Does that mean you do not know, or you won't tell me?"

"Perhaps neither," Charlotte said as she trudged past Elizabeth; she led the way toward the back.

"All right," Elizabeth muttered, following. "Young Miss Taciturn. We shall see what we can do to break down some of those walls you have built around you."

They followed the timbered wall to the back stable yard, an area that bustled with life, as did the farmyard beyond where the dairy house was, and the pigs and chickens that supplied the castle with food were kept. In the large yard, strewn with straw to soak up the mud, stable boys groomed two huge horses while more patiently waited their turn, standing tethered to a rail outside of the cavernous timbered stable. The guttural shouts of men inside the stable told her more work was going on within, and the *clink-clink* of a smith's hammer echoed in a shed that slanted off to one side of the main building. In the center of the cobbled yard just beyond the stable, ringed by a low wall, was the blasted trunk of an ancient tree.

"What is this?" Elizabeth asked, approaching it. She pulled off her glove and touched the trunk, wondering why such a withered example of former arboreal glory had been allowed to remain.

"It is the family tree."

Elizabeth glanced at Charlotte's face to see if she was making a joke, but she likely didn't know the humor of her remark in English. "What do you mean?"

"Ask Uta. She will tell you the story."

"Oh. All right."

From the gaping maw of the stable came a dark horse, ridden by the count. The wolf dogs followed him. He waved as he rode past, on his way to the village, presumably, to speak to the injured girl.

"Is your uncle . . . does he always concern himself with the village goings-on?"

"It is his responsibility," Charlotte said. "He is their . . . how do you say it?" She frowned, and then her face smoothed. "Ah, yes, he is their liege; to them he owes protection, to him they owe allegiance."

"That is an enormous responsibility. But did not that kind of thing die out many years ago?"

Charlotte shrugged. "Perhaps, perhaps not. I don't know." She had lost interest and wandered now around the back of the timbered wing, sloshing through snow that melted on the cobbled surface.

Elizabeth followed. There was a wide courtyard in the center, sheltered by the newer wings of the castle, and it appeared that in summer there was a fountain and a garden. Everything was overlaid with a thick blanket of sparkling white, though, and shapes that could have been benches or shrubs or walls appeared in a vague random pattern that would not reveal its underlying objects until spring had melted the snow.

"Are these gardens?"

"Yes."

"And do you garden?"

"No."

"Oh. Do gardeners only do so, then?"

Charlotte sighed impatiently. "No. Meli gardens; she knows all about herbs and likes to prepare her potions and ointments. If you so much as cough she will try to doctor you. My Aunt Adele, Uncle Bartol . . . even Uncle Max. They are all mad for gardening in summer. I do not understand it."

"I look forward to seeing this in spring," Elizabeth said, glancing around and up to the high windows overlooking the garden. It was unfortunate that her own room did not overlook the garden; instead it had a forbidding view of the dark forest, the edge of it like a black slash in the snowy landscape. But then, the windows overlooking the garden were only corridor windows. She shivered and gazed up; the sky, once brilliant with sunlight, had darkened somewhat. Clouds were gathering above the hill, and her fingers were beginning to numb and her toes were already so cold she couldn't feel them in her boots.

"Shall we go back in?" she asked her pupil. "I think that is enough walking for one morning. With our brains refreshed, we shall begin to speak of what we wish to do for the next few months."

Charlotte was silent.

"And perhaps," Elizabeth continued, "you could help me to learn a little German. I found it very difficult to communicate with the footman, and I don't like to put people out to translate for me continually."

Again Charlotte shrugged and they turned to head back to the front door of the castle.

MEN had been sent out first thing in the morning to pack down the snow with sledges, and so as Nikolas rode he found only a few spots where he foundered. Karolus, his mount, was as steady a horse as could be bought or taught, his breeding from an ancient line of battle horses used to bearing much weight and soldiering through awful conditions.

With so far to go in the snow, he had time to think.

Would he, given his current knowledge of Miss Elizabeth Stanwycke's attributes, her great beauty, and probing intelligence, hire her again if he had the opportunity?

No. From the first night, finding her in his library, he had been aware that he was in a most dangerous position. He was drawn to the woman, and not just for her beauty but for some indefinable quality of deep calm, something he was missing, he supposed. All of men and women's pairings were a coupling of natural desire and a need to fill a void, to find what was missing from one's own heart and soul and fill it with another's. If she felt it, too, though, she was concealing it well. He thought he saw it flash in her eyes once or twice, and he felt it in her trembling when he was close, but she never by gesture or word gave him the slightest hint.

But it was early. She had only been there a few days. Time would tell.

Not that he could afford to take advantage of any attraction she felt for him. Already he had been faced with the consequences of her curiosity and intelligence. It was vital she not find anything amiss; once they were past the next night he would be safe for a while and could plan.

The dogs had been following him, but as he reached the end of his property they stopped and sat, watching, as he trotted down the sloping road into the nearby village. Wilhelm Brandt's house was a three-story home close to the heart of town. As with many of the other buildings, the first story was a store; one had to climb the stairs to find the Brandt's living quarters. He was the burgermeister, or village mayor, by Nikolas's own command, but the man's tenure had not been without trouble. Brandt had an eye for opportunity and was not averse to taking advantage of his position. He had perhaps a too loyal following among the town's men.

An old fellow hurried as quickly as he could from the small stable behind the house and took the reins, gazing fearfully up at Karolus, who was seventeen hands and powerfully built.

"Do not concern yourself, for he will behave." He said a few words to Karolus in Latin and tugged at the reins, and the horse went obediently with the fellow, who trudged behind toward the stable.

Nikolas took the steps two at a time up to the Brandts' door, knocked, and entered, as was his right. Ducking his head to avoid the low lintel, he stepped inside. The interior was tiny and smoky, with little light from the two windows overlooking the street. As his eyes became accustomed to the dimness he could see that Wilhelm's tiny wife was there, bowing her head before him.

"Good morning, Frau Brandt. Where is your husband?"

"Count von Wolfram, welcome to my humble home. I expect Wilhelm in one moment."

"How is your daughter?"

"Better, sir."

"I would like to see her."

He could see the hesitation in the woman's wrinkled face and he wondered if her husband had told her to admit no one to her daughter's bedside, but she dared not contradict the lord from whom her husband had obtained his post. She ducked her head and motioned behind a curtain that sectioned off a portion of the main room of the home.

He pushed aside the curtain to find Magda Brandt sitting on a pallet, her face pale, her expression nervous. He didn't approach closer, merely asking, in as gentle a tone as he could manage, "How are you, Magda?"

"Better, sir."

"Where is the injury?"

"On my arm." She held it out, but all she could show him was a dirty cloth wrapped around the wound.

He sighed. "Frau Brandt," he called.

When the girl's mother came in he gave her a severe look. "Madam, this girl's bandage is filthy. If I am to believe her arm truly on the way to healing, I will see her come out to the light and there you will boil a cloth, cool it, and after you wash the wound wrap it in the boiled cloth."

She gazed at him in incomprehension but scuttled to do as he commanded when he repeated his demand in a steely tone. Magda Brandt slipped past him into the great room and sat down by the open hearth, huddled miserably in her neat but worn dress. She was a pretty girl who would one day be as peaked and wizened as her mother. But this moment she was round and plump, pink and pretty. Even her humble mode of dress did little to conceal her loveliness and the tempting roundness of her figure under the bodice.

She kept her eyes averted as Nikolas examined her. When Frau Brandt did not appear to be boiling any cloth, he repeated his command more slowly. She nodded but did not move to obey.

"Now!" he roared, and both she and her daughter jumped. With difficulty, he restrained his temper, condescending to explain more fully why he wanted them to do what he said. He explained about infection and the necessity of keeping the wound clean.

While he spoke, he hurried the mother along, even though he sensed that far from not understanding, she did know what he wanted but was loath to obey. Finally, he squatted by the girl on the tidy hearth and unwrapped the filthy bandage himself, though she trembled at his touch. He did not want her to be afraid of him, but he supposed it was the natural consequence of their separate stations in life. She knew he could command anything of her family or of her and she would be compelled to obey.

When he undid the dirty cloth, what was beneath was a revelation. "This is no wolf bite," he growled.

He looked up into the girl's eyes and saw terror. When he glanced at the mother he saw terror mixed with evasion.

"But, Count, please, yes . . . yes, it is a wolf bite." That was the mother, wringing her wrinkled hands together.

He examined the wound more closely. There was considerable bruising, but it was red and maroon with a dark center, like her arm had been twisted. He touched it, and she flinched. There was, in addition, some scratching and an abrasion that bled freely, but if the wound had been received in a struggle with a wolf, there would have been some tearing of the flesh. He had expected to see much worse.

Wilhelm Brandt at that moment stormed into the room. With a mixture of bluster and cringing, he demanded to know why the count was unwrapping his precious child's bandage.

Nikolas stood, towering over the mayor. "I want to know why you are passing off this mere scratch as a wolf attack?"

"I? Passing it off? My daughter was attacked on your property, Count . . . or next to your property." The distinction was important; no one from the village had permission to be on his property after sundown.

"This is not a wolf bite. I would say this wound had more to do with some human agent than any animal."

"Then perhaps it was both," Brandt said slyly, his round face twisted in an expression of contemplation.

"What are you talking about?"

"It has been said that wolves are gathering on your property, Count, but perhaps . . ."

Nikolas stared at the man and waited, but when no more was forthcoming, he said, "You have something in mind; out with it, man. Say what you will." If his tone was menacing, he did not care enough to temper it with any softness.

"Perhaps," the man said, looking to the right and to the left, "it is werewolves."

Fury welled within Nikolas, and he tamped down an external expression of it with some difficulty. "I thought you all were past such supernatural nonsense as this! Who has been spouting such absurdity?"

"No one, lord," Brandt said, with a deep bow. "No one but you; for it was you who said this bite had a human source, and yet it was a wolf who attacked my poor Magda. So there is only one solution—werewolf."

Nikolas, conquering his fury with great effort, strode to the man, who cowered before him. "If I ever hear that you are spreading such pernicious lies, such absolute rubbish, and terrifying the good people of Wolfbeck, I will wring your neck with my bare hands."

"Then, lord," Brandt said, his voice quavering, and his gaze sliding away to the hearth and to his wife, "let us put men on your property to guard. I have ten men ready who will patrol and make sure no wolves—nor even werewolves—are gathering."

"No!" Nikolas thundered. He turned to the women, tried to gentle his tone, and said, "Frau Brandt, wrap your daughter's arm in the clean warm rag that you have boiled. Do so again tomorrow, and the next day. My housekeeper will send down to you what you need to look after Magda." He strode to the door but turned before exiting.

"Brandt, hear me good," he said, pointing a finger at the mayor. "If even one armed man steps foot on my property at night, I will kill him, flay him, and nail his hide to the church door. It is on your conscience if it comes to that."

Chapter 9

ELIZABETH AND Charlotte ate lunch together, during which Elizabeth tried to begin the process of instilling appropriate manners in the girl. It wasn't that Charlotte was rude at the table, nor was she slovenly in her dress or personal habits, but there was that in her mode of sitting and speaking that indicated she would stand out unhappily among proper society. She slouched, her stare was often vacant, and she was not careful in her eating habits. She could not—or would not—school her facial expressions and often looked either bored or unhappy.

But after lunch Charlotte begged off any more lessons, saying she felt ill, and she disappeared, presumably to rest in her room.

Elizabeth found herself with free time. After sitting with Countess Adele for an hour, during which she listened to a recitation of the family history from about the year 1100 up to 1300, she felt some sympathy for Charlotte. If the girl had felt anything like the ennui Elizabeth felt in the countess's presence, then her illness was not completely feigned.

And so, free and at loose ends, not really wanting to visit anyone else for the moment while she thought about some of the odd occurrences so far at Wolfram Castle, she explored the building, the warren of corridors and dead ends, new portion and old castle finally beginning to make sense to her in the light of day. But still she could find no explanation for those wooden doors in the base of the old castle. They must lead to rooms not readily accessible—storerooms, perhaps. That would make sense, for stores of food, coal, wood, and other supplies would need to find their way into the house somehow, and how better than from doors near the lane? Those rooms, then, would in turn be accessible only from service areas, pantries, and the like.

She had not forgotten the count's magical appearance in the library the first night of her arrival, but she had thought of a logical explanation; it now seemed to her likely that there was a door in the paneling somewhere that led to his own suite of rooms. How else to account for it? It did not explain, however, the unmelted snow on his cape.

On her way toward the yellow parlor, the room she considered her own little sitting room, she encountered Bartol Liebner and realized that what she had been thinking so strange for the past hour was that she had encountered no other member of the family in her travels.

"Guten tag, Fraulein," he said with a polite bow. "I hope you have so far been enjoying your day."

"Uh, *vielen dank*, Herr Liebner," she said, trying out some of her German and thanking him for his good wishes. "I have been enjoying it so far."

He clapped his hands. "Very good, Miss Stanwycke. Soon you will speak such good German there will be no keeping secrets from you!" He chuckled and gave her a roguish grin.

"I hardly think that is a concern, sir. Languages are not my strength."

"And so," he said, his hands behind his back and rocking on his heels, "have you been seeing the castle?"

"I have. I've gone over much of it, but . . . I think I missed a part," Elizabeth said, peering along the gallery and pondering her route. "I thought there was a . . . a room that had weapons on the walls. I remember seeing it a couple of days ago, and I wished to see the family shield that hung in it again."

"Ah, you mean the sword room!"

"I probably do."

"May I direct you?" He held out his arm in a courtly manner.

She took it. He was just her height and kept up a lively chatter as they walked, relating amusing anecdotes from von

Wolfram family history that Countess Adele had not touched on, and she found herself enjoying a family member's company for the first time since arriving, if one did not consider Uta's interesting oddness and Frau Liebner's familiar comfort. Or the count's intense attractiveness.

They entered a room on the second floor, and Elizabeth immediately recognized it as the open, marble-floored chamber she had seen on her first night's perambulations. How she had missed the door in her travels that day she couldn't say. It made her wonder if she had truly learned all there was to know about the castle or been deceived once again. It seemed simple enough, but once one had doubled back and gone up and down stairs, one was thoroughly confused as to what had been explored and what had not.

"That is the family shield you spoke of, Fraulein," the man said, guiding her to the far wall and indicating above a glass case.

"Yes, I see." She gazed up at the shield, barred diagonally in red and black and with a wolf rampant on one half and a raven with outstretched wings on the other. "What does the motto mean?" she asked of the German words scrolled across the top.

"Literally, it can be translated, 'Run swift. Fly high. Freedom always.' But old Johannes—Nikolas's father, you know, not his poor late brother—once told me it means that, like the wolf, they should run swiftly, like the raven, they should soar, and always, they should hold their freedom sacred above all else."

"Hmm. I've never heard a family motto like that."

"You have never met a family like this," Bartol said, taking her arm and squeezing it. "They are . . . magnificent."

She glanced sideways at him, curious at the thickness of his voice. There were tears standing in his dark eyes. "But you are no blood relation, am I right?"

"No, I am not so fortunate. But always they have been so very kind to me. The count's mother was my eldest sister. I came to the castle to keep my sister company when she married—she was very shy with her new family and wanted her little brother to be with her—and I have been here since."

"Did you never want to leave?" Elizabeth asked, grateful for the explanation of his residence at Wolfram Castle but wondering that he had never wanted his own family.

"Who could? This is my family. I am devoted, like an old dog, you know. And now, how much more dear to me could the children be, even if I had my own? I would die for Charlotte and Christoph . . . or I would kill for them, you know, so precious are they to me."

"That is very commendable," Elizabeth said gently, touched by his devotion. She squeezed his arm to her side. "They are lucky to have you here."

A door at the end of the room swung open, and when Elizabeth glanced up she saw Count Nikolas and Cesare Vitali stride in together, dressed for exercise. The count wore the same tight breeches and open shirt she had seen the evening she arrived, and he appeared just as raffish and handsome, that one dark lock of hair falling over his white forehead. Both stopped when they saw the pair by the glass case of ancient weapons below the family shield.

"Ah, nephew, and Signor Vitali!" Bartol cried out.

"Uncle, how . . . unusual to see you here," the count said, strolling toward them, his boot heels beating a sharp rhythm on the marble floor.

"Yes, is it not? But Miss Stanwycke asked me to guide her, and how could I say no to such a pretty lady? And now you both are here for some swordplay. May we stay and observe? It would be thrilling for Miss Stanwycke."

Elizabeth felt the color rise in her cheeks. She would never have made such a request on her own behalf. When she glanced up at Nikolas she found it impossible to read his expression. He appeared angry, his dark eyes stormy, his brows drawn down. But when his gaze met hers, she felt he was not angry at the request nor even at her presence, but at something that preceded it, likely even before he entered the room. The Italian secretary, who carried their specialized practice weapons, bowed politely as he took off his spectacles and set them on the glass case.

"For myself," he said with a smile, "I would only be embarrassed because my former student—I taught him Italian and fencing when he was at university, before becoming his secretary—has so far outstripped my teaching and will show me to such a disadvantage. It is, of course, up to the count."

Nikolas bowed and said, "You must both do as you wish. We are merely practicing, so it is no exhibition of skill. It will be a poor example of proper swordsmanship, but do what you will."

It was a bad-tempered response, but Elizabeth was intrigued. Was he a poor swordsman, or was he just in a foul mood? "We'll stay, then," she said, released from any compunction about intruding by his ill temper.

Bartol guided her over to a row of chairs lined up along the wall, obviously intended for the express purpose of seating watchers. She took a seat, settled her dove gray skirts, and composed her thoughts.

The two men consulted for a moment, murmuring to each other, and then took their stance, opposing each other with epees drawn.

What followed left Elizabeth breathless. Signor Vitali had been falsely modest, for he was superb, to her untutored eyes. His elegant form, slim and agile, was like quicksilver, lunging and parrying. He was the elder of the two, but on the fencing floor he appeared the younger, as swift and sure in his movements as a dancer.

But the count . . . for most of the practice Elizabeth could not keep her eyes from him. As he appeared to work out his anger and aggression, his muscular build stretched and strained at the bounds of his tight breeches and close-fitting shirt. And as he worked, so did he perspire and his dark hair became plastered to his neck. His shirt dampened and his shoulders were outlined, as clear as if he had been wearing no shirt at all.

It was close to indecent. And yet the more furiously he thrust, the more of that dangerous attraction she felt; her heart pounded uncomfortably and her mouth dried. Her powerful attraction to him was merely physical then, she thought, disappointed in herself. She had thought herself more mature, after her recent trials, and certainly with more sense, than to allow the merely animal to appeal to her. She should be fascinated by the poignant beauty of Cesare's classic style, and yet instead she was drawn to the animal fury of the count's rage.

She watched, clasping her hands together tightly in her lap. She could feel the count's uncle glance sideways at her occasionally. He must be wondering at the tenseness of her attitude, but she could not relax her posture. She felt every thrust and every wickedly skillful plunge of the count's sword as if it resonated within her somehow.

Finally they were done and she felt flushed with mortification as her employer's gaze met hers and held it. She rapidly stood, excused herself, and almost ran for the door.

Nikolas watched her go with a mixture of regret and relief.

"How very masterful you are, nephew!" Bartol said, crossing the floor and clapping his hand on Nikolas's shoulder. "And how very damp," he continued, wiping his hand on his trousers. "I feel sure Miss Stanwycke was quite overcome by your display."

"Why do you say that?" Nikolas asked sharply.

"Why, it was clear, nephew. If you had seen her tension and the way her eyes never left you . . . why, you would have seen what I did." Bartol bowed and made his farewells.

Cesare cleaned the hilts of their weapons and replaced them in their holder as Nikolas wiped his brow with a cloth.

"What was in your heart today, Nik?" Cesare said casually, picking up his glasses and slipping them on.

The count shook his head, noting his secretary's deliberate use of his nickname and recognizing it as the man's subtle way of trying to ease into informal talk. "Not now, Cesare. am going to bathe. Meet me later in the library."

He strode from the room and in half an hour he was soaking in his gigantic copper tub, one luxury he only occasionally allowed himself. It was crafted by the old coppersmith they had once employed to make roofing plates and was large enough for his own body and for another, if he had so desired, though he had never tested that capacity. The steam rising around him, he rested back, allowing the heated water to pull the tension from his body.

What was Wilhelm Brandt up to? Magda's wound was not a wolf bite. He knew that, and no one with a mind and eyes would mistake it. But then Brandt had not intended Nikolas to see it and had been furious when he had. All he knew was it was vital that Brandt not send men onto von Wolfram property that night. He hoped he had made that clear enough; what he could have done stronger than issuing that bold threat, he could not imagine. The mayor didn't have to know that Nikolas would no more shoot a man unprovoked, even on his own land and within his own rights, than he would harm one of his own family.

His family. His torment and his pride. He loved them fiercely and trusted them implicitly, but they did try him with their troubles.

He shook his head, ridding himself of gloomy thoughts, and instead allowed himself to remember the way Elizabeth's steady gaze had followed him as he fought Cesare. He and his secretary would both be sore the next day after such a vigorous workout, and he would not lie to himself: he was showing off for her, displaying every skill he owned and many he had forgotten he possessed, wishing to impress her with his fencing prowess. Pondering that, he realized he had not done such a foolish thing in front of a woman since he was nineteen and on his tour of Europe.

But he had wanted her to watch him, had needed that feminine appreciation, hungered for it, in fact. Even now, just the warmth of her gaze left him feeling light-headed with desire, as irrational as that seemed to his better judgment. But he had wanted her to stay a moment, wished to talk to her and ask her her opinion of his fencing. How imbecilic that was. It was fortunate that she had left so quickly he supposed, for he may have made a fool of himself.

Closing his eyes, he tried to think of something else, *anything* else. As far as he knew, she was a virginal English lady with no more thoughts of sexual relations than any young lady; she certainly was not some *houri* there for his delectation and deflowering. He could no more seduce her, even assuming she was willing, than he could dream of having a wife and family. It was not for him. He had dedicated his life to protecting his family from their own fatal flaws, and to healing the terrible wounds left fifteen years before, wounds that still gaped as raw and festering as that terrible night when Anna and Hans had died together.

On that cold thought, he slid down under the rapidly cooling water, rose again, sputtering, and climbed out of the tub. He needed to rid himself of foolish fantasies, dress, and go to speak to Cesare and then to Adele. They must be ready for the night ahead.

Chapter 10

NEITHER NIKOLAS nor Adele were at dinner that night nor in the drawing room later, and Elizabeth was relieved. She sat for a while in the drawing room, talking to Count Delacroix and Melisande Davidovich, both most gracious, and drank tea served by the unctuous Herr Liebner. It was, he claimed, his honor to serve tea to such glorious company.

She spoke briefly with Count von Wolfram the next day, and both agreed that Charlotte was like a rough gem—she needed polishing. He pronounced himself satisfied with Elizabeth's ideas as to how to go about that, but warned her he would be watching for signs of improvement. They kept their distance from each other, but Elizabeth covertly watched him and could not help but feel that he looked tired and worried, distracted by some deeper trouble he could not share with anyone.

In the next few days a routine of sorts was scheduled. Mornings, she and Charlotte would go to the yellow parlor and spend some time talking about English etiquette. The girl was oblivious to so many things ingrained in the average English girl of the same age and rank that Elizabeth was only beginning to get to the bottom of how much Charlotte would need to learn. She started with simple knowledge, such as how formal affairs differed from informal, and what she could expect at events as different as a Venetian breakfast or a royal ball. She tried to teach Charlotte how to preside at the tea table, but that was difficult when the girl refused to see any use in such skills.

"I do not understand why it matters if I can make a good cup of tea," Charlotte said, her tone sulky. "Do those in England truly judge one on such things? It is laughable, to think such a thing important when there are serving staff to do so."

Exasperated, Elizabeth replied, "You're completely right, Charlotte. It will matter not a whit to those whose opinion is truly worth courting, those of true substance and worth, if you can prepare tea or not."

"Then why learn?"

"The problem is, Charlotte, that people of substance and depth and intelligence are few and far between. Unfortunately we must live in a world filled with people of no substance at all. They can make your life difficult if they so choose, so it is for them that you must learn to curtsey correctly, behave in a demure fashion, and pour a perfect cup of tea." She paused, thought for a moment, and then said with a smile, "And those with true substance will appreciate the ability, too, for a good cup of tea is never amiss in this world."

Charlotte had not replied. Elizabeth wasn't sure yet how to break through the girl's crusty exterior. All she could do was continue to be kind and firm.

Afternoons Elizabeth had free, for Charlotte would only take so much tutoring before disappearing to spend time with Melisande or Christoph. So Elizabeth retreated to the library that Adele had indicated was appropriate or stayed in her room and wrote in her journal, recording her plans for Charlotte and many of her inner thoughts on the odd temper of the household; there was so much she didn't understand, and her journal received all of her thoughts and worries without requiring her to explain herself, a relief when one felt as alone as she often did. Other free time she spent with Uta and Frau Liebner, beginning to grasp the rudiments of the German language and how it differed from English.

For some reason the tension she had felt in the household the first few nights she was a resident seemed to have eased, but perhaps it was merely her own initial unfamiliarity with life at Wolfram Castle that had made the atmosphere seem so strained. And yet she hadn't forgotten the naked woman she saw on the road on their way there, nor had she discovered who among the staff Count Nikolas could possibly have been escorting in under cover of darkness, when she had observed the odd scene from the gallery.

Evenings spent with the family were not yet completely pleasant, but she was beginning to relax and find them bearable. The count generally sat alone and read, seldom joining in with the card games or conversation, but on occasion he would join the family and she saw in him the yearning desire he had for his family to be happy and prosperous. It warmed her to see such devotion to his brother's children, even if it was not reciprocated. Between Christoph and himself in particular there seemed a vast rift, but Elizabeth did not know the full history of that division.

And so she had been there two full weeks. The moon was new and the nights were black, and several successive days of snowfall had made them prisoners in the castle. After dinner they gathered, as usual, in the drawing room; this night was different in that Frau Liebner had attended dinner and joined them for the family time after. She was a welcome sight in the drawing room for Elizabeth, but as Countess Adele monopolized her attention at first, Elizabeth did not intrude. Charlotte and Melisande moved to the piano, which had been brought to the drawing room while the music room was being painted, so Elizabeth sat and listened. Countess Gerta, who had been ill for a week or so with a cold, was finally with the family and though wan appeared quite cheerful. She sat down by Elizabeth.

"We have had, Miss Stanwycke, so little time to talk. I feel I don't know you yet at all, and yet everyone has such good things to say of you."

"Really? How kind of them," Elizabeth replied. She watched Charlotte and Melisande consult over a piece of music, but then glanced at the countess, who had sat down beside her on a settee. The other woman was youthfully slender, though her twins would be fifteen within months. Her expression, often peevish and pouty, was this night cheerful and open.

"Our French friend seems especially taken with you," the countess said, with a glance over at Count Delacroix.

Elizabeth, startled, followed her gaze. The French count was elegantly dressed as usual, and was, with a courtly bow, making his obeisance to Frau Liebner. "I . . . can't say he has ever been anything more than polite."

"Nevertheless I assure you, he finds you very attractive. Is he not elegant?"

"Well, yes, he is certainly elegant."

"I fear my sister is doomed to be disappointed in him," she said, on a sigh.

"What do you mean?"

"Have you not noticed? Adele is terribly in love with him, but he has never even noticed she is female. I say if you cannot make a Frenchman in love with you, then you are barely a woman."

One swift glance at Countess Gerta's piquant, gamine face left Elizabeth more confused than ever, for though the words sounded mean-spirited, the lady could not appear more mild or cheerful.

"The Countess Adele," Elizabeth said coolly, "has been very kind to me."

"Oh, yes, she would be, would she not? She has made such a terrible uh . . . how is it in English? A puddle? Or no . . . a muddle, that is it . . . she has made a muddle of raising Charlotte, and Nikolas is relying on you to correct that, so he has told her to be especially kind to you."

The young Count Christoph, with an unusual smile on his face, took a violin out of a case sitting on the piano and rosined his bow. He joined the two young ladies in a sprightly piece that had them all laughing merrily at the end. Elizabeth, already wearying of the company of Countess Gerta, stood and strolled over to the piano, clapping at their virtuoso performance. "How well you play, Count Christoph," she said.

His pale face flushed and red blotches broke out on his cheeks at the compliment. He bowed silently. Bartol Liebner joined them as Melisande whispered something to Charlotte, and she, out loud, laughed.

"Yes, Christoph," his sister said. "You must play that piece you composed at Christmas."

"No, I . . ."

"Please, you have not played for us for a month almost," Melisande said, her softer accents a sweet contrast to the rough tone of Charlotte's inflection.

"Yes, nephew, you should show your skill more often," Bartol Liebner said, clapping his hands together.

The young count cast his gaze around, and to the others sitting and listening. Elizabeth watched his eyes and could tell the exact moment when he decided to acquiesce. He nodded and brought the instrument up to his chin, closing his eyes.

What she had expected she didn't know, but what he played was exquisitely sad, the strings singing a lament of lost love and heartbreak. By the end of the piece Elizabeth felt the tears welling in her eyes and she realized as she had listened she had become lost in the old pain, the sorrow of discovering she had not only been abandoned, but she had been maligned, too, and exposed.

"That was breathtaking," she said, almost not recognizing the thickness of her voice.

"Yes, almost professional," a new voice said from near the door. Count Nikolas strolled into the room. He had disappeared directly after dinner with a promise to join them all later, and must now have been done with his business, Elizabeth supposed.

"One would surmise," the count continued, "that you spend far more time with a violin bow than a sword in your hand."

His seemingly innocuous words had a radical effect on his nephew, who tossed the violin in its case and stalked over toward the fire, staring into it grimly. Again the ugly tension between the two men had reared its head. Elizabeth knew the count wished his nephew to have a career away from the castle—the army had been mentioned, though it was said the young count had been rejected for poor health—but Elizabeth wondered if that was the root of all of the unease between them or if there was more to it. Certainly Count Nikolas could have been milder in his remark, which had been caustic and captious.

"I don't want to break up this musical party," the count said, approaching the piano. "Miss Stanwycke, do you play? Will you favor us with something?"

Elizabeth hesitated for only a moment and then acceded to his wishes, not wishing to put herself in the position of having to be urged, as some ladies did, out of false modesty when secretly they wished to show off their skills. She did wish to play and so she would.

She riffled through the sheet music that was spread carelessly across the top of the piano and found an old Gluck piece she knew reasonably well as Melisande and Charlotte retreated to some chairs near the fire to whisper together. She sat on the bench and placed her hands on the keys, playing a practice scale to warm her fingers and familiarize herself with the instrument. She had not played in a couple of months, and she would be rusty at first.

She flexed her fingers, finally, feeling them warm and become more agile, and she placed the music correctly and took a deep breath. Then she lost herself in the music, at first needing to concentrate because it had been a while since she had played the piece, and then at the joy of playing once again.

She was momentarily distracted as Count Nikolas sat down beside her to turn her music for her so she didn't need to pause. He proved himself able, for he clearly read music as well as she did, turning at just the right moment so she did not need to break her rhythm. And yet the warmth of him, the feel of his muscular thigh pressed close to hers, was terribly distracting.

More powerful than that was his scent; he smelled musky, like the forest at night, Elizabeth thought, and his scent filled her nostrils, making her light-headed and slightly euphoric. He murmured how well she played and smiled over at her, the shadow of his beard darkening his chin. She lost her way for a moment but then regained control, finding her place in the complex web of music. How dark he was, compared to his niece and nephew, who were so fair, she thought as she carefully worked through the music, her play becoming more mechanical as skill took over in her distraction. They must take after their mother, and yet Adele and Gerta were both slim and blond, so perhaps there were two distinct strains in the von Wolfram family—the light and dark.

She wound down to the end and finished with a flourish that left her breathless and smiling. Applause from a couple of the others made her smile over at them, but then she met the count's intent gaze.

"You are much better than I expected, Miss Stanwycke. It makes me wonder," he said, folding the music, tossing it up on the piano, and turning toward her, "what other hidden talents you have."

The intimate tone of his voice made her shiver, and she felt an unwilling trill of attraction down her spine as he straddled the bench; now the inside of his thighs cradled her in a most intimate position, pressed to her bottom and thigh. Well, so that was his game—he thought to seduce her. Perhaps all that had kept him as chaste as his great-aunt seemed to think he was, was a lack of appropriate targets for his lust. She stiffened as that thought crossed her mind, for she had no intention of becoming his mistress.

Once, another man had given her such looks and spoken to her in such a tone, and all it had left her with was heartache and shame. Seduced and promised marriage, the cold shock of being exposed and then abandoned by the man who had sworn he loved her still throbbed within her, raising her ire whenever she remembered her feelings of helplessness and humiliation as she was tossed from the household as a whore. Never would she allow herself to be in such a position again. She was not ashamed of her actions, but she was ashamed of her gullibility.

The count said, "Miss Stanwycke, I feel you have not been paying attention while I've been speaking." He put his hand over hers where it rested on the piano keys and caressed it with his thumb. "I will forgive you if you will tell me what you were contemplating so seriously."

"Nothing at all, Count." She moved away from him and jerked her hand out from under his, making the piano keys jangle; some of the others glanced over, but there was nothing to see, as there was a foot or more between them now on the piano bench.

At her obvious dismissal, he stood and stalked off, crossing to stare into the fire, away from anyone else.

It was clear that he was mistaken, Nikolas thought, as he stared at the flames licking hungrily at a thick log. He had thought that in their friendly talk of late there had been a faint encouragement, a hint of womanly interest in her eyes and bearing. She had almost leaned into him as she finished the piano piece, and he had felt her warmth invade him, heating his loins with disturbing sensation. A little flirtation, he had thought, would hurt no one, and so, shielding her from the others with his own body, he had enjoyed the intimate sensation of her nearness. Though accustomed to quelling or dispelling his body's mechanical cycle of sexual appetite—any healthy male was so afflicted—there was in his attraction to her more than a purely physical response. It was as though her very proximity breached his defenses and left him vulnerable to waves of sweet and fervent yearning he had thought long dead, defeated by the need to be a harsh and austere master. And yet by her abrupt manner of moving away from him, she had signaled her disinterest.

He glanced over his shoulder, watching as Miss Stanwycke stood and surrendered the piano to Adele, who began a lengthy and technically difficult piano piece, perhaps at his Aunt Katrina's request, for that lady looked on with interest. The lovely tutor joined the group near the fire and stretched out her white hands, rubbing them as if to warm them. But he knew she wasn't cold; her fingers were warm, soft, and supple, like the best Kashmir cloth.

Count Delacroix said something to her and she sat down by him and joined the lively conversation with Charlotte and Melisande. Nikolas's uncle Bartol brought the ladies cups of tea and stayed, standing nearby, occasionally interjecting a comment. But as he watched, Nikolas became aware of the tension in Elizabeth Stanwycke's spine, how rigidly she held herself; she swiftly glanced at him, then away again, and then back, his gaze holding her like a trap.

His stomach roiled with comprehension; she was not indifferent to him. Far from it. She was fleeing the attraction she felt toward him, and the awareness she felt perhaps even now, as she lost the thread of conversation and was brought back to it by Bartol, her cheeks pinkening to a delightful hue of rose.

The tattoo of his heartbeat thrummed through him, pounding an insistent, pulsating rhythm of remembered moments, her gaze turned up to his, her warmth close to him, her lips so close he could almost taste them. How many times had he wondered if her lips were as soft as they looked, or if she could possibly be as delicious? Countless times, even though they had been in each other's company on only a dozen or so occasions in the last two weeks, and out of those times, only a few had been alone.

Circling the room, watching her and not caring who saw it, he felt her consciousness like a blood call, a tingle of anticipation heating him to fevered state. Sometimes she glanced his way, then swiftly averted her eyes, the rapid rise and fall of her bosom betraying her as her stained cheeks and trembling limbs signaled him.

How could he draw her away from the others? How could he get her alone?

But then sanity reasserted its dominion over his brain, if not his body. Swallowing hard, he turned away. He had no right to be thinking the things he was thinking or imagining the two of them in intimate contact, flesh against flesh, desire melting them together. The fact that she was resisting their mutual attraction should shield her from his depredation; she was in his control, and thus safe from him in every way. Only a brute would take advantage of a woman in his employ or control, and that he thought she might feel something for him did not exempt him from honorable behavior. In fact, it behooved him to act with more scrupulous attention to the proprieties. Asserting the rigid control he considered his saving grace, he strolled to a cooler part of the room, regained his composure, and turned back to his domain, swiftly assessing the company.

Christoph had disappeared. He had mishandled the boy

again; his words had been barbed, certainly, but it was frustrating to see a von Wolfram male as pallid and ineffectual as a sybaritic court musician. The lad was oversensitive! Adele was still playing, her music technically brilliant but without the soft accents of Miss Stanwycke's. Gerta, who looked weary now, was whispering to their Aunt Katrina, who nodded and shooed her away toward the door. His sister was exhausted, no doubt, after a week or two of illness, and was on her way up to her rooms. He joined his aunt on the settee and she confirmed his guess, that Gerta was on her way up to her suite, fatigued by the socializing.

"And so, Nikolas," she said, watching his face. "I am still trying to understand this man you have become. Uta tells me much, you know, but . . . are you happy, Nikolas? Tell me truly."

"Are men of our race ever happy? I think it is not in our blood, Aunt. An Englishman might be happy, though he will never admit it. A Frenchman almost certainly will, and will speak of it at length, while an Italian will paint to express his great happiness and his sorrow both. And a Spaniard . . . even desolation will give him some measure of joy. But a German . . . he will always feel sorrow most keenly."

"Perhaps you are right. I often felt, while in England, that those around me experienced a powerful, self-satisfied joy, though they would never admit it, preferring to express soberly and with great pretended humility that they were fortunate by God's grace only."

He chuckled, but then sobered. "Aunt, how did you meet Miss Stanwycke? You never told me."

"She was teaching a couple of silly girls approaching womanhood in the house of relations of hers; she was kin to the master of the house, while my relation was to the mistress. But I fear my cousin—as I said, the mistress of the house—did not like me very well, and that I bored her. She often sent for Elizabeth, and when she joined the company she was good enough to sit and talk with me. I found her . . . interesting. When your letter arrived asking about a tutor for Charlotte, I immediately thought of her."

"And yet you did not answer for a month. Why did you hesitate?" He watched her face and could see in the chilly blue eyes a mist of evasion.

"I visited the house often to observe her, to see if she was truly suited for your task. And I was not sure if she would come, you know. It was quite a leap, leaving her homeland."

"And yet she did, leaving behind those you say were her kinsmen. Why did she do so?"

His aunt's wrinkled face hardened into angry lines and creases. "She was undervalued and ill-paid. I felt sure she would receive better treatment from those who would not take her for granted and who might recognize the brilliance of her mind and the inestimable worth of her heart."

"Ah, now you see, you have told me why she *should* have left, but you said nothing about why she did finally decide to leave."

"Who can say? I am not inside her heart or mind, Nikolas. I spoke to her at length and talked her into it. Enough. Why did you just a while ago get up so abruptly after cornering her on that piano stool? Did you make her an offer and did she reject you?"

Shocked she should so swiftly come to such a conclusion, Nikolas understood how blatant he had been in his quick and impulsive pursuit of her, and how unfortunate that was for them both. He must not expose her to family gossip. "Of course not. Do not repeat such a thing, Aunt."

"I would never say such a thing to anyone but you. How harsh you have become, and how hard," she said, her old eyes filled with sadness and knowledge. "I would not know you now as the pretty, scholarly boy you were."

"My life was destined for other things," he said.

"But you have left behind so much of what made you different from Johannes and the others. What have you become, Nikolas?"

Irritated, he said, "Nothing so very bad, I hope, Aunt." He rose and bowed politely to her. "I must go now. I will visit you and Uta on the morrow, for if I do not, she will complain I am ignoring her."

Elizabeth glanced up and saw the count stride from the room. She excused herself from the others and went to join her friend, who sat still listening to Countess Adele, advancing now to another even more difficult piece.

"How nice to see you enjoying the company of your family," Elizabeth said, sitting beside her, feeling the comfort of familiarity. With this woman, though Frau Liebner was occasionally autocratic and brittle, she knew she had a friend.

"Yes."

She had answered absently, and Elizabeth examined her, the crinkled forehead, the worried eyes. "What's wrong, Frau Liebner? Has something upset you?"

"No. No, it is nothing. Or if it is, it is nothing you can help, my dear." The old woman gazed at her fondly. "I hope I have not brought you from one bad situation to another, Elizabeth. I pray it is not so."

"What do you mean?"

"Things have changed in the last ten years. Nikolas has changed. He is a harder man now."

"Is he? And yet he is devoted to the family and does everything for their benefit. Was that not always so?"

"Yes. When he came back after the tragedies—"

"After the deaths?" Elizabeth asked, pointedly.

"Yes, after Anna and Hans and Johannes died." She glanced over at Elizabeth but did not explain further. "When Nikolas came back, he was still the eager, warm lad he had been when he left on his tour of Italy and Greece. Even in the midst of great tragedy, he kept his . . . oh, how do you say it in English? His humanity, his compassion. And even when I went away ten years ago, he was . . . softer. Now he is like flint, hard and sharp."

There was silence between them, but then Frau Liebner took her hand and clasped it hard. "Elizabeth, if there is anything between you . . . stop!" she said, putting up one hand when Elizabeth would have interjected a negative. "Do not reply. I am not accusing nor asking. I am merely saying if there is ever anything between you, do not let him hurt you."

"What do you mean?" The warning gave her a pang of anxiety.

But the old woman just shook her head. "I do not know. I just do not know. Uta says he is not so very changed underneath, but I'm not so sure. I don't know him anymore."

Elizabeth followed the woman's gaze, but it was only directed to the door out of which Count Nikolas had strode minutes before.

THOUGH Nikolas read for a long while and then retired, he was sleepless. The scene in the drawing room had left him agitated and wakeful. Homer had always put him to sleep, even when he was studying at the Heidelberg University, so perhaps the *Iliad* would do the task once more. He rose, threw on a robe, and made his way to the library, padding silently down the hall, across the gallery, and up to the half-open door but halting abruptly as he saw a glimmering light within.

Who could it be?

Who else, he thought with a swift pulse of satisfaction. He slipped in through the doorway and there Elizabeth was, gazing down and running one finger over the family bible, her elegant brows furrowed as she mouthed words she was trying to make out in the elaborate German text. Swiftly, silently, like a gray wolf in the forest, he moved across the space and said, "May I help you translate, Miss Stanwycke?"

Her gasp echoed and she jumped back from the book on the lectern as if she were scalded by it. He was beside her in a second, the spill of light over her pale skin showing a fluttering nerve by her eye as she stared at him in consternation.

"I . . . I was just trying . . . to . . . to learn your language."

"By looking at my family's history? What word on this page had you so puzzled?"

She was forced to step back toward the book, and he felt her shivering.

Was she forever doomed to be caught by him in acts of secret elucidation? Elizabeth wondered, trying to focus on the bible in front of her and find the word that had puzzled her so.

Sleepless and cold, she had slipped from her room and wandered, but the draw of the forbidden was irresistible and she had entered his domain. Their interaction at the piano that evening and Frau Liebner's troubling warning had only made him more of a tantalizing mystery, for there had to be some force within him that made her so aware of him, even as she was determined to resist that allurement.

Having found the mysterious phrase, Elizabeth glanced back up at Nikolas. A blue vein pulsed in his neck, standing out like a whipcord, and Elizabeth's gaze was riveted there, as Nikolas stood above her.

"Would you like me to translate, Miss Stanwycke?" he repeated, his voice deceptively soft.

"I . . . I would. I'm attempting to learn the language better, Count," she repeated, feeling foolish and trying to master her agitation. "And family bibles . . . well, I can guess many of the words from context, you see." They were so close that she could see where the bristles of his beard shadowed his skin, the dark outline arcing up to his hairline and down under his square chin. His open robe—black-figured satin with silk cord binding it—exposed a naked V, and the dark chest hairs curled flat against his pale skin almost up to where his pulse thrummed at the base of his throat.

Nikolas moved closer and stood behind her, his breath warm on her neck. "Ah, so that is the word," he said, placing his finger next to hers on the page. "That means 'stillborn,'" he said. "We had another brother—he would have been my junior by three years—but it was not fated to be, and my mother lost him."

The pool of golden light highlighted the dark hairs on the back of his broad hand and the gold and onyx ring he wore, with the family crest emblazoned. Hypnotized, Elizabeth brushed her finger over it and heard his swift intake of breath as their hands touched. She swallowed and tried to catch her breath, but it was impossible, suffocated as she as by warring emotions. She closed the bible and moved away from him in the confines of the narrow space between the lectern and the wall of books.

"My aunt," he said, following her, "has told me little of your family, Miss Stanwycke, but that you lived with them and worked for them. Why do you not live with them still?"

"I am an orphan, but I believe you already know that."

"Yes, but you do have family, and were in fact living with them when Aunt Katrina met you," he repeated.

"Yes."

"Why did you leave them? Surely even the role of poor relation is preferable to being an even poorer tutor in a foreign land?"

He was being deliberately cruel, she thought at first, by calling her the poor relation, but when she looked at his expression there was no taunt there, merely curiosity.

She sat down abruptly on a chair. "I . . . I couldn't live there any longer. There were . . . problems."

"Problems?"

"Problems," she said firmly, unwilling to elaborate. She was not going to recount for his elucidation her humiliation and shame and the awful banishment that would have sent her to the streets of London.

Curiosity warred with courtesy on his handsome face. She couldn't stand to see it anymore and rose, swiftly going to the other end of the room and gazing at his big desk. "The first night," she said out loud, "you just appeared in this room, as if you were an apparition. I have figured out that there must a be a secret passage to this room for some reason," She turned to face him. "Why? And is that why I'm not supposed to be in here alone?"

He felt a smile curve his lips upward, even against the concern he felt. Someone at some time had mistreated her, he thought, feeling a rush of protective ire. But though skittish and uncertain, like the female wolf she would rather go on the attack than wait and be meek. As dangerous as that attribute made her, he liked her for it.

But he chose not to answer. "Miss Stanwycke, come out of the shadows," he commanded.

She moved stiffly to stand before him.

"Look at me."

She looked up and shivered, but her expression was not fear or resignation but defiance.

"You are cold," he murmured.

"I've been cold ever since I arrived here. Your country is winter and ice and snow."

"Ah, but in spring, in the mountains, it is full of life and beauty. You will see. Come May you will forget the ice and snow and see the beauty surrounding you." On an impulse, he murmured, "Let me warm you, before you go back to your room and so to bed." He held open his arms.

Irresistible as the invitation was, Elizabeth knew there was a price attached, a price he wouldn't even know she was paying. And yet . . . one more time could she just let her desires guide her? Numbly, fearfully, against her common sense even, she moved into the beckoning circle of his arms and he enfolded her next to his heart; the wall of distrust and fear she had built up to shelter her gave way, the mortar crumbling as she felt his strength and innate kindness surround her. Nothing could shatter the whole structure of her doubt, but her defense was breached.

She looked up into Nikolas's eyes and saw her reflection there in the dark gray. Warmth seeped into her bones and she closed her eyes as the steady *thump-thump* of his heart calmed her agitation. A moment later the warmth was ignited by his lips against hers, just a soft pressure, undemanding at first, but sweet.

When Elizabeth opened her lips to say she must leave, the seductive invasion of his tongue came as an electrifying shock, pulling her back to the first time such a thing had happened to her and her surprise that men and woman did such things. Then she had not known what to do.

Now she did.

She surrendered, allowing Nikolas to take his fill of her as his teeth nipped her lips, suckling with fervor. Clasping her arms around his neck, Elizabeth took back, delving into his mouth, feeling the thrust and parry as a love dance, an enticing match of erotic force. But the feel of his burgeoning arousal budding against her stomach jerked her back to the impropriety of her behavior and she loosed her hold and staggered away from him, her lips moist and plump, her heart pounding.

His dark eyes like liquid coal, Nikolas stared at her in the shuddering lamplight. He was silent.

"I have to go b-back up to my room," she stammered.

"Yes, you must," he finally said, his voice ragged and harshly accented. "You should, and right away." He broke the intense connection between them, the locked gazes, and turned away from her.

Elizabeth headed to the doorway, turned the knob, yanked the door open, and strode into the hallway, almost running in her haste to be gone. Nikolas followed her to the doorway.

"Miss Stanwycke," he called.

She halted in the middle of the hall and stared back at him in the dim light cast by a candle in a wall sconce.

He stared at her, then shook his head. "I . . . it is nothing."

Somewhere a door shut, and both of them gazed up into the darkness of the gallery.

"Sleep well, Miss Stanwycke," he said and retreated back into his library.

Chapter 11

FORGET WHAT just happened, Elizabeth commanded herself. It was an inappropriate and wholly dangerous meeting, and she was utterly to blame, for obviously even in the middle of the night Count von Wolfram's library was not a safe place to be.

Her thudding heart calmed some as she found the stairs and began her ascent. The sound of a footstep above stopped her and her heart began hammering again, but as a figure holding a candle turned the corner she relaxed. It was just the elderly Bartol Liebner descending, one hand outstretched to steady himself against the wall.

"Miss Stanwycke!" he exclaimed, holding the candle so high it cast elongated and ghastly shadows down the stairs. His free hand covered his heart and he rolled his eyes. "I thought I heard something and came to investigate, and then I heard footsteps . . . my foolish heart did a *thump-thump-thump* and jumped, so I thought it would leap right out of my chest!"

"I felt the same, sir," Elizabeth said, smiling up at him in the dim and flickering light. "I was just . . . uh, in search of something to read, you know, but lost my way to the lady's library. In the dark, the castle is very different than in the light of day."

"How well I know it. Shall I confess? I really came down to go to the buttery to see if any of the cake from dinner was still there. Would you join me in my quest?"

She hesitated, but then nodded, not liking to think of the man wandering alone down the stone stairs. It could be dangerous, and he seemed none too steady on the steps. She wondered if he had perhaps imbibed a little too much of the excellent vintage wine served in the drawing room that evening.

They descended the rest of the way, and Herr Liebner led her to the serving area near the back of the castle, which was reached by a door under the grand staircase. He glanced over his shoulder with one finger held up to his lips as they crept down a dark, chilly hallway. "There may still be servants about, you know, and I would not like to get caught at my thieving."

His wink and lopsided grin made Elizabeth seriously consider her thought that he had a little too much to drink. She chuckled softly and replied, "Would a servant not bring something to you in your room if you wished, sir? It would be simpler than roaming the castle at night."

"Oh, yes," he said, "a servant would bring me cake. But it would not be as much as I want. I am greedy, but ashamed, too. You I will trust more than the chattering servants."

The buttery was a long, narrow room with dishes covered in clean white cloth laid out on shelves and countertops. It was cold, and there almost seemed a draft. Herr Liebner uncovered a platter on the marble counter, sliced a large piece of cake, hesitated, cut two more, moved them to a plate, and then uncovered a pitcher. "Milk, to go with the cake, you know. Nothing so refreshing."

He handed Elizabeth the plate of cake and poured two pewter cups of milk, picked up the candle, and indicated to her to lead the way back out of the narrow confines of the buttery. "Now we will go to . . . the yellow parlor? Yes? You will not mind so much sharing your little haven?"

She agreed, and they made their way back to the yellow parlor by a different path than she was accustomed to. The parlor still retained some of the warmth of the day from the banked coals in the fireplace and she welcomed even so slight a rise in temperature. By mutual though silent agreement they made their way to the two chairs closest to the fireplace and sat, both putting their plunder on the table between them.

Just minutes before, Elizabeth had been kissing the master of Wolfram castle, and now she was stealing cake and milk from his larder. How odd her life had become, she thought, as she ate a piece of the rich, raisin-filled spice cake.

Herr Liebner ate with great relish, finishing three-quarters of the cake. Then he dusted his fingers off, put one hand on his paunch, and belched daintily. The food had sobered him, it seemed, but he was in a sentimental frame of mind. "A good life, I have, my dear Miss Stanwycke. Such a good life!" He leaned his balding head back against the cushioned chair upholstery. "And all because Nikolas is such a good nephew. He listened to his mother's dying words and continued to give me a home when he did not have to."

He must have seen her look of surprise, for he continued, "Oh, yes, I know. I am not supposed to be aware that Maria begged her son to be sure I continued to live here and not be sent back to my family."

"If I might ask, sir, why did you wish to stay here? Did you not leave behind family?"

"Ach . . . it is not the same now. All of us old ones are dead, except for me, and the new ones . . . why, I hardly know those others, my other nieces and nephews. This is my life," he said, waving one hand around. "The von Wolfram family, I mean."

"That sentiment does you credit," Elizabeth said, warming even more to the odd little man and his extravagant love of the family. But as she said it, a shadow of pain flicked across his pale, egg-shaped face. He shook his head and his lip trembled. "What is it, sir?"

"Nothing," he said, looking away and swiping at his eyes.

"But it is something. What has made you so sad suddenly?"

He gazed at her earnestly and then leaned forward. "I feel I can trust you. An outsider is just what we need, someone who sees things differently, perhaps." He stopped, though, and took a deep breath, shaking his head. "I don't know. Should I say anything?"

"About what?" His fussy doubtfulness was irritating, but Elizabeth did her best to be patient. She thought he might have something interesting to say, and it was worth drawing him out, considering how few of the rest of the family were willing to talk about anything at all.

"Well, it is . . . have you heard of the family sorrow, the terrible things that took place fifteen years ago, almost?"

Fifteen years ago. The night Anna Lindsay von Wolfram and Hans von Holtzen died. "I have heard hints," she said hesitantly.

"Yes, hints. I feel the family has never recovered, you know, from that awful time. And the sorrow keeps plaguing them. How I wish I could help."

"What exactly happened to Anna von Wolfram and Hans von Holtzen?" she said boldly.

"Ah, now, knowing you know that much makes my way easier." He took a deep breath, leaned over the side of his chair, and said, "They died together in a dreadful fire. It was a terrible night! Oh, so terrible!"

"A fire in the castle?"

"No. Not in the castle. They were . . ." Herr Liebner shook his head and winced. "So sad. They were together in a little cottage on the property, just in the woods. It was the old woodcutter's cottage, but unused . . . or so everyone thought. It appeared afterward that it had been used often as . . . as . . ." He shook his head.

"As a place for secret rendezvous?"

He nodded.

"And it burned down?"

"Well, in a manner of speaking."

"What do you mean?"

He looked confused for a moment, but then he said, "Well, I mean that they died together in the fire, but it did not burn down completely, you see. Someone saw it and called for help, and the workers of the castle, along with poor Johannes himself—it was his wife inside, you know—put it out."

"That's terrible! But . . . Johannes von Wolfram did so much? I understand he died just three weeks later. Was he not sick even then?"

"Oh, no, hale and hearty. He became sick after."

"Because of the tragedy."

Bartol Liebner furrowed his brow and stuck out his bottom lip. "I . . . I don't know."

There was silence for a long moment. "But you were here . . . and you have a guess."

"Well, yes. But it is just a guess." The man furrowed his brow, his pale face shining like a moon in the dim candlelight. "I think," he said softly, "that poor Johannes did not care to live anymore. He adored Anna—she was an Englishwoman, and, like you, very beautiful—and when she was gone he just . . . didn't care to go on."

"You think he killed himself?"

He reared back in shock. "Oh, no! He would not do that. No, Johannes just . . . he just became ill and died. Very quick. Very odd."

"How strange," Elizabeth mused. She sat back in her chair and stared at the fire. "Countess Gerta had her children not too long after that."

He made a noise between his teeth. "Poor, poor Gerta! She has been fragile ever since, you know. Yes, she had the twins, even though her husband had died, and in the arms of another woman, too. How tragic."

"Did anyone know that Anna and Hans were having an affair? And how did they get trapped in the cottage? Surely if a fire started it should have been easy to get out of such a small building."

He frowned down at his fingers tented over his paunch. "I had not thought of that."

"Was there any other way out of the cottage?"

"No, it was a tiny one-room hovel," he said, a thoughtful look on his face.

"Who else was living here?"

He appeared puzzled at that particular question, but she wasn't willing to explain her query just yet. He shrugged and sat back in the chair, looking up into the darkness. "Here at the castle? Let me see . . . Anna and Johannes, and of course Christoph and Charlotte—they were just six and four years old, not even really old enough to know anything but their mother was gone to heaven—and Gerta and Hans, more's the pity, and Adele."

"Anyone else?"

"Well, of course there was Countess Uta. She was still very spry, though if I remember she had begun to use a cane. But her sight was quite good; the darkness had not crept up on her so much then. And my dear sister Katrina, of course, was here. She has been a widow so long, and even then it was not a recent sorrow. She was not living here then, but only visiting with Countess Uta, with whom she had developed a fast friendship. And Maximillian was here . . ."

"Count Delacroix?" Elizabeth asked in surprise. "I thought he only came when the Terror began in France."

"Oh, no, he is an old friend of the family. He has been a guest here often in the last twenty years. Once it was thought he would marry . . . but no matter."

"Marry who?" She thought she knew the answer, but was proven wrong.

"Well, he was very fond of Gerta and would have married her. But Johannes thought the Count von Holtzen was a better match, you know, and so it was done. Johannes was master of the house, you see, as eldest, since their father was gone. But Maximillian, he has always been a welcome guest here. And I believe . . ." He frowned in heavy thought. "Yes, yes, he was here at the time."

Elizabeth pondered that news. Count Delacroix had wanted to marry Gerta and had been thwarted? But still he remained friendly with the family and could have had Countess Adele, if one was to judge by her current feelings. It was no mystery to anyone how she felt for him.

"Oh, and of course Nikolas and Signor Vitali were here."

"The c-count was here?" She stumbled on her words, it was such a shock, for Frau Liebner had said he was not present, that he was traveling Europe at the time and hadn't returned home until after the tragedy. How could she have been so mistaken? Or was it Bartol Liebner who was wrong?

"Yes, oh yes, Nikolas was here. And the Italian. I was told that Johannes sent for his brother to return for some reason, but if it was so no one else had been aware, for his arrival was a complete surprise. He had done with university, you see, where he had met Signor Vitali—the fellow was tutoring Italian—and they had been traveling for a year or so."

"Are you sure you're not mistaken, sir?" Elizabeth said, leaning forward into the pool of light and gazing steadily at his face.

"Oh, no, I remember it all too well," Bartol said, a terrible sadness in his gray eyes. "For it was Nikolas who came to the house to tell everyone the cottage was burning. His hands were black with smoke and his eyes red with tears."

SLEEP, it turned out, was a luxury Elizabeth was not to experience for the rest of the night. Bartol Liebner's awful word picture of the youthful count, just nineteen, coming in shouting that the cottage was burning was too vivid for her not to believe that it was true. It left her sleepless and anxious. Why were there conflicting stories of his presence that night?

But as long as she had work that needed to be done, she could not afford to let it affect her. Curiosity, she reminded herself, was not an attribute to be cultivated in a dependent tutor of elegant manners.

The yellow parlor had been cleaned before she even arrived after nibbling on a very small breakfast, and no trace of her late-night meal with Herr Liebner remained. She ordered, in faltering German, the small table by the window to be laid as if for a dinner party and awaited Charlotte while her orders were being carried out.

Finally Charlotte arrived, and Elizabeth restrained her urge to inquire if it was too much to expect the girl to arrive at the agreed-upon time. Instead she set directly to work, grilling her student on dinner conversation, how to conduct it, and how to divide one's time appropriately between the two gentlemen on either side of one, if one happened to be taciturn and the other an inveterate talker.

Charlotte shrugged when asked what she would do. "Speak to the one who wished to talk, I suppose."

"But no," Elizabeth said, sitting down and facing Charlotte. "For the taciturn gentleman is a bishop, and if you are not seen speaking with him, it will be said you are shunning the church, or that you were uncomfortable in his presence, and it will cause much gossip."

"I don't care."

Elizabeth again stifled an urge to chastise her moody pupil. "You must care! If you and your husband are to travel in all the best circles, then you must be above reproach. Allowing oneself to become the subject of gossip and innuendo is common and ultimately will lead to a kind of banishment from the upper circles of society. The only ones who will invite you anywhere are those who are always on the lookout for titillation and excitement, and they will ruin you."

"Then I will flirt with the bishop," Charlotte said desperately, her blue eyes wide. "Or I will dump a full glass of wine on him. I don't care!"

Just then the door was flung open and Countess Gerta wandered in. "Oh, are we having a little lesson in deportment?" she asked, wandering over to the window and pulling open the curtain. The window rattled as wind hurled snow pellets against it. "It is snowing again. Will it never stop? I want to walk outside, but it is snowing and . . ."

Charlotte and Elizabeth both waited, but the countess did not finish whatever she was going to stay. She just stared abstractedly out the window.

"Countess," Elizabeth said. "We are indeed conducting a lesson here. Perhaps if you could come back later when we are going to have tea?"

Instead of responding, Gerta sat down at one of the place settings at the table. "What lovely china. This is our family crest, you know, Miss Stanwycke. The wolf . . . is he not a handsome beast?" she said, tracing the crest with one shaking finger.

"Countess Gerta," Elizabeth said, eyeing the woman and wondering what was wrong with her. She was different this morning than she had been the night before, her eyes glazed, her manner odd, a hectic flush over her cheeks. "I don't wish to be rude, but—"

"I have a son and daughter, you know . . . twins. Was that not clever?" the woman asked, gazing up at Elizabeth, who had stood and approached her, trying to figure out some way to politely guide her from the room. "Was it not clever of me to have two children at once? But it was terrible, a terrible night the night I had them. Awful." She shuddered.

Charlotte had wandered over to the window and sat in a window seat playing with a curtain sash, weaving it between her fingers. Elizabeth felt like she had lost control, and wondered if she would have to speak to the Countess Adele about her sister.

"Why shouldn't they be here?" Gerta asked of Elizabeth, her narrow face pinched in an expression of misery.

"Uh, 'they'? What do you mean, Countess?"

"Why should my children not be here, at the castle?" she asked, plucking at Elizabeth with grasping fingers. "Why are they banished? Nikolas has no right. He does not. It is cruel, the way he keeps my children from me, and whenever I ask about them I am told it is for the best. For whose best? I miss my babies."

To Elizabeth's horror, fat tears welled in the countess's eyes and began rolling down her cheeks in quick succession. She glanced over at Charlotte, but the young woman was ignoring them. Melisande came in just then, and Elizabeth looked to her with relief, for she immediately assessed the situation and put her arm around Countess Gerta's shoulders, trying to raise her up. Elizabeth was about to ask Melisande if she would help the countess to her suite when the sound of shouts in the hall made them all pause.

Male voices, two of them raised in anger. The quarrel was moving down the hall, and Elizabeth strode toward the parlor door and looked out just in time to see Count von Wolfram and Christoph stop. Count Christoph said something, and his uncle—older, bigger, and far more powerful—took the boy up against the paneled wall, his large hands gripping his nephew's shoulders.

"If you ever say anything that filthy again," he shouted in English, his language of choice whenever he didn't wish the servants to understand him. "I will whip you to within an inch of your life!"

Without thought, Elizabeth bolted down the hall and grabbed the count's arm. "Leave him alone!"

Her charitable impulse earned a wrathful look from Nikolas, but he did release his nephew, tossing him roughly aside like a doll. The boy staggered but then righted himself, rubbing his shoulder, his face blotchy with red patches.

"Miss Stanwycke, I will thank you not to interfere in my handling of family matters." The count's face was dark with anger, his black hair tousled. He swept it back off his forehead with a careless hand.

She should have been alarmed, but the past twenty-four hours had left her feeling raw and ragged and she could not find it in her to care if she angered him further. As rash as it was, she said, "I did not ask for this quarrel to intrude itself upon my consciousness. If you wish to beat your nephew, and you expect me not to interfere, then you must beat him elsewhere."

"I was not beating him."

"You were very close to it in my estimation," she said, aware that they had an audience. Melisande, Countess Gerta, and Charlotte were standing in the doorway of the parlor watching, and Christoph had slunk off to join them.

"You have no idea what you are talking about. You do not know what prompted this quarrel and have no right to speak of it."

"You're right that I don't know what it was about," she said, glaring up at him, her hands on her hips. "But there is nothing that could make it right to physically punish your nephew. He is a grown man, not a child." She shook her head. "Not that it would be right to beat him if he were still a child," she said, exasperated by how rattled she was and how confused her speech. "I did not mean that."

The count mastered his anger, clenching his fists and gazing off down the hall for a long moment. When he looked back it was with a milder eyes. He bowed. "I apologize, Miss Stanwycke, if I alarmed you."

She should let it go. She should just accept his apology and let it pass. But she couldn't. "You have not wronged, me, sir. You should be apologizing to your nephew and not to me."

"I will not be corrected by any woman," he growled, his dark eyes dangerously narrowed.

"Perhaps you ought to be," she said, stiffening her back and raising her chin. "Now," she said, "if you will all behave like civilized creatures instead of a quarreling pack of wolves, I will get back to my job, which is to teach correct manners!" She whirled and strode back into the parlor, pushing past the crowd at the door. Once in the parlor, she stood, shaking with a mixture of rage and dismay. What had she done? It would likely cost her her job, for she had been foolish beyond belief. If she claimed to be an arbiter of behavior, she should take herself to task, for no proper lady would admonish the master of the house, especially in front of his family.

"Charlotte," she said, turning toward the group, "we will continue now, if you please."

With a gleam of interest in her eyes, Charlotte obeyed, sitting down in her place at the table. Elizabeth gazed back toward the hallway; Melisande put her arm over Gerta's shoulders and led her away, and Christoph, with an enigmatic look at Elizabeth, loped off down the hall. Nikolas, she had to assume, had gone elsewhere to quell his fury.

He was the most infuriating man, kissing her tenderly and with such passionate expertise as she had never experienced, and then behaving like a great angry bear hours later.

"What is it between your brother and your uncle?" Elizabeth asked of Charlotte, even though she knew she should not pry. "Why do they quarrel?"

Charlotte shrugged. "Christoph will not do what our uncle wishes."

"Is that all?"

But Charlotte was done talking. She simply shook her head in answer to any more questioning. They finished the lesson, but Elizabeth couldn't say that any of it was making any impression on her pupil at all. She would take in the information, parrot it back to Elizabeth, and then behave the same as she always did. Charlotte swiftly left the moment the lesson was pronounced done. Just as Elizabeth was directing the servants to take away the china, the Italian secretary entered and bowed.

"Miss Stanwycke, the count would like to see you in his library, if you would be so kind."

Elizabeth's stomach clenched and knotted. This was it. She had gone too far and he was going to send her away. Where would she go? What would she do?

"Please, miss, would you come?"

She had been just standing staring stupidly at him. "I . . . I'm sorry. Of course. Tell . . . tell the count I will come shortly."

With an apologetic look, the fellow said, "If you please, miss, he would like to see you now."

She sighed, and it came out as a long, shaky breath that echoed sadly. "I guess I've done it now," she muttered.

"I beg your pardon?"

"It's nothing. Lead the way, Signor Vitali, if you please."

He did so, taking her to the door of the library. But before he departed, he said, his tone unexpectedly gentle, "Courage, Miss Stanwycke. The count is abrupt and sometimes difficult, but he is a fair man, and appreciative of your services." He bowed once more and walked away.

Chapter 12

SHE RAPPED twice and entered, shutting the door behind her.

Count von Wolfram was sitting behind his vast desk, poring over some papers, a faint quivering light from a candle his only source of illumination, even though it was day. He should open the drapes and get some natural light in there, she thought, but restrained her urge to do it for him. It was not her place.

But he would ruin his eyes that way. "You'll ruin your eyes, straining them like that," she blurted out.

He looked up, his expression grave. "Come and sit, Miss Stanwycke." He stood and waved at a chair by the desk, then strolled over to the window to open a curtain.

She glanced around, thinking she'd rather sit anywhere than in front of his desk, but, taking a deep breath, decided to face her fate head-on. She sat down, folded her hands on her lap, and stared down at the thick burgundy carpet. "Count, I . . . I would in the normal course apologize for my behavior earlier. I should, really. But . . ." She trailed off.

"But you still think you were right," he said, as a block of light from the snowy brilliance outside illuminated the dull room. Turning, he gazed steadily at her.

She stared back. He looked so tired, so drawn. It was as if there was something he was facing that he dreaded. There was a terrible knowledge in his dark eyes, an awful sadness and a dread of what the future held. No one should feel so.

"What's wrong?" she whispered.

He appeared startled. "I beg your pardon?"

"What's wrong? Is . . . is everyone well, sir? You

look . . . you just look so sad." Her last word trembled on a sigh, and she took in a deep, shaky breath.

He stared at her, the light trail from the window glinting on his shiny hair, shadowing his face and giving him the appearance of a haunted man. "Nonsense." He cleared his throat and looked away. "Miss Stanwycke, the reason I called you here—"

"I know why you called me here," she said, following him with her eyes as he strolled back behind his desk.

"You do?" He dropped into his chair and leaned back, gazing steadily at her. "Why do you not tell me then?"

"Well, of course you have called me in here to say I won't suit, that I cannot teach Charlotte what I do not follow myself, that I am unsuitable in every way." She bolted from her chair and paced, wringing her hands. "But you're wrong! I know what I'm doing, and if you just give me a little more time . . . oh, I know I shouldn't have railed at you, but . . . but it was just . . . his face! Christoph . . . uh, that is, the young count, he's just so . . . so young and troubled and . . ." She stopped, realizing she had begun to make little sense. She took in a deep breath and calmed herself, resolving to face her dismissal with fortitude. Turning back to face him, she caught his steady gaze on her, and she remembered well the treacherously wonderful feel of those perfect lips against hers, and how . . . she had to stop thinking, for the pink was rising to her cheeks and she hated being revealed by her own involuntary physical reactions to his fascination.

At least the dark and dismal expression had fled his eyes. "So, you don't think I should dismiss you?"

Perhaps there was room for her to convince him. "No. I will do my best not to interfere in family matters again."

"You do not promise to refrain from interference, I notice."

"I can, on occasion, be somewhat impetuous," she said with what dignity she could muster.

"You call molesting me and berating me like a shrew in front of my entire family impetuosity?"

"I beg your pardon?" she said, indignantly. "I did not berate you like a—"

"But you admit you did molest me."

"No! I don't think . . . that is . . ."

He was, she noticed, clamping down on his cheek, and his eyes danced with an unusual light. Was it possible he was—

"You're laughing at me, sir."

He grinned, a wide smile of strange and terrifying beauty. Rarities were often the most appealing of things, she reflected, as one never had the opportunity to take them for granted.

"I am. I find your begging for your job oddly endearing and delightfully absurd." Toying with a gold seal, he tapped it on the desk surface and watched her face.

"I'm not begging. Or . . ." She took a deep breath and let it out. "Yes, I suppose I am. I like my position here."

He dropped the seal. "Do you?" he asked, sitting forward, his expression serious. "We are a morose and difficult family, Miss Stanwycke, and I . . ." He appeared embarrassed and frowned down at some papers, moving them slightly. "I have not made it any easier by taking unforgivable liberties. In truth I called you here to apologize for last night, something my family would tell you I never do."

And never had done. Why he was apologizing to her he could not fathom, since an hour before he had been in a towering rage at her impudence. And yet, he had been on the verge of hitting Christoph, something he had only ever done once before. She had stopped him and he was glad of that, even though what his nephew had said was unforgivable. But Elizabeth had saved him from a deep regret, and he was grateful. "I am terribly sorry, Miss Stanwycke."

He hoped she knew he was apologizing for his rudeness to her in the hall, as well, though he was outwardly apologizing for kissing her the night before. He had not intended to kiss her at all, his resolution in the drawing room earlier in the evening clearly the sensible route of behavior, but it was an impulse to welcome her into his arms, and when she did come so very close her face was against his chest and turned up to him. Her lips were so rosy in the candlelight and her body rested against his with such trusting surrender that he had been overtaken by a tenderness he had never thought to experience since life had sharpened him against the whetstone of tribulation. Desire he could understand, and lust was a familiar foe to be fought down and ruthlessly conquered—but tenderness! There was no room in his life for it, and he would need, obviously, to be wary when near the tempting Miss Stanwycke.

She was staring at him in puzzlement, and he realized he had been silent a long time. "I agree," she said, slowly, watching his face, "that what occurred last night in this room must never happen again. It was . . . it was just the surprise, I suppose, or . . ." She shook her head.

It had nothing to do with the surprise of being together alone or any other mundane explanation, and she knew it, too, even though she tried to explain it away. If there had been merely desire and passion between them he would have welcomed a lusty interlude, but tenderness . . . there was danger in that softer emotion for him. He had no time nor inclination for those gentler passions. Desire could be fierce and powerful, but love could only weaken a man, as it had his brother and even his brother-in-law. Both had fallen victim to a powerful tenderness for the enchanting Anna Lindsay, another lovely Englishwoman. It had proved a destructive force indeed, and he had determined long ago there was no place in his life for that. "Yes, it was the surprise," he said, deliberately hardening his tone. "The surprise I experience every time I find you in my strangely fascinating library in the middle of the night."

She sat down and stared at her hands in her lap. The light from the window played over her cheek and jaw, the fluid line that led up to her delicate ear and down to her smooth neck and sloping shoulder. She wore no ornamentation, no rings, no necklace, nor even a broach, and he wondered as he watched her if it was that she purposely eschewed the vanity of it, or if it just didn't matter to her whether her fingers or neck were adorned.

And yet she would gloriously complement jewels, eardrops and a sapphire necklace to match the azure of her eyes. A gold satin gown of more fashionable cut and with lace trim to mold to her lush figure; he could picture it, almost; her at the piano glowing in the candlelight, and him seated beside her, feeling the warmth radiating from her—warmth that would thaw his frigid heart—sharing the secret between them of what they would be doing once the household surrendered to Morpheus and he could ravish her, pulling the gold satin and pale lace from her body with his teeth while she writhed under him in splendid, passionate abandon. His heart accelerated as his breathing quickened.

"Why do you stare?" she asked suddenly, looking up at him, her expression full of distress and something more—distrust, perhaps.

He cleared his mind of the fog that had misted it. "I am just wondering what truly made you leave everything familiar to come here. It is an adventure most young ladies would not undertake unless pushed to it by severe privation."

She took in a deep breath and examined him. "Why do you question my motives? Is it not enough that I came?"

"Yes. It is enough." He pushed back from the desk. "Do not mind if I seem distrustful, Miss Stanwycke. I have long found that the only people I can truly trust are my family members. That is just how I am. Please know, I am mindful of the difficulties of the task I have set you; Charlotte has not been well taught and requires refinement. I believe you will succeed. But I wish you could have more speedy results. I won't wait forever." He didn't mean for it to sound ominous, but she paled. He couldn't take it back. Perhaps if she was more aware that her situation in the castle was somewhat precarious it would keep her in her bed at night and from roaming where no good could come to her. There were secrets in the castle, secrets he shared with no one. Secrets that could bring her harm.

She stood. "Is this interview over, sir?"

"Yes," he said abruptly, glancing back down at the papers in front of him. One was a letter from Jakob asking if he and Eva could come home and visit their mother, since she had sent them a letter pleading for them to come. How to answer?

"You look sad again, Count. Whatever it is that worries you, it will work out, I hope."

He looked back up to find her steady, intelligent gaze upon him. "I am sure it will, Miss Stanwycke," he said. "You may go, now."

How changeable he was, Elizabeth thought, exiting and shutting the door behind her. One moment approachable, the next impossible. It should be enough to know she was not dismissed, but it wasn't. This castle seemed to hold mysteries within its ancient walls, she thought, touching the frigid stone as she descended to the great hall. Among those mysteries she would have to add the inner workings of the man who commanded it all.

"Mademoiselle Stanwycke," Count Delacroix said as he came in from outside, stamping his feet and blowing frosty breath while a footman stood waiting. "I have been," he continued, undoing the frogged closure, "taking the air." He shrugged out of his dark gray cloak and the footman caught it and left the great hall carrying it before him.

She shivered. "I'm not accustomed to so much snow and ice," she said, rubbing her arms. "I admit, I cannot bring myself to go out as much as I should."

"I will accompany you if you wish to go out with some support, mademoiselle."

"Thank you. I would not like to bother you, though, sir."

"Nonsense. It does me good. We all go out occasionally, even Bartol. He and I have even been down to the village lately. Now that is a bracing excursion, truly. But may I say," he continued, approaching, taking her hand and bowing over it, "that it does us all much more good to have so lovely, compassionate, and intelligent a presence here at Wolfram Castle."

His hand was icy, and she covered it with both hers to warm it somewhat. He smiled at her, his gaunt face illuminated by the charity in his expression.

"Thank you," she replied, touched by his kindness. On an impulse, and remembering her conversation with Bartol Liebner the night before, she said, "Would . . . would you have a moment to talk, sir?"

He hesitated and glanced around, but then nodded. "Certainly, mademoiselle. Is this . . . a private matter?"

"Not really. I mean, I was wondering about something . . ." How was she going to broach the subject?

He took her arm. "Then let us go to your little yellow parlor; we can be comfortable there."

They moved down the hall toward it, Elizabeth beginning to feel a strange tension that she could not place. Doors closed nearby, voices whispered in hushed tones. Servants bustled by, hunched and with worried eyes. It was eerily reminiscent of when she had arrived more than three weeks ago. Countess Adele came out of the lady's library, which was just down the hall from the yellow parlor; she started when she saw them arm in arm, but only murmured a vague greeting before hustling off on some errand.

"Why is this family so . . . so divided. So difficult?" Elizabeth asked of the French count as they entered the yellow parlor and she closed the door behind them. "Why does everyone behave as though there is some deep, dark mystery, or some . . . some secret shame?"

He gracefully threw back the skirts of his jacket and sat in a chair by the fire; elbows on the arms of the chair, he steepled his fingers before his face. "Mademoiselle Stanwycke, I would say to you that your best course to attain success in your position here is to pay close attention to your student and to little else."

Another veiled warning?

"Why?"

He sighed and shook his head. "Do not look at me so, for truly I have no answers."

"But you do. You're an old friend of the family. You were even here the night of . . . the night of the tragedy."

A guarded look entered his weary gray eyes. "I do not know of what you speak."

"I'm aware of the awful night fifteen years ago when Charlotte's mother and Countess von Holtzen's husband died."

"But there is no mystery there. It was sad, yes, but fires occur," he said, with a nonchalant wave of his hands. "The Countess von Wolfram was there in the cabin for some reason—who can say why—and Count von Holtzen, happening past, heard her screams, it is assumed, and went to rescue her, but both perished. Very sad, but no mystery."

That was not the story Herr Liebner had told her the night before, nor had she said anything about it being a mystery. "Was Count von Wolfram here when it happened? Count Nikolas von Wolfram," she clarified, realizing that the elder brother would have been Count von Wolfram then, too.

His eyes held an alert watchfulness in them. "I believe he was still traveling then."

So, had Bartol Liebner lied to her? Why would he? "Are you sure?"

"Mademoiselle," he said, rising, some agitation in his quick movements, "I begin to wonder why you ask such a string of questions. How can any of this be construed to have any purpose for you, who are here to tutor Countess Charlotte only?"

He was right, of course. It was none of her business. "I'm curious by nature, I suppose," she said with a rueful smile to which he did not respond. "I've heard . . . conflicting stories."

"It has been many years," the Frenchman pointed out, mildly. "Memories fade, memories change." He bowed. "I must go. I am to give Count Christoph a lesson in art this afternoon."

"Certainly, sir. I apologize if . . . if I brought back sad memories."

"Mademoiselle Stanwycke, this castle echoes with sad memories," he said, waving his hands in the air. "What this family needs is someone who will bring some light, some joy to it."

She sat for a time after he left and pondered his parting remark. He was right. If there was ever a family that needed joy, this was the one.

WHEN Nikolas entered the drawing room after dinner that evening, it was with a certain amount of trepidation. He had not been at dinner, as he had been wrestling with the letter back to Jakob and had taken his evening meal in the library.

But he was pleasantly surprised. Miss Stanwycke sat at the piano and played a light air that Christoph was accompanying on his violin. The boy was talented, that was certain, for he kept up with her, though she did not play from sheet music and the tune seemed to be a Scottish air, unfamiliar but cheery. He stood in the shadows by the door for a moment, watching. Miss Stanwycke's slim fingers tripped lightly over the keys as Melisande Davidovich and Charlotte watched, chattering and smiling.

But as he turned his gaze around, he saw that not all were so happy. Gerta was huddled in a chair near the fire and Adele was drawing a robe up over her. Maximillian was playing chess at a table nearby, but he kept glancing over at Adele and Gerta, a worried expression on his lean, lined face. Bartol, Maximillian's chess partner, was watching everyone rather than the board, his gaze darting to each vignette, a frown on his normally cheerful and ruddy face.

When he saw Nikolas he motioned, and reluctantly Nikolas joined his uncle, crouching near him to hear him out.

"Nikolas, I do not mean to make trouble, but it appears to me that Christoph is quite smitten with your English tutor. She has been smiling and flirting with him for half an hour, and I have never seen the boy so taken."

Alerted to a possible problem, Nikolas tried to ignore a flare of jealousy in his own heart as he turned his gaze to the group. It was true that Christoph never smiled so, and it was directed at Miss Stanwycke. She was only a few years older than he, enough to appear glamorous and worldly to a boy who had little experience; she was English, too, beautiful, and with a wit and sensibility that would be attractive to any man.

It was not that he expected Christoph to remain chaste, but his sister's tutor was not a proper object for his passions. Nor was she appropriate for the young man to marry. Christoph reached out for some sheet music, and his hand brushed Elizabeth's, and both started back, as if they had been burned.

Consciousness, the first dangerous stage of attraction, Nikolas thought.

Standing, Nikolas said, "I will take care of it. Thank you for your concern, uncle." He crossed the room, caught Christoph's eye, and beckoned to him.

When his nephew reluctantly left the trio of young ladies at the piano, Nikolas pulled him outside the door. He had intended to find some way to make amends for his behavior earlier, if Christoph would apologize for *his* remark, which had been a comment on Nikolas's relationship with Magda Brandt that was not only wholly without justification, but filthy and inappropriate.

But this new worry superseded that concern, and he said, holding Christoph's arm in his own grasp, "What is going on between you and Miss Stanwycke?"

"Elizabeth?"

He had not even allowed himself to say her name out loud; Nikolas's grip tightened on Christoph's arm. "Miss Stanwycke, to you. What is going on?"

"Nothing," his nephew said, pulling his arm out of Nikolas's grasp. He rubbed it and winced. "But what if there was? Have you branded every woman in the castle and village with your own ownership?"

Fury ripped through Nikolas at the insolent tone and sneer that accompanied those words. "I would have you take back that, and your filthy suggestion earlier today about Magda Brandt."

Blue eyes wide and lips a tight line, Christoph shook his head.

"Take it back, Christoph. Apologize. Now."

"No. If she is yours, just say so, uncle. If you are fornicating with her . . ."

Nikolas, driven past endurance, grasped his nephew with both hands and shoved him up against the wall again. "Why will you continue to poke and prod me like this?" he ground out, shaking the boy. "Take back that insolence, and what you said about Miss Stanwycke!"

"I didn't mean that," Christoph grunted as he struggled

against the superior strength of his uncle, his pale face reddening, two blotches of high color staining his cheeks.

"Apologize!"

"I didn't mean anything about Elizabeth . . ."

Nikolas pushed harder.

"Miss Stanwycke. I meant to say Miss Stanwycke!"

Releasing his nephew, Nikolas, shuddering with anger, strode away for a moment and tamped back the emotion. Again he had allowed the boy to push him past endurance. He must master his anger where Christoph was concerned, or one day he would harm him. It was not natural for them all to spend so much time together. Christoph should have been out seeing the world, becoming more worldly and leaving behind the emotional suffocation of their insular world, but he would not do anything, nor would he even allow anything to be done for him. Nikolas was reaching the end of his forbearance. How did one deal with a boy who would not become a man, even given every opportunity?

He turned back and saw that his nephew was slinking off. "Stay! I am not done with you."

"What now?"

Nikolas stared at him for a long moment as the echoes of their angry voices dissipated in the gallery. Once, when Christoph was a little towheaded boy of five, and Nikolas was home for a brief vacation before starting on his tour of Italy, Greece, and the Orient, the child had gazed up at him with wide eyes and told him he loved him. His Uncle Nikolas was an idol then. That was the last good moment between them.

How to mend the years of damage now? If there was a way, he didn't have a single clue to what it was. Everything went sour after Johannes died. All Nikolas could do was keep trying to set Christoph on the right road. "Why do you insist on thinking I am some lecherous demon?" he said.

Silvery blue eyes glinting in the pale light from the flickering candles in the hall sconces, Christoph watched his uncle's face. "It is the way this family works, is it not? How we all work? We take what we want."

"I am astounded you could see things that way. All I have

ever done is try to make a good home for you and your sister." Nikolas found Christoph's cynical words deeply troubling.

"I think you have had a few other things on your mind," he said, one corner of his well-shaped mouth lifting as he stared up at his uncle.

That sneer again. Nikolas felt the ire building, the desire to punish that damnably knowing sneer. He tamped down the anger, trying to defeat the darkness that pushed itself into his weary mind. "Tell me what you think you know, Christoph, so I can tell you it is a damnable lie."

The younger man was silent.

"Tell me!" He lunged forward to grab his nephew's arm as Christoph began to edge away, but just then the door opened and Melisande and Charlotte, followed by Elizabeth, entered the hall.

"Are you coming back, Count Christoph?" Miss Stanwycke said, glancing uneasily from Nikolas to his nephew.

"No."

"Why not? I thought we would try something we both know, and the two girls can perhaps sing."

Christoph just shook his head.

"Why not, Christoph?" Melisande Davidovich asked.

"Ask him," the young count said, his voice quavering with emotion. "Ask my uncle. He'll tell you all about why I am not fit company for any of you. I might cut one of you away from his pack of available females." With that he whirled and strode away, running up the stairs toward his own room.

Nikolas felt his face growing brick red with a mixture of anger and chagrin.

"What did he mean, Count?" Miss Stanwycke asked.

"I have no idea. Return, all of you, to the drawing room."

"Are you . . . going to join us?" the tutor asked, though it was clear to Nikolas that Charlotte, her expression holding nothing but dislike and distrust, would rather he didn't.

"No. No, I have work to do." He had done enough damage for one night; he would not join them and stifle whatever natural joy was left to glean from the evening.

Chapter 13

THE DAY was gloomy and overcast, with a lowering sky that threatened even more snow. Charlotte had pled ill yet again, and Countess Adele had this time supported her in her claim, telling Elizabeth the girl really did have a cold and was warm with a slight fever. Melisande was preparing an herbal remedy as she did whenever the Countess Gerta was ill, and one of her ointments was already being utilized to clear Charlotte's breathing passages. Elizabeth thought that the countess was perhaps overly careful of her sister and niece's health, but it was not her place to protest, and so she had a free morning.

She sent a message to Frau Liebner through Fanny and was invited to her friend's rooms to visit. Though the woman was still in bed, reading, she invited Elizabeth to sit with her.

Holding up her book, she said, "I am reading that Englishwoman Mrs. Radcliffe's newest novel, *The Mysteries of Udolpho*, which Adele received from an acquaintance in England. The woman has a style, but I must say that so far as I have read the hero, a certain Monsieur St. Aubert, seems a bloodless paragon, too good to be interesting."

"Too good to be interesting?"

"Hmm." She laid the book aside and yawned. "He never makes a misstep, so far, and is faultless in his kindness, moral decency, and charity. He is a priggish bore whose conceited, mischievous, and boastful brother-in-law sounds far more interesting."

Elizabeth thought about that description, wondering at its truth and curious about the character. "May I read the novel after you?"

"If you will join me of an evening, you may read it to me

out loud, for I always have enjoyed the sound of your voice, Elizabeth."

"I will gladly do so, madam. I confess to a great interest after your description of the stultifying goodness of Monsieur St. Aubert. I have always thought that goodness and morality were necessary parts of the hero of any novel's character, but perhaps I am wrong and you are right, that a man who is too good is boring."

"We shall find out together. So, how are you finding your first month at Wolfram Castle?" Frau Liebner said, studying Elizabeth's face.

"I'm finding that a lot of notions I had about the German character were wrong," Elizabeth replied, wandering to the window and staring out over the steep fir-shrouded hill that rose beyond the castle. "I was under the impression that German women were strong, stout, and phlegmatic. Instead I find Countess Gerta is frail and fragile, Charlotte is put to bed at the first sign of a sniffle, and even Countess Adele, the strongest woman in the castle, supports them in their imagined afflictions."

"How harsh you sound. Perhaps you need a day of self-indulgence. Do you enjoy your work so much that you do not appreciate a day of rest?"

Elizabeth turned away from the window and sat down by the bed, gazing up at her friend. "I don't mean to be unkind to the ladies. I'm just a little uneasy, I suppose. Please, don't mind my sulky state." She frowned down at the floor, examining the intricate pattern, a Grecian key design that edged the carpet. "It's just that Count Nikolas has made it very clear that my staying on is contingent upon my rapid success with Charlotte, and for that I need time and cooperation, neither of which I am getting in any measure." She brooded for a long moment. "What is wrong with this family?" she went on. She described to her friend the scenes from the previous day between the count and his nephew. "Do they dislike each other so much? And why?"

Frau Liebner sipped her chocolate. "I admit, I do not know what is wrong between Nikolas and Christoph. When I left,

Christoph was still just a child, sullen at times, but bright and beautiful mostly. Something has happened between them, and I do not know what."

"Do you think," Elizabeth said, aware that she was treading on very treacherous ground, "that it could have anything to do with how his mother died?"

"It is no wonder to me you are having difficulty with the inhabitants of this home if all you insist on doing is speaking of that which makes people uncomfortable." The older woman glared at Elizabeth for a long moment and then called out in German to the maid assigned to help her. The girl scurried to the bedside. "I wish to rise now, and I would appreciate it if I could do so in privacy."

Elizabeth was well aware that she had been summarily dismissed. She apologized for upsetting her friend and earned a milder look.

"Go on, go up and speak to Uta," Frau Liebner muttered. "She will like the company even if you are in a troublesome state of mind."

Was that a subtle hint that the eldest member of the family might have some clues for her? Elizabeth nodded and thanked her, then departed, heading to Countess Uta's suite. Mina responded to her light tap and motioned to the chair near the window, the elderly woman's customary seat. The countess was dozing but awoke as Elizabeth sat down in the low chair nearby.

"Ach, *gut*, a pretty face to look at," she muttered sleepily. "Is happy I am to see you. To see anyone. No one visits among the young ones, except for my darling little Melisande. Dat girl is more like a niece to me dan Charlotte."

"I can see you are in an unhappy frame of mind today," Elizabeth said. "I am perhaps not the best visitor, then, for I feel much the same."

"You are troubled, ja?" The old woman bent forward and framed Elizabeth's face in her arthritic hands and turned it to the weak light that managed to evade the curtains.

"I am," Elizabeth said awkwardly, over the tight grip of the woman's surprisingly strong hands.

"What is it, den?" she answered, releasing Elizabeth. "You came to talk . . . speak."

Elizabeth glanced up at Mina, uneasily, for the woman lingered, folding and refolding a towel by the washstand.

"Do not regard Mina. She knows more secrets dan anyone in dis household, and yet dey stay secrets."

"But do you never wish to have a moment of talk without her nearby?"

"No, for it is vital to me dat she know everything I know."

"I don't understand."

"I know you don't. But if it will make you happier . . ." She gestured to Mina and dismissed her with a flap of her hand. The woman turned and disappeared through a door at the back of the room.

Elizabeth sighed with relief and sat back in the low chair. Why Mina's silent presence should irritate her so she wasn't sure, but the woman was always watching.

"Now, what is so important?"

Elizabeth caught the avid gleam in the almost blind eyes of the elderly countess and shifted uneasily. She hadn't meant to imply any importance to her questions, but it was too late to go back. And she did need someone to talk to. "Nothing important, ma'am. It's just . . . I'm uneasy. There is so much turmoil in this family and yet no one will speak of it. Everyone edges around certain topics and I don't understand why. And stories of the past directly conflict. Was Count Nikolas here the day Count Hans von Holtzen and Countess Anna von Wolfram died, or wasn't he? I am told he was, and I am told he wasn't."

"Perhaps you are asking the wrong questions," Uta said.

"What do you mean?"

"People do not like to speak of things dat have truly happened. Rather dey prefer to talk about gossip and scandal and rumor and innuendo."

Elizabeth was silent. None of that appealed to her. Gossip and innuendo had ruined her, and she despised it and the people who spread it, but she couldn't say that to the countess.

It had not escaped her notice that the elderly woman, too,

had evaded her pointed question. Perhaps she would never receive a definite answer.

"And curses," the old woman said, her face turned to the hazy light from the window. "Curses are always good; people love to speak of dem. Dis family is bewitched, you know."

"I don't believe in curses," Elizabeth said, but then her curious mind teased at her, and she knew she would ask. She leaned in to Countess Uta and said, "What was the curse? Who laid it?"

"See?" The old woman cackled in delight. "Even you, my rational English friend, are not immune from curiosity and excitement of dat which is unknown."

"I don't say I believe it, ma'am, just that I am interested." This was better, Elizabeth thought, edging forward. At least the old woman was entertaining, which was more than she could say for the rest of the brooding, melancholy family.

"Well, dis started long ago, thirty, forty years. Or perhaps longer. Yes, longer . . . the rest is faded in mist now, my memory like fog rolling over meadow on a spring evening."

"What started?"

"The curse of the von Wolfram heir. Once, von Wolfram men were as sturdy and robust as the wolf pups in spring."

"I certainly would call Count Nikolas robust," Elizabeth remarked dryly, thinking of his broad shoulders, muscular frame, and commanding presence.

"True. But he is only young yet."

"He's in his middle thirties, ma'am. Hardly young."

"Youth or age . . . dat depends on from what end you see it, young lady. From your view, so young you are, he is middle years, but from my twilight he appears callow and unformed, not nearly the man he will be, gifen time."

"I interrupted your story, ma'am. Please continue," Elizabeth said, not wanting to think of the disturbing and altogether too fascinating count. His recent behavior toward his nephew had been appalling, to Elizabeth's tender sensibilities, but then, she didn't know what had proceeded his disciplinary action. If it didn't excuse it, it could possibly explain it.

"I remember now . . . it was longer dan forty years. Perhaps fifty."

She gazed into the distance, her lips moving, and Elizabeth waited patiently.

"Yes, fifty years ago or maybe more, for I was a young woman, ripe, ready to wed, wanting a husband and babies. I had four brothers, you know, each more handsome and healthy dan the last. Jakob, Nikolas's father, was youngest of the boys. We had bad winter, and wolves, dey were starving. It was terrible year. My brother Jergen—he was eldest—shot many wolves dat year for depredations on our cattle. Dat summer a band of gypsies roamed by and camped on our land. My father went to dem and told dem to get off, dat dey were not welcome. He shot one for insolence."

"Shot one?" Elizabeth gasped.

"It was just a gypsy," the old woman said with a shrug. "Dat was how Papa saw it. One less gypsy, one less thief."

Elizabeth swallowed back her indignation that any human life could be treated so casually. It was not her story, and not her family. "What did they do?"

"Old gypsy woman came to the courtyard . . . where old tree is now. Was good tree then, big, strong. She stood in courtyard on night of full moon and . . ." The old woman stopped and stared into space. Her eyes closed.

Elizabeth, in some alarm, was about to stand and administer assistance, when the old woman's eyes flew open again.

"She was dat man's mother. The dead one. She shrieked out dat the full moon would see us cursed. Never would a son of our house prosper. All would be blighted and cursed, blasted like the tree in the courtyard."

The tree . . . the withered and blackened stump Elizabeth had commented on to Charlotte. The family tree.

"My father laughed. He said the tree was as strong as the family, and dat she was just an old crazy woman. He drove her away, but dat night a storm blew in, and lightning struck. The tree was split and burned, though still it lives on, a few sprigs of it alive every spring."

She fell silent again and Elizabeth waited, thinking about

what she had said. But finally she asked, "What happened to your brothers?"

"Friedrich died dat spring of fever. Karl . . . he went . . . hmm, I don't know in English. *Verrueckt. Ach, ja,* I know word now. Crazy, he went, and killed himself. Or so we think; no one would ever say it, but I know it was true. And Willem . . . sweet Willem. He was the best of brothers. Too good for dis world, my mother said."

After a pause, Elizabeth gently asked, "And Willem? What happened to him?"

"My father made Willem go into army, you know, as officer, though he was like Christoph and liked to hold violin more dan rifle. He was cleaning gun and it went off, killed him. So dey say. My mama did not believe dat."

Silence fell between them until Elizabeth, puzzled by one thing the old woman had said, asked, "Why did you talk about the wolves in the winter . . . your brother killing them?"

Uta remained silent for a long time, and then said, "It was nothing. It was . . . just how I remember dat winter, and the spring after. It was the winter of wolves."

She would speak of it no longer, for her mood had turned somber and dark. Elizabeth, concerned that she had led the poor woman into talking about worrisome things, stayed and asked if Uta would teach her some German, for she was determined to pick it up. She had learned some in the month she had been there, but she still had a long way to go. Her ploy worked, and she soon had the old woman laughing at her fractured pronunciation of the long string of syllables that made up so many German words.

At the end of two hours, Mina came in and with a wave of her hand indicated that Elizabeth should leave. Though she was about to protest, she glanced down at the elderly woman and saw the strain on her gray face. She really had taxed her too much. Heartsick, she gave the maid an apologetic look, then leaned down and said her good-byes, laying a kiss on the wrinkled brow. The countess was already asleep.

At loose ends, Elizabeth wandered down to the gallery and stood at the railing overlooking the great hall, thinking about all she had learned. It still seemed to her that the family's troubles had a more recent vintage, and that was from fifteen years ago, when tragedy struck. The uneasy feeling she had noted in the castle still overlaid it like a dark shadow. Even Fanny, that morning, when she had come to Elizabeth's room to pull open the curtains, had appeared tense and worried, though when accosted by Elizabeth she claimed there was nothing wrong at all. She didn't like being driven to question the servants; it wasn't seemly and she would resist the urge when next it appeared.

As she brooded she could hear the sound of horses outside, the jingle of sledge bells and voices. A heavy *thud-thud-thud* on the front door sent footmen scurrying, and when two opened the big oak doors, a flood of men pushed into the great hall. Their voices raised, they demanded to see, from what Elizabeth could understand, Count Nikolas.

Snow swirled into the great hall as the servants slammed the doors shut. Cesare Vitali scurried down the stairs past Elizabeth, not noticing her in the shadows, and faced the group, telling them in excellent German to leave and await the count's visit in their homes. They loudly refused and were arguing vociferously with the secretary when Nikolas himself strode into the great hall from some other room. They hushed immediately, and every one, even the man in front, regarded him with some trepidation.

Nikolas planted himself in front of the group, his feet wide apart, his hands on his hips, his very stance confrontational. "What do you want?" he asked of the leader, in German.

Elizabeth crouched down by the railing and watched, her gaze taking in the leader's cape, the thick, gray fur dark-tipped and silvery in the weak winter light from the big windows that lined the north side of the great hall.

The leader said something, but Elizabeth couldn't understand his thickly accented and rapid spate of words. From his intonation she guessed he was the village mayor, perhaps the father of the girl who was attacked, and he was demanding something of Count Nikolas.

But Nikolas merely told him to leave and never come

back. Those words were simple and clear. From there the confrontation devolved into a shouting match, with Cesare Vitali trying to intercede and getting roughly shoved out of the way by one of the village men, a stout fellow with a thick cudgel.

"What is going on?"

The whispered voice made Elizabeth jump, but it was just Bartol Liebner at her side.

"I'm not sure," she said. "I don't understand all of what they're saying but . . ."

Herr Liebner was listening intently and shook his head. In the dim light of the gallery Elizabeth could see his frown and his anxious expression.

"What are they saying? What do they want?"

"Terrible, this is. Awful."

"What is?"

"They . . ." He paused and listened some more. "That man in the wolfskin cape, that is Wilhelm Brandt, the mayor of Wolfbeck. He is saying there are werewolves gathering in the von Wolfram forest, and he is demanding that . . . that some of the village men be allowed to patrol the forest at night."

Nikolas was speaking and Bartol Liebner stopped to listen. Elizabeth could catch much of what the count said, that he would never countenance villagers patrolling his woods, and that they were being fools to believe in such superstition anyway. There were no werewolves; Magda Brandt's wound came from some other source than a wolf, let alone a werewolf.

When the village mayor spoke again, Bartol Liebner translated. A werewolf was sighted in the last full moon, and now the moon was waxing full again. What would Nikolas do in the nights to come? How could he assure them safety in their bed? How could he say he would not allow them to protect their women and children?

His voice loud, rage in his very stance, Count Nikolas said that if even one of them dared to step foot on his land at night, with or without a weapon, he, Nikolas, would shoot him, flay him, and send his skin to his family. With that he gave a command to his footmen and strode to the stairs, bounding up them two at a time. Seeing her and Bartol Liebner at the railing, he glared at them, then strode off to his library.

Quivering, Elizabeth watched the aftermath as the footmen, bolstered by a couple of stout stable hands, herded the villagers out as snow again swirled into the great hall and wind made the pennants flutter and dance.

She turned to Herr Liebner as the big doors were slammed shut and bolted. "Why do they think what they saw was a werewolf?" she whispered in the sudden silence. "Don't werewolves supposedly look just like wolves? And why didn't the count try to reason with them?"

"I don't know why they think there are werewolves here," the man said, his expression grim and his cheeks pallid. "Nikolas did try to reason . . . he told them werewolves are just fairy tales used to frighten little children, and that he had thought better of them than to believe such nonsense."

Herr Liebner looked frightened, Elizabeth thought, but it was likely that the anger of the villagers had alarmed him. Cesare Vitali, having overseen the exit of the villagers, disappeared and the great hall grew calm, the only remnant of the confrontation a hank of fur from the mayor's cape on the stone floor.

Quickly, Elizabeth raced down the steps, snatched up the hunk of fur, and retreated back up the stairs as Bartol watched in fear. In the weak lamplight she examined the patch, a square of fur around four inches. The fur was soft and thick, gray with dark tips.

"You should get rid of that," the older man said, backing away from her.

"You don't believe in werewolves, do you?" Elizabeth said, looking up at the man, surprised at his fear.

"No. No, of course not," he said. "But is bad luck to keep it. Excuse me, please, I must . . . I must go."

Count Nikolas could not have handled the delegation more badly if he had set out to infuriate them, Elizabeth thought, rubbing the fur between her fingers. How could a man so intelligent not see that they were badly frightened and needed to be reassured, not threatened? And how could he threaten such a barbaric punishment anyway? But it was not her business. She should go and read a book, or prepare a new lesson for Charlotte. Or go speak to Frau Liebner or Melisande.

She strode down the hall and without knocking flung herself into the library. "How could you treat those poor men so cavalierly?" she said, crossing the room to the desk, where Nikolas sat. "All they wanted was to protect their families."

When he looked up, she fell back two paces. His eyes were dark with shadows under them, and his mouth was set in a grim line. He stood, slowly, his height imposing even in the high-ceilinged library. "Am I to understand that you are questioning my handling of the villagers?"

"I . . ." She stiffened her resolve. "I suppose I am."

"And where do you get your right, from your vast store of knowledge about ancient superstition and German village affairs?" His tone was a growl and his expression grim.

She quailed at his look but, holding the hank of wolfskin as a talisman, took a deep breath and straightened her backbone. "I have no right," she admitted. "But—"

"But you are going to tell me your opinion anyway."

"Yes, if you will just listen. How did railing at them and threatening them soothe their worries? They are clearly fearful and upset. They clearly believe that there are such creatures as werewolves and that they are in imminent danger from them. How did threatening to kill them further your cause, which must be to calm their anxiety and reassure them? They cannot help their superstition. You should have been more patient."

His expression, dark with fury, calmed. It was like a tide receding, the darkness ebbing from his eyes. "Miss Stanwycke, did anyone ever tell you that you should not speak about that which you know nothing?"

"Yes," she admitted reluctantly.

"And has that ever stopped you?"

"No."

Her simple response, said with all the dignity she could obviously summon, was like a sunray to him, peeking through a dark cloud. She stood before him, hands folded in front of her, back straight, expression sober, and admitted her inability to stay out of that which did not concern her. His mouth split wide in a grin that he could not contain. "I do not know how you do it, but always, no matter how angry I am—and no matter how angry I should be for your interference—you make me laugh."

"I prefer not to be laughed at, sir," she said.

He sobered. "I'm not laughing *at* you. But you bring a levity to the situation by pointing out to me the error of my ways in such a precise and knowledgeable fashion that I cannot help but laugh."

"Most men would dismiss me," she acknowledged with a returning smile.

"Most men would be afraid that you would see right through them and their bluster and puncture their inflated sense of their own worthiness. I am not most men."

"So you don't fear that?"

"No. I know my own worth very well, and I fear no one's ability to puncture it. It is not overinflated, you see."

"From any other gentleman I have ever met, that speech would have been hopelessly pompous, but from you, I believe it is simply the way things are."

It was said with a smile, and he could not tell if she was serious, or if she was placating him, or if she was laughing at him in return.

"I admit," she continued, "I have always been too ready to tell gentlemen my opinion."

He chuckled. "I see now why there are no adequate positions remaining for you to fill on the island you call your homeland," he said, a dry edge to his voice. "You have frightened all the men."

An expression of pain darkened her lovely face—she had been hurt by some memory, he thought—and he rushed back into speech. "That was unkind, Miss Stanwycke, and I apologize. I am always apologizing to you, for some reason, even when you are the one who should be apologizing."

"That is because you are a gentleman, sir, and beneath your bluster, and . . . and your temper, I believe you to be kind. Which is why I was so puzzled by how you treated the villagers who were only asking to be allowed to protect their women and children. No matter how you view their superstitions, you should have been more patient."

He quelled his impatience with her interference. Nothing but an explanation would do for Miss Elizabeth Stanwycke. "Sit!" he commanded, pointing at the chair in front of his desk. "I do not in the normal course of my day feel compelled to explain my actions to anybody. Nor do many in this castle question me." He watched her face, but she was not inclined to hasten into speech and reassure him that he need not give her any explanation, and as irritated as he was he respected that unfeminine stolidity in the face of his admittedly imperious manner. She remained silent, merely watching him. He had to look away, for there was a tendency when he was in her company to get lost in the azure of her eyes.

He sighed. Nothing but the truth then, in this one instance.

"First, they came into my home and upset my staff. If they had a concern, they could have asked me to visit and I would have met with them. I accede to every reasonable request. No, Miss Stanwycke," he said, holding up one hand as she was about to speak. "They know this. I will address any concern they have." That last part evidently silenced what she was about to say.

"Second, what they are asking is unthinkable. Posting armed villagers in *my* forest? Never!" He shook his head. "You don't understand, Elizabeth," he said, then realized he had used her Christian name as her cheeks pinkened. Enchanted by her embarrassment, he stopped for a moment and watched her. "Uh, what was I saying?"

"That I didn't understand," she said, looking down at her hands.

"Yes." He looked away, up at the dry and dusty tomes of Greek philosophy and Latin theory. "Think, Elizabeth," he said, relishing the sound of her name on his tongue, "how dangerous it would be to have men—superstitious, frightened men—roaming my forest armed with guns. Suppose something happened? Suppose I needed to send one of my staff to the village for the doctor? Suppose one of the servants was coming home late from visiting a family member? The full of the moon is when I allow my serving staff to visit their relatives in the village, for they can come home by moonlight."

She nodded and met his gaze. "Yes, I can see your point, but still . . . surely there was a better way to put it? You are too reasonable a man to rule by fear."

"I have tried reason. They respond better to fear, and in this I require absolute, unequivocal obedience. And there is something else going on . . ." He stopped himself from divulging all of his thoughts and worries, though the temptation to talk to her was overwhelming.

She waited a moment for him to finish, then said, "I understand. Truly, I do." She paused, her mouth pursed in thought. "Sir, why do they think there are werewolves? Have they always believed this?"

"It goes back many centuries, and is ingrained in them. Religion has not conquered it, nor can reason." He watched her for a long moment, then said, on impulse, "Are you happy, Elizabeth? And may I call you Elizabeth in private? I like your name, and I like talking to you."

She flushed a pretty pink again and smiled. "I'm happy most of the time," she said, not agreeing to his use of her name, but not denying it, either. "I wish I could get through to Charlotte, but I've not given up hope yet. I think it would help if I could tell her I don't believe you will marry her off to just anyone. Nor send her away arbitrarily. She's afraid of that."

"Do not think I am not aware of her feelings. But I will and must do what I think . . . no, what I *know* is best for her. These are trying times, Elizabeth, with the French knocking at our door and my country in danger. Who knows what will happen in the future?"

"Then I will do my job as best I can." She rose and put her hand out across the desk.

He took it and rubbed his thumb over the soft skin, feeling again that unwilling lurch of his heart. "That is all I ever ask of anyone."

Chapter 14

THOUGH HE was forced to absent himself once again from the dinner table—there were things that had to be done and could not wait—Nikolas moved toward the drawing room where his family and friends were gathered with a mixture of trepidation and excitement. He could not conceal from himself that the excitement was almost wholly because he would see Elizabeth again. The trepidation was for other reasons.

He entered quietly, staying in the shadows of the overhanging entryway and observing. As master of the house, he knew that the moment he was known to have entered, everything in the room—every person's behavior—changed, sometimes for the better, sometimes for the worse.

Bartol was by the fire playing ombre with his sister-in-law. Nikolas smiled; his Aunt Katrina had little use for her brother-in-law, and so this must be penance on her part for some imagined wrong. But he was happy to see her feeling well enough to join the company. In the ten years since he had last seen her she had aged and slowed considerably. Adele was doing her needlepoint, a vast canvas on a wood frame, the subject of which was a bloody battle from three centuries before. In years gone by she would have been a warrior princess, he thought, watching her, the silvery blond hair neat in a coronet braid around her head like a crown. She was intelligent and well-disciplined and would always, always, do her duty, as she saw it.

Maximillian was in a quiet corner playing piquet with Gerta. Nikolas frowned as he watched his sister reach out and caress her opponent's hand. The Frenchman smiled at her, his expression unguarded and gentle. Adele, he saw, had noticed as well, and she placed a wrong stitch, jabbing her finger and stifling an exclamation of pain.

Nikolas grimaced, knowing that no matter how much he wished things to be a certain way, he could not command people's hearts. Adele had always loved Maximillian, and the Frenchman . . . who knew his heart? Certainly not Nikolas, even though they were old friends and he valued the man for the excellence of his mind and the gentility he displayed always.

But now . . . now he could turn his gaze where he wished. Charlotte and Melisande were at the piano playing a quick piece, and Elizabeth? She was dancing the quadrille with Christoph. Quelling a quick stab of jealousy and concern, Nikolas refrained from striding forward as was his instinct, staying in the shadows to observe.

There was no coquetry in Elizabeth's manner toward Christoph. It was clearly a sort of lesson, for she was commanding Charlotte to watch her as she curtseyed and took the younger man's hand. What Christoph might be feeling he did not know, but for his niece's tutor, this was an extension of the day's work.

After a moment Elizabeth released Christoph and went to the piano, pulling Charlotte up and leading her to her brother, setting them in place for the dance. She corrected Charlotte's position, putting one hand to her back and making her straighten and pull back her shoulders. In her fashionably high-waisted gown—the exaggerated silhouette still looked odd to him, but his sisters had assured him as he paid the seamstress's weighty accounts that it was necessary to make over their entire stock of gowns in the new fashion—his niece looked more attractive immediately for her improved posture. Charlotte took Christoph's hand and they went through the paces of the dance not perfectly, but with some measure of grace and elegance, considering the quickness of the steps. It was astounding. There was a vast improvement and even Christoph was smiling, an increasingly rare occurrence.

Nikolas turned his gaze to Elizabeth's lovely face and saw in her smile a joy that was from her student's performance. She was a born teacher, one who taught from a love of people rather than a love of any particular subject. With intelligence, discretion, and perspicacity as her weapons, she enjoyed the game of teaching an unwilling mind, he thought, and of interesting the student in the subject and tricking them into learning. Even Christoph was benefiting from her ability to intuitively find a common point of interest for young people. He was about to turn and leave the room, loath to disturb such a pretty scene, but Elizabeth saw him and gestured for him to join them. Christoph's expression froze, but he made no murmur against it.

"Come, sir," Elizabeth said eagerly, taking his hand and leading him to the pair dancing. "Dance with me for a moment, while Charlotte dances with Count Christoph, for I wish to display the form of the line, and we need more than one couple for that."

His mouth dried, but as Melisande launched into another sprightly piece on the piano he had no choice but to bow, take Elizabeth's hand, and dance. His vision narrowed to one single face among the others; he watched Elizabeth, even as she did her turn with Christoph and he with Charlotte. She was grace personified, and he thought he had never seen a form so lovely as the lithe lines of her body, as she did the leaps and turns necessary.

Out of breath as the music stopped, her cheeks pink from exercise, she smiled up at him and then turned to Charlotte. "Now, Charlotte—"

"I know all of these dances," Charlotte said, a pout on her face, still sniffling from her cold. She was restive now that Nikolas was there.

"Ah, you know the steps, but you don't know the true art and purpose of dance. Watch." Elizabeth looked up at him and said quietly, "Will you perform with me a few steps of any slow dance, sir?"

He acquiesced, and they began.

She curtseyed daintily and then took his hand as they

began the intricate, stately figures. "How pleasant to see you again, Count von Wolfram. Are you enjoying your time in . . . uh, in London?"

He gazed down into her eyes as they came together and was caught by the smile in their depths, a gentle good humor that attracted him, soothing his agitation. "I am enjoying it more than I ever could have thought possible."

"How wonderful! And have you seen the sights yet?"

"I've seen everything beautiful that I could want to see," he murmured. "Whatever else is here, I don't care about."

Her cheeks deepened in color, and he smiled to himself.

"I am so happy to hear that you are enjoying your time here," she replied, keeping her tone serene. "It is unseasonably cold, though, I think. Do you agree?"

"On the contrary, I am finding it rather warm."

She broke away then and said, turning to Charlotte, who watched, wide eyed, "You see? One should keep up a conversation. It is incumbent upon you, even if the gentleman is silent or gauche. One should never speak too rapidly, though, nor should one speak of certain topics."

"Certain topics?"

Elizabeth had returned to the piano and feverishly leafed through some sheet music. Nikolas followed her and leaned on the piano close by, watching her quick, nervous movements.

"Yes. One should not," she said, turning to Charlotte, "relate gossip that is ill-humored. Gossip about general topics is acceptable. Nor should one speak of other ladies, their clothing, their companions. Nor should one speak of ailments, deformities, personal subjects—"

"Anything at all, it seems!" Charlotte said with a peevish flounce. She sniffled and wiped her nose with a handkerchief.

"Oh, no . . . there is much to speak of. One can, as I was, speak of the weather, or literature, or the opera, or music. One can ask after common acquaintances."

"Or one can speak of nothing," Nikolas said, sliding his hand along the top of the piano, toward Elizabeth's arm.

"What?" Charlotte asked.

"Never say 'What' in English, Charlotte," Elizabeth said, turning away from the piano toward her pupil. "One should say, 'I beg your pardon,' if you did not hear or didn't understand." Elizabeth turned back to him. "But what did you mean, sir?"

He gazed at her. "Let us dance again and I will illustrate."

Her hand was naked and soft, no gloves impeding the sweet warmth of her touching him. He led her into the figures as Melisande played and said, "Miss Stanwycke, if English ladies are to be compared to roses, I must say you are the fairest bloom in a lovely bouquet."

"You are impertinent, sir," she replied.

"I dare only because the dance offers so little time, and a gentleman must always tell the truth. Should I say any lady here was lovelier than you, I would lie."

She pulled away. "I don't think that is suitable conversation. Commenting on a lady's looks is not acceptable."

She had backed a few paces away and he smiled at her. "But ladies do flirt, Miss Stanwycke. And so do gentlemen. Charlotte must learn, for men expect a little flirtation before the serious business of marrying is approached. It indicates a wit and lightness of humor that is delightful."

"As long as it does not indicate a lightness of character," she replied soberly. "One is best to err on the side of discretion and risk appearing humorless, for a reputation of ill-considered levity or inappropriate conversation is ruin for a young lady. And a reputation, once damaged, is too often irreparable."

Something lay beneath her words and he longed to take her aside, to delve into her past. She had been hurt, but whether it was by a man or by society at large, he could not guess.

"Are there not harmless little devices that every lady knows . . . things she does to fix a gentleman's attention?" he said.

Charlotte's expression was rapt; Elizabeth glanced at her, and her clouded expression turned lighter again as she regained her equilibrium. She snatched up a fan that lay on the piano. "Certainly, sir. Charlotte, gentlemen, wielding all the power in the world, deserve to be taunted and teased a little, and to be kept in doubt of a lady's regard. Those in society of more serious casts of mind consider it mere foolishness and gamery, but I happen to disagree. If men require such tomfoolery to aid in attraction, then I consider it merely part of the courtship."

"Can I not just tell a gentleman that I like him, and ask if he likes me?"

"Oh, no, Charlotte," Elizabeth said, with some bitterness in her tone that belied her brilliant smile. "A lady will never give away too much of her feelings before she is certain of the gentleman's. Men, being men, will take advantage. Worse, they will value you the less for being so honest and forthright, for what they value in other men they take in women as being unladylike and forward."

It was a hard little speech, and Charlotte stared, openmouthed. But Elizabeth had already turned away from her student. She drifted over to Nikolas and as she stood in front of him she fluttered the fan, covering her mouth and only displaying her remarkable azure eyes, which flirted up at him beneath her lashes. A dimple on her cheek winked but then disappeared, and she sighed and turned slowly, throwing one long, lingering look over her shoulder as she strolled away, the hem of her gown twitching in a most bewitching way. She was well-versed in the art of silent flirtation, even if she had never deigned to use it, Nikolas thought, his heart thudding. Were they in any common ballroom he would follow her and beg the indulgence of one single, solitary dance. And then he would draw her out to the terrace for a stolen moment, a kiss, a touch. She would submit for a brief moment and then draw back, abashed, the better to entice him. He remembered the old games from his days at university in Heidelberg and the ladies of the town, and then after, from his year on the Continent, doing the tour.

But how well such delicate stratagems worked to attract men, for he had to restrain himself, and he knew that he had even surged forward a step before awareness returned to him. He glanced around and caught Christoph's steady gaze on him. It was a moment when he could have perhaps said a word, something, anything to break the tension between them, but he was speechless, caught in a web of tangled feelings.

Abruptly he bowed. "Very good; please excuse me. I . . . I have to speak to . . . to the others. Carry on with your lessons, Miss Stanwycke." He turned and strode away.

He said a brief word to the others but could not bear to stay. It was painful to want something—or someone—so desperately and yet know one's desires were doomed to be disappointed.

The night was a long one, and Nikolas awoke the next morning aching with desire from dreams that left his sheets damp with sweat. A plunge naked in the snow may have helped his feverish state, but work would have to suffice as an antidote to desire. Whether it was just the result of long abstinence or something about Elizabeth Stanwycke herself that had his blood boiling with need, he didn't know.

He rode to the village in the morning and spent several hours speaking to people, reiterating his commands, trying to counteract the effects of Willhelm Brandt's poisonous dread. He then finished his letter to Jakob, telling him this was not a good time for him and Eva to come back to Wolfram Castle. He met with his estate manager regarding plans for the spring planting and birthing of new milk cattle, and he met with Adele, trying to disregard her frozen expression and pained demeanor, knowing she was aching to spill her troubles to him, but with no patience to deal with them when he had his own concerns.

Finally Nikolas was alone in the library, and he laid his head down on his desk and felt weariness shudder through him.

A sharp rap at the door made him straighten, and he shouted, *"Kommen sie."*

The door opened and Charlotte sidled in, standing just inside the door.

He stood. "What is it?"

She faltered for a moment, her pretty face a mask of confusion. But then she stiffened, much as he had seen Elizabeth do when she was bracing herself to say something to him, and said, "I'd like to talk to you, uncle, if I may."

"Certainly. Come. Sit," he said, indicating the chair in front of his desk. "What is wrong?" When she flinched, he realized how brusque he sounded. Could he never soften his tone? She was his niece, not a servant or subject. With great effort, he said, "If you have any concerns or worries, Charlotte, you may always come to me."

She gazed at him steadily, skepticism in her blue eyes, and he could see her mind working, trying to find a way to say what she wanted to say. It was likely the same old argument again, the fact that she did not want to marry an Englishman, did not want to go to England, and in fact didn't want to go anywhere without her brother. Nikolas had determined that for her own sake she must leave, and with things the way they were in the castle and the situation as it was on the whole of the Continent, he thought it would likely be that summer. He was not willing to bargain, nor back down. Though Nikolas could not force Christoph into any action, Charlotte was his ward and would be until she married. He only hoped he had not left it too long.

"How are you feeling? Are you over your cold yet?" he asked, as she sneezed once and blew her nose.

"No. It is still with me, though Meli's potions have done me good."

Silence fell between them again, but finally she met his steady gaze. "What really happened to my mother?"

He sat back, stunned. She stared at him, waiting, and he realized that if he had had nothing to hide from her, he would have spoken immediately. "You know what happened. She died very tragically, in a fire."

"But how? Why?"

He considered, as he gazed at her, how much he should tell her, meaning how much she needed to know to be satisfied. "You were so young when she died. I'm sorry you never really knew her, for she was . . . a lovely person. She was very kind to me."

"Were you in love with her?"

"What? Who told you that?"

She looked frightened. "No one. No one at all, uncle. I just wondered . . . the way you just spoke of her . . ."

But he knew she had come in thinking that, and that someone had fed that lie to her. "No, I was not in love with her. She was kind to me, but just in the way an older sister is to a younger brother. Like Christoph is to you."

She looked away, a gleam of a tear in her eye.

It took every bit of determination to do what he knew was right. Nikolas got up, circled the desk, and crouched by her, gazing up into her eyes. "Your mother was indeed a lovely person, and your father loved her very much. She was out at a cottage on the property—no one is sure why, but we think she may have been looking it over, thinking of redoing it as a little retreat for her and your father—and somehow, it caught on fire. I think a lamp spilled and caught on a curtain. Hans, your Aunt Gerta's husband, had gone out for a ride, and though we don't know for sure, we think he must have heard her cries and rushed in to try to rescue her."

Tears dripped down her cheeks and onto her clenched hands. He put his larger hand over both of hers and squeezed. "I . . . I had been gone some time, on the Continent. Cesare and I were just coming back that night; he had stayed behind in the village with our trunks, but I was eager to get home and had come through the woods—it was the full moon, lots of light—and . . . and I heard the cries. I found the cottage in flames and tried to rescue them, but it was already too late. I could not get in. I couldn't save them."

Charlotte wept silently for a minute, then, sniffling, she said, "What about Papa? Why did he die?"

Nikolas sat back on his heels. "I don't know. He got sick. We tried everything, called in a specialist from Vienna, but he was gone three weeks after Anna . . . your mother."

"He didn't . . ." She shivered. "He didn't kill himself?"

"Who has been feeding you those lies?" he said, standing to his full height and towering over her.

She scuttled out of the chair and toward the door. "No one!"

"Charlotte! Wait!" He hadn't meant to frighten her. He thrust his hands though his hair and squeezed. He must learn to temper his responses. "I . . . I did not mean to shout. I am not angry at you, but if anyone is telling you such despicable lies, I want you to tell me who."

"No one! No one. But . . . it has just been whispered that he did not have to die . . . that he should not have died."

"No, he should not have died." He shrugged helplessly. "But he became ill. He died. That was all."

She nodded, her lips in a tight line.

"Charlotte, I—"

"Good day, uncle. I will not disturb you again," she said, slithering out the door and racing down the hall away from him.

He flopped back down in his chair and covered his eyes. Even if his soul was not already damned to hell, it would become that way from the lies he was forced into again and again. When would it end? *How* would it end?

Feeling at the end of his tether, he bellowed to a footman, who scurried off to do his bidding. Ten minutes later, flustered and harried looking, Elizabeth Stanwycke hustled into the library.

"What is it? What is wrong?"

"Did you put her up to that?" he growled.

"Whatever are you talking about?" she said, crossing the room and staring down at him.

"Did you plant those evil lies in Charlotte's head? She never did ask such things before, and I know you have been snooping around the castle, prying into things that don't concern you . . ."

"Whatever is wrong, Count, do not pull me into your schemes and stratagems. I have said nothing to anyone. What are you talking about?"

He gazed up into her mystified eyes and knew she was telling the truth. "I'm sorry. I'm sorry!" He rubbed his eyes and then stared back up at her again. "There I go, apologizing to you again."

"Well, if you would stop trying to bully, accuse, and torment me, then you would have nothing to apologize for."

As brisk as the words were, he could hear the exasperation in her voice, and though he felt it was better than he deserved he was grateful that she said no worse. "Elizabeth, Elizabeth. Do you know, I think in truth I just wanted any excuse to see you."

"You could have chosen something else rather than base accusations to bring me here," she said, her tone still stiff.

"You are right. Again, I apologize. Will you sit with me for a moment, if I promise to be on my best behavior?"

"I will sit," she said, perching on the chair across from him, "but I doubt if you can keep your promise. You must tell me first what it was you were talking about with my pupil."

"Charlotte came to me; she had some ideas about her parents' deaths. I don't know where she can have gotten some of them."

"In particular . . . ?"

"She asked me," he said, precisely, "if I was in love with Anna, her mother. I was not. And she asked me . . ." It was too painful; he could not go on. He bowed his head and felt the weariness and misery of his life descend upon him. He could not go on, trying and failing constantly to deliver his family from the pain of the past and the uncertainty of the future.

The room was quiet and cold and he felt so empty inside. Had Elizabeth left him alone? He couldn't blame her if she had. But then he felt a warmth nearby and she stood before him and her hand was on his hair. He felt himself dissolve, and then, before he realized what he was doing, his head was against her stomach and she was stroking his hair. Relief trickled through him like a clear, cool stream, and he lost all sense of time and place.

Her scent filled his nostrils; her heartbeat filled his ears. Fingers threaded his hair and stroked his neck, and with his eyes closed he could sense every touch; it took him beyond forgetfulness to bliss.

"I know," she murmured against his hair as she bent over him like a sheltering willow.

Without knowing what he was saying, he had been muttering, over and over, in German, "I'm weary, so weary." She had understood him, but whether it was his words or his tone she was responding to, he didn't know and didn't care. He raised his face, eyes still closed, and lips touched his eyelids and his cheeks, and the soft kisses rained on his brow and over his lips. He reached out, encircled her waist, and pulled her to him, onto his lap, urgently seeking her sweetness, tasting the wetness of her exquisite mouth over his. He nuzzled her neck and nipped her soft earlobe, hunger building in his stomach like a fire heating a forge. In a heartbeat he traveled from tenderness to desire.

But in an instant it was over, and he was cold again, bereft, for she had wrenched herself from his grasp. "What is wrong, Elizabeth?"

"I . . . I meant only to offer you a moment of solace, sir, for I know how weary your burdens make you." Her voice was breathless and she was standing on the other side of the desk again, her body half turned, ready to flee like a deer before a wolf.

"No, don't go," he said, rising and putting out one hand.

"I must. You know that. Truly, I must go. I . . . I hope you're feeling better. Don't worry about Charlotte; she's just questioning everything right now, I think."

And then she was gone, the door silently closing behind her.

THE day was long and felt like drudgery after the sweet moments of utter bliss, being in Count Nikolas's arms. Elizabeth endured the afternoon, then visited Countess Uta, and after, before retiring for the night, she read *The Mysteries of Udolpho* for a while to Frau Liebner. The count, luckily for her fragile hold on rationality, was absent from the dinner table, and she excused herself from the after-dinner ritual of the drawing room, pleading a headache. Charlotte was still not feeling well and so had gone back to her bed.

And then silence and solitude. Blessed, blessed solitude in

her own room, cold and lonely as it sometimes seemed. Reflecting on the moments with the count, touching his hair, feeling him melt against her, his strength deserting him as she sheltered him against her bosom, she wondered if she had ever felt so about John—the tenderness and solicitude—even in the midst of thinking she loved him and would forever. But she had been deceived in those emotions. She felt barely a twinge about John now and experienced only disgust when she remembered their times together. Those precious stolen moments that had once felt sacred right now seemed, in retrospect, hurried and wicked, the merest satisfying of bodily urges with neither tenderness nor affection to sanctify them.

But what had possessed her when she saw the count so weary and troubled to take him to her breast like that? It was the action of a moment, the decision made somewhere else than in her mind. And what followed had been heady, sweet, thrilling . . . and dangerous.

Sleepless, she abandoned her bed and instead huddled in the window seat of her room, which looked out over the back and side of the castle, the stables dark, the snowy fir-clad hills beyond gleaming from the light of the full moon. How long she had been awake, she didn't know, but it had been hours, some spent pacing, some spent laying on her bed gazing at the ceiling, and now, in the window seat, staring out.

As she gazed down at the stables she saw that there was one solitary light burning, and it was moving. Fascinated, she watched. A stablehand—though she now knew some of them by sight, she couldn't tell which one from her height, for his form was foreshortened—came to the door and looked out, then paced the stable yard and went back in. After a time, he did the same thing again. Was he merely sleepless, too? She didn't think that was likely; the stable hands worked too hard and their life was too grim. Sleep must be a kind of refuge for them, a release from the unutterable weariness of their long day.

It was one of the older men, she could tell by his walk, which listed to one side as if he had a bad leg. As she watched, she saw him stiffen and hold his lantern up high; he stood so as a rider galloped into the yard, splashing through the slush. It was a large man in a black cloak, and he was burdened by something . . . or someone. For it was, in his arms, no inanimate object, but a child, or a woman.

Her hands pressed to the cold glass, she watched, but her breath kept misting the window, and she didn't see him in the act of dismounting, distracted as she was by wiping the fog away. Where had he gone?

And then she saw him, still burdened and striding out of the stable. He headed toward the castle, his step sure, his pace hurried.

Who was it? And what, or whom, did he carry?

When he disappeared from sight, she grabbed a robe, slipped it on, and fled the room, moving down to the gallery, but there was no one in the great hall. If it was a servant she might never catch sight of them, for they would enter by a servant's entrance. She paused and waited in the shadows, but still there was no one.

Shivering, she retreated back up toward her room but heard a noise and shrank back against a wall. A heavy tread— of a large man in boots, perhaps? But from where? Any sensible woman would retreat to her room . . . or would have stayed in her room in the first place. But she couldn't.

Down the hall . . . her own corridor! She crept along the wall in the shadows toward the servants' stairs at the end of the new wing, for she could hear the footsteps get closer, and then the door that topped the staircase opened. A cloaked figure pushed through, and there he was, with his burden. But who? She moved slightly and the man turned.

Nikolas! She gasped and he caught sight of her, his face almost unrecognizable, it was so twisted in fury. The cloak that covered his burden shifted, and one silvery blond ringlet fell out. She started forward but in that instant, as he growled, "Go back, Elizabeth," a cold hand clutched her and yanked her backward, through a door.

She shrieked, but a hand covered her mouth. She fought, but the figure was stronger than she.

Chapter 15

"HSST, BE quiet, Miss Stanwycke!"

She struggled free and righted herself and saw, by faint candlelight, Cesare Vitali in his dressing gown. She had been hauled into his dressing room, it appeared by the wardrobes lining the walls; she had known his suite was beside her own room but had never seen it. "That was the count!" she cried. "But who . . ." She fell silent, not sure she wanted to know what was going on, nor who the blond girl or woman was.

"You should stay in your room at night, Miss Stanwycke."

She stared at him, wondering at the hint of threat in his voice. "What's going on?" she whispered, her voice trembling.

"Nothing that should concern you."

He did not say another word but merely poked his head out and looked up and down the hall. He pushed her out and said, "Go to bed, Miss Stanwycke, and from now on stay there. And stay out of business that is not yours."

The door slammed behind her and somewhere else down the hall another door closed, but whether it was in the same corridor or in the old part of the castle, she could not tell. Shivering with fear, she scurried to her own room and shut the door, pushing the chair from her desk in front of it. That was the last time she would wander at night; she was cured, she hoped, of curiosity forever.

And yet, even as she crawled into her bed and blew out her candle, she was plagued by one thought. *Who, of all the woman in the castle, did that silvery blond lock of hair belong to? Who had the count been carrying from the stable and beyond?*

She slept, but it must have only been for three or four hours. The questions she had gone to sleep with still plagued her when she arose and sat at her desk in the faint early morning light from her window. Who was the blond woman and why was Nikolas carrying her home from somewhere in the middle of the night? What was he hiding? In the pages of her journal she asked all the questions she was afraid to ask of anyone in the castle, made all the conjectures she did not dare to voice, and then she hid the calfbound book in her wardrobe. It would never do to leave it somewhere it could be discovered.

Whatever was going on, clearly it was something at least Cesare Vitali knew about.

But more, what had come to her as she lay fitfully dozing and waking, was that Nikolas must be the man she had seen the night she arrived at Wolfram castle. Surely it would be too great a coincidence to believe that the man in the black cloak chasing a blond woman and Count Nikolas in a black cloak carrying a blond woman were two different sets of people.

Her whole body ached with weariness. Blond women had run through her dreams all night, and every time it was a different one—Adele, Charlotte, Gerta, and even Melisande, whose hair was honey blond but had streaks of flax through it.

But why did she confine the choices to family members? It could even be Fanny, she thought, as the maid entered. She watched the pretty blond maiden going about her business, drawing open the curtains and serving Elizabeth tea, her preferred drink in the morning. Could she ask her? If it was Fanny, though, the girl must be in some kind of trouble and may be loath to speak of it.

"Did you sleep well, Fanny?" Elizabeth asked, taking a sip from the porcelain cup. An awful thought occurred to her in that moment—that if it was the young maid that Nikolas was carrying home, did that mean perhaps he was having some kind of illicit relationship with her?

"Yes, Miss Stanwycke, I always do sleep well."

Nikolas's part in the whole thing might be innocent, though, or perhaps even heroic. Elizabeth's rich imagination constructed possibilities and probabilities. If Fanny was having some kind of affair with someone else, that man could be abusing her, and Nikolas could have rescued her from the clutches of the villain, though that didn't explain the blond woman being chased by the cloaked horseman the first night of her arrival.

And from where could Nikolas be bringing her the previous night? Why would Fanny leave the castle, unless her lover was someone from the village, perhaps? And that same question followed if the blonde in his arms was someone other than Fanny—Charlotte or Melisande, for example.

"Fanny," Elizabeth said.

The girl turned to her just before exiting. "Yes?"

"I want you to know," she said carefully, watching her face and eyes, "that if ever . . . if you ever need someone to talk to, someone a little older than yourself, I am always here. You can tell me anything."

The puzzled expression on Fanny's face spoke volumes about her complete innocence of any kind of subterfuge or secrecy. She said, "Th-thank you, Miss Stanwycke."

So, if Elizabeth was as good a judge of character as she fancied herself, and that alone was in question given recent events in her life, then Fanny was not the blonde in Count Nikolas's arms. She sat in her desk chair staring at the floor and pondering. It was most certainly not Adele, for she was taller, nor could Elizabeth ever imagine the eldest sister of the von Wolfram family falling in a faint or creeping out to meet a lover. Of the other three possibilities, who was most likely the one?

Inescapably, she concluded the most likely candidate was Charlotte. The girl was upset about something and, as she well knew, an affair going awry could cause a woman turmoil and desperation.

Her thoughts a confused jumble, Elizabeth dressed and descended to the breakfast room where she was, as often occurred, the first at the table. She ate slowly at first, as Count Delacroix came in. He was always rather quiet in the morning, and so Elizabeth merely said a good morning to him and continued her meal. Bartol Liebner was next to enter, and he came in with a cheery greeting for her. He asked after her sleeping, and smiled and nodded when she said she had a fitful sleep.

"I, too, was troubled in my sleep. I thought I heard something, and indeed went to my door and peeped out, but nothing there was in the hall. Were you likewise disturbed, Miss Stanwycke?"

She was saved from answer by Countess Adele, who entered and glowered around at those gathered, saying, "Has Charlotte not descended yet? I begin to think she is malingering. I saw her playing the piano with Melisande yesterday and walking with Christoph. If she is well enough to do all that, then she is well enough for morning lessons. Miss Stanwycke, I promise I will ensure the girl is in the yellow parlor at the proper time this morning. No more excuses."

Countess Gerta fluttered in, planted a kiss on the French count's silvery hair as Adele scowled, and took a piece of toast from the silver rack on the sideboard. "I feel so invigorated this morning. Did everyone sleep as well as I did? It was a blissful night." She winked at the Frenchman and smiled innocently at her elder sister.

Charlotte and Melisande entered together just then, whispering to each other. As Charlotte sat without greeting anyone Elizabeth examined her and didn't like what she saw. There were dark circles under the girl's eyes, and her complexion was pale and puffy.

"Charlotte," Countess Adele said, her demeanor severe. "I will have no more excuses. You will, from now on, attend Miss Stanwycke in the yellow parlor in the morning, or I will require you to see a physician."

It was not a commandment inspired to bring Charlotte to her in a frame of mind amenable to tutelage, and Elizabeth fretted about how the day would go. But there was no way of correcting the impression the countess had left with the girl that Elizabeth had been complaining about the lack of application on the part of her student.

Melisande Davidovich, watchful and sympathetic,

squeezed Charlotte's hand. She whispered something, and the girl scowled and shook her head.

"I promise, Charlotte," Elizabeth said, trying to soften the countess's command, "that today will not be onerous."

"What . . . shall I pour tea again, or walk with a book on my head, or pretend to speak with some aging English earl so he will grace me with his presence in the marital bed?" Charlotte stood, her voice rising and her face getting red. "I have decided I will no longer take the idiotic lessons," she said, trembling all over. "I am done. And my uncle can punish me as he wishes, but I will not be some Englishman's sow to breed healthy babies."

Cesare Vitali came in that moment, and hearing the last words, looked shocked. "Countess Charlotte!" he exclaimed.

"No, Cesare, I will not be silent any longer."

Elizabeth stood and watched, waiting for some explanation. She glanced between Charlotte's face and the secretary's. His was the more unreadable, his eyes shadowed behind the glinting glasses, but it seemed that he was trying to communicate something to her.

"Things are not right in this house," she began. Melisande reached up and took her hand, squeezing it in a silent sign of support, but Charlotte faltered and did not go on, her gaze locked with Cesare Vitali's.

Bartol Liebner, his expression troubled, had stood as well, and said, "My dear niece, tell us all. Tell us your troubles. Surely as a family—"

"Shut your mouth, Bartol," Countess Adele said, her tone offering no quarter. "Charlotte, you are hysterical. Go to your room and I will come up and speak to you."

Gerta giggled inappropriately but then stifled her laughter and bit her lip. Elizabeth heard, but she could not tear her eyes from Charlotte's face.

The girl quailed visibly but rallied and began to speak again. "I just wanted to say—"

"No! Do as I say this minute." Adele was a force not to be resisted, and Charlotte caught Cesare's eye, then turned and fled the room.

Melisande ran after her and Adele, with a stifled exclamation, left, too.

"My goodness," Gerta said, primly. "Such hysteria this morning."

Bartol Liebner nodded. "Something is wrong with that girl, but I do not know what." He sat back down and finished his meal in silence.

Elizabeth was no longer hungry, though, and left the room. Looking for her one friend in the castle, she was unlucky; Frau Liebner, it appeared, had been recruited by Countess Adele to try to talk to the girl about England and why it was not such a terrible place to go. Since Charlotte's primary objection did not seem to be so much to the country itself but to her marital prospects and the anticipation of being separated from her brother, Elizabeth did not see what good it could do, but it was their business not hers, and as she had been reminded so often, she should stay out of that which did not concern her. She was not on terms with Charlotte that would make her interference of any help, anyway. Disconsolate and at loose ends, she wandered up to Countess Uta's suite, not sure what to do with all that she had seen, heard, and learned in the last day or two.

The old lady was, as usual, avid for gossip, but Elizabeth had already determined not to mention what she had seen the night before. What point could there be in disturbing the poor old lady's peace when she could do nothing about it? Nor would she have any answers to Elizabeth's many questions.

Instead, Elizabeth spoke of her life in England and how much she enjoyed teaching eager young minds. At the end of her cheery speech, the old lady sat silent. Mina had made her comfortable and then had gone off on some errand Uta had initiated with a series of hand gestures.

"All very pretty," the old lady finally said. "But I think dis is not what is in your mind and heart, ja? You are gifing prepared speech, rehearsed and prettily said. What is wrong, Elizabeth?"

"Nothing, ma'am."

"What is wrong?" Her blind eyes staring into space, she

reached out and touched Elizabeth's face, her knobby fingers caressing the curves, touching her mouth.

Elizabeth submitted patiently, but she was not prepared for what Uta said.

"You are fearing very much dat you are falling in love, and dat the gentleman is unworthy or . . . or unable to reciprocate."

"What nonsense! I'm sorry, ma'am, but you have been misled by someone into believing—"

"Do not speak so hastily, and do not get up." She put out one strong hand to stay Elizabeth, who had indeed begun to rise. "I do not hear dis from anyone but only speak what I haf been thinking. Why do you fear men so? Is it the nature, the physical part only?"

Elizabeth, fretful and anxious but held firm by the old woman's grasp, said, "No, there is just nothing—"

"Haf you ever been in love before?"

"I thought I was."

"Ach, gut, tell me of dis." She released Elizabeth and settled back down in her swaddling wraps. "Dis is what I want to hear, not such nonsense about how much you love the teaching and how you love castle and how you love Germany. Tell me things about you, about your heart."

As harsh and grating as the old woman's voice was, Elizabeth felt a tug at her heartstrings. Even Frau Liebner, who knew everything, had not been willing to speak of it, and the past lived still, shameful, hurting, aching in her heart. Shivering, she whispered, "Please, ma'am . . ."

"Just tell me. It is like telling wall, or whispering to pillow, for as much as I like to hear, I do not tell."

Elizabeth felt the truth of it and started, faltering at first, but becoming stronger and more determined. "Before coming here I was a governess in a great house, the home of my distant relatives." She stopped, and then said, "I suppose I should say, first, that my mother and father died when I was young. They were very gay, very happy. My mother was the daughter of a viscount, but my father . . . he was somewhat beneath that rank, and yet he loved my mother, and she him. Or so I was told anyway. There were many arguments and many tears, but always they made up their quarrels afterwards. However, when they died together in an accident, it was discovered that as much as they loved each other—and despite my mother's many complaints about my father's treatment of her, it seems that they loved each other very much—it appeared they had failed to love the progeny of their union as much, for no provisions had been made for me, and I was penniless. They had squandered Mama's dowry."

"Dat is not love of each other, for if a man loves the mother of his child he provides for dere baby. Dat is selfish love of oneself only, dat sees reflected in one's wife or husband's eyes only the youthful, undying vision of yourself."

Elizabeth frowned down at her skirt and plucked at the fabric. Perhaps the countess was right, and it was not that she had been innately unlovable, but that both her mother and her father were just too wrapped up in themselves to truly care even for each other. It would explain much, she thought, about their arguments and her mother's histrionics. "As a result," she went on, "I lived during my youth as the charity child of some cousins. When I grew, and it was clear that there was no money to launch me on society, much talk was expended on what to do with me until some kindly third cousins offered to give me a home in exchange for the tutelage of their spoiled and despicable little brats."

Elizabeth swallowed back the bile of her humiliation at the hands of that family. With the approbation of their church commending them for their kindness in giving her a home, they had been firm in treating her as something below a chambermaid in importance, all the while paying her only in pin money and her clothes—made over from the mistress of the house's wardrobe—and food.

"You did not like your little cousins."

"For the most part they were foul little beasts, and they were allowed—nay, encouraged—to treat me badly. Every attempt at discipline I made was countermanded by their doting mama and papa, to my detriment, for the children soon learned that even the butler must be listened to before me."

"Why was dat? Did you whine? Did you grovel?"

The lady's harsh words brought Elizabeth back to earth with a thud, and she laughed. She reached over and squeezed the old woman's hand. "How clever you are, Countess. I believe I did, rather, at first. I had not developed the firmness of mind to deal with the problem. I was very young, just eighteen when I went there. I expected my cousins to support me in what I wished to do with their little girls. I thought that naturally they would want well-disciplined and well-behaved young ladies for daughters."

"All parents want dat, or so dey say, but not all know how to accomplish it. Some have too much pride and mistake poor behavior in dere children to be a sign of precocity."

"You are wise, Countess Uta."

"Go on. What did you do?"

"Well, nothing for a few years; I suffered and did my best, becoming more . . . more beaten down, more unhappy as the children became more insolent. But then I did something calculated to horrify my employers; I fell in love with the master of the house's younger brother."

Uta snickered. "Understandable reaction to rejection and frustration, dat was. Go on. Did the young man return your affection?"

"He certainly gave every appearance of it. He said tender words, squeezed my hand, and gazed at me longingly. He made every effort to find me alone. He begged me to meet him in the hedgerow."

"Ach, yes, certain signs of love . . . the love of a spoiled young gentleman, anyway. And what happened?"

"The age-old song, ma'am. I thought myself in love, thought that I was certainly the first and only to feel that tingling in the limbs when one's beloved is near, and that singing is in the heart. His soft words and fond gazes captured me completely, and when he wrote me a sonnet, I was utterly bewitched."

One knobby hand covered hers. "Do not think yourself too foolish, Elizabeth, for many a girl has been captured so."

"Oh, I was more than captured, I was seduced. Or . . . to be fair, he did not have to ask me a second time to meet him in the attic, where a deserted divan became our haven. My life was so miserable, and in his arms I found happiness, however brief it was. I was ready and willing, and . . . and I capitulated utterly, giving even my maidenhood as a sacrifice at the altar of my love."

If she expected a gasp of shock, she was to be disappointed. Uta merely said, "And was the joy of such a union worth the illicitness of it?"

"No. At least . . . not the first time." It was terribly odd to discuss the affair so coolly, with so little emotion. "But John was a considerate lover, and I came to enjoy it. Somewhat."

"You did not get with child?"

"No," Elizabeth said, feeling the heat rise in her face. "I . . . there are certain things he taught me . . ."

"He was experienced in debauchery."

"Odd how that didn't occur to me at the time, how he had learned such things. I was just grateful that he seemed to care for me so much."

"You were very fortunate, for such means are not foolproof, young lady. In future, you must be more careful."

"There will be no 'future' to take care in, ma'am," she said, drawing herself up. "You cannot think me so foolish as to be taken in by a man's blandishments again?"

A half smile lifted Uta's wrinkled mouth. "Are you saying you will never fall in love again?"

Elizabeth was silent. No, she couldn't say that. She had proven to be surprisingly susceptible to a certain gentleman even now. "No, I suppose I can't say that. But if I have learned anything, it is that men are not to be trusted."

"How did the affair end? Badly, I suppose?"

"Yes. Oh, yes. He had promised me marriage, and I do believe he thought he was being honest when he offered it. But he apparently raised the specter of such a misalliance to his parents, and he was forbidden and then enticed with the offer of independence from the parental purse if he allied himself with a certain young lady of good birth and better dowry."

"So he abandoned you?"

Elizabeth nodded, feeling the pain, but noting that it was considerably dulled. It was now more allied with her stupidity in believing him than anything. "Yes," she said. "Yes, he abandoned me with some blithe words. He wished me well and hoped I found a husband, but it would not be him."

"Good. Would you be happy in dat marriage?"

"Ma'am," Elizabeth said, shocked. "It was certainly *not* good! When he abandoned me he confessed everything to his brother, over whose children I had governance. So shocked were the little darlings' parents that I was not only dismissed, but I was warned that if I ever tried to get a position teaching children I would be exposed as a whore across the whole of England! After five years of service, that was their treatment of me. Any marriage would certainly have been better than the degradation, humiliation, and utter shame I suffered at their hands."

"I suppose. But you would be married to a man of such terrible lack of strength. Would be a sorry life for a woman of your character, to find such a thing."

Elizabeth fell silent again as she considered it all. It had been a terrible time, but thinking about it now, she could not imagine being married to John. With the mist of love receded she could see his vanity, his want of intelligence, and, of course, his weakness in the face of threats from his family. Marriage to such a man would involve many compromises, and he would have soon resented her for the sacrifices of worldly wealth he had made to wed her. Ridiculous to even think of such an eventuality, of course; he had never truly intended marriage, and it occurred to her then that he may have been using her to try to wrench his independence from his clutch-fisted parents' hands with the threat of an unsuitable alliance.

When she looked up it was to see that Uta had fallen asleep and Mina was coming back in. With a gesture, the fierce maid indicated that Elizabeth should leave. She obeyed, laying one soft kiss on the old woman's forehead under her lacy cap. When Elizabeth looked up she noticed a softer gleam in the maid's gray eyes, though it vanished in a heartbeat.

And after that she wandered, depressed somewhat by her recitation of her sad little tale. It had been a blow, being dismissed, but worse was the hatred in her cousin's face as he accused her of seducing his younger brother, just so she could marry into the family. And then he had said some vile things to her, ending with a disgusting offer to take care of her if she would make herself available to him. She had slapped him, and she still did not regret that.

Her employment there was over and she was discarded with no notice and no care. What was worse was that she had just been learning that with growing confidence and stronger behavior she was actually beginning to make some progress with her charges, especially with the eldest girl in her care, a child of thirteen years who was beginning to show promise.

Frau Liebner had been a visitor to the house often, as she was a distant relation of the mistress of the house; that woman disliked her, so Elizabeth had often been sent for to make conversation with the older lady. They had discovered a kinship of sorts, a meeting of minds. She hadn't realized it at the time, but Frau Liebner had been set the task of finding a tutor for Charlotte and had been considering Elizabeth as a possibility, which accounted for her frequent visits in the last month. On the very day she was being dismissed, Frau Liebner was coming, she said, to offer her the position, though she did not have much hope of success, at that point, until she learned of the trouble.

Elizabeth drifted to the yellow parlor and opened the drapes on the prospect of snow blowing around the house. She remembered that day; it was October, and the wind had turned chill . . . or what she considered chill at the time. She had never experienced the cold of a German winter before. She had burst into tears when Frau Liebner had offered her the position, mostly because of the lady's kindness, and because she had just been wondering where she would go without a recommendation to help her to another position. She had felt compelled, though, to tell the lady the truth, sparing no detail, for she did not want the story to reach Frau Liebner's ears from the poisonous tongue of her cousin.

Though Frau Liebner listened to the story stiffly, Elizabeth had soon learned the depth of the woman's friendship. Frau Liebner marched from the room, confronted the master of the house, told him what she thought of him, and then commanded and oversaw the packing of Elizabeth's trunks. Together they had retreated that day to Frau Liebner's rented house, and preparations began to travel to Germany.

She had not had time to think, after that, nor to ponder the decision she had made in haste. Crouching on a settee, she stared at the frosted panes of leaded glass and traced out her initials. She was cold, but perhaps she had become accustomed to it, for she barely thought of that anymore.

She might never see England again, she truly realized in that moment. Her life had taken a different path, and if she was very fortunate she would find similar work to this position with another German family, and then another. She might, perhaps, travel, to Italy or Greece. But England—dear, misty England—was in her past, as surely as her childhood.

Finally she wept. She covered her eyes and sobbed, admitting her fear of the future, her desperate need to succeed in her task, and all of the loneliness for an almost forgotten way of life. And for a part of herself—trusting, naïve, and sweet—that she had lost along with her innocence.

"Miss Stanwycke . . . Elizabeth, what is wrong?"

It was the count! Elizabeth wiped at her eyes, but she knew there was no hiding the tear trails and damp cheeks. She met his gaze as he crossed the room, not knowing what she would find there after the night before, but seeing only concern on his darkly handsome face. "It is nothing, sir, please don't worry . . ."

"No, Elizabeth, it is something," he said, sitting down on the settee beside her and taking one of her cold hands in his large warm ones. "You are so cold," he said, rubbing her hand. "I . . . I came looking for you, and . . ." He stopped and frowned. "Are you unhappy? I know things are unsettled, and I know Charlotte is difficult . . ."

Half laughing and half weeping, Elizabeth said, "Difficult? She is a paragon compared to the children I taught before I came here. You're too hard on her, sir. Charlotte is a lovely girl, and she is never rude to me. She is unhappy, yes, and I fear something is troubling her, but I . . . I like her very much."

"Then why do you weep, *Liebchen*?" he asked, touching her face and gently wiping one tear trail with his thumb.

She turned her face into his warm palm for one second, but then drew herself up, trying to regain her composure and some iota of her fractured dignity. "I . . . I miss England . . . I miss life there, the rain, the mist, the countryside."

He looked stricken, but once she was started it was like a bubbling spring—it would not be capped. "Oh, I miss hearing English all day, and I miss being warm, and walking in the woods, watching the birds."

"Do you . . . do you wish to go back?"

"You don't understand! This all happened so quickly," she said, taking a deep, shuddering breath as she began to understand her own tears. She gazed out the window and felt him take up both of her hands and caress them. It was a comforting gesture that required nothing from her in the way of response. "I'm mourning the loss of my childhood, I suppose, and my country, and my former life. I'm like a plant, uprooted, searching for a place to grow again. Once I thought I might eventually have a home of my own, a settled place, a husband, children, a life. I thought I would have a place to let those roots grow deep and strong." She was stricken by the thought that she was certainly saying too much, being too honest, but it was too late to turn back now. She had come to this place thinking she would be able to fit herself into some narrow definition of womanhood, retiring and reserved, but it seemed that impetuosity would not forever be stifled.

She needed to explain to him, though, so he did not think her hopelessly ungrateful. Aware that he still held her hands, and trying to decide if she most felt stirred by his touch or wary, she said, "I have accepted that my life will be different from what I once envisioned. But when you lose something, even if it is just the chimera of what you think will be your future, you mourn, and then . . . and then you take a deep breath and move forward." She did, indeed, take a deep breath, feeling a calm enter her, strength reasserting its dominion.

"So . . . you don't wish to go back?" he caressed and squeezed her hands, now warm from his solicitude.

She searched her heart. This life she was living, though fraught with difficulty and turmoil, was invigorating and fascinating and she had come to genuinely care for some of these people, even though she was doomed to leave them, probably just when she had come to love them. It would be hard, but with that knowledge came the additional knowledge that she would survive. She always would, and she would gain strength.

"No . . . no, I am mourning the past, but I would not go back. I was weaker then. I couldn't go back to being that insubstantial girl that I was." When she met his eyes, it was to see shining in their dark depths some fierce emotion, and she quailed before it, not knowing what to make of him.

He reached out and touched her cheek, his other hand still holding hers. "So strong, you are, and I thought I was bringing a mild, mousy Englishwoman. Instead I bring Boadicea to my home."

She took a deep breath. "Sir, what was going on last night? Who was that you were carrying into the house? And why?" She had blurted it out before she thought, but she would not take it back. She needed to know. He seemed so forthright, so strong, so honest, and yet there were so many secrets in this cold castle.

His eyes shuttered and he withdrew his hand, drawing back from her physically as he pushed away her queries. "I can't tell you that, Elizabeth."

"Yes, you can. What is going on in this house?"

"Nothing that need concern you," he said, standing. "You must just believe in me, Elizabeth. I am involved in nothing sinister . . . trust me."

"I'm trying," she said, gazing up at him, wishing she dared ask how he felt he had earned trust. "But you're not making it very easy."

He gazed steadily at her. "I know." He bowed, his expression remote again, and said, "I hope you are feeling better, and that . . . and that you are happy here."

She watched him stride from the room and let out a long, exasperated sigh. He was so far from what she had thought he would be from Frau Liebner's description of him. And yet what she sensed at the core of his soul was a man devoted to his family, and willing to make any sacrifice for their happiness. Even in his treatment of Christoph, as misguided as it appeared to her, she could see his exasperation and desperate want to help his nephew.

Strangely, she did believe that what she saw the night before had not been sinister from his aspect, though she still could not fathom why he could not just tell her the truth, if it was nothing to be concerned about. She shook her head and rose, thinking to go see if she could speak to Charlotte, or even Melisande.

Her curiosity would just not allow her to leave the family turmoil alone until she got some inkling of what was going on that had them all so agitated.

Chapter 16

"I AM not quite sure what to do about Miss Stanwycke," Nikolas said to his secretary, as Cesare stacked some papers in front of him.

"She is far too intelligent and much too curious," Cesare said, pointing to a spot that needed a signature. "She is bound to make discoveries. I think you should send her away, and Charlotte, too."

Nikolas dipped his quill into ink and signed, then sanded the signature. "Charlotte is not yet to be trusted away from Wolfram Castle. And I won't send Miss Stanwycke away."

"How do you know *she* is to be trusted? What if she finds out too much? She's English; the English are easily shocked by anything . . . out of the ordinary."

Nikolas looked sharply up at his secretary, but the fellow's eyes were obscured by the firelight glinting in his glasses. He relied upon Cesare and felt sure of his loyalties, but there was always, behind his brown eyes, a hint of the shrewd and devious Etruscan mind. "This is more than just shocking, Cesare, and more than just out of the ordinary. My entire life encompasses that which is more than just out of the ordinary." He dismissed his secretary with a curt word and bent over his paperwork. He could not get out of his head the sight of Elizabeth weeping, and then her talking about all she had left behind, and all of the hopes she had of her future, dashed.

He didn't know much about her past but what his aunt had told him, but it seemed that if she truly wanted a husband, there must have been some fellow willing to marry her in England. She was, after all, beautiful, desirable, intelligent—

combined with an elegant bearing and regal manner. Even penniless she had to have captured someone's eye.

She had certainly dismissed her future possibilities too easily. In German society there would be many men eager to wed her, he thought, dowry or no. Her family background was more than adequate. So why was she so sure that that was an impossibility?

Or was it that she wanted more for herself than life as wife to someone she could not love? Just any husband would not do for someone so full of life and passion and intelligence. He thought back to his sister-in-law Anna and how difficult her adjustment had been to life at Wolfram Castle; her marriage to Johannes had been arranged for them, but for Nikolas's brother it had been a love match from almost the first moment. And yet he had to admit that as much as Johannes had loved Anna, he had not made her life any easier, demanding from her obedience when he should have given her compassion. Was that what finally drove her into Hans' arms? It was far too late for answers to the questions that still plagued him fifteen years later, but he didn't suppose he would ever stop wondering.

He worked on for a long while in silence, realizing some hours later that he had forgotten about dinner and no one had come to get him. His usually efficient household was preoccupied and scattered. He left the library, roaming the house, but it was much later than he had even thought and all were gone, even from the drawing room. Or perhaps, given the events of the last few nights, all were absenting themselves on purpose. Charlotte had been told to keep to her room until the next day, and Melisande, a fast friend, would likely keep her company. His Aunt Katrina had pledged to spend some time with her to try to convince her that England—and English men—were not so bad. But there was something more to her abysmal behavior of late than just Charlotte's resistance to his plan for her. If he only knew what it was. She and her brother both were becoming more and more distant, lost to him as he never thought they would be.

But he had even more pressing worries. He gazed out the

drawing room window and saw the moon rising, casting a silvery glow over the snowy landscape. Beyond the drive to the castle were the dark woods, their deep green depths full of danger for the unwary. A chill ran down his spine, a superstitious dread stealing over him at the thought of what it all meant to him, to his family.

He heard a stealthy step in the hall and raced to see who it was, alarmed that he had so lost track of time that it was moonrise, but it was just Mina. He gestured to her and whispered his wishes into her ear. She nodded and slipped down the hall past the bend, her night just beginning, watchfulness her duty.

About to retreat to his library, Nikolas heard another stealthy step, and by instinct he faded back into the shadows. He watched, and across the silvery trail of the moon, down the carpeted center of the hallway, stole Miss Elizabeth Stanwycke. Stifling a muttered curse he waited, and when she was about to pass him he reached out of the shadows and grabbed her arm.

She shrieked and fought him, thumping her fist against his arm with all her might, but he held on and pulled her back into the moonlight, letting her see his face.

"Why do people keep grabbing me from behind?" she muttered. She shook off his hand. "What are you doing, grasping me so tightly and frightening me like that?" Her face was as pale as the moonlight, and her dusky hair, streaming down her back and over her shoulders, gleamed with a bronze sheen.

"I should ask you what you are doing creeping around my castle after you are supposedly gone to your bed for the night?" He grasped her arm again and roughly pulled her across the gallery and into his library, his anger at her intransigence making him harsher than he was in the normal course of dealing with any woman.

"I . . . I was going to go visit . . . Frau Liebner," she stuttered as she stumbled after him. "For I was worried about Charlotte and thought we would have a conversation about the girl, and what I can do to help."

She was making it up as she went along, he could tell, though she was a quick thinker, for it was a plausible enough explanation and she was headed in the right direction. He was still holding her arm tightly and she disengaged herself, pointedly rubbing her upper arm. She was infuriating, he thought, and at the same time entrancing . . . gloriously beautiful and fascinatingly independent. If an alliance with her weren't dangerous to his duties, he would be tempted to seduce her into his bed. She was not indifferent to him, and his blood coursed at the thought of feeling her under him in his enormous bed, brought to passion again and again.

But given her questing nature, she would abuse the intimacy, no doubt, and try to get him to reveal all his secrets. And that, he thought, brought back to cold reality by the idea of it, would end all converse between them, for she would shun him if she learned the awful truth of the lengths he was forced to go to protect his family from the poison that saturated it.

"I apologize," he said stiffly, "if I hurt your arm, Elizabeth." He was treading a fine line, he knew, for he wished to frighten her enough to keep her in her bed at night, and yet if she became too frightened, she would leave the castle, and he didn't want that. He couldn't bear the thought of it, though he knew it was more for his own sake, for the pleasure of seeing her and talking to her daily, rather than for the benefit she was undoubtedly giving Charlotte. It was a dangerous self-indulgence.

"I . . . . I wish to speak with you," he said, trying to think of any reason to keep her there for the time being. "Come, sit by the fire, for I believe you are chilled."

She was reluctant and glanced at the door. He wondered if she had heard or seen something she was not willing to share with him, and that was why she was out of her room in just her nightrail. He let his gaze travel her form, appreciating the rosy outline of flesh under the white muslin if her gown. The cold had peaked her breasts, and the nipples jutted enticingly under the filmy fabric. As scandalous as their midnight meeting was, he didn't care. Let anyone castigate him who dared; no one would, for he made his own rules to live by.

He took her hand and sat her down in the chair nearest the fire, letting his hand cup her shoulder and his fingers brush her jutting breasts. His awareness was such that he could see, throbbing in her neck, her pulse, quickening as he touched her. He took the chair next to her and watched for a moment, as she, conscious of his gaze, crossed her arms over her breasts. He shifted, uncomfortably aware of the blood rushing to his nether regions.

But discipline was his byword; always would the animal part of his male being be defeated by rigid discipline and harsh self-command. He demanded of himself far more than he ever asked from any of his serving staff or family members.

"What do you want?" she asked, turning to face him, having regained her own self-command.

"Do not speak to me so, Elizabeth," he said, keeping his tone deliberately hard. "I have already given you more quarter than I would any other person in my employ."

She nodded and, as difficult as it was for her, he could see, said, "I'm sorry, sir. I did not mean to be impertinent. I was still a little shocked at such rough handling."

"I apologize. I hope I have not bruised you, but you must learn to stay in your own room at night." The veiled warning in his tone did not escape her notice, and she bit her lip, looking away to the fire. "I appreciate your care for Charlotte, but let her be. I will speak to her in the morning again."

She was silent. And yet he felt sure that beneath her calm exterior she was musing on his reasons for insisting that she stay in her room at night. Unquestioning obedience was not her natural response.

"Do you know, some say I ought to have married," he said, hoping to distract her from her thoughts. The only way to deflect an intelligent mind from working on a problem was to give it a new line of thought to ponder. "I ought to have brought a womanly, motherly influence into this house to care for my nieces and nephews, it has been said."

She glanced over at him, her interest quickened. It was something she had wondered about, evidently. "Why did you not marry? Not for their sakes, I mean, but for your own?"

The real reason he would never marry was powerful, and being reminded of it cooled his blood like an ice bath. "I have been devoted to my family," he said. "It cannot have escaped your attention that they are a troublesome lot and require much of my time. Marrying and having a wife and children would have taken too much of my attention, that being reserved for my family only."

"It has always been my impression," she said, staring over at him, "that marriage does not take much of a man's time, though a woman might devote her whole life to the art of being married. Are not wives formed to serve and help a man? Is a wife's sole purpose not to take the onerous burdens of life from her husband's broad shoulders?"

There was an edge to her voice, and he thought she felt more about that observation than she had shared. But he imagined it for a moment, imagined having a wife, say . . . Elizabeth. Instead of sitting in the library that moment separated from her by the space of three feet, he would be in her bed making love to her. And in the day he would be teaching his sons to hunt and his daughters to ride. Oh, yes, in his life it would take much of his time to be a husband and father, for he would never leave such a family to their own devices. Some fathers did—his own father, for an example—but he never would. He put his head back. Wholly caught up in the dream, he pictured the scene, even: on his lap a gentle girl like her mother—only not so curious—and beside him, in front of the fire, a handsome boy, like his father but . . . and there the image popped, disappearing like a luminous soap bubble.

Impossible. His head drooped. Marriage was out of the question, and even more so was having children. He would not perpetuate the taint of his family trouble. If he succeeded, it would end with his generation; that was the work of his life, the cause to which he had committed himself, and it required all his dedication and all his sacrifice. The end would be worth it; he had to believe that and keep working towards it.

"Nikolas," Elizabeth whispered.

She had knelt before him while he was pondering his fate, and he gazed down into her blue eyes, the golden brown hair streaming over her shoulders glinting brilliantly in the glowing firelight. It was like his daydream come to life, her face before him, her loveliness shining in the fire's glow.

"Nikolas," she said urgently, "you look . . . sad, so terribly sad. What is it? How can I help?"

"Elizabeth, don't look at me so," he whispered, sitting forward and putting his head in his hands. "If you knew me . . . really knew me . . . you would shun me. I am a brute, a hard man not deserving of your compassion."

"That's not true," she said, raising his head, her hands framing his face. "You were so kind to me just hours ago; I will *never* forget that moment." Her voice quavered with emotion, but she mastered it and went on. "You were concerned that I was crying, and I have never met another man who would have behaved as you do. Most men shun tears and avoid women in pain. You are good, I feel it, so don't speak of yourself so; I'll not allow it."

He scooped her into his arms and held her close on his lap, all of his good intentions swept away in her sweet negation of his terrible self-doubt. For long minutes he just held her close, feeling her heart beat, hearing their two hearts establish a common rhythm. Always would their hearts beat in time now, he knew, for he had learned something in the last few minutes; he had learned how easy it would be to fall in love with Miss Elizabeth Stanwycke, and how close he was to that perilous precipice. He must push that truth away, must command his emotions more rigidly, must—

She kissed him, framing his face again, her fingers thrust through his hair, raining soft kisses over his cheek and mouth. She wore nothing under the nightrail, and through the thin fabric he could feel the warmth of her flesh, enticing, exciting, arousing. His passion rising, he held her close, licking her mouth, tonguing her with fierce need. Responding feverishly, she twisted and was straddling him then, and he trembled from head to toe, feeling her inner warmth seep into him where their intimate parts met for the first time, her dampness communicating to him how sweet would be the velvety depths of her.

With trembling hands he cupped her breasts as she gazed down at him, lips parted, eyes clouded with ardent yearning. He hardened beneath her dampness and her awareness of his arousal—her eyes drifting closed, lashes fanned down over her velvety pink cheeks, as she pushed down against him—sent him to some cloud-strewn land of forgetfulness. Thumbing her nipples, feeling her strain into his hands, he pulled her to him and laved them through the fabric, wetting her nightrail, the nipples pebbling sweetly in his mouth as he suckled. Throbbing urges tore though him, and the temptation to open his breeches and have his way, knowing that she was naked under the nightrail and her passion was dampening him even then, was almost painful.

But impossible. He stopped his caresses and summoned all of his considerable will to defeat the mists of passion that had rolled over him, enveloping them both. Gently, he disengaged her arms from around his neck and set her back in his chair. He strode to the cold side of the room and battled, fighting his body, quelling with ruthless control his aching need.

The chill of her dampened nightrail and Nikolas' rapid disengagement brought Elizabeth back to herself rapidly. What had she been thinking? She was mortified by her own wanton behavior and embarrassed that he had been the one to draw back, not her. Confused and torn by conflicting emotions, she sat and shivered, folding her arms over her stomach, which churned with the warring urges she experienced.

In truth, after her conversation with Uta and Nikolas's kindness to her in the midst of her pain, she had felt so raw and afraid. What was she feeling for him, she had wondered. Was it just physical attraction? She knew she liked him and respected him, but she didn't fully trust him, nor should she, given how many secrets he was evidently keeping. She acknowledged that secrets were not necessarily a sign of any guilt, but still, there was not between them the level of intimacy a man and woman should have before sharing their bodies.

And yet with John she had shared her body and her soul, thinking he was sharing all, too, and it was a sham. He had lied about loving her, for she knew he suffered not a bit when he deserted her at his family's behest. At least Nikolas was honest about what he could and could not tell her, and in a moment when he could have taken advantage of her passionate response to him, he had exhibited self-control beyond what would be expected of any man. It was humiliating, in a way, when it was she who had sworn to herself never to submit to any man's passion again, and yet she had made the overtures towards a sexual liaison. Apparently she was not made for chastity.

He returned and gazed down at her. "How beautiful you are, Elizabeth," he said, his voice velvety sweet. He caressed her shoulder and stroked her hair.

Beautiful but ultimately resistible, she wanted to say but didn't. She would not allow injured feelings or shame to rule her tongue. "I . . . I must go, Nikolas," she said, allowing his name to roll from her tongue as she slipped from the chair. She longed to throw herself at him and tempt him with kisses; he wanted her, she knew it deep inside her being, and his arousal had not subsided even now, though he had mastered it. But it was better this way, better for her certainly.

"I know," he said simply. "I know you must go."

There was something between them, something powerful and glorious, but she had sworn to herself never to capitulate, not because womanly passion was wrong, just because the consequences were far too severe. She must learn from his example of rigid self-control and never let this happen again.

She left the library and stole up the stairs and along the passage toward her room, wondering, still, at the source of the noise she had heard that had originally drawn her from her chamber. Voices raised in what sounded like an argument or a confrontation had made her want to investigate, but all had been calm when she crept along the hallways, at least until Nikolas had grabbed her and hauled her into the library. Was his one of the voices she had heard? If so, to whom did the other belong?

At her own door she heard something and stopped. But the sound came from past her room, down the hall, and she padded down the carpet toward Gerta's suite; there it was, a high-pitched giggle. The countess was in a fine fettle this evening, she thought. Perhaps she was reading something humorous. But then the sounds changed, and the small hairs on the back of her neck rose as she heard an outcry.

She tried the door but it was locked, and then she backed away as she heard, unmistakably, the guttural sound of male urgency and the answering cry of a woman in the throes of passion. She knew the sound . . . had uttered ones like it, she supposed. Countess Gerta had a visitor, it seemed, and there was only one possibility. Count Delacroix. So they were lovers, as she had begun to suspect.

Pity for Countess Adele welled into Elizabeth's heart as she scurried back to her own room, wanting to hear no more. When the affair was revealed there would be a painful scene, no doubt. How it would end was anyone's guess. But perhaps the two would marry, and perhaps that was the best outcome to be hoped for.

Chapter 17

RIDING AT dawn, breakfast alone in his library, then a long walk outside and talk with Charlotte, who was still sullen but promised to attend lessons with Miss Stanwycke: all of those activities were calculated by Nikolas, after a sleepless and restless night, to quell the thoughts and memories that still taunted him with rich detail. He could capture Elizabeth's scent in his memories, feel the filmy fabric of her nightrail under his tongue, and the sweet peak of a pebbled nipple under the cloth.

He could feel her silky hair tickle his neck as she straddled him, her arms wound around his neck. He could even taste her mouth, like nectar, warmth blossoming through his body at the memory of her weight on him, her hips under his hands, the curve flaring over him. And he could see her face, shadowed but visible, glowing in the flickering firelight. He closed his eyes and leaned back in his desk chair, envisioning the clouded gaze, then how her lips parted, her hair streaming down as she threw her head back in passionate abandon.

But it would surely drive him mad if he continued to think of it. He sat up, rubbed his eyes, and tried to concentrate on the paper on the desk in front of him, a request from the mayor for another meeting before the next full of the moon. It was only February, and he had to hope that the still-snowy landscape would keep the good burghers of Wolfbeck safely in their homes and beds, but he couldn't rely on it. He would have to meet with Wilhelm Brandt and see what he wanted now.

A tap at the door roused him from his torpor and he shouted, *"Kommen sie."*

Bartol Liebner entered and approached, trepidation in his cringing position. As irritating as that was to Nikolas, he had to realize Bartol's life at Wolfram Castle had not been easy. With no real blood ties to the family, he had always known he was there on sufferance. On her dying bed, Nikolas's mother had asked that he always be given a home, since it was all he had known from his youth, and Nikolas, of course, had agreed. He didn't begrudge the old man the shelter of his roof, but Bartol always seemed to feel his inferior and dependent position keenly. For that reason alone, Nikolas attempted to be kind and milder of temper.

"Nikolas, how tired you look!" Bartol said, approaching the desk. He tapped the surface and then folded his hands together. "You must take better care of yourself, nephew. What would this family do if you ever fell ill?"

"I am never ill, you know that," he replied. "What is it, uncle? I don't wish to hurry you, but is it not something that can wait until dinner?"

"You did not come to the table last night," Bartol said, taking the chair opposite Nikolas across the broad expanse of desk.

"I was working and did not want to stop."

"You should make time to eat a proper meal, nephew," the man chided, waggling his finger.

Stifling his impatience, Nikolas said, "I will tonight. Can this not wait until then?"

The old man shifted in embarrassment, his cheeks red. "No, I don't think so. It really is something we must speak of in private."

"What is it then?"

Bartol grimaced. "You know me, I am the last person ever to make trouble. I am devoted to this family, though, and have all of your best interests at heart, especially those of the fair ladies in our masculine protection. I always say to Maximillian that we cannot do enough for the ladies, for their tender sensibilities—"

"Enough," Nikolas said, his patience stretched to breaking. "Please, uncle, if you have a point, let me hear it."

"This is so difficult," he fretted, a sheen of perspiration breaking out on his balding head.

"Then leave it until you can more easily speak of it."

"No, it must be said. Thank you for your bracing attitude, nephew," he said, dabbing his forehead with a handkerchief. "It is what I need. I fear Charlotte is in danger."

Nikolas stopped and stared across at the man. "What do you mean?"

"I do not mean her physical health, God willing," Bartol said. "I mean . . ." He stopped, looked around and leaned across the desk, lowering his tone to a whisper. "I am not one to retail gossip, but I have heard . . . Miss Stanwycke is not who she appears to be."

"What?"

"I fear . . . yes, I must tell you. Charlotte must be protected from invidious influences. Miss Stanwycke is not who she appears to be; one would think, looking at her fair face, that she is an innocent young woman, but in reality she is far from it."

His pulse quickened and anger began to build. "Tell me all, uncle. I need to know everything that you have heard."

"I have heard," he said, in a confidential tone, "that she is not an innocent, she was . . . she was the mistress of a young man of the family she last worked for. She seduced him and lay with him many times, wishing, no doubt, to beget his child and so ensnare the poor gentleman."

Anger built, stoking and burning like a forge fire. Nikolas couldn't speak, for his fury was choking him.

"She was dismissed as a whore," Bartol said, his tone sharp now as his outrage built. "And she was told—rightly so, to my mind—that her infamy would be published throughout England if she looked for work teaching innocent young minds. My sister was undoubtedly taken in by some sad tale, for you know women . . . they are ever soft of heart and—"

Nikolas stood. "Get out! Get out, uncle, before I . . ." Summoning up every ounce of control, he lowered his tone from a harsh shout. "But first, I warn you," he said, leaning across the desk and pointing his finger in Bartol Liebner's pale face;

the man was shrinking back, unprepared, clearly, for such a reaction to his information. Listening at doors and eavesdropping on private conversations to collect odd bits of gossip like so many fascinating trinkets was a nasty habit of Bartol's that Nikolas should have curbed long ago, but now it would end. "Do not spread such vile and poisonous gossip around this household or I will not be responsible for the consequences." He pointed to the door. "Leave me now."

Bartol stumbled out of the chair and toward the door. "But I only was thinking of the best for poor, dear Charlotte, and—"

"Get out," Nikolas roared.

"Of course, nephew, if you think it is all a lie, or if you think it is all right, I respect your opinion, and I swear I will never say another word." He scurried from the room.

IT had been a long morning for Elizabeth . . . long and tedious. Though Charlotte was in the yellow parlor and nominally ready to apply herself, she was moody and dreamy the whole morning. Very little was accomplished. Though Elizabeth could see some subtle differences in Charlotte's behavior—her posture was better, and she had taken on some neater eating habits—would it be enough? Would others notice the changes?

Elizabeth had spent the afternoon in Countess Uta's suite, entertained by the elderly woman's tales of the family legends—wolves and werewolves, shape-shifters and demons. As folklore it was fascinating, but she was afraid the old lady really did believe some of it. Dinner was quiet and the drawing room cold without Nikolas there. All day she had alternately blushed at thoughts of him and turned cold at the knowledge that he had rejected her. If his emotions were engaged he would not have been able to, she reasoned, but an attraction that was merely physical he could master. Her own feelings toward him were a tumultuous mix of longing, tenderness, and fear . . . fear of her own desire for him and fear of what he might be hiding beneath the facade of gentlemanly behavior. Kissing him had left her with the sense that beneath the veneer of grace and dignity raged a seething cauldron of bestial impulses and urges both frightening to her civilized self and enticing to the voluptuary within her. Her greatest fear was that her attraction to him would overcome her better impulses finally, though she did not intend to let that happen. Though judging by his behavior the night before, she supposed she could trust in his rigid self-control should they be so tempted again. She was plagued by an awful question: Did she most want to test her own resistance, to prove to herself that she could master her wanton impulses, or was it that she really wanted to see his restraint break under unconquerable attraction to her?

She sat by the fire in the drawing room, and though Melisande had engaged Charlotte and Christoph in a difficult and lengthy piece on piano and violin, she was not tempted to join them. Let the young people be, for a while, without her trying to inject some lesson or homily into the evening.

Countess Adele was absent, and Countess Gerta played at piquet with Count Delacroix, her playfulness appearing to wear even on her lover after a while, for he excused himself and came over to sit by her. She could sense from him some desire to engage her in conversation, but she was too weary and confused to help him along. And she also was a little peeved by the gentleman who would refuse to see the love Countess Adele clearly held for him, preferring the sly and coquettish Gerta over the solid worth of the elder sister. It was ever thus, though, she supposed. Men would always value youth, beauty, and availability over worth, modesty, and courage . . . at least for a bed partner.

The Frenchman cleared his throat finally and said, "Miss Stanwycke, I need to broach a subject of some delicacy with you."

Oh, Lord, Elizabeth prayed. *Please do not let him confess his affair to me!*

"It concerns you intimately," he said.

She met his gaze. "I beg your pardon?"

He lowered his tone, casting a glance around the room, and

said, "I must say, this is exceedingly difficult for me, but I truly like you, mademoiselle, and I think you need to be told what is being said about you. I fear it has already reached Nikolas's ears."

"What is it?"

"I will not hazard a guess as to the truth or falsity of the gossip, but really it does not matter." The courtly Frenchman looked extremely pained, his gaunt face twisted in a grimace, but finally, he said, simply and with great dignity, "A source has informed Count Nikolas that . . . that you were dismissed from your last position for having seduced a gentleman of the house and becoming his mistress."

"When?" she said numbly. "When was this told to the count?"

"Today, mademoiselle. I'm so sorry. I felt you needed to be told so that if you were . . . if you were spoken to about this, you would not be taken by surprise." He stood and bowed. "I must go back to Countess Gerta, but . . . but I hope all works out well for you."

Nikolas hadn't come to dinner again, nor to the drawing room. Was he even now making the decision to dismiss her as an evil influence on his niece? Was her own behavior with him a confirmation of sorts, and did he now look back at their passionate interlude with more jaded eyes? Who had told him? Immediately, she pushed the question away. Frau Liebner, she was certain, would not have. But Elizabeth had confessed herself to Uta, and who knew what the old woman would let slip accidentally?

After thinking about it from every angle, she stood and moved to the door, numb but sure of her actions. She would not live with this awful sword hanging above her head. If he was about to dismiss her, she needed to confront him and find out while she held strong.

She sped from the room, ignoring Melisande's plea to join them at the piano, and made her way upstairs toward the library. That was where he would be. It was like his lair, where those who needed to see him bearded him in his den. Cautiously, she approached, standing outside the door for a long while, clenching and unclenching her fists.

"Whoever it is, come in; do not stand outside the door," his voice roared from within, speaking German.

She understood. She had learned much, and though not fluent she could understand a lot more than she could speak. She entered without further ado and crossed the room swiftly to stand in front of his desk, like a schoolgirl ordered to come to be chastised. He stared at her, not smiling, but not grim, either.

She knew what she needed to say. "I have been told, Count, that you have been informed of some unsavory aspects of my personal history."

He frowned and sat back in his chair. "How word travels in this place."

She put up one hand and said, "Sir, I ask you not to speak until I am done."

He observed her for a long moment, his expression neutral. "Very well," he finally said. "Sit. Tell me what you wish."

She sat down across from him, composed herself, and then told him the story, unvarnished, not sparing herself, and yet not shouldering the entire blame for an affair that did not begin with her but with the man who told her he loved her.

Finally he said, "So, you were seduced . . ."

"Not against my will."

". . . and abandoned."

"Yes. And . . . and I understand that in your eyes that must make me unfit to tutor an impressionable girl like Charlotte. I understand that you will dismiss me, but I ask that you give me time to find a new position before asking me to leave. And . . . and if you could see your way to giving me a recommendation, or even telling me if you know of anyone who might look for a tutor of English . . . I know some German, now, and—"

"Wait!" he said, putting up one hand. He sat up straight and continued in a formal tone. "As far as I can tell, Miss Stanwycke, you have behaved with the utmost dignity and rectitude while in my employ."

"Except for kissing you," she said, feeling the heat rise in her face.

"Except for kissing me," he agreed. "But I am hardly likely to complain of that, since I was there and taking part as well. It would be most unfair to hold against you our mutual lapse from good judgment. What makes you think I will want to dismiss you?"

She was silent.

Nikolas watched her face and saw beneath the pretense of indifference the fear and trepidation that was evident even as it began to dissolve in the face of his question.

"You mean . . . I may stay?" she asked, her voice quavering, dangerously close to tears now that she had no need of courage.

He stood, circled the desk, and took her hand, pulling her up and leading her over to the fire. "Sit, you are shivering with cold." The chairs held dangerous memories of the night before for him, but he determined to stay rigidly focused on her needs in that moment. He added another log to the fire and used the bellows to good effect. "Miss Stanwycke," he said, turning back to her. "Elizabeth . . . your past is personal to you. Even if I were inclined to criticize you—which I am not—I respect the opinion of my Aunt Katrina, and she thinks you are quite special. As . . . as do I. You have this position until you are done with your task, just as before."

"Thank you," she whispered.

He sat in the other chair, weariness overtaking him. He knew how much courage it must have taken for her to face him, to march in and confront her future like that, but he wished it had not been necessary for her sake.

"He was my first . . . my only," she whispered, staring at the flickering fire.

"He took your virginity?"

She nodded.

"Why did he abandon you?" he asked, wanting to understand. With so much beauty, intelligence, courage, and fierce sensuality, he could not imagine any man letting her go once he had experienced her; even an inequality of station would not explain it, for she would be worth daring much disapprobation to possess. It was a lesson to himself, that revelation, for he knew that he feared her power, feared that if they did make love, he would move heaven and earth to keep her, even to the detriment of his plans for the future of his family.

"His family found out," she said. "At first he told them he intended to marry me, but then . . . then they offered him something he wanted very much in exchange for abandoning me with no further ties. They offered him an estate and an independent purse if he would marry where they wished. It was too much to ask that he say nay to that."

"Coward," Nikolas growled, feeling her pain.

Her hands trembled as she smoothed the blue fabric of her dress. She said, her voice quavering, "He . . . he offered me . . ." She shook her head, squeezing her eyes shut to quell welling tears. "He offered to keep me on as his mistress once he married. He enjoyed my company, he said, and would gladly set me up in a little house of my own for however long we happened to be together."

He reached over and took one of her hands, squeezing it. "What did you say? How did you feel? Were you . . . tempted?"

"Never! I realized in that instant how we had been looking at our relationship differently. I had thought it was a force of nature, with real love and devotion on both sides equally. It would end in marriage, surely, I thought, for how could such a grand passion not? He saw it as a passing fancy, although it did not stop him from telling me, early on, that he loved me dearly and would marry me when he could convince his family to give him his independence."

Nikolas could see it in that instant and knew the root of her cynicism concerning men and marriage. It must have changed how she saw everything. It was only surprising how open and caring she still was, given the pain she must have suffered. "You were in love with him?"

"I thought I was. I don't know now . . . perhaps it was just the first time anyone had made me feel . . . good."

"You . . . came to enjoy . . . uh, intercourse?"

She reddened even deeper, the blush spreading to her neck

and breast. "I suppose. It felt . . . it felt like he needed me. It pleased me that he wanted me so badly."

It wasn't what he was asking, and he frowned, remembering her passionate response to his touch the night before. "But the lovemaking, how did that make you feel? Not for his sake, but for your own?"

"You are asking the most impertinent questions. But I suppose," Elizabeth said with a faint smile, "having done what I have done, I should not indulge in false modesty. I did enjoy it, yes."

Watching her face he felt deeply that she did not even understand what he meant, that she didn't know what it was for a woman to fully enjoy sexual intercourse, or even sexual play. And yet she had a passionate nature. However, he knew from friends' talk that they did not expect nor even wish for their women to enjoy lovemaking too much, feeling it indicated an unfeminine character. He felt differently, having been initiated into the delights of female sexual adventurousness by an older woman while he was at university and then, as he traveled Europe, by a gorgeous Italian courtesan who took pity on him and taught him much.

"Your lover . . ."

"He is married now, and he is some other woman's prize."

Her tone was venomous, and he was not reassured. "Do you still care for him?"

"I . . . I don't know that I ever did," she said slowly. "I think I was lonely, and his attention flattered me; I was happy to believe myself in love."

Nikolas nodded. "If he could give up a woman of your worth so easily and for mere money, then he is a puerile fool not worth being named a man."

She glowed, her smile radiant, and his heart hammered uncomfortably. "Do you remember, Liebchen," he murmured. "How you felt last night?" He swallowed hard and tried to master his feverish longing for her. "How your body felt?"

She looked down, abashed, but nodded. "I do."

"Did you feel thusly with your lover?"

"No. No, never." Her response was quick and firm.

"I could show you what he never did, Liebchen, let you explore how a woman truly feels."

She moved to stand, but he reached out and held her arm firmly. "Do not run from me. I am not asking to become your lover. I . . . I cannot take that risk for reasons not worth canvassing. But there are things I could teach you . . . you need to know how to be pleasured so in future, with . . . with another lover, you will know what to ask for. Men are indubitably dull-witted where women are concerned and do not know what to do to make them experience sexual fulfillment."

"You know that's not possible," she whispered, searching his expression. "For you . . . and I . . ." She did not finish.

"It is possible. I swear, I will make no demands from you. But I could teach you the rewards of passion."

Regretfully, she shook her head. "No. No. Impossible."

He stood and pulled her to her feet, wrapping her in his arms. He was aroused and knew she could feel he was so, but he held her without demands. "Elizabeth, if you change your mind, come to my room. No woman so lovely as you," he said, kissing her ear, "should live without knowing what it is to be worshipped and adored. I will not ask you to submit to any sexual demands. I will never ask anything of you. I want only to show you what it feels like to be a woman of sensuality."

He guided her to the door and she fled, trembling, to her room. *Worshipped and adored.* Stripping her clothes off in the dark, she huddled under her sheets, Nikolas's words sending shivers down her susceptible body. She had never felt this fever of anticipation, and she was tantalized by his suggestion. What would he do? What would he show her? What did he mean?

With John, while he was entering her she had felt the beginning flush of excitement, and then he would take his joy and be done, and she would think it was likely that what she had felt was all there was. And yet . . . with a trembling hand she touched herself, remembering the feel of Nikolas's erection pressed to her, and she was damp with desire. She knew the damp softening of her flesh was a natural preparation to make it easier for the man to enter her, but now she began to feel, as she touched, that there was something more.

Her skin heating with desire, she remembered Nikolas at her breast, suckling, as she had straddled him, feeling him pressed to her, knowing instinctively he would have given much to enter her then and there, and yet he had restrained himself and conquered his urges. Her fingers moving more quickly, she arched and felt deep within herself a shivering sweet release as she imagined being with Nikolas, touching him and feeling him enter her.

Falling into the first deep sleep she had known for weeks, she drowsily wondered, if she visited him, what would he do?

Chapter 18

DAYS PASSED. Charlotte was quiet and obedient; Elizabeth worried that she had been brought to heel with threats, and that the girl was falling into depression. Her eyes were often glazed and though she appeared to listen attentively, she learned little. When asked a direct question she often shrugged listlessly. Perhaps, Elizabeth thought, her illness had not been exaggerated after all, and she was still suffering the aftereffects. When approached about the problem, Countess Adele merely shook her head with a worried look in her chilly eyes.

And so Elizabeth went about her routine, teaching, visiting Uta and Frau Liebner, reading aloud to them both, then dining and spending time in the drawing room. Tensions in the household had eased again, inexplicably, and some seemed almost happy. Certainly Countess Gerta did. Would some announcement come soon of a wedding? Only time would tell.

But throughout every day and into the night she thought about what Nikolas had said. He glanced at her often, a world of meaning in his gaze, but he did not seek her out, nor did he try to sway her. They had no more private meetings, and she kept to her own room at night.

But finally, one sleepless night many days after their chat, she slipped from bed, drew on a robe, and padded down the stairs and down the hall past the sword room to his suite. Perhaps she would just ask him what he meant. But what if he had changed his mind? Her heart pounding with fear, she turned away, but footsteps on the staircase beyond the count's chamber decided her action, and she slipped through the door.

It was a large and opulent room, with a door leading to his sitting rooms and dressing rooms beyond, no doubt.

Nikolas, lying in his enormous full-testered bed, looked up from a book. His expression gladdened. "Elizabeth," he said, tossing aside the book.

"Nikolas," she whispered, leaning back against the door. "I . . . I did not come for that, I just came . . . I just came to ask you . . ."

He smiled, slipped from the bed, and padded over to her. She glanced down, shocked at his bare legs and feet under a nightshirt.

"Come," he said, taking her hand. "You are freezing. No matter what you want, come under a blanket while you ask."

She obeyed, stumbling after him on numb limbs. He scooped her up and dropped her into his bed, pulling up the luxurious midnight blue covers over them both as he reclined next to her. He gazed down at her as she lay back, her head resting on his pillow as his scent bathed her nostrils. The warmth of his bed and his body filled her with an agitated excitement, but it calmed as a languor overtook her.

Why was she so nervous? She was not some green girl, and she had had sexual intercourse before. If she was so attracted, what was there to stop her from taking advantage of his proposal? There was no risk involved, nothing expected from her; he had made her a promise, and if anything, she had learned that he was to be trusted implicitly. Curiosity was burning like a pit of coal inside of her. And yet . . . Count Nikolas von Wolfram was a much more impressive man than John had ever been, and so much more dangerous in many ways. And so much more enticing.

"What do you want to ask?"

"What did you mean, Nikolas, the last time we spoke? What would you do?"

"First this," he said, leaning over and kissing her gently on the mouth. "And then this," he said, taking her in his arms and pulling her to him.

She wrapped her arms around his neck and submitted to the kiss again, letting herself go and feeling his tongue enter her, taking it in and thrusting her own back. It was what she had come there for, after all, though she had lied even to herself. She lost track of time and space, just closing her eyes and feeling the delicious sensations winding through her, down to her belly and between her legs. A sweet, hazy intoxication stole through her, but when she first felt his fingers, delicately touching her, exploring her, tickling her thighs and the soft flesh of her stomach, she gasped, torn out of the haze by a stab of alarm.

But then, seduced by the tenderness of his touch, she found herself spreading her legs a little as he probed further. His thick forefinger gently separated the folds of flesh, and as he kissed her, laying her back, he delved in, thrusting gently, leaving her weak and moaning aloud. She muttered his name, and as her wetness coated him, and he plunged deeper, she arched and felt a spiral of ecstasy shiver through her body, so much more intense than when she touched herself that there was no comparison.

She clung to him, and as the waves subsided she opened her eyes to find him staring at her, a look of such gentleness on his handsome face that she wanted to cry. But still, he didn't stop. He teased her more, and she was so sensitive she bucked and writhed, but as he kissed her, still delving into her wetness, she felt the madness come again; it erupted deep within her this time, like a bolt to the core of her being.

In the sweet moments after, trembling as he held her close to him, she felt him, thick and heavy against her thigh. With one shaking hand she reached down and sheathed him with her fingers, gasping at his size and thickness, but he groaned and rolled away.

"No, Liebchen, for if you do that, I will no longer be the responsible one." He got out of bed, pulled on his black satin robe, and scooped her up. "I am taking you back to your bed before you fall sleep."

She came to him the next night, unable to stay away, and the night after. It was a madness that had gripped her, and every night she thought she would be strong enough to resist, but every night she tossed and turned and finally submitted, going to him, slipping in, and letting him pleasure her. And always he would carry her back to her bed, stealthily slipping down the hallways along the shadowed perimeter. As tender as he was, and as gentle, he still never indicated by word or deed that he considered their liaisons as more than a passing sweet interlude. She should be ashamed, she sometimes thought, but she wasn't.

And yet inevitably their nighttime meetings had a cost. During the day she could hardly think. She found herself daydreaming about him when she should have been teaching Charlotte; a more astute pupil would have noticed, but her student was still preoccupied. It could not continue, though. She resolved that she must stop once and for all. Nothing that encouraged her to neglect her proper tasks could be normal or healthy. She was stronger than this madness and would call a halt to it. He had proved his point; she now knew what a woman's passion felt like, and had experienced fulfillment, but she must get over what was becoming an obsession with the master of this castle, for it could have no good ending, she feared.

And so that night, she stayed in her own bed. She might not sleep, but she would not leave. An hour passed, and then an hour more, as she stared at the ceiling.

A faint shuffle alerted her to someone outside her door, and she sat up, alarmed. "Who is there?" she called out softly. Her door opened and Nikolas slipped in, crossed to her bed, leaned over, and took her mouth in a deep wet kiss.

"I could not stand it. I knew by the look in your eyes today that you had resolved not to come to me. I could not stand it, and so I came to you." He rubbed her shoulders and climbed onto her bed, pushing her back against the pillows.

"Nikolas, no!" she cried, pushing him away. "We must stop! I can't think during the day, can't attend to my work, and . . . and your niece will suffer."

"Not so much as I will if I cannot touch you. Let us experience this madness while we may," he said, caressing her face, and then her neck and bosom. He pushed her back until she was reclining once more on her pillows. "Life is hard and serious, tedious often. Why should we not enjoy this until it fades?"

His reasoning was enticing; they were doing nothing truly wrong; why should she not enjoy this delicious madness for a time? She trusted him fully now and knew he would never take advantage of that trust. She gazed up at him, although he was nothing more than a dark shadow looming above her. "But . . . you will not allow me to . . . to touch you. Why?"

"This is about you, Liebchen." He crawled under her covers, cradling her in his arms. "I have my release later, just thinking about you and what we have done. It is too dangerous for me if you touch me, for I truly fear I will lose my will to restrain my urges."

A quiver of alarm, enticing in its dangerous thrill, trickled through her. "You wouldn't . . ."

"No . . . no," he whispered, touching her cheek gently. "Hush. I did not mean to frighten you. I would never force myself upon you; no man of honor would. But powerful urges denied can have, for a man, painful consequences."

She relaxed against him; the darkness, his heat, and the knowledge of what he wanted to do filled her with agonizing desire. "I'm afraid that someone will find out," she whispered, sheltered in the curve of his arms. She traced his form, his hard stomach quivering under her fingers, up to the ridge of his collarbone, down his shoulder and upper arm to the cording of thick muscles across his forearm and the dense mat of hair she knew to be black against his pale skin. "I have caught looks, glances . . . I know I am different . . ."

"Yes," he said, pulling her nightrail up over her head and tossing it aside. He covered her with his body and kissed her breasts, wetting her nipples with his tongue. "You are different, but no one will ever dare say anything to you."

"But what if they know?" she cried, shuddering as the delirium of sensual delight invaded her body.

"Then they know," he growled. "I care not."

She surrendered then, giving in to the feelings as he teased her nipples into peaks and stroked between her spread legs.

Afterwards, she cradled his shaggy head to her breast, feeling the roughness of his chest hair against her stomach, relishing the differences between them, the enticing sense that this man in her bed was a powerful force of nature, and he cared for her, truly cared for her, in ways no one else ever had.

"Nikolas?" she said into the darkness.

"Hmm?" he murmured.

"Have you never . . . never had a woman here?"

"Do you mean here at the castle?"

"Yes."

"I have not."

"Why?"

He was silent for a long moment. "It is difficult to explain. It is important to me that I give to my family all of my time and devotion; it consumes me, I suppose."

"But is there to be nothing for you? No . . . love, no caring?"

He was silent again, but then said, "I had given up on such things."

"Then why . . . why this?"

"I do not know. I am going against everything I had promised myself, everything I have forsworn in the last years."

"Is it only because I am the first unrelated female to reside here?"

"Oh, Elizabeth, no. Do not think so." He gazed up into her eyes in the dimness and touched her cheek. "I have never met any woman such as you. You have a . . . gallantry that pleases me, a courage I admire. You are a woman such as I never expected to meet in my lifetime."

She had no answer then, for she feared her voice trembling at the unexpected sweetness of his reply. And yet, the tenderness of their relation did not change all that she had earlier said, all that she feared. She still knew she would have to make him stop. They could not go on this way without both of them suffering ultimately. If the madness would not subside, then she must be the strong one this time.

The next night she stayed dressed. She couldn't think when he touched her, and she gave in all too easily. If she kept her dress on, perhaps she could make him understand that it was becoming too difficult. She knew her own feelings and was terribly afraid that his tenderness had defeated every good intention she had had of keeping her heart intact. People were beginning to wonder if she was all right, and even Countess Adele had asked her just that day if she was quite well. It could not go on. If she had had any hope that their deepening tenderness would end in marriage it might have been worth the risk, but he had made plain his intention never to wed. So when he tapped and entered her room that night she was still up and waiting. He smiled as he crossed the room to where she stood near the fire.

"Hmm . . . shall we play a new game tonight?" he asked, a devilish glint in his dark eyes.

His dark tousled locks, broad shoulders, and square features made him dangerously handsome, even attired in a nightshirt and robe.

"We have to talk," she said, her voice quavering. "I'm serious, Nikolas, we cannot continue this way."

"Are you ashamed of how you feel?" he asked, caressing her cheek and pushing back her veil of hair.

"No. I'm not ashamed."

"Then why should we stop? We are hurting no one."

That wasn't true, she thought, watching his face, tracing the square jaw and noting the bristly beard and drooping dark curls. She was beginning to ache for him, to long for his touch and want more than just the petting game they indulged in. It was dangerous to *her*. She had thought the pain of John's abandonment was ferocious; she now felt much more for Nikolas, and every day brought deeper emotions. How would it end? She would not let herself be destroyed.

He tried to take her in his arms, but she pushed him away. "No, we have to talk . . ."

But the rest was lost in a kiss. All of her good intentions died with that sweet beckoning feeling that budded whenever he touched her. How could she resist when every fiber of her being longed for him?

"I will be your abigail," Nikolas said huskily, helping her

from her dress until she stood just in her chemisette and stays before the fire. "Be still, Liebchen."

"I will," she whispered, abandoning hope of ever resisting him.

Standing in front of her, his big hands trembling on the laces of her stays, his knuckles brushing her already erect nipples through the soft fabric, she shuddered at every touch. She stared at his face, the high planes of his sharp cheekbones casting his jaw into shadow, the set of his full, sensuous lips firm. She had promised to be still, but it was terrifying and she quivered. She was close, so close, and she knew now what she was feeling, and why it frightened her so.

She knew the difference now between infatuation and true love.

He paused and looked into her eyes, a questioning gaze; he was sensing something.

"No, Nikolas, please, don't stop," she murmured. The forgetfulness of delirium would be welcome, this time, when sanity was too hard to bear.

She needed to say no more to urge him on. He bent over and pulled at a knot with his strong teeth and then jerked the lacing open. Cool air flowed over her breasts as he pushed back the fabric, but he covered them with his large warm hands. He brushed the nipples with his thumbs and kissed her.

Helpless with desire, if he had asked her that moment, with his hands over her breasts and his lips suckling hers, she would have surrendered to anything. He put one arm around her then, and pulled her close, and his other hand touched her leg, pushing up the short skirt of her chemisette. He caressed her bottom and cradled her against him. His arousal pressed against her belly and he lifted her, cupping her bottom with both hands as he held her firmly to him. He filled her mouth with his tongue, thrusting in an imitation of the love act, and she parted her legs so he was supporting her wholly with his hands on her bottom and back.

A light tap at the door startled her and she reared away from him, stumbling back down onto her knees.

"Elizabeth, what is wrong?" he asked.

He hadn't even heard! The knocking was repeated, and Frau Liebner's voice, sounding muffled by the door, called out Elizabeth's name. "Are you there? I heard a voice. Are you all right, my dear?"

Elizabeth got to her feet and put one finger over her lips in a shushing gesture to Nikolas, whose glazed expression did not portend well for him understanding the need for silence. She opened the door and poked her head around it. "Frau Liebner, I was . . . was sleeping."

"But I just heard a voice." The woman's face below her white lace cap was set in worried lines.

"I . . . that was just me. I was just saying to wait for a moment."

"May I come in?" the woman said, pushing against the door.

"No!" She had almost shouted that, and she repeated, more softly, "No, I'm not dressed."

"You will be in your night attire, certainly, and that is enough for me."

Elizabeth felt rather than heard Nikolas's presence behind her and gasped when his hands cupped her bottom, pushing up the fabric of her chemisette and caressing her naked bottom.

"Are you certain you are well, my dear?"

Frau Liebner held up a lamp and Elizabeth cringed, thinking how disheveled she must look, her cheeks red from Nikolas's whiskers, her lips plump from kissing and her hair tousled.

"I'm perfectly well. I . . . I'm sorry I'm yawning," she quickly said, faking a big yawn, "but I'm so very tired. Can we, can we t-talk in the m-morning?" Her stutter was caused by the count's hands kneading her bottom. He was pressed against her now behind the door and Elizabeth could feel his erection butted up against her bottom. One of his hands snaked around and caressed her belly, then moved down, his thick fingers tickling the damp curls between her legs.

"I have something of great import to discuss with you. It cannot wait, Elizabeth."

"I couldn't attend properly, Frau Liebner, I am s-so t-tired."

One rough finger caressed and parted her, stroking her with insistent rhythm. Elizabeth trembled and sighed, putting her cheek against the cool door. She was caught, unable to protest, and Nikolas had to know that. She longed to relax and enjoy his capable hands. She longed to close the door and tell him he was evil and then surrender to his skilled petting. She longed to tell Frau Liebner she had other things to think of. Or at least that one big distraction, pressed against her.

But she could not arouse suspicion. As Nikolas's thick finger gently parted the folds of her skin, the very roughness of his hand enthralling, she begged her friend, "Please, Frau Liebner, I'll come to your room first thing in the morning I p-promise, I promise . . ."

His finger, stroking more quickly, delved deeper and then came up to tickle the nub, the center of feeling, and she felt a physical shuddering quiver through her as if she were in a carriage over rough road. An abrupt euphoria seized her, swallowing her whole, and she closed her eyes, sagging against the door, as wave after wave of glory surrounded her in brilliance.

"Elizabeth?"

Dizzy still and her cheeks flushed with exquisite heat, she opened her eyes to see the lovely old wrinkled face of her friend. "Yes?"

There was knowledge in the wise old blue eyes. "I will see you in the morning, my dear, but if it is not first thing, I will not be surprised," she said and then walked away, lamp held high.

But her voice came floating back down the hallway towards Elizabeth. "And Nikolas, you should go to bed, too, you rogue. Let the poor girl sleep, if she is so *very* tired."

He shoved the door closed with his foot and carried her to bed, this time staying with her until she was asleep.

Chapter 19

HE COULD not get enough of Elizabeth. He hungered for her day and night and had taken to staying in her bed until she was asleep, just holding her close, deriving what satisfaction he would allow himself from that delicious warmth. Often she tried to reciprocate his love play, and he knew that he could have made love to her long ago, but he knew also that it could never be.

And yet that, perhaps, was why his hunger grew until just the scent of her in the hall, just the sound of her voice at a distance, made his body tremble with desire. His aunt knew and had told him in veiled words that if he hurt Elizabeth, she would do something; she was not sure what, she said, but it would not be pleasant. He assured her, in tactful language, that he had not taken the ultimate step; they had not made love and would not, for he knew his duty to his family and his future.

No one would deprive him of what little he could have with her, though. Doomed to be parted ultimately by fate and the separate paths of their lives, he felt a desperate need to drink his fill of her, to touch every sweet inch of skin, to memorize for all time her scent, her gaze, her soft expression, the tremulous sound of his name on her lips as he brought her to fulfillment.

But inevitably she was caught in the hallway at his door one night, and by his uncle Bartol of all people. Though he had never told her that Bartol was the one who had exposed her past indiscretion to him, he knew that finding her outside his door in the middle of the night must have caused the old man to make some assumptions. A sick conviction in his stomach grew; Bartol Liebner, though not cruel by nature, had a fastidious moral side and would confess his discovery to someone. If it was only to Maximillian, the Frenchman would keep the secret, but what if he went to Adele? How would he explain himself to his sister? It was not that he feared her disapprobation; he feared no one, for he was master and all in the castle knew that one fact.

But . . . he was going against every stated intention he had ever spoken of in his many talks with his one remaining sensible sibling. Adele had given up as much as he had, and it was not fair to her that he should have such a sweet entanglement when no opportunity for love would ever lighten her burden. So it was his own hypocrisy he was running from, the revelation of his own fall from grace that he feared. And yet night after night he surrendered, finding in Elizabeth's arms relief even from his lack of respect for his own actions.

After the discovery by Bartol, she was terribly embarrassed and did not want to venture to his room again, so, though he had not intended to, he decided to tell her one of the secrets of Wolfram Castle.

"Come here," he said, after she told him of her fears of discovery. She had crept to his room one last time, she said, to tell him they must not continue. He took her hand and led her to a corner of his room, where the wood paneling had an odd join.

"Why?" she asked, pulling back.

He depressed a panel and pushed, and it slid sideways, opening to a corridor hidden along the outside wall.

She gasped and stuck her head in the passage. "Nikolas!" she cried and then sneezed. "Oh! What . . . where does this lead?"

"I'll show you," he said, chuckling at her consternation. He picked up a candle and led her into the passage, down a long narrow corridor, up some stone stairs and down again, through a twisted turn, and along a straight portion. She was shivering and sneezed again, for the passage was drafty and frigid, as well as dark and dusty, but finally he came to a portion of the interior wall where he stopped. "Here; push that wooden panel."

She did as she was told and it slid sideways just as the other had. She gasped. "What . . . what room is this?" she whispered, not daring to poke her head through.

"Step in," he whispered. "Step in, and you shall see."

She did as she was told, and stepped into the room and then gasped again, whirling to face him as he stepped in after her. "This is my own room!"

"It is, indeed," he chuckled, pulling her to him.

"A secret entrance into my own room," she said, shaking her head in wonder. "And I never knew it. How many of these passages are there?"

"The castle is threaded with them, some not even along outside walls, but within the walls. I'm not sure even I know them all."

She turned in the circle of his arms and gazed at the walls. She shivered and her expression was wonder mingled with trepidation. "Nikolas, how many of the inhabitants know about these passages?"

"I know. Uta and Mina know. Cesare knows. Also Adele." He thought and then nodded. "That is all, for I have guarded the secret carefully. The rest are in ignorance of the existence of these corridors, and I mean them to stay that way, so do not worry about anyone else finding their way into your room; it will never happen, I guarantee that. You must be careful not to get lost, and you must always be careful you are entering the correct room."

"This is how you appeared in the library that first night. I thought there must be a secret passage, but I never imagined . . . many of them? Where were you coming from that night?"

He turned her around, laughed, and said, "That I do not need to divulge," and then he kissed her.

So, she thought, as he carried her to her bed and undid her robe, he trusted her enough to tell her about the secret passages, but not enough to tell her where he was and why he felt the need to use a secret way into the castle. It was the one thing that still clouded her joy—he was holding back from her, not telling her things about himself. She felt it deeply, but what it was that he still kept secret, she was not sure. In fairness, it was possible the secrets were not his own, and so he felt loath to share them. But there was something . . . something about himself, too, some element—

Blissful fog began to invade her brain as he touched and caressed her. She ran her hand down his hip and to the ever-present bulge under his robe that spoke of his constant desire for her. His whole body jolted as she touched him, and he stayed her hand.

"No, my sweet Elizabeth, do not do that."

She gazed up at him in the dim candlelight. "But I want to," she whispered. "Please, Nikolas, I want to. You're so good to me and have taught me how much I love your touch, but I want . . . I want to give you back all that you give me."

"Elizabeth," he said, impatiently, "can you not just take for once in your life? This is for you, not for me."

And not for them together, she thought sadly. She pulled away from him and he stared at her, a puzzled expression on his face. "Why? Why, Nikolas? Why will you not let me give back to you, when I want to so very badly?"

He shook his head but didn't answer. He was afraid of something, she could see it in his haunted eyes. There was some deep pain in him and she longed to soothe him. So much about him was noble and good; that she had learned in the past weeks. When he lashed out in anger toward Christoph, it was an expression of his frustration with the boy's recalcitrance, and he held in much more than he ever expressed.

But still . . . by not letting her give to him, by holding himself aloof, he was protecting some part of himself. He was afraid of something. Was it that he was afraid that if they made love, he would come to care for her too much?

She melted back into his arms, hating herself for inspiring the wounded look on his face. "Just hold me tonight, Nikolas. Just hold me."

They wound themselves together in a loving tangle, and

warmth penetrated both of them: warmth, a sense of safety and trust that defied all reason, and a melancholy devotion.

They had slept for hours. When Nikolas awoke and felt her there, asleep in his tight embrace, he stroked her hair and lay still, listening to the soft, even puff of her breath. "Oh, that I could tell you all," he whispered against her hair. "But you would turn from me in revulsion, and I would suffer such torment if you did. Better you stay in blissful ignorance, Liebchen, than that you should know too much."

He loosed his hold and slipped from her bed, gazing down at her in the weak morning light from the half-open drapes. Her hair splayed across the pillow. She was all curves, he thought, watching her: her cheek, her shoulder, her breast beneath the muslin of her gown, her hip as it flared, gently mounding the blanket over her. She moved and murmured, touching the warm spot where he had lain just moments before. Her fingers, as they caressed that warmth, sent shivers down his spine, and he knew he feared the hold she had on him. He should have sent her away, but it was too late. He could no more tell her to go now than he could tear out his own still-beating heart and toss it to the hills.

The door latch moved and he could hear Fanny's soft tread outside the door. Swiftly he crossed the room, exiting by way of the secret passage.

"IT'S almost March," Elizabeth said, padding over to the window in Frau Liebner's room and gazing out. Two days of rain had melted much snow, and now she could see the green coniferous blanket over the hills that stretched beyond and above the back of Wolfram Castle.

"You have been here two months, almost. Much has happened in that time, eh?"

"Yes," Elizabeth answered absently, toying with a tassel on the tie that held back the curtain.

"Elizabeth, attend me please!"

Elizabeth turned to gaze at her friend, who stared at her

from her bed; having a cold had kept her there a few days. "What is it?"

"Elizabeth, I have never asked you about your relationship with Nikolas, but—"

"Please don't," Elizabeth said hastily. "I wouldn't know what to tell you."

Frau Liebner stared at her. "What have you done?" she whispered. "I brought you here to rescue you from that despicable cad, what he and his family did to you, and then you—"

"Please, ma'am," Elizabeth said, perilously close to tears. "I . . . I cannot . . ." Unable to continue, she said, "I must go. Charlotte awaits me."

Coward, she said to herself as she fled. Frau Liebner was right; she had only spoken out of concern that Elizabeth had tumbled herself into the same difficulties that had forced her out of England. But Elizabeth was ill-equipped to talk about what she didn't understand herself.

Swallowing back her tears, she retreated to the yellow parlor. Charlotte awaited her there, staring absently out the window. They were to handle the British peerage today, so that Charlotte might never make the mistake, as hostess, of seating someone in the wrong order, or greeting someone improperly. Elizabeth retrieved from a drawer the book she had used to make some notes, but then sat down at the table and bowed her head.

"Miss Stanwycke? Is . . . is everything all right?"

She looked up to find Charlotte's lovely eyes fixed on her and a worried expression on her face. "I don't know," she answered. "Is it? Charlotte, I know you don't wish to follow your uncle's orders and go to England, but there is much more than that bothering you. If you cannot speak to your aunts about it, nor to me, why do you not try to tell your uncle? He cares about you and Christoph so much and only wants the best for you."

The girl's lip trembled, and tears welled into her eyes. "Uncle Nikolas?" She shook her head. "You do not know him as I do." She frowned, trying to sniff back the tears. "I do not know what is wrong. Truly, Miss Stanwycke, I do not. There is some trouble for Christoph, but he will not tell me what it is. It has been going on for a couple of years, but has been getting worse and worse. Sometimes he is gone from his room all night, and I do not know where he goes, and . . . and the next day he is almost wild and tells me he hates himself. I am afraid, so afraid! Oh, Miss Stanwycke, what if . . ." But she shook her head, unable to voice her worst fears.

"Charlotte!" Elizabeth, alarmed, went to her and stood before her, grasping both shoulders with her hands. "Have you asked him yourself?"

"Of course! All he does is tell me I need to look after myself. He is . . . is evil, he says, and not f-fit . . ." She broke off, finally weeping openly.

Elizabeth brought her kerchief out and dabbed at the girl's tears, but just then the door opened and Countess Gerta drifted in, as she often did. Making an attempt to shield Charlotte from her aunt's gaze, Elizabeth turned. "What is it, Countess?"

Countess Gerta frowned, a puzzled look on her peaked face. "I . . . I do not know. I came in here for something, and now I cannot remember . . ."

"Perhaps if you go out again—"

"No. I will stay, certainly." She sat down and glanced around the room. "Where are Eva and Jakob?"

A prickle of presentiment crawled up the back of Elizabeth's neck, making the small hairs stand away from her skin. Gerta's expression was unfocussed and blearily puzzled.

Charlotte, having recovered, said, "Aunt, they are away at school, remember?"

"Oh. I thought they would be here." She got up then and drifted out of the room.

Elizabeth sat down and stared at the door. "Has she always been like this?" Over the past two months she had often seen the countess in an abstracted state, and sometimes she appeared confused, but to ask if her children were there when she knew they were away at school . . .

Shrugging, Charlotte said, "I suppose not. She cannot have

always been like this, but she has been for many years. At times she is quite normal, but then at others . . . losing her husband . . ." She shook her head. "And then she had the twins; Aunt Adele says she was never the same after. She was very ill for a long time, and then she was weak in the head for a time after that."

"I've heard the story," Elizabeth said, "of how her husband and your mother died in a fire."

"But why were they together?" Charlotte whispered, her expression twisted with pain. "No one will tell me that."

The conflicting stories came back to Elizabeth, and her own puzzlement over them.

"I have heard," Charlotte said, her voice wooden, "that my uncle Nikolas was there . . . that he could have saved them, but did not even try."

"Who told you that?" Elizabeth asked sharply.

Looking frightened, Charlotte said, "No one . . . I just heard it."

"From whom?" Elizabeth asked again. "Charlotte, to whom do you speak? I have noticed looks between you and Signor Vitali. He hasn't . . . you aren't involved with him, are you?"

"No!" Charlotte said, her blue eyes wide. "Cesare is . . ." She hung her head. "I . . . I thought I was in love with him once, but he told me . . . he very *kindly* told me he could never care for me. I do speak to him sometimes, but he has always just advised me, as you do, to trust my uncle Nikolas."

"Then why do you not, when all around you . . ."

Charlotte stood and wrung her hands together. "I am not feeling at all well. I am going to my room." She raced from the parlor and disappeared and Elizabeth was left alone again with her own troubling thoughts.

That night Nikolas came to Elizabeth, but she could tell he was distracted. Many times he started at some imagined noise, and once he got up, paced to the window, and gazed out at the moon, which waxed fuller, almost a complete disk. She held him close, but when he imagined her asleep, he crept stealthily from her room.

With the full moon the next evening came snow . . . not as much as before, and in pellets, tiny freezing balls of ice that pattered against the window like gravel. Elizabeth awaited Nikolas in her own room that night, but he did not come. The next morning at the breakfast table he whispered to her that he was exhausted, but she felt his attention drifting.

Was it over? Had she bored him finally? Was there something she should have done differently, or some way she should have seduced him into lovemaking?

That night she resolved to visit him one more time and make him tell her the truth: What secrets tormented him? What did he fear? Why would he not make love to her? All desire to resist had fled from her mind; now she wanted him, and needed him. And was so afraid she had again given her heart to a man who could not return her love.

Late that night she crept down the cold secret passage, but she stopped when she heard a loud sound that reverberated through the corridor. Trembling with fear, she hastened her footsteps, getting lost once, making a wrong turn another time, but finally finding a panel that slid open. But was it his room?

Shaking with fear as much as cold but not willing to wander all night in the walls like a ghost, she stepped into the room. It was Nikolas's! She breathed a sigh of relief and padded across the carpet to his bedside, the light from open curtains streaming into the room and turning everything a luminous pewter.

But he wasn't in his bed, though it was disturbed; he had been there, she could feel it, and in fact the bedclothes were still warm from his body. Where had he gone? Puzzled, she wandered to the window and peered out.

There, in the stream of moonlight that crossed the snowy path, she saw him, and he was heading towards the woods! She knew him so well now that she could see him in the set of his shoulders and the length of his stride. What secret business was he about that could tear him from his warm bed in the middle of the night?

The woman ... the blond woman he rescued time and time again!

Furious and perplexed, Elizabeth could not contain her ire nor her curiosity. She fled to her own room, donned her warmest cloak over her nightgown, and pulled on boots over woolen stockings, then speedily descended the stairs. She left the building, grateful that once again she had evaded any servants, though most were long gone to their well-earned beds. She followed his path, clearly delineated in the fresh snow, over the long lawn and across the lane and an expanse of grass to the forest edge.

And there she stopped, her frigid breath coming out in frosty puffs. He had already entered the forest, home of wolves and other predatory beasts ... home even of werewolves, if such folklore was to be believed. She shivered and hesitated, wondering if she truly should plunge in and follow him or go back to certain safety. Even now she could go back to the house and forget it.

Though she wouldn't; if she retreated now she would wonder forever after what Nikolas's midnight venture was about. Living with doubt was tearing her heart out; answers would calm her again, for better or for worse. She could see his path; it was clear and even in the forest, with the moon full, she could find it.

She would follow. Five minutes. She would go in, venture forward five minutes, and then retreat if she could not catch a glimpse of him. "Surely I am the greatest fool God ever put on the earth," she muttered, hiking up her cloak and feeling the cold snow drift into the tops of her boots. Her cheeks and ears stung with the bitter cold, and tears froze on her cheeks. Though the woods were eerily beautiful, with silvery branches stretched up like lacy fingertips to the pregnant moon above, she still shivered with cold and nerves as she plunged through the drifted snow in Nikolas's path, not daring to call out for fear of alerting someone—or some*thing*—to her presence.

And then she heard a rustling; she stopped and waited and heard it again, but not ahead of her—to the side—and then it stopped. She took two steps and it started again, but when she stopped, it silenced. She swallowed past a lump, her heart beating so hard she thought her breastbone would rip open.

Forward or back? Or not to move at all?

Off to her left she caught sight of a movement, but it was low, slinking through the wooded underbrush. Moonglow caught it, and the figure was gray and black, low to the ground. "Wolf," she whimpered. A sob caught in her throat. This was ludicrous. She must leave; her decision made, she backed away, stumbled on a rut but righted herself, her feet numb with the cold and feeling like icy stumps. *Flee*, her terror shrieked; *don't*, her common sense whispered. *Don't alert anyone to your presence.*

In the distance, beyond where she thought she saw the wolf, another figure moved, a slim figure in a gray cloak. Human! A woman? She squinted and could see the hood; as the figure moved, the hood fell back to reveal hair that streamed down across the gray of the cloak—silvery hair rippling in glorious waves.

She whimpered again, torn between her raging curiosity and her terror. Another sight of the wolf made her decision, and she ran away, her breath catching in great gasps as reason fled to be replaced by primal fear. Wolf! She ran and ran, the taste of fear like blood in her mouth, bitter and metallic, but then she saw that there was ahead of her no path, no great footsteps left by Nikolas, nor even her own. She had gone wrong and was off his path. Where?

She turned and turned, her cloak flinging snow up in a shower, but the only footsteps she could see were her own, back the way she had come. If she followed it, perhaps she could see where she had gone wrong. She tried, but soon terror gripped her as she realized it was leading her into deeper wood; bile backed into her throat, the bitter taste choking her. She didn't remember where she had gone wrong, didn't know what to do. A branch cracked somewhere. Human or beast?

"Nikolas!" she screamed. He was there, somewhere. Nikolas would know what to do. "Nikolas!"

Just as her fear threatened to overwhelm her and her

heart's thumping was the only sound she could hear, she heard another noise, and there he was, a dark figure, moonlight glinting from his raven hair. "Nikolas!" she cried, running to him.

"Elizabeth," he cried, clutching her shoulders and shaking her. "What are you doing out here?"

"I . . . I saw you leave . . . I wanted to know—"

"Never mind," he said, roughly turning her and guiding her forward. "You must go back." He pushed her ahead of him and soon she was at the edge of the forest; she could see that she was just a hundred feet along the forest's edge from where she had entered.

"Go! Back to the house."

"Come with me," she said, turning back to him.

He stood on the edge of the forest, his bulky figure a dark blot against the silvery gray and deep green trees. "No. Go, now!"

She obeyed, afraid to do anything else, but when she turned back to look, she saw his figure melting back into the woods. Scared, cold, and bewildered, she raced back to the house, up the stairs, and to his room, where she stirred the fire, adding another log, then waited in the window seat, her wet feet becoming warmer, though still soggy.

There, across the white snow, she saw him carrying the woman. Who was it? She couldn't see, couldn't tell. She raced out to the landing, but he never appeared in the great hall, nor did he come down the passage. Where was he? She thought to descend, then hesitated, trying to imagine which way he had entered. She would go back to his room and use the secret passage, she thought finally. Maybe that would be where he was. She entered his room and there he was, flinging aside his cloak and pulling his wet boots from his feet. He had indeed come in through his secret passage.

"Who is she?" she whispered.

He looked up, his face haggard and harsh in the firelight. "It is not your business, Elizabeth."

"Nikolas," she said, striding across the room to him. "I—"

"No! Do not ask again," he thundered, standing. "I warn you, stay out of this, or—"

"Or what?" she asked, standing before him.

He slumped down in his chair and buried his face in his hands. "Just go. Leave me."

"No," she whispered, refusing to be driven away. She squeezed into the chair beside him and took him in her arms, cradling him against her breast while she watched the fire burn merrily. He was cold but gradually warmed, nuzzling her neck but not attempting to kiss or caress her. When she looked down at him, the weariness had eased from his face and he was asleep, his stubble-darkened cheek resting on her breast. She stayed where she was, cradling him until early morn when he awoke enough to stumble to his bed.

SHE had come to some conclusions. The woman he rescued from her nighttime wandering had to be Countess Gerta; it fit with her madness, or weakness, or whatever it was. But why would Nikolas not just trust Elizabeth enough to tell her? He couldn't think she would betray that trust, after everything they meant to each other. Though perhaps that intimate connection emanated more from her than him. Was it all an illusion, then?

She stayed away from him that morning, which was not difficult, since he did not join the family for breakfast, nor for luncheon. Countess Gerta was in her own room, "ill" it was said, which bolstered Elizabeth's conviction that it was she who slipped out at night. But was it madness that sent her out into the cold and the danger of the woods, or did she slip out to meet a lover? And yet Count Delacroix was right there, inside the castle, and they could be together whenever discretion allowed.

Did she have another lover, then? If that was her the first night Elizabeth had arrived in the castle, that would explain her nakedness, but not why Nikolas was chasing her as if she were a deer. The mystery was infuriatingly obscure.

That afternoon as Elizabeth sat in the lady's library, reading a new book that had just arrived, she heard the sound of male voices shouting. She raced out and down to the great hall, and there, again, was a group of villagers. This time she could understand every word they said as they confronted Nikolas.

"This is the skin of a wolf we caught last night on the edge of your property, Count von Wolfram," the eldest man said, tossing down a bloody silver fur pelt that left a streak of dark red as it skidded across the marble floor to Nikolas's feet.

Elizabeth gasped; was that the skin of the wolf she had seen the night before? She hid by a pillar, listening and watching.

"What were you doing in my woods?" Nikolas thundered. "I told you truly, if I caught any one of you there I would flay you alive and nail your hide to the church door."

"But you did not catch us, we caught the wolf!" That was the mayor, Elizabeth now knew, an older man with gray hair beneath his knitted cap. He had not even removed his hat as he should have before his liege. His sneer was insolent and bitter. "We told you, if you do not let us patrol, we will do it anyway! Our dogs will be with us, and we will do what we must to protect our women and children from the awful teeth of these beasts."

A terrifying thought occurred to Elizabeth: when Gerta slipped out at night, Nikolas was afraid she would be caught by wolves, or perhaps even worse, caught or killed accidentally by the terrified townspeople. Pity overwhelmed her and she slumped down by the pillar. Poor Nikolas, caught between his loyalty to his sister and the terror of his subjects. No wonder he looked haunted.

All day she pondered; she had heard that the full moon exacerbated some people's madness. Perhaps that was behind the tension in the house that she now knew to associate with the cycle of the monthly full moon. How little she knew, though. Was the moon truly full for more than one night? And why did it act as such an irritant?

And who else in the castle knew about Gerta's affliction, that the entire household should become so filled with unease? Did some of the serving staff know? And how much of the family was aware of the countess's nocturnal ramblings? Not Charlotte, she thought, though she could not be certain.

Questions plagued her, wretched curiosity blended with a real concern for the poor woman she had initially disliked but now pitied from the bottom of her heart. If madness was her curse, why could they not manage to keep her confined, since escaping was such a problem and such a danger? One person to watch her was all it would take, for she was slim and frail.

If any of Elizabeth's musings held the truth, then she glimpsed it only faintly, like an image seen beyond smoky glass.

After the men left, she did not see Nikolas all day. Whether he was avoiding her, or if he was just taken up with his troubles and busy, she did not know. But how could she demand of him when he so clearly had deep troubles? The responsibility of those tribulations was wearing him down, she had felt it in his anxious restlessness, had seen it in the grooves that were beginning to band his high forehead. She was beginning to wonder if perhaps she had discovered the real reasons behind his refusal to marry. His deep sense of duty had taught him that there was no room in his life for more than he already tended.

Night fell, and the rhythm of the household slowed. The drawing room had been sparse, populated by only Count Delacroix, Bartol Liebner, and the Countess Adele, all of whom had retired early with murmured excuses of exhaustion. Elizabeth, restive and worried, had spent some time in the yellow parlor, wondering if she was accomplishing anything with Charlotte or if it was all just a futile exercise.

Finally, though, she decided to retire and quietly slipped along the corridor toward the great hall and up the stairs up to her room. But as she entered, she heard footsteps; she hesitated by the pillar and saw Gerta von Holtzen, silvery blond hair exposed, slip out the front door.

Nikolas, Elizabeth thought immediately—*he should be told*. But if she stopped to find him, Gerta might be lost in the woods forever. Undecided, she glanced around her but saw no ne, nor was there a single sound. If she screamed or yelled, people would come running, but then . . . then the secret of Countess Gerta's odd nighttime perambulations would be known, and Nikolas had worked so hard to conceal her weakness. She raced after the countess to the front door, tore open the huge oak portal, and gazed out. "Countess Gerta," she shouted into the wintry night as the figure retreated. The woman stopped for one second, and then she ran.

Shivering but determined, Elizabeth could not risk losing her and ran after her. She was fast; she would catch her before she got to the woods and stop her. Then she would know the answer to the mystery: madness or intrigue? No time for a cloak, no time even to tell anyone or to get word to Nikolas . . .

She raced across the snowy lawn, down the slope, slipping and freezing, and across the gravel lane. Gerta was swift, certainly, but still, if Elizabeth could just get to her before she entered the forest . . . and yet the race was a losing one. The woman ahead of her was truly fleet of foot, like a doe, dancing through the feathery mounds of moonlit snow to the dark edge of the forest, and then she plunged in and disappeared.

Chapter 20

ELIZABETH ALLOWED herself one moment to curse roundly, in language she had learned but never used, but then gathered her courage like a mantle around her and plunged in after the countess. The twists and turns of the countess's flight were like the twists and turns of her life lately, Elizabeth thought briefly, her breath becoming ragged and the wet cold numbing her feet. "Curse these impractical shoes," she muttered, gasping, flexing her frigid toes.

If it were not for the fact that she had seen the bloody pelt of the forest's wolf with her own eyes, she would have sworn that she could see the animal following her. She stopped and stared through the dusky thicket of naked gray trunks, her breath puffing in clouds of fog. There could only be one hunting animal in a forest, couldn't there? Wouldn't the dead beast have run off any others? Predators were by their very nature solitary creatures.

She moved on, trying to find the path. Damn and damn again! She had lost sight of the woman. Elizabeth stopped and realized her ragged gasps for air were echoed by a rustling close at hand. Was it the countess? She twisted and turned around, trying to see in the dim reaches of the wood, but she was at a spot in a fringe of conifers where moonlight, even as brilliant as it was on this snowy night, did not penetrate easily. It was dark and dank, the smell of snow and bark and pine filling her nostrils. Where was she?

A rush of air, and something brushed her cloak, falling at her feet. She cried out and jumped, but it was just a clump of snow fallen from one of the fir trees. Whimpering, she fell to her knees. What was she going to do?

A howl reached Elizabeth's ears and she sobbed, terror replacing worry. Wolf? How was that possible? And yet . . . she listened, stuffing down the fear and trying to be rational. The sound was not like the wolf howl she had heard the first night. It was . . . it was higher, and with a keening edge like . . . like a woman's wail of pain.

It was human!

She staggered to her feet and followed the sound, all the while castigating herself as mad, and heard it again as she came to a large clearing where the snow was well-trampled and the moonlight lit the opening. There, in the middle of the trodden snow, was Countess Gerta. Elizabeth breathed a deep sigh of relief and took one step forward, but then the countess threw back her head and let out a long, keening howl while she undid her cloak and flung it to the ground.

"Countess," Elizabeth said, starting forward.

The woman turned and Elizabeth fell back, alarmed by the distorted expression on her pale pixie face. The countess tore at her dress collar and howled again, the sound echoing in the woods.

Taking a deep breath and swallowing back her fear, Elizabeth approached, holding out one hand as one would to a growling dog, and speaking in what she hoped was a calming voice. "Countess . . . please, Countess Gerta, let me help—"

The woman lashed out with crooked bare fingers and snarled wildly, her bloodshot eyes starting out from their sockets. She tore at the sleeves of her dress, rending one with a terrible ripping sound.

"My God, what is wrong with you?" Elizabeth muttered, almost weeping with vexation and horror.

"She is ill," a voice said, behind her.

Elizabeth whirled. "Nikolas! Thank God you're here; help her!"

"I have every intention of doing so," he said quietly. "As I always do." He approached his sister, talking soothingly, but she snapped and growled even at him. He wrapped her in his arms and she struggled wildly, then abruptly it was over and she fainted. He mantled her in her cloak and lifted her in his arms. "Come with me, Elizabeth," he commanded, but she was already following him.

What a strange parade they were, she thought, following him through the woods, across the lawn, and towards the castle edge. He followed the path along the base of the castle to a small wooden door.

"I suppose I should never risk coming in the front door," he said and grunted as he squeezed through the door and down a narrow corridor with his burden. "You caught Cesare and I at that once, carrying Gerta through the great hall."

Wordless, she followed him along one of the dark secret passages, then up stairs—many, many stairs—him grunting with his burden on the precarious stone steps as they made their way to a room. He pushed open a panel and staggered into a tiny room with his burden.

Mina shot forward and pulled the woman from his arms, carrying her to a narrow bed by a humble hearth. It was some kind of small dressing room or servant's closet. Elizabeth looked around herself curiously but did not recognize the room as one she had ever been in or seen.

"How did she get out this time?" he demanded of the silent servant, who had already begun to strip the wet clothes from the unconscious countess. When he got no response, he grabbed Mina's shoulder and she shrugged him off, then made some gestures, pointing to her own head where a red welt marked her forehead.

"I'm sorry," Nikolas said and patted Mina's shoulder. She gave him an enigmatic look and then went back to her business.

"Come," Nikolas said to Elizabeth. "You are shivering, too, and freezing." He grasped her shoulder and guided her back through the secret door and through the maze of passageways to her own room. Once there he sat her down near her fire after stirring it to life, then pulled off her sodden slippers and stockings and chafed her feet.

"Tell me," Elizabeth said, staying his hands and gazing down into the weary gray eyes she had come to love. She knew what haunted him now, and she felt so sorry for him. Perhaps it would help if he was able to talk about it.

He retrieved a blanket from her bed and wrapped her in it, then sat down on the floor at her feet. Silent for a long time, he finally spoke as Elizabeth almost slept, she was so weary. But his tale awoke her.

"The death of her husband and her terrible time bearing the twins did something to Gerta. She was well before that happened . . . or at least I think she was. I wonder now, for Hans brought her back here to calm her, he said. But she always was . . . nervous; I thought then that he just meant that."

"When did this . . . this awful delusion start?"

"A couple of years ago. She . . . oh, Elizabeth," he said, hanging his head. "She thinks she transforms into a werewolf. All the old stories have infiltrated her poor weak brain, and she really believes it. Thus, at the full of the moon she goes into this . . . this trance, and escapes."

He laid his head on her lap, his hair a mass of dark curls that glowed with threads of silver among the dark. He was wearing himself out in the service of his family, she thought, tenderly stroking his great shaggy head. "My God, Nikolas, how terrible this is for you. But can you not . . . confine her somehow?"

"I will not use restraints," he said, gazing up at her with a fierce light in his dark eyes. "She is not an animal; she is my sister."

"I don't mean restraints," she said with a soothing tone that calmed him. "I mean locks. Bolts on the door."

"That is what we have always done. That small room is her prison, to my shame, when she is in this state." He bowed his head once again. "I have never wished to distress my poor, poor sister, but as the moon waxes full she becomes ill, feverish, agitated, and I have always used that . . . that illness as an excuse to have her looked after by Mina in that tiny closet. I thought it secure; until recently it sufficed, and we were able to confine her during this time with a lock on the door and the ministration of Mina, who is fiercely loyal and utterly dependable. And we—Uta, Adele, and I—could conceal her weakness from the rest of the family with tales of fever or frailty. It has long been known that she is not well. But . . . something has changed. The delusion has deepened, and she is becoming more clever. Even through a bolted door, and tonight, even past a wary guard, she escapes." He sighed. "It started to worsen a few months ago. That was indeed my sister and myself you saw as you arrived at Wolfram Castle; Gerta had escaped that evening and gone farther than I would ever have thought possible. She had wandered far afield and I had to chase her down on horseback. I was afraid she would freeze to death before I found her! I am only fortunate that in her madness she returns to the same spot again and again."

"How terrible that the old folklore has transformed in her mind into this . . . this delusion."

He nodded. "But it is a powerful hallucination, defeating every attempt at reason I have made. She thinks . . . once she is in her right head she truly thinks she became a werewolf in her trance. I have tried reason, I have tried ridicule, but the idea remains. And she . . . she enjoys the idea of it, the power, the thrill of becoming the animal of our family's lore. Even when she is quite well, during the waning moon, I think she still glories in her secret knowledge. This I do not know how to defeat. How will it end?"

"Nikolas, I'm so sorry," she said, her voice gentle as she touched his hair.

He looked up at her, his cheeks ruddy in the firelight. "Elizabeth, no matter what, you must promise me you will not go into the forest again. There are truly wolves there!"

"But . . . but the villagers killed it."

"They are pack animals, and there are many more. In the nighttime it is their forest. Undisturbed, they are harmless, but confronted, if they think they or their offspring are in danger . . ."

She shivered. "I followed her tonight because I saw her as she left, and I thought I could catch her before she entered the forest."

"Please, do not do that again." He reached up and squeezed

her hand. "A wolf, though not violent left alone, will defend one of its pups, or its mate, to the death."

"Rather like you," she said, petting his head and kissing him. "I think you and those wolves have much in common."

"Come to me, Elizabeth," he said, standing and pulling her up. "My sister will sleep the rest of the night now, and into the day. After one of her delusions she always falls into a kind of faint and is weak until the moon rises again."

"But Nikolas—"

"No," he said, wrapping his arms around her. "I need you tonight, Elizabeth . . . please. No more talk. Just hold me."

She hesitated only a second and then whispered, "Come to my bed."

They lay together and she kissed him deeply, wishing she could tell him all she felt, all she wanted, but knowing that this night he needed just to be held close by one person who would not demand anything of him. He fell deeply asleep and so did she, but he was gone from her bed when she awoke the next morning.

Fanny brought in tea, but Elizabeth lay in bed staring up at the coffered ceiling and ornate depiction that centered it, a painting of cherubs and heavenly messengers.

"Miss . . . will you be going down for breakfast?"

Rousing herself from her reverie, Elizabeth swung her legs over the side of the bed and shivered wearily. She met the girl's gaze and realized that Fanny knew that Nikolas had been there. Her stare was wide-eyed and wondering. Once again Elizabeth was in the position of being involved with a man and having the servants aware of it. They likely whispered the gossip in the servants' hall.

"Yes, I will be going down for breakfast. Thank you, Fanny."

The girl left, and Elizabeth collapsed back on the bed. She couldn't hide it from herself any longer. Love for Nikolas coursed through her veins with every drop of blood. She curled into a ball, holding her pillow to her stomach. How was she going to continue to face him day after day, knowing that he didn't feel the same, knowing that her love was doomed to remain unrequited?

He cared for her, she could feel it in his touch, but love . . . did he even have that to give? He had never asked anything from her, nor had he ever promised her anything. While giving unconditionally to her, he held himself aloof.

Why? She frowned, arose, and began to dress. He cared for her and he was physically attracted for her. She had never met a man so perfectly formed to be a husband and a father, and yet he claimed family responsibilities kept him from marrying. As unreasonable as that seemed to her, he clearly believed it. She now knew that those family responsibilities included the care of a sister descending into madness. That was a burden indeed, and she could understand his weary resignation in the face of it.

But what kept him from consummating his illicit relationship with her? The fear of getting her with child? When had that ever stopped a man from taking what he wanted? Perhaps he was that rarest of beings, an honorable man, the kind her mother had sworn did not exist.

And yet . . . perhaps his reticence to go beyond what they had already done together was best. If he was simply incapable of loving her as she had come to love him, then making love could only add to her pain when the inevitable parting arrived. She had to know the truth. With her feelings engaged, she would not let him simply push her away anymore. She would have an explanation.

"GERTA is sleeping peacefully still, nephew," Uta said, groping for Nikolas's hand.

"Good. I suppose Mina has told you that Elizabeth knows all . . . or almost all, now?"

"Yes. You should have told her all of this long ago instead of going to her room every night and diddling with her. She is not a pet: she is a woman of strength and intelligence."

Nikolas grimaced in impatience as his great aunt took his

hand and squeezed it hard. "Easy to give such sage advice," he muttered.

"Do not be impertinent with me," she said, her imperious voice still steady, despite her years. "Did you think I did not know? Of course I know. I know everything. Katrina and I are in agreement; you should marry Elizabeth Stanwycke."

"You of all people in this household know why I cannot marry her."

"I know why you *think* you cannot marry: you are a great fool."

He jerked his hand away and stood. He would not be called a fool in his own house, even by someone he venerated as he did his great-aunt.

"Do not pout because I dare to call you a fool," she said, gazing up in his direction. "I think you a fool about a great many things. You think you are the only one who can care for this family, the only one who can set to right the wrongs of a generation. You are crippling them all by trying to carry their weight. Let them aid in their own salvation; let them shoulder their own burdens."

"If they were truly their own burdens, perhaps I would, great-aunt," he said carefully, tamping down his anger at the old woman's interference. If anyone had earned the right to give him advice, it was her. "But this is up to me to do. I will brook no opposition on this point."

"Fool," she muttered. "Never was there a greater fool than a man who believes that only he is capable of saving his family from destruction while they do nothing to aid themselves." She brooded for a moment, but then said, "Gerta will require watching again tonight. I am going to have her in this room with me, for I do not trust the lock on the dressing room anymore; it seems to melt away in the face of her madness. If I were as superstitious as people think me, I would say it was unnatural how that happens every time. But I think that it is just that she is getting more crafty and cunning with every cycle. And I am going to give her laudanum, no matter what you say."

"I will not have my sister stupefied with drugs," he said, his voice deliberately calm. No one would do that to her, he had sworn to himself and to heaven.

"You will not have her drugged, you will not have her restrained! You truly believe only you know what is best for her."

"And what if that is so?"

She was silent for a long minute, her head bowed and lace cap askew, and Nikolas began to think she had fallen asleep, but she roused herself and said, "No, no, I know that you are correct this time. I will not give her laudanum. I do remember her reaction last time, and how ill she became. Despite appearances, Gerta is dear to me, if only . . . if only she could be again the girl she once was." Her weary old voice broke.

Nikolas knelt down again and took Uta's hand, squeezing it gently, touched by the tears that rolled out from under the wrinkled eyelids. "The best we can do is care for her."

"Nikolas," the old woman said, urgency in her tone. She reached out and touched his face with her crooked, stubby fingers. "You must not give up every hope of a normal life for yourself, for the sake of taking care of your family. You deserve a family of your own, and—"

He stood and said, "No more interference, aunt. I will do what I see fit."

"Stubborn. You will never listen to me!"

"Reflect but a little and you will understand my choices."

Miraculously, the next couple of nights were quiet. Gerta was passive through much of the night, only occasionally evincing a need to go out. This was restrained by constant vigilance, a necessity he was grateful for, as it left him little time to commune with Elizabeth.

But inevitably the full moon passed.

He visited the drawing room after dinner as the waning moon glowed pale and weak over the snowy landscape. With the enormous crimson curtains drawn and the fires burning merrily, the drawing room had a cozy and homely look for which his weary mind and body were starved.

Adele was playing chess with Maximillian; with Gerta still too weak to join them, she was the proud possessor of his company and glowed, if such a harsh, austere woman could ever be said to glow. Christoph, looking happier than he had for a while, played the piano with Melisande, while Charlotte looked on, her expression a trifle melancholy but not depressed.

Elizabeth, in an emerald gown he had never seen her wear, was by the fire reading.

"Is the book satisfying?" he asked, leaning down and whispering into her ear. He took the chair opposite her and drank in her beauty.

"It is." She had stiffened and offered him not one smile.

"Have I . . . offended you?" he asked. He wondered if his troubled family life was finally taking its toll on her.

"No, of course not," she said, reaching out her hand and then hastily drawing it back as she glanced around the room.

He understood the impulse. With the growing closeness he felt for her, it was difficult to restrain the urge to touch her hand or her arm, to murmur an endearment, to offer a caress. He touched her hand briefly and said, "Would you . . . would you come to my room tonight?"

"Only if you will talk to me."

"Instead of other things?" he said, gently jesting.

Her lip quivered and she looked away. Damn, but he wanted to cradle her in his arms and kiss her! He wanted to tell her that she deserved more than him, deserved better, and that there were a thousand men who merited her affection more than he . . . but not one who needed it more. And if he was to be fair to her, he could tell her none of that. Nothing that was in his heart. It would only hurt her when their association inevitably came to an end.

"As . . . as well as other things," she said, her tone breathy. The pulse in her neck quickened.

He carefully controlled his own breathing, for her intimation was that that night, they would again engage in love play, and he had plans for her. "Come to me after midnight," he said, "and we will talk . . . and other things."

BATTLING her doubts, trying to decide how to confront him about his reluctance to admit any feeling for her beyond desire, Elizabeth fled through the secret passages, her heart thumping like a military tattoo.

As she eased herself into his room and saw him standing bare-chested by the fire, his head down, his profile lit by the glow, she again felt the suffocating wave of tenderness mingled with despair. She knew now that it wasn't the same as it was with John. Her feelings for that fellow had been driven by loneliness and lack of respect for herself and her autonomy. The love she held for Nikolas was for his innate worth, his decency, and the heart beneath his breast, a heart devoted to the care of his family. Sure now of her own strength, she respected his and loved him deeply.

Would there ever be any room in his heart and life for her?

She ran to him and flung herself into his arms and he lifted her from her feet, carried her to the bed, and kissed her, covering her with his body. Her heart sang out with love and joy as he covered her mouth and kissed her tenderly. They lay together on the bed and twined themselves in each others' arms.

"Nikolas," she said, gazing at him.

"Mhmm?"

"Your aunt told me that once, long ago when you were traveling, you wrote to your brother that you intended to marry. Whatever became of that girl?"

He grimaced. "I was so young, Elizabeth! Young and green. It was while I was in Italy. I had just gone there; Cesare was with me. I met him at university and engaged him as a tutor and traveling companion, for he is very knowledgeable about the world. She was . . . a woman I met there, in Italy."

"That tells me nothing," she said, hoping to pry from him why he was once ready for marriage but now considered it impossible.

He stared at the ceiling and sighed. "Why must women always know about their predecessors?"

She was silent. It hurt to imagine him ready for marriage to someone else, when he would not, or could not, offer her the same. Resting her head on his chest, she stared up at his chin and throat, the pulsing throb at the base strong and steady.

He sighed and glanced down at her. "You want to know, don't you?" When she nodded, he sighed again and said, "She was very beautiful and much older than I. I was nineteen. I believe she was thirty-five or -six. Though I didn't know it at the time, she was a courtesan."

"How could you not know that?"

"As I say, I was young. And she never treated me like a patron. She never asked me for jewels or teased me to pay her accounts. She just . . . just taught me much about women."

"Oh. But you wanted to marry her."

"I *thought* I did, Elizabeth." He rubbed a strand of her hair between his fingers and gazed into her eyes, his own a softer gray then she had ever seen. "It would have been a terrible mistake, for I was so young. It was like you with your fellow; I didn't know enough to know it would never do. There was never any risk, though. I did ask her, but she only laughed at me."

"Is . . . is that why you have vowed not to marry?"

"'What? No. Lord, no, Elizabeth. Do not bring that subject up, if you please."

He kissed her again to soften the words and they lay for some time, kissing, as their breath mingled. He undid her robe and tossed it aside and peeled the neckline of her nightrail back, raining soft kisses over her breasts as her nipples hardened under his expert handling.

"Nikolas!" she gasped, clutching his muscular shoulders, trying to resist his seductive power.

"Yes, Liebchen?" He continued to lavish attention on her.

"I . . . I wanted to talk," she moaned.

"And so we have, and so we will again. But not this moment."

He pulled her on top of him and she felt his hands snake up under her nightrail to caress her bare bottom.

"Nik . . . oh, Nik!"

"Do you trust me Elizabeth?" he whispered, still caressing her naked bottom and cradling her over his bulging erection until she thought she would scream with desire.

"Yes, Nik, oh, yes, I trust you." Perhaps now, she thought, surrendering to the blissful hope she had not even dared to entertain. Perhaps now he would make love to her completely, fulfilling needs and desires that had been building inside of her for weeks. The sweet release he always gave her was wonderful, but to be thoroughly satisfied she would need him inside of her.

"Then lay back on the bed . . . and trust me."

Breathless, she slipped off of him and lay back and waited. He got up, and her bare legs became chilled as he left her for a long few minutes. "What are you doing, Nik?" she called out, wondering if he was disrobing.

"Close your eyes," he said.

She obeyed, shivering with excitement mixed with fear. He lifted her and pulled her to the edge of the bed, so her legs dangled over. What would she feel next? Would he introduce it to her slowly? Would he give her time to become accustomed to it? But the sensation, when it came, was not what she expected. He parted her legs, and then warm water trickled down her thighs; his big hand began to caress her with soapy foam. "Nik!" she said on a gasp, "what are you doing?" She struggled to see.

"Stop! Do not move even the tiniest bit, my sweet."

Cold steel. And it scraped away at the hair between her legs. Mortified but resisting the urge to wriggle, she cried out, "What are you doing?"

He chuckled, a wicked, enticing sound that made her shiver with yearning. "You will see. It is a trick that lady of my acquaintance—the one we just spoke of, when I was but a callow and inexperienced youth—taught me. I learned much later, after she had regretfully sent me away, that she would ask select men to do this for her, and then she would allow them unexpected pleasures after, as you will allow me when I am done."

Swallowing back a quick and biting retort on knowledgeable courtesans, she stayed patient and still, her legs spread trustingly for him, afraid of what would happen if she didn't. Mortified as she was by how she must appear before him, her legs spread, her womanhood laid out for his view, she still found it intolerably exciting. She hoped it was as arousing to him as it was to her. Protecting her most delicate parts with his thick finger, he patiently scraped away every bit of hair, but at last he stopped and then patiently bathed her in fresh, warm water, his fingers fondling her, tickling her as he dabbed with a towel. Was he done at last? What next?

But then an unutterably delicious sensation filled her as a warm and probing entity caressed her most sensitive spot, tickling and then thrusting until she writhed with a fierce and dizzying need. His tongue! She gasped and cried out; it was hot and devouring, and her clean-shaven pubis was sensitive to the wet delight of being licked and suckled and finally entered by his tongue.

She gripped his hair and almost screamed, pleasure coursing through her body as she was flooded by the familiar euphoria multiplied many times over. He thickened his tongue, then softened it and lapped, then teased with the tip. She released his hair and stretched back full length, surrendering to sensation, shuddering as wave after wave ripped through her. As the waves receded and she became aware again, she felt his fingers touching her legs and bottom, his caressing fingers tickling the sensitive nubs of her nipples.

Weak and quivering as he slid up to her and she felt the pulse of his erection against her bare leg, she knew she could wait no longer. She gave him one long, wet kiss on his mouth, then boneless, lithe with sensuous delight, she slid down off the bed and knelt before him between his knees; he was fully naked and she kissed him tentatively, the unexpected velvety texture of his thick shaft surprising her with its eroticism. She felt his whole body go rigid, and he cried out "No! Elizabeth, no." But she would not be denied. She might not know what to do, as he clearly did, but she would do what she wanted and see what happened.

She laved him with her tongue. He tried to sit, but she pushed him back. "Nik, please," she whispered. "Let me."

He calmed, though his whole body quivered, and she inhaled his musky scent, touching the shaft, feeling the thickness of it with her hand and then sliding her tongue all the way from the nest of curls from which it sprang down to the end, finally taking the knob in her mouth as he thickened more, pearly droplets oozing from him in his excited state. She could feel a pulse in his engorged member and experienced a joyous sense of command over this powerful man as he lay quiescent and trembling under her ministrations, moaning her name and crying out endearments, drifting into hoarse and guttural German, using words she could not understand but fully comprehended.

She knelt before him and stroked him with her mouth, letting her hands run up under his bottom, feeling his muscles tense and relax as he struggled, holding back his inevitable release. Surrendering, as she knew he must, she was finally able to taste him, at least, if she could not have his length inside of her completely. His release was swift and wild, and he growled and howled with fearsome delight as she inexpertly licked and sucked and teased, doing what she hoped was right.

Later, in the dark, after tender ministrations on her part with a damp cloth and a bowl of water, she timidly asked if she had done things correctly. He chuckled hoarsely as he stretched his naked body across his big bed like a great, happy cat.

"I do not think any woman could do that particular thing badly, but I must say, your adorable enthusiasm more than made up for your inexpert handling." He kissed her then, and as they twined together, naked at last under the covers, she felt his member, slumberous and thick, against her bare leg.

"I have so wanted to give you . . . release."

He sighed. "I hope, Elizabeth, that you did not just feel

some weight of obligation; I have never wanted you to feel some debt to me."

"No," she whispered. "It never felt like a debt. But when you . . . care for someone," she said, choosing her words carefully, "you wish to give them pleasure."

"You did do that. I do not think I have ever felt such . . . such exquisite passion in my entire life. I have no words to explain my feelings."

"You don't need to explain it. I'm so happy," she murmured. "Nik, I lo—" She stopped abruptly, fighting the urge to tell him her deepest feelings. Telling him now would change everything, and she did not want his memory of the tenderness of that night to be altered by a confession of love. Inevitably he would feel he was expected to reciprocate, and she wanted him, for once, to be able to have pleasure with no burden of expectation of return on his shoulders.

"Mmm?" he murmured. He kissed her neck, sleepily.

"I loved doing that. It . . . it pleased me, too, deeply."

He kissed her down to her breasts and fell asleep with his head cradled there, her fingers threaded through his thick hair.

Chapter 21

HIS VERY blood sang with joy in his veins through his morning duties and paperwork. He could not concentrate on anything, it seemed, and yet he felt more relaxed than he had in months. Though she had crept from his room before dawn, he had seen her at the breakfast table, and she had blushed as he stared at her, watching her lick honey from the corner of her mouth, ravenous for every last second of seeing her.

It was not the first time he had experienced that particular sensuous delight, but there was something profoundly special about it . . . different from any lovemaking he had shared with any other woman. What was it?

He sat at his desk and stared absently at the paper in front of him.

It was her . . . the expression on her face. In the glow of candlelight the night before, as she knelt before him, more powerful than her submissive pose would seem to suggest, he had caught a glimpse of her face. Her eyes were closed as she suckled and teased him, but her expression was . . . what was it?

It was as if . . . as if she was savoring him, tasting him, not just his body but his deepest self, and sweetly smiling as she gave to him; just the sight had made him feel . . . loved. He went cold and a shiver raced down his back. Was it possible? Could she . . . could she love him?

It had never occurred to him, and yet he knew she was fond of him. But what he had felt the night before from her was love . . . pure, sweet, unexpected, and unfelt before. Love shone in her eyes and beckoned him, like a warm light.

Caught between the heaven of her love and the hell of his life, he trembled, on a razor's edge of sanity.

His mind told him he must draw back—there was no truth in her love, for it was based on an illusion of what she thought he was—but his heart told him to take what he could, for he might never feel so blessed again.

"MA'AM, why do you all think Countess Gerta's condition is irreversible?" Elizabeth asked Frau Liebner as they sat together awaiting Uta. She had learned from the elderly countess that Frau Liebner knew all about the turmoil that went on during the full moon, and so she could speak of it openly. She was keeping her mind strictly on anything other than Nikolas, for she caught herself dreaming of him at every moment. Even through a difficult morning with Charlotte, she had not been able to chastise the girl for inattention when her own was so divided.

"It is progressing, this sickness. What could anyone do?"

"But doctors—"

"When she was young, she went to Vienna to see a doctor who said that she was frail and must be sheltered. Even then she was . . . difficult. Emotional. Unstable. Nothing like this, but of course it is getting worse." She shrugged. "It is simply how it is."

Elizabeth sat back in her chair and thought. What worried her was that the same things they said about Gerta when she was young also applied to Charlotte now. Was the poor girl doomed to live as her aunt did, eventually going . . . quite mad? Oh, she prayed it wasn't so. And yet there were days when Charlotte was completely normal. Whatever was bothering her was getting worse, though, it seemed. Christoph, too, was moody and unpredictable.

Perhaps . . . Elizabeth stopped, her eyes widening as she thought. Was Nikolas afraid that the instability in his family was inherited, and was that why he had decided he could not risk having a family? At that moment Mina carried Uta from the dressing room and gently set her down in her chair by the window. Uta, to cover her embarrassment—Elizabeth could tell the proud old woman disliked being seen carried—fussed with her shawl.

"Ma'am," Elizabeth said, touching her hand, "I hope you slept well?"

"Oh, I slept very well. Did you, young miss?"

There was an archness in her tone, and she and Frau Liebner both snorted in amusement. What it meant she could not tell, but just thinking about how she slept, wound in Nikolas's loving embrace, made her blush.

She was far too aware that morning, for she could feel the unfamiliar nakedness in her nether regions, and she was so sensitive that she felt the difference simply walking. She swallowed and tried to turn her mind elsewhere, but nothing worked. Nikolas . . . he was all she could think of. He was all she had ever wanted.

After some commonplace conversation she excused herself, thinking some outdoor exercise was in order. She invited Charlotte out for a walk, but the girl was closeted with her brother and would not move. Elizabeth descended to the great hall, dressed for a walk, but undecided as to whether she would go. The dogs worried her, and she wasn't sure she wanted to go out alone.

At that moment, Bartol Liebner strolled into the great hall from the serving area beyond. "Miss Stanwycke," he cried out. "How lovely to see you. Are you going out?"

"I was considering it. It appears to be a beautiful day, but . . . no one wishes to walk, and so perhaps—"

"Let me accompany you."

"Are . . . are you certain, sir?"

"I would be delighted," he said with a courtly bow, "to accompany so lovely a lady. It would be a great favor to me."

Muffled against the cold, they ventured out. Herr Liebner took her arm to support her, and they walked the perimeter of the huge castle, dwarfed by the stone walls but sheltered from the wind by their fastness.

"How are you finding your mission here, Miss Stanwycke?" The cold of the air had taken her breath away at first, but the exercise was welcome, and she soldiered on, glad of even the support of the older man's arm, for the wind was whipping up and becoming stronger. "It's not without its challenges. Charlotte is a delightful girl, but—"

"But too morose, yes, I know. I worry about the family often, miss."

"It's so wonderful that you care for them so much," she said, glancing over at him.

His balding head was wrapped in a scarf, but his lively black eyes were visible. "They are my life," he said simply. "They are everything to me."

"It must have been difficult, though, when you were young, to leave your family and come here."

"Ah, but I was coming with my sister, Maria, and she was the only one in my family who truly cared for me. The rest . . . they despised me."

"But why?"

He shrugged. "I do not know."

"But Frau Liebner . . . she married your brother, am I right?"

"Yes, but always she has disliked me, too, I feel. I fear my brother, Viktor, poisoned her mind against me. Have you never noticed? Has she never said anything?"

"No . . . I don't think so," Elizabeth replied. She thought about it. "No. Not at all."

"Ah, perhaps she begins to see my devotion to this family."

"Has she questioned it in the past?"

"Oh, yes, she has thought terrible things, that I wish to interfere. It is not my place, but she thinks I push."

"Oh." They walked on in silence for a while.

"It is just my worries for the family, for poor, frail Gerta." He shook his head and made a sound between his teeth.

She glanced at his expression. Did he know everything? Did others, despite Nikolas's circumspection, know the secret?

"You must have noticed how she is?" he continued. "Ill. Often ill. And . . . not quite right in the head. I suggested a doctor, but no, they are too proud to expose her to medical help. Always it must be kept quiet, and yet poor Gerta . . . how can they not get help for the dear girl?"

It was so exactly what she had been thinking that Elizabeth was astonished into silence. Was it true, though? Did pride alone keep Nikolas from getting help for his sister? He certainly hid her weakness, shielding her as best he could, and Elizabeth had thought of that as a loving gesture, but if it kept her from getting help—

The wolf dogs bounded out from the stable area and Elizabeth couldn't help it, she started back. They stopped in front of her and Bartol, snarling uneasily.

"Perhaps . . . perhaps we ought to go back," she said. The dogs, with their wolf faces and aggressive attitude, still worried her. They must not be out at night, she realized, for she had not been confronted by them when she went out with Nikolas to rescue Gerta.

"Ach, they are mere puppies," Bartol Liebner said, but he turned with her and guided her back the way they had come. "Have you had enough of a walk anyway, perhaps?"

She glanced at him and saw the beginning signs of weariness on his face and thought he might have asked more for his own sake than hers, so she said, "Yes, I think I have. But I appreciated your arm, sir."

"And I appreciate your kindness and beauty, miss. It has enlightened the days at Wolfram Castle. And we all see in Nikolas a difference."

"I beg your pardon?"

"Oh," he said, gasping, "I should have said nothing. I am so sorry! Forget I said anything at all, Miss Stanwycke."

Mortified by how far the gossip about her and Nikolas had evidently spread, she said not another word until they parted with mutually friendly words.

She had completely lost sight of her original stiff resistance to the count's charms, she thought, in a maudlin mood that afternoon. A few kisses, some petting, and she had lost her way, falling in love with a man unattainable by his own admission. But did it change anything? He evidently had no intention of marrying, and yet she had allowed herself to get entangled and become . . . well, his mistress in all but deed.

"I need to talk to him," she said to her reflection that evening as she undressed for bed. "I need to tell him this can't go on." As many times as she had made that resolution, and as many times as she had failed to keep it, she hoped to be strong, finally.

She slipped along the chilly passages one more time to his room and slid open the passage doorway. He had asked her to come to him, for he had a surprise for her, he said, and so she would. Perhaps for the last time, though. She must find the strength to regain her autonomy. If their lives were never to be merged, then their bodies should not be.

He was ready for her with twenty or more candles lit, and his "surprise," as he had named it, in the middle of the floor. Her eyes widened.

"What is that?" she asked, circling it.

It was large and copper, long and wide. He smiled as he watched her, knowing she had never seen anything like it, for he had had this made just for himself. "It is, my sweet, a bathtub, one made for two." He reached down and splashed some of the fragrant, steaming water, spattering her.

She stood by it and reached down. "It's so hot!" She swept her hand through the water. "Mmm, how lovely!"

"It is my own design," he said, smiling at her expression of joy at the warm water swishing through her fingers. His poor Elizabeth! He feared she had been often cold in the months since arriving at Wolfram Castle, but for this one night she would feel warm, if he had his way. And he intended to have his way. "The problem was in keeping this much water hot while enough was heated to fill it. So there is a basin at the bottom that holds heated stones, and it keeps the water warm much longer." He circled and took her hand, stroking her palm with his thumb. "As long as needed."

She looked at the tub and then up at him.

"Yes," he said to her unasked question. "Would you like to try it out?"

She closed her eyes and sniffed the steam. "Lavender.

How heavenly, Nik." She bit her lip and looked up at him, then squeezed his hand. "It's tempting. May I really? I . . . I shouldn't . . . I truly should not."

She was hesitant, and he worried he had taken her too far the night before. He must not expect as foregone what he wanted to pass, he thought. He must allow her to experience this with no pressure to go further than she had already gone, or even as far. She looked . . . frightened. He took her in his arms. She laid her head against his chest, by his heart. She loved to listen to it, she had told him, and it seemed to him the strength of the beat was a reassurance for her. "Elizabeth," he said gently, threading his fingers through her unbound hair, twisting the silk between his thumb and forefinger, "I promise you nothing will ever happen that is not your choice. I care about you very much. If you wish I will stay out of the room and you may bathe alone, or I will confine my participation to washing your back. And other parts." He could not resist adding the last part.

She flushed an adorable pink. "You're wicked," she said breathlessly. She wrapped her arms around his waist and gazed up into his eyes, her own the blue of the Aegean. "No, Nik, I . . . I'd like to be with you, but . . . but just kissing and touching. I . . . I can never do the . . . the other."

The other. Making love. He had thought her wishing his advances, perhaps even waiting for them—or at least that was the sense he had had the night before—but either he had been misled by his own desires or she had doubts that were taking a toll on her attraction. He felt desolate, and though a fragment of his disappointment was in knowing he would not see fulfillment that night, he felt pain for her and the deep hurt she had suffered when a man so carelessly broke her heart and deserted her, for he had the sensation that her reluctance that night was due to a reawakening of her old pain. He would cheerfully plunge a dagger in that man's heart for hurting her thus.

And yet, if she truly was fond of him, if perhaps she even loved him, what was he going to do but break her heart anew?

Wretchedly confused by his own warring emotions, he could only let it go for this one night.

"It shall be exactly as you wish, Elizabeth," he whispered.

He undressed her, taking his time with her robe, and then slipping her nightrail up over her head, delighting in the warm tones of her lovely alabaster skin flushing to pink underneath, the rosy nipples hardening at the rush of cool air. Where he had shaved the night before was soft and sweetly folded like a tight, secretive bud, concealing intimate delights that made him hunger and ache. He took her hand and guided her to a stepstool he had placed by the side of the copper behemoth and watched her delicately walk up and climb in, relishing this candlelit sight of the curves he had come to know so well by touch. As she sank into the water, her breasts bobbed enticingly.

She sighed and closed her eyes. "Oh, Nik, this is heavenly!"

He swallowed hard and caressed her neck. "May I . . . may I join you?"

When she looked alarmed, he continued, "You have my pledge. I shall wash your back, but no more. You know me, Elizabeth. Trust me." *As you did last night,* he finished in his mind.

She nodded shyly.

He pulled his clothes off with trembling hands and climbed in with her. She floated on her stomach, her arms over the back of the tub and her head in her arms; her rounded bottom rose above the milky water like a pale ripe peach. He slid his hands up her legs to her hips, and she moaned softly as he soaped her bottom, taking exquisite care, enjoying the ripeness of her curves and how her pale skin flushed as he touched and caressed.

The room was in darkness except for the twinkling light of candles softly glowing and the gentle radiance of the firelight; he felt a peace in his heart, a deep welling of gratitude for this woman and this moment. Even if they never made love, he would remember this as the sweetest of nights.

He moved onto his stomach, too, and floated between her

legs, squeezing her delectable bottom and nipping one plump cheek with his teeth. She squeaked a protest but then splashed and giggled. He was enchanted, having never seen her so relaxed and languid.

He nipped again and circled her hips with his hands, lifting her slightly above the water, nibbling both cheeks and teasing and kissing her. When he let one hand drift down her belly in front to caress her between her thighs, he could feel how ready she was for his touch. His arousal ached and throbbed, but he kept his mind on his task, and that was to surround her in love and safety. Never would he be one to use her when she trusted him most. He pushed from his mind the fear he had of ultimately having to betray that trust, in the need to take care of her in the moment.

Drifting and floating over top of her, his hard shaft slipping between her legs, he felt her jerk nervously.

"Do not worry," he whispered into her ear. "I cannot help what I feel, but it will stay so, and I will take no liberties." He nipped at her earlobe.

She sighed, and her body sagged into the water under his weight. Concentration was required, because it seemed to him her instinct was to entice him. Her legs parted, and with every motion his swollen rod nudged her fastness just behind where he tickled and rubbed, his fingers delightfully aware of her vulnerable nakedness and the softness of her skin. He kissed her neck and felt her body warm and plump under his touch, ready and willing to accept him into her.

Surely she would like it, and maybe she needed urging. Perhaps she needed him to take command before she could allow herself to enjoy what nature made for them to share. After all, he had taken command the night before, and he remembered how joyous was her acceptance of his advances. Beyond her first embarrassment at the intimacy of his attentions had lain a sensual submission to his tutelage.

He shook his head, clearing the fog of lust that overtook him, deliberately cleansing his mind of such seductive fantasies. He had been unwise to put himself in such a position, just inches away from delirium. She arched her back and moaned, as he touched her, and he felt her edging toward climax, her buttocks pushing up urgently as she bobbed and pushed down onto his fingers.

She writhed wetly, crying out, "Yes, Nik, please . . ." as she pierced herself on his thick fingers, two inserted as he teased the sensitive nub with his thumb.

He spread her wider with his fingers and his arousal fit itself to her plump cleft, nudging her open as she reached satisfaction. Her invitation seemed clear, the raised bottom, the spread legs, and he surged over her, the mist lowering over his sight and reason, his instincts flooding his body with heat even as his organ was engorged with blood and seed. Kissing wasn't enough. He needed to taste her, her tender skin beneath his lips inviting. He bit her neck gently and her back arched more in response, changing her position slightly, ready for mating.

He thrust into her and groaned aloud, feeling her velvet slickness sheath him, and he bit harder, pulling out and stroking in again, almost crazed with the need to fill her, to command her . . . to claim her as his woman. He muttered endearments in German, over and over, telling her of his need for her.

"No!"

The word bit into his consciousness and he groaned. But he pulled out fully, his organ pulsing and swollen. He doubled over for a second with denied need but then kissed her shoulder where he had left a red mark. "Elizabeth," he whispered, shaking with the urgency of his desire. "I am so sorry, my dearest . . ."

"No," she whispered, turning under him in the water. "No, don't apologize." She reached up and covered his mouth with one finger while she stared into his eyes. He hovered over her, hope in his dark eyes, yearning in his expression. "Don't say another word, Nik."

She could still feel a throbbing within her where he had been and she felt empty, unfulfilled, desolate now that he had withdrawn. She ached to be filled again, stretched to surfeit with his delicious thickness, for there would never in her whole life be another moment like this one. What was life, if it was lived in safety? Her decision was swift, and she would allow no possible future regrets to taint this sweet moment. She pulled him down and he floated between her legs, gazing up at her, his chin resting on her wet stomach, the bathwater lapping at his jaw. "Not from behind," she said, staring into his eyes, sending him the message. She framed his face, pushed back the dark wet curls off his broad forehead and kissed it. "Not like an animal, Nik."

As she watched, he began to playfully tongue her navel. She giggled and he licked her wet belly and then moved up to her breasts. Closing her eyes and stretching her arms above her, over the edge of the tub, she felt his tongue rough on her nipples, and they pebbled hard under his laving. He suckled, drawing each one into his mouth, leaving it pink and hard, erect.

"Yes," she moaned, "face-to-face, Nik." His arousal nudged against her as he moved up and covered her mouth with his. She spread her legs wide, helpless against the wave of need, convinced against her more reasonable mind. "Yes," she whispered into his hair. She pulled him up and kissed his ear, inhaling his musky scent, murmuring, "Come home to me."

His hands cradled her bottom and he fitted himself to her, then pushed in, slowly, his thick stiffness countered by her swollen, sensitive softness. She watched what she could see of his face, riveted by the ecstatic expression on his face as he took her wholly, pushing fully into her body, water sloshing over the edge of the copper bath from his tightly controlled movement. The fit was strained, and she felt a moment of pain as her body adjusted to his swollen shaft, but then a tremor of resolute joy overwhelmed the pain and she sighed, spreading her legs wider and clasping her heels behind his back.

And then he began stroking, pushing in and withdrawing, thicker and heavier with each movement. She lost all thought or consciousness but the feel of him taking her beyond anywhere she had ever been, beyond care, beyond pain, toward a misty distant shore named ecstasy. It was so much more than mere touching and tickling and teasing and tonguing. Swept along by the fervor of his movements and rapture in his eyes as he gazed down at her, she felt the moment coming, and then, together, they clung to each other.

She cried out and her nails dug into his muscled back, raking his skin as he pushed into her and convulsed, his body doubling and bucking as he filled her with his release. She clung to him, her legs wrapped around him; her arms rigid she held on, weeping with shuddering joy as the water splashed and sloshed in the huge tub.

Then they drifted as the water became tepid finally and the divine madness of their mutual desire receded. They kissed, their mouths sealing, their limbs tangling and their bodies still joined in intimate union.

I love you, she thought, but dared not whisper.

I love you, he felt, but dared not believe.

Chapter 22

SHE STAYED in his room; after their loving bath, he dried her on the rug in front of the fire, carried her to his bed, and made love to her again, slowly, and after a few hours of sleep, as the morning light began to peek around the crimson curtains, again they found happiness together.

He fell back into a deep sleep as morning tiptoed into the room, and she watched him, his chest rising and falling, the dark whorls of hair still damp from his excitement. Delicately she patterned the hair and touched his nipples and lay her hand possessively on his hard stomach. It was intensely exciting to own this man, if only for a while. His vitality was enthralling, his energy flowing out of him and into her at his merest touch. His hard jaw was dark with stubble, and his sensitive lips, the site of so much delicious enjoyment, were slack and full in his repose. She bent over him, her hair falling over his chest, as she kissed his lips. He opened his mouth slightly, even in his sleep, and she kissed him deeply before slipping from his bed, her female region throbbing from his vigorous lovemaking.

Stiff from the sweetest exercise, she slipped back into her room just a moment before Fanny pushed the door open with her bottom and entered with morning tea. The girl gazed at Elizabeth with an odd expression on her face, perhaps startled that her mistress should be out of bed and near the wardrobe. Elizabeth carefully kept her gaze from the sliding panel.

"Good morning! Is it not a beautiful day?" Elizabeth said lightly.

"It snows again, miss," Fanny said primly, setting the tea down and opening the curtain.

"Yes, lovely, lovely." Elizabeth caught a glimpse of herself in the vanity mirror and what she saw startled her. There stood a woman very much in love, her cheeks rosy, her body voluptuous under her nightrail, her lips pursed in sweet happiness; she looked completely different from the pale and nervous wretch who had entered Wolfram Castle just two months before. She swallowed over a knot and stared. Was this young woman she saw in the mirror, so full of devotion and passion, doomed to dwindle when Nikolas inevitably deserted her as his family's needs took precedence?

She raised her chin. She would not! First, she would not lose him if she didn't have to. She was no feeble female—she was strong, and she loved Nikolas von Wolfram. Whatever he intended, he didn't know how powerful a force was a woman deeply in love.

But if he did desert her . . . then she would go on. She would not crumble in the face of it, but survive and thrive. She might never stop loving him, but she would never let it embitter her.

And yet even as she made that stern resolution, a part of her mind was plagued by uneasiness. How could she be thinking such thoughts? If he was the sort of man who could make love to her so thoroughly and then desert her, as she was contemplating, what did it mean? It meant, surely, that he was not the good, kind, wise man she thought him. And what did it say of her that she could not have full confidence in him, and yet had joyfully made love with him? She had sworn never to be touched again by a love that could not be returned, and yet she was giving herself wholly to a man who held secrets, who still reserved a part of himself back.

Was she doomed to always be so sure of him as long as he held her, and so uncertain when they were apart?

Fanny had slipped from the room and Elizabeth dressed, then descended for breakfast. That, in itself, was not easy, knowing that many in the household were speculating and gossiping about her relationship with Nikolas. But she was not a weakling; she would hold her head up high since she did not think she was doing anything wrong. Her religion told her she was sinning, but with the love she felt, and fearing it could never have the end she wished, she still felt justified in taking her meager allotment of joy, perhaps the only true joy that she would experience in her life. It was a compromise, yes, but what in her life had not been?

Her philosophy would be tested, she had no doubt, in the months ahead, as she learned her fate at the hands of Count Nikolas von Wolfram. Despite his determination not to marry, she felt, with him, the possibility of such great love could have no other end than matrimony. And more; she felt deeply that as much as her situation in life would be elevated by marrying a German count, she knew, too, how much she would be able to give to Nikolas. His own life would improve immeasurably by having someone who loved him and was devoted to him and who would put his needs first, as no one else, not even himself had or would do. She had hope, hope that her steadfast love would show him that marriage would give him all that he needed and thought he could never have.

And it was possible she was an even greater fool that minute than she had been when she let her first lover seduce her with promises of marriage. This time she had been seduced without even promises, and had hope without reason. Perhaps that was the very definition of a fool—to hope without reason.

She entered the breakfast room with her head held high, only to find her stern discipline unnecessary. Only Countess Adele was there, and she was distracted and worried, staring down at a letter on her plate. Elizabeth was ravenous, so she piled her plate with food, then sat near the countess. But after she sated the sharp edge of her hunger, she noticed the nerve jumping at the corner of the countess's eye.

"Ma'am . . . ma'am, is something wrong?"

Her hand trembling, Adele picked up the letter and held it between her index finger and thumb as if it contained poison. "This has come for Nikolas."

"Who is it from?" Elizabeth said, experiencing a prickle of fear at the countess's tone.

The countess did not answer for a long moment. "It is from . . . it is from Melisande Davidovich's father, I think."

"Miss Davidovich? I didn't even know her father was living. I mean, I assumed—"

"He is living, we just did not know where he was. Until now."

Elizabeth fell silent, unable to continue a conversation that would at some point force her to become an inquisitor or babble without sufficient information. The silence stretched. The countess sipped tea and watched the door as Elizabeth finished her meal.

But finally Nikolas strode in, with an exuberant stride. "Good morning, sister! Good morning Eliz— Miss Stanwycke."

Elizabeth blushed and smiled up at him, while Countess Adele looked stiffly disapproving. Her brother paid her no mind though and piled his plate high. "My hunger is sharp this morning."

"That seems to be common," Adele said, gazing at Elizabeth's nearly empty plate.

"Good appetite, Miss Stanwycke?" he asked with a sly smile. "Our air must agree with you. Or something must."

"Nikolas! Pay attention," the countess said. "I have a letter here; it seems to me that it is from Mikhail Davidovich."

He immediately halted, laid down his fork, and grabbed the letter. He ripped it open and read it. "Tiresome wretch," he said as he read. He threw the letter down with a deep sigh and began eating again.

"What does he say?"

Elizabeth, at sea and not knowing the source of tension concerning this Mikhail Davidovich, let her gaze alternate between Nikolas's face and his sister's. Nikolas finished chewing, slurped some coffee, and banged his cup down.

"I have to go."

"Not yet! Tell me what is going on," Adele demanded.

"That is what I mean. I must go to meet him. He is in Brandenburg, and he is in trouble."

Adele said something rapidly in German, but it was colloquial and quick and Elizabeth didn't understand it. She stood. "Count, if I am interfering in family business—"

"No, sit! Adele, English. Miss Stanwycke is to be trusted, I feel certain." He turned to her. "You will not repeat what you hear, will you?" He smiled.

"No, I won't."

"Good. I trust you, and I may need your help to keep Melisande calm through this; she seems to like you and feel comfortable with you, which is more than I can say for my sister, who frightens the poor girl, unfortunately." He turned back to his sister, whose expression was stiff with fury. "You know you do, Adele." He summoned his thoughts and said, "Mikhail is in Brandenburg, but the Russians are demanding he be held; he has sent me a plea to help, and for Melisande's sake, I must go, for I fear he will be used as a political pawn. There is a tension right now, with the Russian action in Poland, and France pressing to the south and west."

"What has Davidovich been doing?" Adele said, her tone icy.

Nikolas shook his head and said, "I am very much afraid he is up to his old tricks." He turned to Elizabeth. "Mikhail Davidovich is . . . a troublesome sort. He is, by his own representation, something of an art dealer. But what that often means is—"

"He is a thief," Adele said succinctly. "Do not be diplomatic, Nikolas, if you say you can trust her." She rose and continued. "I suppose you will go and rescue Davidovich yet again. I think you would do Melisande no harm if you let her father rot in prison."

"I cannot do that," Nikolas said, his expression mild but his tone steely. "I have sworn to Maximillian to protect her no matter what, and that, of necessity, extends to her father."

"Maximillian does not expect you to face danger—"

"Would you rather he go in my stead? I think not. There will be no danger for me in Brandenburg," Nikolas said.

"There is danger everywhere lately," Adele said, her voice harsh. "What we have heard from Mainz lately, about the French, and now Poland to the east is falling to the Russians."

She shook her head. "We live in dangerous times, hemmed in, surrounded. I will go and instruct Heinrich to pack; you will take him with you, of course?"

"Yes. And Cesare will go, as well. I may need his diplomatic skills. And he speaks a little Russian, whereas I do not."

"Just so you are back before"—Adele cast Elizabeth a swift look, and continued—"before too long."

Elizabeth knew she referred to the next full of the moon and Countess Gerta's unbalanced state. When she left the room, Elizabeth said, "Nik, must you go? Will it indeed be dangerous? Countess Adele seems to think—"

"Adele worries too much." He stood behind her and massaged her shoulders, glanced around, and dropped a kiss on the top of her head. "What I will miss most is you." He sat beside her and took her hands in his. "I had thought," he said huskily, "that tonight we would continue where we left things this morning. Will you come to me tonight?"

"Of course, Nik," she whispered, staring down at her plate.

A noise outside of the door sent them separate ways. Elizabeth waited for Charlotte in the yellow parlor, but when she did not come, she decided to go to the girl's room and find out what was keeping her. She rapped and a maid answered. Elizabeth struggled to make her desires known in German and slipped past the girl at the door, crossing the dim room to the bed where Charlotte lay, curled into a ball.

"Charlotte," Elizabeth murmured, touching her shoulder.

The girl moaned but did not answer.

"Charlotte!" Elizabeth said, shaking her shoulder. In German, she demanded of the maid, "What is wrong with your mistress?"

The maid huffily answered that nothing was wrong, the young mistress was just tired. She was often like this and for a few days would do nothing. That was what had happened the last time she was ill.

Elizabeth gazed down at the girl's pale, puffy face. So, when she had supposedly had a cold, she was just like this, in a state of lethargy. Her breathing was even and deep, her complexion waxy, but there seemed no danger of any sort. What could she do?

The house was charged with an energy as the master prepared for his trip to Brandenburg, a city some hundred miles to the east of Wolfbeck. It was unfortunate that he had been called away at such a time, for Elizabeth had hoped, over the following days, to be able to probe his mind and find the source of his resolution never to marry or have a family. They had taken a chance the night before, making love as they did, for though it was an unlikely time of the month for her to conceive, she knew it was not impossible. He was worth risking much for, but a child, when he had no intention of marrying? With the flush of passion waning, she fretted, and yet could not, in good conscience, accost him that day to question him.

The day wore on in tedious anxiety. Her worries piled one upon the other. Why, when he did not intend to marry, did he think it all right to risk conceiving a child with her? She knew him to be responsible; was he leaving that worry up to her? And what about Charlotte? Should Elizabeth mention to Nikolas her worries that the girl's symptoms were so very much like what she had heard of Gerta's first symptoms years before? Or had he already thought of that? And why did he refuse to have Gerta attended by a physician, when a specialist might be able to do something for the poor woman?

In that fretful state of mind the day toiled on, until finally it was time for the drawing room assembly, which Nikolas had asked everyone to attend, though he would not be at dinner that night. And so they gathered. Countess Adele hovered over her sister, who was well-wrapped, sitting in a chair, though she looked cheerful enough and her bright eyes darted from face to face eagerly. Elizabeth watched her, haunted by the memory of the same woman in the midst of her delusion, snarling and snapping as she rent her clothes from her. It was a sight she would never forget for the rest of her life, and yet Countess Gerta seemed to have no memory of those dark times in her lucid periods. Perhaps that was a kindness.

Christoph was there, his sullen presence a dark blot near

the calm beauty of Melisande Davidovich. Bartol Liebner and Count Delacroix played chess near the fire.

Nikolas entered, and all eyes were on him. He greeted everyone and then clapped his hands together as he paced near the fire. "I am forced by circumstances to go away for a week, perhaps ten days. I will be traveling to Brandenburg; Cesare will accompany me, of course. I expect you all, in my absence, to go on with your daily routine. Adele will be obeyed, please; consider her acting in my stead."

Christoph snorted, and Melisande put one gentling hand over his.

Nikolas turned his gaze on his nephew. "Did you have something to say?"

"Would you listen if I did? I doubt it."

"Say it," Nikolas commanded, his tone steely and his gaze never leaving Christoph's face.

"All right," the younger man said, straightening and strolling out from the shadows. "I think as the next male in line I ought to be head of the household in your absence."

"Do not be so absurd," Countess Adele blurted out.

Nikolas put up one staying hand. He strolled to meet Christoph in the center of the room, for all as if it were a duel they were about to conduct. "Give me one reason why you believe I should trust you with the care of this family."

Christoph, two patches of red burning on his pale cheeks, glared at his uncle. "I am your inheritor."

"Only if I say you are."

"But—"

"No! You have neither proved yourself nor earned my respect. You continue to act as a sulky child denied a toy, and I will not put the safety of this family in your inept hands. Adele will be in command. That is all." He whirled on one heel and strode to the door.

"You are a pompous ass!" Christoph roared.

In the wake of his insolence, the room got deadly quiet. Bartol dropped a chess piece and the sound reverberated in the silence.

Nikolas turned slowly and gazed at his nephew with contempt on his face. It was an expression Elizabeth hated, for she felt that though the division between Nikolas and his nephew seemed wide, he was making no effort to bridge it. As well as she felt she knew him, in that moment she didn't recognize her gentle, tender lover in the haughty, arrogant nobleman before them all.

"You will apologize to me now," Nikolas said, strolling back towards his nephew.

Christoph sneered, but behind the defiance was fear. "For saying the truth?"

"For your disrespect, which knows no bounds."

The hard stare between them was long, and Elizabeth could hear her own breathing. But finally, when it seemed one of them must flee or fight, Christoph broke his concentrated gaze, muttered a brief, *"Entshuldigung,"* and fled the room. Elizabeth watched Nikolas's face and was grateful that there was no triumphant sneer, just a sad acceptance.

He bid them all good night, shared a long look with her, and then left the room.

Soon after, she excused herself for the evening and made her way upstairs to her room. But she did not long remain there, heading to Nikolas's room by way of the secret passages.

"Elizabeth," he whispered, catching her to him and kissing her long and hard, then more softly.

They merely held each other for long minutes and then moved to the fire, he sitting down in a chair and she sitting in his lap, cradled against his chest. She warred in her mind with how to raise the multitude of topics about which she wished to speak with him, and whether to bring them up at all, considering he would be gone the next morning for a week or more. This night should be their farewell, not a discussion about serious matters. And yet, some things couldn't wait.

"There is something on your mind, Liebchen," he whispered in her ear as he stroked her back and shoulders.

She looked down into his eyes. "How do you know that?"

"How could I not? Even before we began, I watched you so often; I know the wrinkle of your brow, I know the pensive expression in the eyes, I know, too, the heart of you," he said, touching her breast with one finger. "Did my trouble with Christoph disturb you?"

She thought. "Yes. You seem a different man than the one I know in your dealings with your nephew."

"I am a different man. He is my heir. If something should happen to me, despite what I said, most would consider him the liege of this castle and of the people hereabouts. But he is weak, and I feel . . ." He shook his head and frowned, a dark lock of hair falling over his forehead.

She swept it back. "What is it, Nik?"

But he shook his head again. "I cannot say. It is all . . . dark suspicion, fear, worry. But not fair to share until I learn more from him. He does not trust me, and I do not understand what I have done to deserve his distrust."

"Nik, you treat him as if he is a child still!"

"Because he behaves as one!"

She clung to his neck as he moved in agitation. "Calm, Nik, calm!"

He settled back in the chair. "I apologize, my sweet, but it is troublesome to me. It does not concern you, though, so do not worry about it, please. I have something of utmost importance to ask you."

Her pulse throbbed. Something to ask her? "What . . . what is it, Nik?"

He touched her cheek tenderly, and his dark gaze caressed her. "This is very important to me, Liebchen. Will you keep a watch on my sister for me? I will be back well before the next full of the moon, but . . . what is it, Elizabeth?"

She had been expecting—or wishing for—something else and moved slightly in her disappointment, she realized, but she calmed her breathing and settled again. "You want me to watch Gerta? But she'll be fine until you're back, and Adele is here, after all."

"But Adele . . . she will have much to concern her in looking after the household. Do not worry, but just watch. Other than you and Adele, only Uta and my aunt Liebner know of

Gerta's condition, and I wish to keep it that way. The rest just know she is often not well."

"That is one thing I am concerned about, Nik. I was thinking . . . surely her condition is not incurable. Perhaps a physician—"

"Elizabeth, please stay out of those things which do not directly concern you."

She was silent for a moment but then climbed from his lap, feeling undignified and that the position no longer reflected her closeness to him. Perhaps that closeness was an illusion fostered by their intense physical attraction to each other. She stood before him and gazed down at his shadowed face and troubled expression, the set of his jaw stubborn and impassive. "Don't push me away," she whispered. "I say what I say because I care for you all."

"I know, Elizabeth," he said, holding out one hand and beckoning for her to come back to him. "But you have not been here all this time and you do not know—"

"Perhaps that's why I see more than you do," she said, keeping her distance. "That very fact that I have not been here long and so see things with a different eye. Haven't you noticed Charlotte's behavior of late? Doesn't it remind you of Gerta's as you have described it to me from a few years ago? And doesn't that worry you?"

He pushed his bottom lip out and reflected, but then shook his head. "No, no it cannot be. Impossible."

"Cannot be, or you just aren't willing to think it might be happening to your niece, too? Are not these kind of things hereditary? Isn't that what worries you, Nik?"

His face darkened, a red flush rising from his neck to his cheeks. "Elizabeth, I warn you—"

"Don't warn me, Nik. Don't treat me as if I have no stake in this!"

He rose and towered over her. As big as he was, she did not feel menaced but could see he was suppressing his anger. "You *have* no stake in this, so do not pretend you do," he said coldly.

It was like a knife to her heart, and the pain plunged

through her; he couldn't love her and say such a thing. Her joyful determination of the morning was replaced by desolation. So it was only a sexual relationship between them, after all, and nothing more. And as much as she wanted to persist, her sense of pride would not allow her to beg him for his love. What good was love grudgingly offered anyway? "I don't think I can stay," she said, and she wasn't even sure if she meant with him that night, or at Wolfram Castle.

"Elizabeth," he said, his expression distraught. "I'm sorry. Please stay; I need you."

"I don't think you really do," she said. She headed to the door. "You may want me, but you don't need me." She frowned, thinking perhaps he just didn't wish to acknowledge that he needed her, and it amounted to the same thing. "I'm through with creeping through the walls like a ghost, Nikolas. I'll go by way of the corridor, and gossip be damned!"

She fled down the hall, tears welling in her eyes and impeding her view. She lost her way, turned, and stopped, blinking away the wetness. Where was she? She doubled back, ascended some stairs, then realized she was in her own corridor near Countess Gerta's door, and there again was the high-pitched giggle and then the amorous sounds of a woman being loved.

Pain in her heart, she padded along the corridor, but her tears blinded her; she wandered past her own room and soon she stood in the hallway near the gallery wondering what to do. Where could one go to escape the pain of a breaking heart? Voices below on the staircase made her stop and sidle into the shadows. Despite her bold words to Nikolas, she did not relish being caught where she ought not to be. There was enough gossip in this place without adding to it. She recognized the cultured accents of Cesare Vitali, but he was speaking Italian, and Elizabeth, though she knew French and English and now a decent amount of German, had never learned much Italian beyond the basics.

That raised an interesting question to her curious mind. Who else in the household knew Italian besides Nikolas? The voices were getting louder as the two conversing climbed the stairs and paused on the landing. Cesare was speaking long and earnest, with no break. About to furtively return to her own room, Elizabeth sidled out of the shadows and caught a glimpse of the two on the stairs; a tall, stooped figure moved up to the next stair into her line of sight, replying to the secretary in perfect Italian. It was Count Delacroix!

But . . . Elizabeth looked back towards her own hallway. If the Frenchman was here, then who was with Gerta von Holtzen in her room? Some noise she made must have alerted the two men, for they both looked up and caught sight of her.

Count Delacroix, with his customary aplomb, bowed and said, "Mademoiselle, may I guide you anywhere, or—"

"I think she knows perfectly well where she is going . . . or where she has been," the secretary said, a peevish tone in his voice.

Elizabeth felt her face heat, and she said, "Excuse me, gentlemen, if I interrupted your conversation. I was about to . . . to go to the kitchen and get some milk, but I think I will retire instead."

With more questions than answers, Elizabeth turned back to her own room. She stopped in front of her own door, but all was quiet in Countess Gerta's chamber. She retired to her bed, staying awake awhile, wondering if Nikolas would come to her to try to make up their quarrel, but he did not come.

She arose the next day and raced to dress and descend, anxious to speak to Nikolas before he left. She had a sleepless night, thinking of him and how she had left things. But she was too late; he and Cesare had left at daybreak.

The day drifted on, and she learned some about Melisande's father from Countess Uta, who told Elizabeth that he was a useless kind of man, part art thief, part swindler, a man who had pretended to be Russian aristocracy to seduce Melisande's poor mother and then abandoned her after going through some mockery of a wedding ceremony.

That topic could not hold her attention like her concerns for Charlotte, though, and Uta agreed with her that there was some cause for concern. The old woman urged her to go see

Charlotte again, and so Elizabeth, as the late winter sun sagged toward the horizon, made her way to Charlotte's room.

Christoph was there by her side as she lay sleeping. He was staring at his sister with a worried expression. Elizabeth had not spent much time with Christoph, and then only in the company of others, so she hastened forward, putting out one hand when he would have arisen to give her his chair.

"Please, Count, don't get up. I am delighted to find you with your sister."

He gazed at her distrustfully, and she realized the gossip had no doubt made its way to him and he likely considered her in league with his uncle.

"I'm worried for Charlotte," she said, sitting on the edge of the bed, gazing down at the pale form.

"I, too, worry for her."

Elizabeth glanced over at him and caught his speculative eye on her. He looked conflicted, as if he had something he wished to say but was undecided as to whether it was appropriate. "I'm especially concerned right now, while your uncle is away," she said.

He snorted, and her suspicions were confirmed. He was ready to talk to someone, and perhaps he may speak to her, if she persisted.

"You seem . . . skeptical, Count, as to your uncle's devotion to your sister. Do his plans not auger well for her future?"

"He just wishes to get us both out of here, out of the country."

She waited.

"He doesn't like anyone clearheaded, or anyone young and strong, who might put a stop to his plans, to know the truth."

Confused, Elizabeth thought for a moment and then decided just to say what she felt. "What do you mean? I don't understand."

Christoph frowned and shook his head. "My . . . my English is not so good as Charlotte's, so perhaps I do not explain. Uh, how should I say it?"

She waited longer.

"He is hiding secrets," he said finally.

"Secrets?" She wondered if it was his aunt's condition of which the young man spoke.

"His past. Our mother. He killed her."

The shock hit Elizabeth like a fist, and she grasped the bedclothes in her hand. "What . . . what do you mean? How is that possible? He wasn't even here that night . . . or at least, not until it was too late."

He nodded wisely. "You have been told the lies."

Elizabeth stayed silent, trying to understand what was being told to her. "No," she said. "No, I can't believe it. You've been misled."

"Ah, but I know from one who was here that night and who knows everything. Everything!"

"Sources like that can be wrong, or misled, or . . . or malicious," she said gently, more sure of her ground now.

Christoph gazed down and took his sister's hand in his own. "I wish that were true, Miss Stanwycke . . . I only wish that were true. But he was here that night, and he set the fire, for he wanted my mother for himself and was maddened that he could not have her. So he lured her out there, set fire, and then stood and watched . . . and listened while she died."

A shiver coursing through her at the vivid image, Elizabeth whispered, "Who has poisoned your mind against your uncle? If that was true, then why was your Aunt Gerta's husband, Hans, in the cottage? Why did he not save your mother?"

"I do not know. Perhaps he tried to save her; I do not know."

"Who told you all of this?" Elizabeth said impatiently.

He looked up into her eyes. "So he has you under his spell, just as Charlotte said."

Even her pupil knew of her relationship with Nikolas? Had she been so very indiscreet? "Did Charlotte tell you this ridiculous story?"

"No, she does not believe it either. She thinks our uncle merely could not save our mother, but she does not believe he killed her."

The tangle of stories was tightly knotted, but there was some snarl at the center, some binding mystery. It was as if there was some dark presence, some overarching deviltry here that confounded reason to untangle. But if that was true, did it indeed go back fifteen years?

"And now," Christoph whispered, with tears in his eyes, "and now, he is poisoning Charlotte!"

"Oh, that's ridiculous!" Elizabeth said, fear cleansed by the absurdity of such an accusation. Charlotte stirred, so Elizabeth leaned towards the young count and lowered her voice. "You cannot believe such a story! You cannot believe your uncle capable of cold-blooded murder. For what purpose?"

He looked confused, blinked, and said, "I don't know what to think."

What was clear to Elizabeth in that moment was that someone was originating these wild tales and implanting them in the impressionable young people of the von Wolfram family, and she would not stand for it anymore. She was going to find out the truth. She remembered that moment Charlotte's worry for her brother, and how he had told her he was evil. How did that figure into this snarl of lies and mystery? Or was it a separate knot?

"Count," she said gently. "As difficult as your relationship with your uncle has been, you must know he is not guilty of such a heinous crime as murder . . . and of his own sister-in-law? Wherever you are getting this idea from . . . perhaps that person is mistaken. Or misled themselves." She considered that. She had been told differing stories of the night Anna von Wolfram and Hans von Holtzen died, too. Why was that so? And who did she believe?

She gazed at his pale and beautiful face, his blond hair glowing like an aura in the flickering candlelight. His expression was contemplative, and she thought he appeared like the saints in the stained-glass windows she had seen in the chapel room. Perhaps she had given him something to consider. She hoped so, for as angry as she felt towards Nikolas, she still believed in him.

"Who told you these tales?" she asked.

Christoph, though, was done talking and resisted any further interrogation, merely shaking his head at her questions.

Perhaps he needed to think, or perhaps he would come to her if she just left it alone for the time being. "If you ever wish to talk to someone, Count, please consider me a friend." She touched Charlotte's forehead and then left the room.

Chapter 23

SOMEONE ELSE had to know something. Perhaps her two old friends would have some ideas. Elizabeth made her way to Countess Uta's suite, where she found the old countess and Frau Liebner communicating with a distraught Mina. Caught immediately by the frantic gesticulation, Elizabeth crouched, wordless, at her friend's side while the maidservant whimpered and gestured. Countess Uta, her almost blind eyes wide, peered at her maid with a horrified expression on her face.

"What is it? What's going on?" Elizabeth muttered to Frau Liebner.

"Hush. I don't know yet. I have only ever been able to make out a little of Mina's wild language; it is just between them."

Uta's face was gray and her expression became bleak as a wintry sky. When Mina was done, she bustled off to the other room on some mysterious errand.

"What is it? What was she babbling about?" Frau Liebner said.

"I . . . I cannot believe it." The old woman stared off in the distance, one tear sliding down her cheek, meandering through the maze of wrinkles and crinkles that webbed her face.

"Please, ma'am, tell us," Elizabeth said, putting out one hand and laying it on the old woman's blanket-covered arm, "so we may share your trouble."

"I sent Mina on little trip last night. I haf been so concerned for Gerta, you both know why." She did not even need to talk about the countess's terrible times of madness and her midnight excursions; they both understood. "To me it seemed dat the key to her trouble lay not in dose times when she is hallucinating, but in dose times when she is not."

Elizabeth, startled by the thought, realized the wisdom behind it. "Do you mean, ma'am, that you don't believe Countess Gerta is . . . mad?"

"I do not know. But even if she is, I had suspicions, concerns . . . I believe her to haf a lover."

Startled, Elizabeth said, "Yes, I think she does. I have . . . heard things."

Frau Liebner said, "Heard things? I . . . I never considered it, but true it is that she was ever in need of a man, and I cannot believe she has gone without all this time. She would have no fear of conceiving a child. After the birth of Eva and Jakob, the doctor said she would never have another child; she was left barren."

"I had thought it was Count Delacroix," Elizabeth mused out loud, "but . . . but I now know that is impossible." She explained her meaning briefly.

"So who is it? Do you know?" Frau Liebner asked of Uta.

The old woman had been silent; she looked ill and clutched at the arm of her chair. "I know for fact dat she once seduced the music master; it was why Nikolas dismissed the poor man so summarily and never engaged another. But of late dere was no man I thought a target for her seducement. I had suspected Vitali—he *is* Italian—and I had believed the man involved in her declining health in some sinister way. Vitali is difficult fellow to fathom; he is secretive and sly. It was connection I was looking for . . . the link between her illness and her hallucinations."

"But it's impossible that her lover should be Signor Vitali," Elizabeth said. "I . . . I know that for a fact." She further explained what she had heard, and her intrusion on the conversation between Count Delacroix and the secretary so soon after.

"It does not matter; I know now who it is who goes to Gerta's bed," Uta said grimly.

"Who?" Elizabeth and Frau Liebner said simultaneously.

"Mina did not want to tell me. She has held the awful secret all day, merely telling me she did not know, could not say, but now . . . she has decided she cannot keep it from me any longer."

"Who is it?" Elizabeth said, her breath catching in her throat. She was afraid she already knew.

"It is Christoph," she whispered, her voice cracking with emotion.

"No!" Elizabeth exclaimed, shocked beyond horror; and yet her worst fear and her last guess were confirmed. "But she is his aunt!"

"Oh, this is terrible," Frau Liebner whispered, her hands clutched together.

"Mina has just told me he was . . . he was with her last night."

Feeling ill, Elizabeth held her stomach. "Are . . . are you absolutely certain?"

"I think it is so. The boy . . . the boy is so terribly wounded. I know not whether dis terrible affair is the result of dat, or . . . or the cause of it."

Elizabeth tried to tame her wildly racing thoughts; after the initial shock, her mind sped over her recent conversation with the young count and his beliefs about Nikolas's culpability in his mother's death. She considered Christoph's statement to his sister that he was evil and that she should not be around him. She shared some of what he had told her just that evening and then said, "Is it possible that Countess Gerta has been . . . has been harboring these awful suspicions all these years and has fed them to Count Christoph? Is that where he has gotten these beliefs from?"

"Yes," Frau Liebner said, understanding dawning in her eyes. "Perhaps that is so. Gerta was never easy after Eva and Jakob were born. She told me then she had enemies. I didn't know what she meant—it sounded so dramatic, and she always was a girl who liked to be the center of all attention, so I thought she was just making things up, you know, to be more important—and then I forgot about it, for she never said it to me again."

"Where would she get that idea, though, that Nikolas killed Anna and Hans?"

"Who knows?" Frau Liebner said. "Out of her own weak mind, perhaps."

But Elizabeth thought not. "Is it possible . . . is there anyone . . ." She stopped and shook her head.

"What are you trying to say?"

"I'm not sure. It's just an idea. Let me think about it." Slowly, she said, "I have been wondering something else, too. Are there any drugs or plants or substances that can cause that awful lethargy that Gerta and now Charlotte sometimes suffer from?"

Frau Liebner's eyes widened and Uta gasped.

"Mina!" Uta shouted.

The maid came running, and the countess gesticulated to her as she asked the question. The maid nodded.

"She says yes, dere are," the countess said. "She knows much about plants and herbs, learned at her mother's knee."

"What are the . . . the plants?"

Mina, her lined face pale, shook her head in frustration. There clearly were no gestures for what she needed to say.

"Write it down," Elizabeth said.

Uta replied, "She does not write."

Mina hurried away but came back almost immediately with a piece of paper and charcoal. She drew something and showed it to her mistress, but Uta could not see it. She handed it to Frau Liebner, who shrugged.

Elizabeth snatched the paper and gazed at it intently. It was a crude sketch of a flowering plant, but the shape of the flower was distinct. "Of course!" she gasped. "It's a poppy. Are poppies grown here?"

"Yes, in garden," the countess said. "The seeds are used for cooking."

"And maybe for other things," Elizabeth said. "Do you think Gerta could be taking opium herself, and maybe . . . maybe feeding it to Charlotte?"

"No, she would not do such a thing," Frau Liebner said. "Would she? Why would she do such a thing?"

"I do not know," Uta said, her face gray.

She was exhausted; Elizabeth stared at her for a moment and then said softly, "Countess, please, say nothing to anyone of what we have been speaking. Let me do some investigating."

Frau Liebner took her old friend's hand and said, "Yes, it is not for us old ones to solve this, but for the young ones." Still holding the countess's hand, she turned back to Elizabeth. "But you must wait until Nikolas has returned."

Elizabeth didn't promise, having plans of her own. Instead, she said, "Do you think Countess Adele suspects any of this is going on?"

Frau Liebner sniffed. "Adele is intelligent but terribly unable, sometimes, to see what is directly before her."

"And who would suspect such an awful thing?" Uta added. "I do not know what to think about Christoph. Is he bad seed? Is he evil? Or is he terribly misguided, abused?"

"Ma'am," Elizabeth said, slipping down onto her knees and taking the old lady's two hands in her own, moved by the woman's pallor and trembling. "I'll do everything I can to find out the answers. But while I do, try not to brood on it. Just until we know more."

Elizabeth left the two ladies alone to console each other. She knew she would have to be careful. She didn't feel there was any danger in asking a few questions, but discretion would be important. She could not confront Countess Gerta or Count Christoph without upsetting the household and possibly endangering Mina, the source of the information. When Nikolas got back, there would be time for open discussion, but not before.

Her first thought was to interfere in any way she could with the illicit and incestuous relationship between Countess Gerta and her nephew. If she could do that and get to the bottom of Christoph's deep hatred and suspicion of his uncle at the same time, it would be a miraculous feat. She pondered all of the twisted threads of the awful family secrets hidden by the thick walls of Wolfram Castle as she wrote in her journal that night. It helped to lay out all of her conjectures and worries on paper, for it aided in her logical assessment. One thing she decided as she wrote: they were right about interfering between Christoph and Gerta. It was a necessary first step.

That night there would be no danger, for Christoph had spoken openly of his resolution to stay by his sister's side while she was ill. Elizabeth sent Fanny to sit with the two of them.

The next day Countess Uta feigned an illness she did not feel and asked if one of her nieces would stay with her that evening as long as she needed. Countess Adele would have done so, grudgingly, but Uta asked if Gerta would attend her bedside, and somehow, with the promise of relating old scandal, she managed to get the woman to stay. It was a poor measure and bound to fail quickly, for Countess Gerta could not maintain concentration for any length of time. Quickly alternating between lethargy and an awful feverish excitement, she was unpredictable, and their hasty plans could fail at any time. At least there was no full moon, the period that exacerbated her condition so terribly.

The three of them—Uta, Frau Liebner, and Elizabeth—agreed among them that they could only do so much, and that would have to be enough. Not one of them considered Adele a possible confidant, for her temper was uncertain and her relationship with Gerta such that she would be unable to keep a secret from her sister; she was sure to reveal it in spite or in shock, and not one of them wanted to risk the consequences of such an untimely revelation.

Again that night in her own room, Elizabeth took up her journal and quill and wrote for a while, trying to work out the mysteries surrounding Wolfram Castle and the turmoil that roiled within. Why, she mused on paper, would the young count be the aggressor in the relationship? It just didn't seem to her as something he would even consider as possible, though she was a newcomer and so not aware of all of the undercurrents and stresses in this odd household. But when did it start? Was it possible that the Countess Gerta, disturbed and unhappy, turned to her nephew for comfort, and that it became something else as he got older?

And did the countess purposely drug herself, or was there a far more sinister explanation for what was going on with Countess Gerta, and now probably with Charlotte? She stopped writing and gazed at herself in the mirror above her desk; she was pale and frightened looking, quite a contrast from the woman in love she had seen just a few mornings ago. But her life had taken an odd turn, and now she had become the unwilling repository of a disturbing family truth, and without even Nikolas to confide in.

She stopped the ink bottle and wiped the quill. A terrible thought occurred to her: What if Gerta was not the one drugging Charlotte? Who was, and why? There was no action taken in life by any person that did not have some goal.

Perhaps Charlotte was the one they should be watching over. She had awoken during the day and had seemed better, but she was still weak. Christoph was not to be trusted as a guardian, in Elizabeth's own estimation. The night before, though he had said he would stay with her, he had wandered out in the middle of the night and had not come back, Fanny had told her. Fanny was again going to watch over the girl but had first to ready herself for another sleepless night, so she was that moment downstairs.

The house was dark and quiet as Elizabeth slipped out of her room into the hall. She was filled with an uneasy feeling that she could not explain as she padded quietly down the hallway to her pupil's room. Surely she was imagining things? Christoph was supposed to be with her, and Charlotte had a maid just in the next room to hers; this was a well-run household, with people coming and going and servants around most of the time. She tapped on the door but didn't hear anything, so she opened it and peered into the darkness. There was no Christoph, certainly, for he would not sit in the room without so much as a candle to light the darkness.

"Charlotte," Elizabeth whispered, slipping into the room. She heard a noise in the darkness and tiptoed across the room, following the sound, holding her flickering candle high. What was it? Where had it come from? A click, and she fell back in fear and horror. A panel in the wall had moved!

She gathered her courage and raced to the section of the room where the noise had originated, but it took her a moment to find the panel, and when she slid it back and entered the secret passage, it was too late; whoever had been there was gone. Perhaps it was only Mina, she tried to tell herself. It was possible the vigilant servant had had the same thought and feared for the young countess's safety but had fled when she heard someone coming. Elizabeth retreated and slid the panel back in place, moving swiftly to the side of Charlotte's bed and gazing down at the pallid girl. She was motionless and pale, but her breathing was still even.

Elizabeth set the candle on the table and took a seat at her bedside, not sure what to do. Her mouth was dry from her rapid flight. She raised the glass of cool water by the bedside to her lips and was about to take a drink when she saw, through the bottom of the glass, an unstopped bottle on the table. Why was it there, and with the lid off? What was it?

She put the glass down and picked up the bottle, sniffing its contents. It was almost odorless, whatever it was, with no hint of laudanum, and it was more than half empty. And it was clear, like water. She dumped both the contents of the bottle and the glass into the slops pail and set the glass on the table near the door. A chill ran down her spine as she wondered—had she just interfered in something? Had she just stopped the young countess from being drugged yet again, or had she been too late?

She stood and leaned over, watching the young countess's face in the light of the candle she held. Charlotte's color was better than it had been and she was deeply sleeping, but it did not appear to be a drugged state. In any case, Elizabeth was not leaving the room for the rest of the night, and she would be sure that Charlotte was transferred to Frau Liebner's room the next day even if she had to batter back Countess Adele's objections. It would be worth the risk of dismissal to protect her charge. She settled in the chair by the bed, prepared for a sleepless night.

Resolute, she wore down all resistance the next day, buoyed by the support of Frau Liebner, whom Countess Adele at least respected. Though she had considered other alternatives—Melisande had offered to take care of Charlotte and had even pleaded that it would help her keep her mind off her father's difficulties—it came down to a matter of trust. Only Frau Liebner and Uta had her absolute faith. How she had come to be the arbiter of such a grave matter she didn't know, but by virtue of her love for Nikolas and her care for Charlotte, she would take this task seriously, as though her own life depended upon it. And when she thought of Nikolas away on his journey of compassion, she somehow knew that she was doing what he would want. No matter the state of their own relationship, she would do for his family whatever she could until he came back to reclaim the authority.

And Charlotte, over a period of a few days, recovered from her stupor; it was as though a different girl emerged from the lethargy, one with a sharper wit than Elizabeth had thought her student possessed. The drawing room finally saw them all again as the count's journey numbered seven days and the moon was again waxing toward fullness.

Frau Liebner was an anxious visitor, sitting in watchful silence by Countess Gerta near the fire. Bartol Liebner stoked the fire and adjusted a screen for his sister-in-law. Count Delacroix, his usual bonhomie present, played chess with his niece, whose distressed countenance was becoming more gaunt with each passing day that delivered no news of her father; Charlotte sat nearby, well wrapped and quiet in a comfortable chair, reading a book. It was an unusual sight, but one Elizabeth welcomed. Countess Adele played the piano softly, instructing her nephew in the intricacies of a difficult piece as he tried it on his violin.

For the casual observer it would seem a harmonious family scene, but Elizabeth, knowing them all as well as she now did, was too aware of the tensions present and the terrible implications of even the most innocent glance. Count Christoph watched Countess Gerta as he did badly at his violin piece, and Elizabeth could see that woman's flighty, flirtatious conversation with Count Delacroix nearby was as painful to him as it was to his stoic aunt, who pretended not to hear as she played softly the difficult chords. Melisande Davidovich was making every effort to appear normal, but concern over her father's fate was causing her attention to drift, and she lost match after match to her uncle, even when he coaxed her to make certain moves.

But underlying it all Elizabeth felt an odd strain, as of a string pulled taut and plucked by mischievous fingers. Bartol Liebner felt it, too, she thought, for his normal joviality was absent. He sat down by her.

"Miss Stanwycke," he said. "I am worried. Do these precious people appear all right to you?"

"What do you mean, sir?" she asked.

"Is something wrong?" he asked quietly, turning to her, his ovoid face shiny with perspiration from his efforts with the fire screen. "I have the terrible sense that all is not right with my dearest family."

"Have . . . have you ever felt this way before?"

He shrewdly glanced at her and then back at the others. "Many times has this family suffered. First, fifteen years ago, when so much tragedy . . ." He shook his head, tears welling in his eyes. "But this last while, with poor, dear Gerta and Charlotte . . . both of them not well. Is it some family weakness, I ask myself? Or is there something else, something that haunts this whole family?"

He was so close to the truth, and she didn't know if she most wished him to guess or not guess. She had sworn to take no one else into her confidence, but he was so close. "Do you . . . are you postulating that the two things are connected, sir?"

His black eyes widened. "Connected? The tragedies of long ago and the young women of the household's illness?"

She had said too much; she didn't even know what she was guessing at herself and did not want to imply that she did. Shaking her head, she said, "No, that is far too great a chance, is it not? It is impossible to suppose."

"I do not see why you would even consider such a thing," he said, his eyes wide in wonder. "Unless . . ." He leaned toward her. "Have you heard or seen anything? Have you learned something?"

"No, nothing at all," she said, turning her gaze to him and meeting his eyes. "Not a thing." She was beginning to imagine conspiracies everywhere, she thought in despair, for she could have sworn she saw a hint of suspicion in his expression. Her wretched imagination was running wild.

The next few days passed easily enough. Charlotte was finally well enough to be up and around, but Elizabeth didn't even attempt to resume their lessons. Instead she asked if Charlotte would like to go up and sit with the Countess Uta and Frau Liebner. The girl, still wan but with a sharper gleam in her eyes than Elizabeth thought had ever been present, said, "Only if the old ladies will tell some of the ancient stories."

"I think you might convince Countess Uta to divulge some tales if you ask prettily. You may think her a bloodthirsty old dame," Elizabeth added, with a soft smile, "but she was very concerned for you when you were ill."

Ignoring the last addition, Charlotte slowly rose and indicated her readiness to visit her great aunt, then said, "May we ask Meli to join us? She's so worried for her father and the diversion may do her well."

"I think that would be a lovely idea," Elizabeth said, pleased to acknowledge such a kindness, although she knew that even in her time of worry Melisande Davidovich had not shunned her daily visits to the grand dame of the household.

And so they took tea with Countess Uta and Frau Liebner.

The elderly countess had been examining her old jewelry, heavy monstrosities in gold and silver, laden with dusty gems and enameled panels. "Much of dis will be yours someday, Charlotte," she said, holding one particularly hideous piece up close to her eyes, pawing it with her crooked fingers.

"Thank you, aunt, but . . . but please feel able to give it away elsewhere."

"I would not think of it. Family is all we haf, my girl." She tossed the piece to Charlotte and said, "What do you think of dat, eh? What a wonderful piece of work!"

Charlotte held it up. "It is truly awful!"

"What is it?" Melisande asked, leaning forward.

"It is . . . a wolf's head?" Charlotte said, grimacing.

"Of course," Uta said. "It is family pin. We are descended from wolves and ravens, you see, from the animals of the forest and the air. And back to dem we shall go someday."

"I am not going to be a dirty dog, nor a molting pigeon."

Uta's expression grew grim. "Disrespectful you may be, my girl, but dere was a time when the family history was not so, when dis family was about to perish, and it was only our ability to become other dan we are dat saved us."

"What do you mean, ma'am?" Elizabeth asked, watching the interest sharpen on Melisande's face and happy to see something other than worry there.

"I mean in the old times, many years ago—three hundred, perhaps more—dis castle was under invasion from the barbarians from the east, near Berlin. Long ago the chief of dis place was Friedrich Jakob von Wolfram, but laying claim to the castle was one Arndt von Bruckstadt. And he brought his army and he lay siege in the depth of terrible winter, but Friedrich left the castle in the night through . . . through a secret way he knew, and he entered the forest where Bruckstadt's men were sleeping, waiting for morning's light, and as he ran, he donned a pelt, the pelt of a gray wolf, and he said a spell and became a wolf, for truly we are a family of wolves and ravens, powerful and swift."

Elizabeth glanced at the girls and had to suppress a grin. So, it was old fairy stories that could capture their interest like nothing else. And there was no one who could tell a tale like Uta, her gritty, heavy accents perfect for relating tales of ancient enmities and dark lore.

"He became a wolf?" Charlotte whispered. "How is that so?"

Uta waited one long moment and then said, "Werewolf! Half human, half animal, a terrible state, but when his family was threatened, Freidrich had no choice but to become dat awful, soulless beast."

Frau Liebner shook her head. "I heard this story first from

your grandfather, Charlotte, but in his relation the hordes at the gate were from Poland and the siege occurred in summer."

That deflated the mood of tension, and Elizabeth sighed as Melisande and Charlotte giggled.

"Imagine a man becoming a wolf!" Charlotte laughed, her blue eyes sparkling like sapphires. "I once had a governess who believed all of the silly old tales, and she said I should be stolen away by imps if I did not do as I was told."

"My mama told me that fairies had kissed me as I slept, and that was what the little freckles on my cheeks were from," Melisande said, her smile fading, perhaps as she remembered her mother.

Charlotte squeezed her arm and laid her head on her friend's shoulder. Elizabeth watched and saw a difference in her pupil. There was a clarity in her gaze and a buoyancy in her manner that had never, to her view, been present. She exchanged a glance with Frau Liebner, who was observing her niece, too.

Had Charlotte been systematically drugged for months? Was that the sole source of her lethargy? But if that was so, who had done it? And why?

After dinner that evening Elizabeth sat alone for a few minutes in her own room, trying to formulate a plan to protect both Gerta and Charlotte from some unseen and unknown enemy. As many times as she had tried to come up with a reasonable theory that would explain the horrors that had befallen this family, she had failed. The serving staff she did not suspect. Their movements were too circumscribed, and they just did not have enough freedom to do all that must have been done if one was to believe in some concerted plotting.

That left the family members and those guests who were present: Adele, Gerta, Nikolas, Bartol Liebner, Christoph, Charlotte, Melisande Davidovich, Count Delacroix, and Cesare Vitali. She curled up in the window seat and gazed out over the darkening landscape and tried to order her thoughts in a logical manner. Charlotte and Gerta, as victims, could be stricken from the list. Adele and Nikolas could have no possible motive that she could imagine, but if she was going strictly on possibilities it had to be admitted that both the siblings had full access to the house. So though she considered them unlikely, she could not strike them from the list of her suspected villains. If it was to be believed that the old tragedy of fifteen years before and the latest troubles were tied together, then Melisande was out of it, as was Christoph, too young at the time of the deaths to have had any part in them.

Who did that leave? Bartol Liebner, Cesare Vitali, and the Count Delacroix. Elizabeth yawned and rubbed her eyes with her knuckles. She must go back down to the drawing room, she supposed, and soon. As she widened her eyes against the weariness she felt and gazed out her bedroom window, the sight she did not want to see was before her past the open curtains. The moon was almost full. Still uncertain of the source of Countess Gerta's hallucinations, all they could do was protect her as well as they could until they figured it all out. Nikolas would surely be home the next day, or the one after that at the latest.

She was so tired, and she longed for Nikolas to come home and assume the burden of his family's care once more. She laid her head on her arms and stared out over the blanket of snow. Nikolas. She had been so worried and busy the last week or so, and had not allowed her thoughts to drift to him, the feel of his arms around her, and the sense of him possessing her body and soul as he had the night they had made love so thoroughly.

Perhaps it was that Elizabeth was afraid to think of it, given her resolution to break free of her fierce need for him. His lack of ability to love her as she loved him frightened her, for it meant she had done the unthinkable and given herself once again to a man incapable of love . . . or at least incapable of loving *her*.

She opened her eyes wide and sat up, gazing around. The room was brilliantly lit; it was fully daylight! How had that happened? Fanny pushed into the room that moment carrying a tray. She gazed at Elizabeth and dipped a curtsey.

"You are awake early, Miss Stanwycke. And dressed already!"

"What?" Elizabeth wiped sleep from her eyes and gazed out the window over a scene of reflected sunlight sparkling off a blanket of snow.

Fanny set the tray down and gazed at the bed, her face pale and her expression a mask of mystification. "Your bed, miss . . . it has not been disturbed."

Cramped and aching, Elizabeth swung her feet over the edge of the window seat and stretched. "How embarrassing! I . . . I must have been so tired I fell asleep right here, in the window seat!"

She didn't even remember laying down, nor falling asleep, Elizabeth thought, disturbed. She must have worried herself to exhaustion. But . . . how did it happen? She had come up to her room after dinner to sit for a moment before joining the others in the drawing room, and she had fallen asleep.

And had slept for . . . it must be ten hours! She never slept more than six. How very odd.

She went about her business that day, having to explain to several people why she did not join them in the drawing room as she had said she was going to. Bartol Liebner told her he had been concerned and had thought they ought to go up to her room and make sure she was all right, but the others had quashed the notion.

"Thank you, sir," she said. "I wish you had prevailed. It is so unlike me to fall asleep like that."

He stared at her, worry in his dark eyes. He put one gentle hand on her arm and said, "If that ever happens again, Miss Stanwycke, I promise you I will insist."

Touched by his concern, she thanked him. "Sir, it was almost as if I was . . ." She was about to say "drugged" but shook her head.

"What is it?"

"Nothing. Nothing at all. Just a foolish notion."

Perhaps Nikolas would be home that day. She hoped so, for the moon was almost completely full that evening, and anything could happen.

Chapter 24

WHY WAS Nikolas not home? He had been gone for weeks! Elizabeth paced from window to window that evening, as they all gathered in the drawing room. This night she had not gone up to her own room after dinner, even though she sorely needed a moment to think, but she had a superstitious dread of the same thing happening as had happened the night before.

"Elizabeth," Frau Liebner said loudly, "come and sit by me and talk!"

She obeyed.

"Stop this incessant pacing," the woman said in an undertone. "We must decide what to do this evening. Last night was very dangerous for Gerta. Though she did not leave the house, she wandered and was found by Bartol near the outside door. He came to me with great worry and said she did not seem herself. It is the full moon. Though Gerta seems lucid, she is fretful."

"I know. She's excited . . . agitated. I don't like it."

"What shall we do?"

"What excuse can we use to keep Mina in watch over her? It's getting more difficult to contain her." Elizabeth said and pulled at her bottom lip with her teeth. Nikolas's last words, his plea for her to look after Gerta, nagged at her. Why wasn't he home yet? He was the only one Gerta obeyed without question; he was the only one who had the authority to order her confined, if the need arose.

"Ladies," Bartol Liebner said, bowing before them. "May I bring you some tea?"

"That would be wonderful, sir," Elizabeth said.

"Do what you will," Frau Liebner grumbled, waving him away as if he were a pesky fly.

"Why do you not like your brother-in-law?" Elizabeth asked. "He's so eager to please, so desirous of helping wherever he can."

"It is an old prejudice," the woman said. "I do not expect to defeat it now."

"But what was its genesis?"

Frau Liebner hesitated, grimly frowning, and then said, "Ah, just an old tale. Perhaps not true, perhaps true; I don't know."

Her damnable curiosity tugged at Elizabeth as she watched the older man making up their cups. He was slow and bent and took a while making them to the exact specification he had long memorized. It was one of his little courtesies that he liked to make up the ladies' cups for them; he had done so even at dinner the night before, insisting on bringing her a special glass of blackberry cordial distilled by his own methods. He was something of a vintner, he had said modestly. "But what is it? What is it that turned you against him?" Elizabeth asked, turning her attention toward Frau Liebner.

"Viktor told me once that the reason his brother was sent from home was . . ." She stopped and shook her head.

"What?" Elizabeth prodded, feeling a frisson of alarm for some reason that she could not place.

"He . . . he was suspected of taking advantage of a child . . . the child of one of the family's serving staff."

"Taking advantage of a child? What does that me . . . oh." Understanding, when it came, turned her stomach. "How . . . how old was the child?"

"She was twelve . . . perhaps thirteen? Viktor was vague. It was not proven and he denied it; they had only the girl's word for it, and children, especially of that class, are so unreliable. And so her family asked Maria to take him with her when she married, and she did. He has never, to my knowledge, done anything so since. This is why I say it could be true, or perhaps not; more likely it is not. I have never known what to think, but it remained in my memory all these years."

The man brought their cups, carefully, and set them down on the table. "This is yours, Miss Stanwycke, with the cream. And, sister, this is yours . . . just the way you like, with nothing in it."

Elizabeth watched him but saw no monster in the bland, pale, smooth face. Surely if he was such a wretch as to take advantage of a child, it would show. She would know it, she decided. She was a good judge of character, after all. Rumor, she well knew, and innuendo, could ruin a person, and she refused to judge him based on old stories related at second hand. She had suffered from just such cruel gossip, and she would not hold him accountable for suspicions never proved. "Thank you, sir. You are so very kind."

"I live but to serve this family, and those in its employ," he said, then bowing and making his way back to where Gerta was sitting by the fire near Count Delacroix and Countess Adele.

"He has perhaps been cruelly misjudged," Elizabeth said to her friend. "I know what it is to be so misjudged and I will not inflict that pain on another. I was named a . . . a fortune-hunting whore, and it hurt deeply." She raised her cup to sip the tea, but her gaze was caught by a faint smudge of dark powdery residue at the edge of the vessel. With shaking hands she put it down and stared at it, trying to imagine some reasonable explanation that did not mean what she feared it meant. But too easily she could see the truth behind it. Her mind raced from surmise to logical assumption, and thence to a dreadful certainty. When Frau Liebner raised her own cup to drink, Elizabeth put out one staying hand. "Ma'am, do not drink. I think . . . I think I may know why I fell asleep so deeply last night."

She explained some of her thoughts to her friend, and together they came to some conclusions. But still, they had no authority to act. All they could do, Elizabeth said, was to protect Gerta and Charlotte and hope Nikolas came home on the morrow. If he did not, they would need to do something drastic.

Later, their plans in place, Elizabeth retired after much

public yawning and weary rubbing of her eyes. Supposedly she went directly to her bed to sleep, but really she stole through the secret corridors, which she had spent some time mapping out in the last couple of days, towards Charlotte's room. They had managed to trick Gerta into sleeping once again up near her aunt Uta with yet another tale of a bad spell on the old grand dame's part. It would not work another night. Mina was set to maintain a vigilant watch over the most unstable of the household, and Elizabeth had confidence that no bump on the head would occur this time, for Mina was now wary of the seemingly fragile but surprisingly tough Countess Gerta.

She and Frau Liebner had discussed the possible culpability of Bartol Liebner; was the smudge of dark powder a sleeping potion? And if so, why? Again it was not provable, but it had set her to thinking, to wondering. Was Bartol Liebner a perpetrator, or a pawn in some larger game? Was he the sole villain of the piece, or was there another hand as yet unseen? She didn't know.

She slipped like a ghost through the walls, first to a room where some answer might lay. She slid the panel open and there was the library, cold as a tomb without the master of the house. She shivered but resolutely held her candle high. This very secret door was where Nikolas had entered the library the first night she had been there. Knowing all his secrets made her feel closer to him, but in truth he could still be miles away. Word had come that he was expected, but no one was sure if it was the next morning or still another day. His message had said simply that he would explain all when he arrived.

She stole over to the shelf she remembered to have contained encyclopedias of plants and herbs and ran her hand along the leather bindings, looking for one in particular. There it was, the red calf and gold-leaf lettering shining in the flickering light. She pulled it down from the shelf and laid it on Nikolas's desk, leafing through it, aware that she should not be taking this time when she had grave concerns for Charlotte's safety that night.

But just one moment more . . . yes . . . there it was. Laboriously, she made out the German lettering. Her verbal skills in the language were much better than her reading skills, though she had been reading all she could get her hands on to improve herself. A small line drawing accompanied the text, and from what she could tell the descriptions were chillingly similar.

Agitation. Wild, vivid hallucinations. Episodes of frantic movement while holding the conviction that one had become an animal. Learned men had studied folklore and had determined a rational explanation; it was unfortunate that in all the years of suffering no one had opened this particular book and read this particular passage. Perhaps it was just that in times of tribulation the mind leaped to conclusions, oft times that confirmed one's worst fears rather than searching out a more mundane explanation.

The book fell from her hands, and Elizabeth felt a chill down to her marrow. Countess Gerta was indeed being systematically drugged, and possibly by more than one kind of substance. One would make her sleepy and lethargic, as they had postulated, but another would cause the hallucinations. She had never even suspected that was possible, that such delusions could be induced in such a manner. Was Charlotte the next objective of the fiend's scheme? And why? And was this truly Bartol Liebner's doing, or was there some mastermind behind it all, some devious plot that reached beyond what she had so far discovered?

There was no time to ponder. She hastily put the book on the shelf and slipped back into the walls to make her way to Charlotte's room. She would watch over her herself, if need be, but nothing was going to happen to her charge, and when Nikolas came home she would lay it all before him. As the master of the house he would ultimately have the responsibility of figuring it all out. But as awful as it was, what a relief it would be for him to learn that his sister was not mad, but drugged! It was later than she had thought, Elizabeth realized when she stealthily emerged into Charlotte's room, candle held high, and saw the full moon rising above the deep green forest. Her charge was sleeping calmly, the soft, regular breathing an assurance that she was well. Elizabeth tiptoed to the window and looked out over the moonlit landscape.

"No," she whimpered as she looked down. "It's not possible!"

But it was. There, staggering across the snow, was the cloaked figure of Gerta von Holtzen, headed directly for the forest and the wolves.

"Damn! And damn again!" Elizabeth cried. "Can no one contain her?"

"What? Who . . ." Charlotte awoke and sat up in her bed, her pale face a mask of fear.

Elizabeth whirled, the flame of her candle flickering wildly. "Charlotte, listen to me," she said, moving toward the door. "Listen well! You must awaken and tell your aunt Adele or your aunt Liebner . . . or anyone who will listen!" The need for secrecy was eradicated by the greater need to protect Countess Gerta in the absence of Nikolas. "Tell them that your aunt Gerta is in trouble and in the north woods. And then stay with one of them! I am going now to get her . . . she's not well . . . just tell someone!"

She bolted from the room and realized she did not even have the few moments it would take to alert someone; she would just have to trust that Charlotte had listened and would heed her. But still . . . she must do everything that she could. As she raced down the steps she caught hold of a footman and said, in the best German she could manage, "Tell Countess Adele to send help, into the north woods. Countess von Holtzen is in trouble!"

The man gazed at her with wide eyes. Did he understand? Did he not understand? She had no time to figure it out, for every second she delayed took the countess closer to the woods and nearer deadly danger. She raced out the front door, leaving it open behind her, but when she glanced back she saw framed the portly figure of Bartol Liebner.

"Miss Stanwycke," he called out. "Is everything all right? Do you need my help?"

She turned away from him and ran. But she was already

too late. The cloaked figure was even now plunging recklessly into the forest edge, as if she knew she was being followed. "No, oh no," Elizabeth whimpered, floundering through the fresh powdery snow that had fallen just that morning. "It's March . . . does winter never end in this land?"

Her cries echoed and disappeared in the night air, and in the distance she heard a sound that stopped her in her tracks and raised the goose bumps on her arms. Wolves. The keening cry soared and wailed, beckoning the countess to her destruction. Why, if she was to hallucinate, could she not have imagined she was a mouse and needed to find some hidey-hole to burrow into?

Elizabeth trudged through the snow, slipping in her haste and tumbling into a drift. She extricated herself and finally found where the deluded woman had gone into the woods. She followed, no choice left to her by her own humanity and by Nikolas's plea. She must protect the countess from herself. Soon . . . soon Nikolas would be back and would sort the mess out. Soon they would figure out what his uncle had done, and why. Soon, God willing, soon.

The woods had gone silent, the absence of howling even more ominous to Elizabeth than the sound had been. In the woods it was not as easy to follow the trail, for the snow had drifted unevenly and some patches were bare. Muttering a prayer for guidance, Elizabeth called out, "Countess! Countess Gerta, please, come back!"

No sound greeted her, and really, she had not expected it, for the woman had proven to be incapable of hearing reason when in such a state. If her suspicions were correct, Bartol Liebner must have found a way to administer the hallucinogenic herbal concoction to Gerta, but how had she slipped from Mina's guardianship this time?

It was no time for wondering such things. She staggered on, pulling up her skirts and wading through a drift; there had been no time to retrieve a cloak, and she was in danger, she knew, from the cold. But so was the countess in that same danger. It was only by her brother's concerted effort that she had not frozen to death any of the times she had disappeared into the forest.

Then Elizabeth came upon a bare patch, which though welcome made it harder to see where the countess had gone. She stopped, panting, to catch her breath and heard a rising wail once more, but this time it was the reedy sound she knew was not the wolves but the countess. She plunged on through the snow with a renewed fervor, knowing now she was on the right track and that the countess had likely stopped. If she could just get to her . . . .

There was a clearing ahead, perhaps the same one the countess had chosen last time, and Elizabeth made her way there. If it had not been for the full moon gleaming down on her as she came into the clearing in the middle of the woods, Elizabeth would have thought she was hallucinating.

There, standing on a patch of beaten snow, Gerta von Holtzen stood. She had stripped off all her clothes and they lay in a circle around her; her unbound hair rippled down over her shoulders and back, glimmering silver in the blue white light of the full moon. She still wore stockings, but they sagged on her thin legs and were coated in ice. Her shoes she had discarded with her garments. Her slender white body exposed to the cold, she stood, arms spread wide, and howled, the sound a keening wail that raised the hairs on the back of Elizabeth's arms.

"Countess," Elizabeth called softly as she approached, stretching out her freezing hands in a beseeching gesture. "You must come back with me, please! Gerta, you must—"

Snapping and snarling, the woman turned on her and growled, her eyes wide and her teeth bared. She swiped at Elizabeth with her fingers crooked into talons and then barked, before throwing back her head and howling again. Without warning she made a rush at Elizabeth and swiped again, scratching Elizabeth's bare hand with her fingernails.

Shaking with fear and shock, Elizabeth retreated, trying to think logically what to do. If only she could, but her mind was whirling, trying to know what was right, trying to come to some decision. She held her blood-streaked hand close to her body, the scratches throbbing with a fierce heat. What would bring the countess out of her strange delusion?

She had to try.

"Countess, please, just let me help you," she said, keeping her voice soothing.

Gerta bared her teeth, her pale eyes glittering. "I am the wolf woman, I am woman by day, wolf by night," she cried in guttural German and threw her head back, ending her words on a keening howl.

Elizabeth, with the improved knowledge of German she had come to over the past months, understood every eerie word. "No," she whispered, then said more strongly, in German, "No! Countess, you are simply a woman, a graceful, fair woman . . . a mother . . ."

"I am wolf woman!" Gerta howled, then she stared at Elizabeth, growled with an ominous, throaty snarl, and took one step toward her, her gaunt, naked body white in the gleaming moonlight. "I am wolf woman, I am a huntress, I seek blood, and my teeth grow long as the moon waxes full . . ."

A rustling in the woods interrupted her and a huge wolf bounded into the clearing and stopped abruptly, as if appalled by the sight of the two women. It stared, dark eyes watching Elizabeth with almost human intensity. Gerta turned to it with a glad cry and outstretched arms. Elizabeth, fearing for her own safety if she rushed at the beast to retrieve the countess, turned and stumbled to the far edge of the clearing, trying to master her fear of the wolf, trying to think what to do. The beast was enormous, with a mantle of dark bristling fur over its heavy shoulders and a thick ruff of black sliver-tipped fur around its face. If only Nikolas was back! Perhaps he was even now on his way home; perhaps he was taking a shortcut through the forest and was close enough to save them. With an odd thrill racing down her back, she felt his presence with her; if she needed him, he would come, she was sure of it.

"Nikolas," she cried out, peering back into the forest in the hope that aid was coming, the sense of his presence was so powerful. But then she looked back at the clearing and shrieked at the sight that greeted her eyes.

Chapter 25

THE WOLF convulsed and writhed on the ground, paws stabbing at the air, eerie howls rending the night.

"Nikolas, help!" Elizabeth shrieked again in desperation as Gerta tried to bend to help the wild creature.

But it snapped and snarled and convulsed again, twisting and writhing wretchedly in the beaten snow; even Gerta suddenly staggered back, screaming in fear. In horror Elizabeth watched as the creature swelled, becoming larger, longer, even as the snout shrank and the fangs, too. The wolfskin split and changed, hanging in rags from the body on the snowy ground.

The human body. A man lay curled in the snow, his hands over his face. But then he stretched and knelt and stood up, a ragged wolfskin kirtle that reached to his muscular thighs his only clothes. It was Nikolas, and with an enigmatic look at Elizabeth he caught his sister and murmured to her in German, then lifted her cloak off the ground. Gerta had gone limp with the reaction of horror, and he surrounded her in the cloak and said, his voice harsh in the silent forest, "Elizabeth, I know you are shocked, but you must help my sister. There are villagers . . . hunters . . . near; I saw them leave the village as I came through, but I could not stop them and they are after blood. Take her up to the castle, and I will follow."

Elizabeth stood staring at him, uncomprehending, her mouth covered with her quivering hands. Nikolas? Nikolas, with whom she had lain and made love, and whose tender hands had unclothed her and touched her, and he was . . . an inhuman beast? She backed away and stumbled, her legs trembling and weak with horror as she retched convulsively.

"Elizabeth! Listen to me!" he shouted. His arm over his sister's shoulders, he moved forward, urging Gerta on, protecting her with his strength. A dog barked in the distance and his eyes widened. "Elizabeth," he said again, but his tone was pleading, filled with urgency. His eyes were silvery in the moonlight and glittered oddly. "You are the only one I can rely on. Now you have seen the worst and know what I am. But . . ." His voice softened. "Help Gerta, for her sake, for the sake of another woman. For her children. She is only sick, not what I am. Help her. *Please!*"

Elizabeth still stared, and he pushed his cloaked sister towards her and then backed away, as if he knew she couldn't bear for him to be near her. Gerta sagged against her and Elizabeth supported the other woman's weight with difficulty.

"I will draw them away, but you must help me . . . or help Gerta," he said. "Please, Elizabeth, I am begging you." Then with one long, sad look over his shoulder at her, he walked back into the forest. Then he began to lope, and as he melted into the dark woods Elizabeth saw a flash of silver-tipped fur.

Dogs barked and bayed, closer now, their wailing cries echoing through the forest. Hunters from the village! They had to retreat before they were found, Elizabeth knew, or they could be killed. Elizabeth gathered up the scattered garments, roughly took Gerta by her narrow shoulders, and guided her back out, supporting her when she stumbled, urging her to move faster, following their footsteps in the snow that still lingered there, in the depths of the woods, as she searched for the path to the castle.

The torment of what she had seen would tear at her gut, Elizabeth knew, but now her duty was clear: get Gerta out of the woods and back up to the castle without anyone suspecting what horrors had occurred that night. With the hounds sounding even closer and fear pounding through her veins, she urged the woman on.

IT was over . . . it was all over. He had done what he had to do and had drawn off the hounds and the hunters, back towards the village. He hoped he had confused the dogs so much that the men would give up and return to their homes. Trembling from exhaustion, Nikolas crouched at the edge of the forest, having reclaimed his human form once more and his clothes, too. He gazed up at the gray front of his home, his inheritance, his legacy; bitterness filled him and bile erupted into his mouth. He crouched, retching into the snow, spitting and heaving as the horror of his life overwhelmed him.

He would almost have given his life rather than have Elizabeth see what she had seen.

But worse, he must now make his way up to the castle and resume his burden, make sure his sister was all right, and try to see Elizabeth, to reassure her that he was no danger to anyone . . . or at least not to anyone who did not harm his family.

Aching within and without, a searing pain in the empty cavity where his heart should have been, he trudged up to the castle and entered, wet, cold, and miserable, through one of the two doors that led to the secret passages. Heinrich, Cesare, and Melisande's father he had left behind in the village inn, for in truth when he learned as he came through Wolfbeck that the hunters had headed to his castle, he had not known what he would find when he got there. Melisande's father was in terrible condition, beaten, barely well enough to be carried to an inn and back to the carriage as they traveled, and Nikolas could not deal with any more burdens that night. They would be safe in the village until the next day.

His silent servant, Heinrich's son, bustled to his aid when he entered his own chamber through the sliding panel, and he let him know he would need clean clothes and hot water, as well as some wine. He needed a restorative before he dealt with the consequences and exigencies of that night.

Dressed in warm clothes, he sat by the fire in his room, allowing himself one minute, knowing from messages sent and received that Gerta was safe up in Uta's suite, where Mina, too, was being cared for, having been drugged, which explained his sister's escape. She was becoming crafty in her madness, and he faced the awful possibility that for her own good she would have to be confined or surrendered to someone else's care.

He bowed under the terrible thought; perhaps he had failed after all this time.

ELIZABETH slipped into Nikolas's room, only her steely determination and need to speak with him forcing her to go beyond the horror and fear of what she had witnessed. There, by his fire, he was, his head buried in his hands, his shoulders slumped in defeat. His shaggy hair, threaded with silver, gleamed in the firelight, his long fingers thrust through it as he clutched his head. How could she feel such overwhelming tenderness and such loathing at the same time? With the knowledge of his duality, her conflicting emotions had erupted, too, and they warred in her breast. One would win, and she feared it would be the loathing of his inhuman side; for how could it be otherwise?

"Nikolas," she whispered.

He bolted to his feet and instinctively she withdrew a few paces, searching his face for traces of the beast he had been.

"Elizabeth," he whispered, holding out one hand. Then he let it fall to his side. "I will not approach you, I promise," he said, his voice breaking.

"How long?" she asked, staying a good distance from him. "How long have you been—"

"A werewolf?" he said, perhaps knowing she could not utter the word. "Fifteen years."

Her eyes widened. "Fifteen years?" Was he then involved in the deaths fifteen years ago? No, she knew that was not so. Or . . . did she? So many things she had thought she knew were now proven wrong. And yet beneath it all was the knowledge that everything he did in his life he did for his family; he was no murderer. "Explain . . . I don't understand . . ."

"This is no time to explain. I need to know—"

"Just tell me!" she cried out. "Tell me why!"

"Why I am as I am?" He shook his head and shrugged.

"Every von Wolfram male has the potential within him, but it does not always come out. In most cases it is only to protect our family that we begin to transform."

"How does it happen?"

"Elizabeth, there is not the time necessary—"

"Yes, there is! Gerta is safe; I saw to her myself, and you know after this she'll sleep the night away. Just answer me! Please, Nikolas, help me to understand."

He collapsed back into his chair and rested his head in his hands again. "After all, what does it matter?" he muttered. He took a moment and then began. "Many years ago, I began to feel . . . to feel different. I knew all the old stories, but I thought . . . God help me, I thought it was ignorant folklore. But then, one night . . . the fire."

Elizabeth trembled, waiting, watching. Still keeping her distance, she circled and watched from the hearth. He didn't look up. "The night of the fire," she prompted him.

"It was summer. I was on my way home from Italy; we— Cesare and I—made it to the village, but I was anxious to come home to the castle. So, leaving Cesare behind in the village to bring up my trunks the next day by cart, I was coming by a path through the woods in the full of the moon. I saw a figure near an old abandoned cottage; the fire started, I heard voices calling for help, and I tried to save them. I tried. I tried to beat down the door, but it was impossibly locked, I still do not know how, nor who it was I saw move away in the shadows that night. I ran after him . . . or her, and then towards the castle, for I needed to get help. As I ran I felt this change come over me. But I did not transform. I did not yet know how."

"What happened?" she asked. "Did you get help?"

He nodded. "I got Johannes and others, but it was far too late. It was a terrible, terrible night. We got the fire out and then discovered the bodies inside . . . the bodies of Anna and Hans. I never spoke of the figure I saw, for I feared . . ." He shook his head and didn't finish. "The clearing where the cabin was is still where Gerta goes, every time she is in her awful state."

"Oh," Elizabeth said, understanding finally some of his

fears and worries. There was silence for a long moment. But then she said, "How does it feel to be . . . to be . . . and is it voluntary? Do you control it?"

He looked up at her with exasperation. "How can you ask this? Why do you want to know?" When there was no answer, he sighed and shrugged his shoulders. "Now I control it; I learned how. Uta . . . she sensed a change in me, even more so after Johannes died, and she told me then that the old family tales were true. In the chapel was hidden a relic, the wolfskin kirtle. She gave it to me but told me to use it wisely. At first I was fascinated by the ability and I shifted often. I ran in the forest, glorying in my power."

"Is it not dangerous for you . . . the other wolves . . . the forest?"

"No. No, it is not dangerous. They know me . . . they . . . they fear me. I am like them, but not like them, and they know I could kill them in that state. They sense the difference and stay away from me."

"Oh," she said, feeling a shiver run down her spine. His world was dark, different, filled with sensations she could not even imagine.

"It is why . . . the first night of the full moon I go into the forest . . . I run. It drives the other wolves away . . . it warns them. But it was a fertile year for them. They have increased in numbers, and their fear wanes. It is why they have begun to watch us . . . Gerta, you . . . even me. They will never attack *me,* but if you or Gerta appear to present a danger to them, they might hurt one of you."

There was silence for a long minute, then she said, "You were telling me . . . how you began to . . . to glory in the power of the change."

"Yes. I began to enjoy the power and the secret. And that was when I discovered the danger."

"You enjoyed it? How can that be?" Elizabeth asked, horror welling up in her again. "And is that the danger?"

"Of course that is the danger!" he said roughly. "How could I not enjoy it? There is an intoxicating power to being a wolf. It is life as no man has experienced it; one can smell things, feel things . . . and one is swift and sure, and there is no question in one's mind about what is the right thing to do, no moral ambiguity." He sagged, his gaze drifting. "That was when it came to me that I had to stop or . . ."

"Or?"

"Or it would take me over. That is the danger. Man is a creature full of contradictions. We think of everything, ponder the moral implications of our actions. The animal and the human war in our breasts, and that is how we are meant to be . . . it is what makes us human, that war between instinct and reason. It is the only thing that tempers our behavior, and without it, with only our intelligence and our instinct to dominate, our drive, we would be the most dangerous beasts that live. A wolf does not do that, does not question its behavior. One protects one's family pack, even if it means killing another to do it. It is seductive, that sureness, for as a human we weigh things, make decisions, then ponder those decisions. But a wolf . . . once a course of action is begun, he never thinks again of the right or wrong. It just . . . is."

"Is anyone else in the family . . . afflicted?"

He flinched at her choice of that word. "Not to my knowledge, though I fear for Christoph. It is why I am so harsh with him; I must make him my subordinate . . . he must fear me a little. Until I am sure of him, I cannot let him become as I am, or I fear he would be lost to the seduction of it, of being an animal. It is why I wanted him in the army; that ruthless discipline over oneself, that is what is needed."

She thought how lonely Nikolas's life must have been, all these years, carrying his secret. It explained much about his aloofness, his rigid self-discipline, his . . . aloneness. "Does anyone else know?" she whispered.

"Adele knows, though she has never asked for anything, any confirmation. Uta knows . . . she is the holder of all the old stories. She knows, and as I said, gave me the kirtle . . . told me to use it wisely. Cesare knows. He is the only person in this world I trust implicitly." He glanced up at her. "Or he *was* the only person." He gazed back down at the carpet.

"Is it only males, then, who become . . . ?"

"Yes. It is how I always knew Gerta was not a true were-wolf, no matter how much she wishes to be."

That brought the present back to her, and what she needed to discuss with him. She watched his face, trying to overcome her repugnance, but it was not to be. Whether all love for him was gone she could not say. She doubted that was possible, but still . . . he was not the man she had thought him, and it would never be the same, she knew that for a certainty. Summoning all her determination, she said. "M-may I . . . sit?"

"Please," he said, indicating the other chair. "I will . . . stay away from you, Elizabeth. I understand how you feel."

She doubted that he truly did, for no one could understand the sundering of a human heart into two fragments; that was the pain she was feeling that moment. She sat and felt his warmth radiate towards her, and there was still that part of her that longed to hold him close. The terrible pain she saw in his eyes tore at her, for she knew it was put there by her own re-action to him. It was out of her control, though; she could not change how she felt. "Are you always part wolf . . . or part human?"

"There is that within me that is wolf always," he said. "But no, Elizabeth, I am fully a man. Even in my wolf state, the man exists; I have willed it so. And yet there is that about me that is always wolf . . . your scent, it drives me to distraction. I can tell when you are near. I could find you in the darkest forest just from the hint of your scent on the air. There is that much wolf left within me in my fully human state."

She resolutely pushed away the many questions that were still unanswered. What she had to tell him could wait no longer. "I have to tell you what I have discovered," she said, staring at the fire. Questioning him further about his transfor-mational powers seemed useless when she could not bear to be in his presence much longer. The need to tell him what she had discovered superseded her need for answers. "I know you have been told what happened this night, that Mina was drugged. But I have learned much, and suspect more. Niko-las," she said urgently, meeting his gaze once more. "It is your Uncle Bartol! I suspect that all along, from the beginning, he has been drugging Countess Gerta. There is a compound that can easily be made from plants, herbs, even potatoes exposed to the sun in growing . . . any one of the substances contains an ingredient called atropine . . . Nik, it causes hallucinations! It makes people think they are transforming into an animal, or that they can fly!"

He was astounded, and his face paled. "But why? Why would he . . . ?"

"I don't know; someone else might know that, but I'm almost certain I'm right. He drugged me, Nik." She told him of her odd night's sleep and her discovery of the powder on the edge of her cup the very next night. She suspected that he had been reading her journal, perhaps threatened by her quest to figure out the dark secrets of Wolfram Castle. "And there's more." She told him all she knew, including their discovery of the relationship between Christoph and his aunt. Whatever else she believed, she knew that Nikolas was the only one who could handle all of these things and straighten out his troubled family. "But Nik," she said urgently, reaching out to clasp his arm before remembering and drawing back. "Nik, one of the affects of this drugging is . . . is to make the person promiscuous and unable to distinguish inappropriate behavior. Poor Gerta . . . she was unable to control her behavior for that reason, I'm convinced. And it is possible," she continued, gaining conviction as she went, "that Bartol even drugged your nephew to a lesser degree. It could account for his behavior and for his improper relationship with Countess Gerta. He's so tormented . . . . I feel that from him and pity him from the bottom of my heart. I think that Bartol wanted to use the confusion and pain of the family to further his own ends, whatever those might be."

As she watched Nikolas's face, a frightening change took hold. His dark eyes gleamed silver and a ferocious expression like a shadow overtook him. If he had shouted or broke down it would have been terrible, but even worse, a cold, dread certainty steeled his whole frame. She would not have been surprised if he grew fangs or fur in that moment, for the animal part of his being was powerful.

He stood, his movements fluid. "I am going to kill him," he said, his voice a growl.

She stumbled from her chair and backed away, but when she met his gaze again he had calmed and there was pain in his eyes.

"Elizabeth," he whispered, reaching out one hand. His signet ring glittered.

"No, Nik, I can't," she said, answering his unvoiced plea. She could not touch him, could not go near him. That was over.

He nodded. "I know." He looked down at the floor for a long minute and then back up at her. "I am going to speak with Bartol."

"You're not truly going to . . . to kill him, are you?"

"Not until I'm sure. And not until I understand why."

Nikolas left Elizabeth, unable to bear the distrust in her eyes and the fear in her expression. Though broken of heart, he admired the strength of will it took in her to come to him alone to tell him her suspicions and findings. Selfishly, he had breached the barriers of her heart, and now she suffered. Too late he understood how much he loved her, and how great his pain would be once he allowed his heart to feel what it was to find one's life mate and then lose her.

But not now. Now was the time for blood. He was gaining a fierce determination to at long last put down the terrible evil that had laid hold of his family when Bartol Liebner had come to the live at Wolfram Castle. Though he had been blind to the man's pernicious influence, now he could trace back a hundred—nay, a thousand—instances when Bartol had the opportunity to infect his sister and his niece and nephew with his dark domination.

As he made his way to his uncle's quarters, Nikolas remembered all of the terrible happenings of years gone by. Was it possible? Could much of that turmoil be laid at Bartol Liebner's feet? He would learn the truth if he had to shake it out of him.

But where was he? He was not in his quarters, nor was he in any reasonable place he was likely to be. The dark house was alive with servants rushing here and there, and he took a moment to reassure himself that all was well with his family.

Elizabeth had gone directly up to Charlotte, who was confused and frightened; he looked in on them but said nothing to either. Adele was with Uta and his aunt Katrina, who were keeping watch over Gerta; she slumbered on a cot in the corner of the room, her complexion pallid, her pulse slow but regular. The women beset him with questions, but all he did was ask if any one of them had seen Bartol. Not one of them had, and he would not answer when they asked him questions. There was no time for explanations.

Nikolas, baffled to know where his uncle was, stopped everything and closed his eyes. The full moon called to him, and his animal heart felt the threat of the fell presence that tainted and imperiled his family. If only he had felt this before, or at least understood what he felt, for he had, indeed, sensed the evil permeating his home. Sadly, he had always feared that he himself was the evil presence. Now he knew the truth.

Where was Bartol Liebner?

His eyes closed, his head thrown back, his nose flared, a hundred scents traveled through him; he could hear a scrabbling in the walls, like a rat crawling to safety. Blood heating like pitch, Nikolas's heart throbbed and pulsed and fury gripped him.

Bartol. He was in the secret passages. He knew them and was slithering like the serpent in the garden with his poisonous message. That was how he had done much of his ill deeds, perhaps, slipping into rooms, spreading his venom.

Raising his hands and stretching to his full height, Nikolas tamped down the urge to howl and instead shouted, "I will find you Bartol Liebner!"

Bolting into his library, he pushed back the panel. He had no need of a candle or lantern; his eyes were sharp with the animal blood of the full moon, and he loped along the passages, crouching and listening at times and padding quietly often, but then the scent of fear reached him, assailing his nostrils with its foul odor. The man was near, and the urge to transform was like a hunger that gnawed.

However, never had Nikolas done so in his own house, and never would he, even though he didn't even need the wolfskin kirtle anymore to change; that was a relic of bygone days. He used it to speed the transformation, but as angry as he was, and as hard-driven to protect his own, he could make the change in seconds if need be.

But no; in his home he would face his mortal enemy in his human form.

The passage rose and fell, steps, then a flat run, and then . . . he grabbed hold of cloth and Bartol squealed with fear, his whole plump frame shivering. Roughly, Nikolas hauled his uncle through the passages and into his library, throwing him on the floor.

"Nephew," the man cried, one hand up in a pleading gesture, his palm scraped and bleeding. "What has come over you? What have I done to displease you?"

"What have you *not* done? That question is more to the purpose, Bartol Ignasz Liebner. I accuse you of drugging my sister and my niece, and perhaps even my nephew."

"How can you say such things?" Bartol whimpered, pulling himself up with the aid of a chair arm. "I live only to serve your family. I have given my life in devotion—"

"You have given nothing! But why? What have you wanted that you did not get? Why have you poisoned this family with your evil?" Nikolas pinned the man with his gimlet gaze and waited.

Bartol squirmed. He shuddered, and then his eyes darkened, the pupils large and dark and the smooth ovoid face twisting with malice. "Do you want the truth? I saved you all pain! Your sister-in-law and brother-in-law . . . they were fornicators! Anna Lindsay fled to Hans and told him lies about me, and then they began their filthy little intrigue, pawing each other in secret and escaping to that dirty woodsman's cottage to pursue their scandalous affair. I cleansed this family of that filth!"

A wave of dizziness passed over Nikolas as he understood

the implications of Bartol's confession. For years he had feared that Gerta, heavily gravid and emotionally unbalanced, had set the fatal fire herself—he hadn't any proof, just a deep-seated fear—but his poor sister had been innocent. It was Bartol; he was the plump figure scuttling away in the dark, he had set the fatal fire, and perhaps even . . . had he even poisoned Johannes? He looked at the man, trying to understand. "You say Anna told him lies about you. Did you . . . did you try to seduce her?"

Emotion flicked over Bartol's face: fury, fear . . . guilt.

"You did. Or perhaps worse. And she told Hans. But why did she not tell Johannes?"

There was silence. He was not going to answer. He began to creep towards the door, but Nikolas thundered, "Stop!" and grabbed the man and hauled him back to the center of the room, throwing him down like a doll. "She did, didn't she? She did tell her husband, my brother."

"Lies!" Bartol shouted, rising to his knees. "All lies! But Johannes, he was a good man. He didn't believe her filthy lies."

"And so she went to Hans, and that was how the affair started, no doubt. I remember Anna, she was beautiful and kind, but she was weak, too, and would have turned elsewhere if Johannes expressed some doubt."

"She was a whore, and yet I was not good enough to bed a whore?" Bartol raged, his watery eyes gleaming with hatred. "Your father was just as bad! I was never good enough, not good enough to marry Adele, not good enough even for feebleminded Gerta!"

Nikolas felt a sick lurch in his stomach as he finally understood it all. "You wanted to marry one of my sisters?"

"And why not? If my sister was good enough for your father, why was I not good enough for one of his daughters? I would finally have had a life away from my family . . . away from you all. I watched them in their cradles and planned my marriage! I would have been a good husband, I would have been a kind husband. But no! Jakob said no."

Horror seized Nikolas. "You watched them in their cradles? You . . . you planned this even as Gerta and Adele were children? And then . . . you killed Johannes. You killed my brother!" He had heard enough and he knew enough; it didn't matter anymore why Bartol had killed Johannes, it was enough to know he did. "While you were at it, you should have killed me!" he shouted.

"I tried," Bartol said, hatred in his sneer. "I tried but you . . . you would not die!"

With a roar of fury, Nikolas lunged at the man, seized his collar, and hauled him toward the door. At the very least he was going to horsewhip Bartol Liebner to within an inch of his life, and then . . . and then . . . would he kill him? The call to blood was fierce. But the human was stronger; Nikolas would take him to the village and the fiend would be tried for his crimes. A court of law would decide his death or life.

But the door burst open just then, and Fanny, the little English-speaking maid he had assigned to Elizabeth, tripped in, breathless and wide-eyed with terror. She could not speak and stood staring, whimpering.

"What is it? Fanny, speak, I command you!" he thundered.

"I don't know what this means," she cried out, wringing her hands. "I don't understand the message, but Miss Stanwycke . . . she said to tell you or I would not have burst in on you like this ever, sir . . ."

"What is it? Give me the message!"

She closed her eyes against his ire and said, "Countess von Holtzen awoke and tricked Countess Uta and Frau Liebner, telling them she needed privacy to relieve herself. She has slipped away from them and run towards the woods again, and Miss Stanwycke has followed. She tried to warn the servants, but they will not listen. She needs your help, Count—"

But Nikolas had already pushed Bartol away. "Enough! I understand." He turned to his uncle and stabbed a long finger at him. "You stay here on pain of death. I am not done with you, but if you do or say one more thing, I swear I will kill you, and I promise it will be painful and slow."

Chapter 26

THIS COULD not be happening again! Would this awful night never end? The moon was beginning its descent, and the night was even more chill, the scent of fresh snow tanging the air. And again Elizabeth had been forced to run after the countess, for she had no idea where Nikolas was, and given the happenings of earlier that night could not risk the countess being alone in the woods with the hunters possibly still there.

And the idiot servants . . . again they had all gazed at Elizabeth as if she were a lunatic when she told them to get help. They would not try to get help, nor would they even find Countess Adele or Count Nikolas for her. It was her sex, she knew, for though the Countess Adele wielded some power in the household, no other woman had any right to give them orders. It was infuriating, and her only hope was that Fanny, with her intelligence and grasp of the English language and ready understanding, would get the message to Nikolas.

The one person she did not want to send the message through was Charlotte; her charge she had told to stay in her room, bar the door, and allow no one entrance. Until she knew where Bartol was, she was bent on not allowing Charlotte to be exposed to his hateful, insidious influence.

The countess was already in the forest; Elizabeth swore she would guard the woman herself for the next few nights, for she seemed too clever and too determined in her hallucinatory state. If no one could confound her wily ways, Elizabeth would herself. She would sit on her if need be.

But first she had to find her before the hunters or the wolves. That might be terrifyingly easy, since she could hear the sound of men shouting and dogs baying. She crashed through the forest, hoping she wasn't too late, terrified of what she might find. The snow was slippery and her feet went out from under her; she crashed to the ground, her bare hands grasping at snow-frosted branches and twigs, scraping them raw. No nightmare could be this terrifying, this horrible, she thought, clambering to her feet, weeping from pain and frustration.

Where had Gerta gone? Elizabeth was forced to pick her way, for there was a ridge she had not encountered before, a snowy hill, and then . . . there it was, moonlight still slanting through the trees to it. That same damned clearing! She had found the way, even though she had approached from a different angle.

Now she knew the significance . . . it was the place her husband had died, and in the arms of another woman. How that awful night must have haunted the poor woman! With fresh determination Elizabeth surged forward, bent on protecting Gerta from herself and from the despicable actions of her diabolical kinsman.

Elizabeth and the hunters reached the countess at the same moment. Gerta, gowned only in her nightrail and with her silvery hair streaming down her back, howled and swiped with her clawed hands while dogs crouched nearby, barking and circling her. Men with torches stood near, their dark, hooded forms menacing, the golden flames battling the silvery moonlight for supremacy.

"Countess," she shouted, trying to approach the woman.

But the dogs snapped and snarled, and the countess did, too, pointing her chin to the stars and howling in an eerie, keening bay that was answered by the confused and incensed dogs. The men strode forward, and one took her arm, roughly.

He shouted in German, and Elizabeth understood only part of what he was saying. But she did understand by his gestures and movements that they intended to take Gerta with them to the village.

"No!" Elizabeth shouted, racing forward. But she was held at bay by the snarling dogs. "Leave her alone! Let her go!" It came out in English . . . she couldn't think how to say it in German, and the man just stared in her direction with a baffled expression.

Countess Gerta twisted and struggled, her countenance holding more fear now than madness. Summoning every bit of her courage and inner resources, Elizabeth moved forward again slowly, speaking in her best German. "Please, you must see that the poor countess is only sick and troubled, not dangerous. She is just a woman; do not harm her. Let me take her home."

"She is a werewolf," the man replied, his dark visage twisted with fear and loathing. "She has hurt my daughter. She must be killed."

"No!" screamed Elizabeth. Shaking, she covered her mouth with her hands, thinking, trying to figure out how to get to this man, how to reason with him past his superstition. "No! There *are* no werewolves, just a woman unhappy and troubled, perhaps even drugged. You see there is a drug—"

But another man took the countess's other arm and they turned and roughly hauled her toward the far edge of the forest, in the direction of the village. They would kill her; Elizabeth knew it deep in her heart. Whether they intended to or not, that is how the night would end if she did not find a way to intervene.

And then, out of the forest a great, shaggy silver wolf erupted and stood, paws splayed, lip curled, his black and silver ruff of fur sparkling in the moonlight. The men gasped and fell back.

Nikolas! Elizabeth almost whimpered his name aloud but held back; when she called his name last time, that was when his involuntary transformation back to human form took place, and that would be death to him here. But it was him; she knew it by the look in his eyes and by the intensity of his stare as he first gazed at her and then at the newly released Gerta, who stood quivering and bewildered.

Elizabeth understood and didn't need to be told again. With steely determination she refrained from calling out to him, and instead dashed forward and grabbed Gerta's arm.

She stumbled away, roughly hauling the countess with her. She paused at the edge of the forest, thankful that Gerta was no longer resisting, and looked back.

The dogs were circling Nikolas, and his fur bristled as he readied for battle. One dog lunged at him and Nikolas leapt on the animal, his big mouth clamping down on the dog's throat. The dog yelped and staggered away, blood coursing down his pale fur. Elizabeth felt her stomach twist in revulsion, but then it settled, her fear for Nikolas making her wish him success, no matter what he had to do. These men would kill him in an instant if they could.

The hunters, though, even the lead man, were staying well back, their fear of Nikolas in his bestial form as evident as their intention to do him grave harm. One raised his bow to his shoulder.

"Ni—" Elizabeth bit down on her tongue, exchanged one long look with the wolf, and knew her duty and Nikolas's wishes, even as her heart clenched in pain and fear for the man who still existed even in the wolf form. She turned and without a look back pulled Gerta to safety in the woods and towards the castle. But behind her she could hear the sound of a battle and an animal howling in pain.

It seemed to take forever to retrace their steps. She went wrong a couple of times and had to refind their path. She was almost to the forest edge, almost to the castle, when she heard a crashing in the forest behind her. Only one creature or human, though, she thought, turning to see her fate, dread filling her mind with a certainty that if it was one of the hunters, she and Gerta would both die.

But it was Nikolas in human form, stumbling and reeling through the fir trees, naked but for the wolfskin kirtle and his black cloak.

"Nik!" she cried as he made his way to them.

He stumbled to the ground and gasped out, "It is all right, they are gone, chased away. My own wolves will guard the castle for the rest of the night, but . . ."

He collapsed in the snow. Elizabeth ran to him, pulled back his cloak, and saw the bloody haft of an arrow sticking out from his shoulder. He was pale, his handsome face drained and white in the last glimmers of the sinking moonlight.

"It . . . it must be tipped in wolfsbane," he struggled to say as she crouched by his side. "Nothing else would . . . would . . ."

"Nikolas?" Gerta whimpered. "My brother? Hurt?"

"I need to get you both back into the castle," Elizabeth said, putting one hand under Nikolas's arm and hauling him to his feet. He was far too big a man for her to do that alone; it required much effort on his part, but with him resolutely pushing past the pain he suffered, they struggled together across the open field and up to the castle.

The courtyard beyond the castle was ablaze with light, and there were shouts.

"What's going on now?" Elizabeth muttered.

They struggled to the back, Elizabeth hoping to find some help, for she knew Nikolas was fading, the loss of blood beginning to tell on his ability to move. She could not carry him up stairs, she could not even support him further, for his strength was fading with the effects of poison.

One of the stable boys, eyes wide, was holding a horse, and it was rearing up as the wolf dogs snapped and snarled around them. But the most frightening sight was Bartol Liebner, surprisingly strong for such a supposedly frail man, holding Charlotte against him, her eyes closed, a knife to her throat.

He was hollering at the stable boy who was saddling the horse, but his hold on Charlotte kept slipping as the girl slumped heavily against him. The stable boy, doing as he was bid, led the horse to a mounting block.

"Bartol Liebner!" Elizabeth shouted. She was terrified for her student, for the knife near her throat kept wavering and it was large, easily big enough to slice her with the wrong movement. After all Elizabeth had done, she had failed in her one most important task of keeping Charlotte safe. Though she had warned the girl to stay in her room and bar the door, she had failed to specifically name Bartol as the enemy. Fury enveloped her. "Bartol!" she screamed again.

He turned and there was fear in his eyes, but defiance, too, and hatred. "Get away, or I will kill her, I swear it."

"What do you think you're doing? Where will you go?" Trembling with fear for Charlotte as the knife nicked the tender skin and a single ribbon of scarlet trickled down the unconscious girl's slender white neck, Elizabeth was frozen, afraid to move, afraid to startle him lest he slice her throat. She had not foreseen this awful turn of events, believing that Bartol was confined in Nikolas's care. Poor Charlotte! Bartol had seemed so inoffensive to Elizabeth for so long; how much more so must he have seemed to one so naive as Charlotte, who had the long habit of trust in him to deceive her? If he came to her door, offered her solace and a soothing drink—"You cannot succeed; you must know that," she said, trying to reason with him.

"Leave me alone! I am taking Charlotte; she will be my wife. I mean her no harm, but you will force me into it if you do not get back now."

Nikolas slid down to the ground as Gerta started forward, toward Bartol. She was whimpering and crying.

"Bartol, what are you doing?" the countess said. "I do not understand."

"Get back. You are nothing to me now. If they had let me marry you . . . but you are getting old, and too mad even for my use."

"No!" she cried out. "You love me; you have always said so! I am your precious, your own."

"You are mad and barren! Ugly, old . . . skinny . . ."

His cruel words enraged her, and she shrieked out her hatred for him, running at him with fists flailing.

"No!" Elizabeth screamed, and she lunged after the countess, at the last moment grasping Charlotte's arm and pulling her away as the old man moved to defend himself against the countess's flailing fists.

What happened next occurred so quickly Elizabeth could only reconstruct it later. One of the dogs, on Nikolas's shouted command, leaped between Countess Gerta and Bartol, knocking the man down, and in that instant a dead quietude rolled over the stable yard, all activity brought to an end by the sight of the motionless body of Bartol Liebner, blood pouring from his head into the dirty slush.

Gerta crouched by him and wailed, the dog cringed back, and Nikolas, with a superhuman effort, staggered to his feet and stumbled to the scene of grave suffering, bending over his sister and trying to raise her up. Charlotte lay nearby; Elizabeth ran to the girl and was reassured by the fluttering of a nerve in her neck and the rise and fall of her chest in regular movement.

Alone, his head split open by the mounting block, Bartol Liebner lay, a black and red blot on the ground of the stable yard. As servants raced out and Fanny took Charlotte's care over, Elizabeth went to the man, whose pulse was slowing.

His dark eyes flew open, though, and he looked up at her and groaned, as his eyes fluttered closed again, "Damn you to hell! All my plans for naught . . ."

But he said no more, and Elizabeth whispered, "Whatever your depraved plans were, they were doomed from the start, and for the pain and suffering you have caused, I think you are the one consigned to burn in hell."

Chapter 27

A DAY passed of such unutterable weariness that Elizabeth, when she finally did find an hour to sleep, slumbered deep and dreamless, even though she had thought she would dream of that awful scene in the stable yard.

Uta and Frau Liebner, horrified by the terrible happenings of the night, had bundled both Gerta and Charlotte into Uta's suite and with a recovering Mina—her strong constitution had thrown off a drugging that would have killed a lesser woman—guarded the two. Though physical danger was past, they were intent on discovering the extent of damage to their emotional well-being.

Heinrich, Cesare, and Melisande's father had arrived at dawn, and Nikolas, bandaged against the wound in his shoulder, had descended to the village. From what she understood, Elizabeth assumed the villagers still had no proof of a werewolf, and certainly did not know that their liege was the beast. He had gone down, Cesare reluctantly told her, to calm their fears and order an investigation. He had long suspected that Magda Brandt's wounds were not inflicted by an animal at all, but by a human source, and Cesare had learned, in his stay in the inn, that the girl had a secret lover who was a brutal and vicious man. Among the women of the village it was thought that he beat Magda, but in her fear of him she would not confess it easily.

Elizabeth was in the library with the door open doing some more research on the herbs used to drug Gerta when she sensed a presence and turned. It was Christoph. His eyes were red and his face pale, his shock of blond hair in wild disarray.

"Is she . . . is she all right?" he said, entering but staying near the door. His sensitive hands fluttered, but then he passed one over his wildly tousled hair, an echo of his uncle's habitual movement. "No one will tell me anything. No one will let me see her. Is she all right?"

Not sure if he was asking after Gerta, his erstwhile lover, or Charlotte, Elizabeth was silent for too long evidently, for he groaned and covered his face with his hands.

"My poor sister! I should have taken her from this awful place! I should have protected her, but instead I stayed . . . to my shame . . ." He fell to his knees on the floor and wept, beating on the rug with one fist.

Appalled, Elizabeth raced to his side and knelt beside him, putting her arm around his shoulders. "Count, it was not your doing. You could not have known—"

"I should have! I should have guessed. But I didn't understand what was happening to me. Sometimes . . ." He gazed into her eyes and clutched her hand, his forehead creased in puzzlement. "Sometimes it was as if I was in a dream, and as if it was all happening to someone else and I was only watching, a ghostly spectator, not in my body at all," he said, his words spilling from him in a rapid stream. "I . . . I was afraid I was going mad, and sometimes I wasn't even sure if I was doing what I thought I was doing. Am I mad?"

She hadn't intended to tell anyone anything, preferring to leave that up to Nikolas, but it seemed to her that given the difficult nature of Christoph's relationship with his uncle, that the information was best coming from another source. Nikolas and his nephew had enough to work out without needing to go over all of this. "Count Christoph, Bartol Liebner was an evil, evil man. His purpose seemed to be to foment trouble in your family . . . to break the bonds of your close ties. He had been planning and devising his scheme for many years. What his original plan was, I do not know; I think his ultimate objective was to wrest control of this family from your uncle and take it over himself, though I cannot imagine how he thought it possible. But this is what I know to be true; he was drugging your poor aunt, and he was beginning to drug Charlotte . . . and I think . . . I think he was drugging you." She explained what she had discovered, getting the book down from the shelf and laying it on the carpeted floor. She pointed out to him the references that made clear what hallucinations and aberrant behavior could be blamed on such concoctions.

He calmed and became thoughtful, his beautiful face shadowed by terrible knowledge. It reminded her of Nikolas's face, and she could finally see the resemblance between them. He stood, regaining his detached demeanor, and helped her to her feet. "Thank you, Miss Stanwycke. I think . . . I think I have much to apologize to my uncle for. In truth, I thought he was responsible for my mother's death, and even my father's. My . . . my aunt told me that, but now . . . now I realize how gripped she was by that monster's lies, and how I aided by being unwilling to go to him, man to man, and ask him for the truth. I will never be so misled again."

He had not once said Countess Gerta's name, Elizabeth realized, and perhaps that was better. "He was a horrible, jealous, deranged man. He was trying to sow the seeds of this family's destruction."

"He would have succeeded if not for you."

"And your uncle," Elizabeth added softly, not willing to take credit for all when without Nikolas, the night would have ended in tragedy for both Charlotte and Gerta.

The count nodded, then bowed and slipped away.

IT was very late; moonlight had guided him home. Nikolas wearily gave up his horse to the stable boy. He had prevailed, as he knew he would, in the village and had quelled Wilhelm Brandt's insurrection when he revealed his daughter's cruel lover, freeing Magda from the brute's domination. His bandaged shoulder ached from the long and tedious day. He felt sure he would collapse if he let down his guard, and yet he could not even feel relief yet, there was so much that needed to be done. There was no doubt in his mind that the moment he was in the house he would be beset by questions and problems and dilemmas at every turn. What to do about Christoph? And Gerta? And Charlotte?

But instead, there was an eerie calm. Adele and Count Delacroix were closeted together with Gerta, he was told, in Uta's suite. Frau Liebner was sitting with Charlotte, who still slept, but with an encouraging pink tinge to her pallor. No one knew where Christoph was. Cesare told him all this as Heinrich undressed Nikolas and tended to his wound, replacing the bloody bandages, since he had done much harm by riding when it was so fresh. It had taken all of his endurance not to allow the villagers to see that his shoulder was wounded, for he wanted no one to even begin to make the connection between the Count von Wolfram and the great silver wolf that had driven the hunters back twice that night.

The day had been so long and it was late; Cesare suggested he retire and let everything wait until morning. But that moment there was a rap at the door.

Cesare answered it, and Count Delacroix slipped in past him, approaching Nikolas diffidently. "Are you well, Nikolas?" he asked, his brow furrowed and his silvery hair glinting in the light.

"As well as can be expected. I will recover." Nikolas watched the man, wondering who among the household knew his secret.

"I will not keep you. I just thought I would give you some comforting news. It seems to me that Countess Gerta, though weak and ravaged by the occurrences of the past, will eventually recover, physically at least. It will take time and care, but she will have that and more."

"Good."

Hesitantly, the older man bowed and said, "There is something of great import I wish to discuss with you . . . but not now," he hastily added at the end of his sentence, perhaps sensing Nikolas's great weariness. "I will just say that . . . the Countess Adele and I have been talking while we watched over her sister. It appears that she has long been under the mistaken impression that I held a degree of warmth towards the Countess Gerta, and that . . . in short, Count, I have . . . I have asked the Countess Adele to be my wife, and she has agreed. We would like to marry and then make our wedding journey to Italy. With your permission, of course."

Nikolas sighed, wearily. Perhaps it would be a good thing, but he could not imagine how he would deal with the household without his most valuable sister, and with Gerta, Charlotte, Christoph, Eva, and Jakob to take care of.

"And we would like to take Adele's sister with us. We both feel that a change of scene from the terror of this last while, and the warmth of Italy, will do poor Gerta a world of good. I have . . . I have a sister there, and we could stay at her villa where a physician of her acquaintance also resides, my sister fancying herself ill often."

Nikolas felt light-headed with relief that one problem, at least, had a tentative solution, but he merely nodded.

"I will leave you alone," the count said, bowing and moving back to the door. "And we will speak of this tomorrow."

Heinrich, seeing his master's unutterable weariness, hastened even Cesare out of the room and turned down the bed. Nikolas crawled in, but after the candle was out he lay for a long time staring at the draped bed canopy. He had not dared to see Elizabeth; he had no right and could not bear the look in her eyes. She had seen him attack the dogs of the villagers, she had witnessed his animal behavior, and she would loathe him. Even if it was not so, with all she had done she was likely sleeping at this hour.

But . . . an idea crept into his brain, and once it had taken hold it would not release him. He could at least gaze at her as she slept; she would never need to know. One last time he could look upon her lovely face and bid her adieu from his heart. Seized by the notion, he knew there would be no sleep for him until he acceded. His whole body aching, quivering with pain and weariness, he slipped down the well-known passages, remembering every sweet moment of their time together. Her room beckoned him as a haven of warmth and love . . . warmth he would never share again and love that had fled with the knowledge of what he was.

He silently slipped into her room, the waning moon lighting it faintly, and moved quietly to her bedside, where he could hear the even puff of her breath. He stood close, not daring to even reach out and touch. Her face was pale, and her chestnut hair was splayed splendidly across her snowy pillow. The covers were pushed back and he could see the rise and fall of her breast.

She would go back to England, no doubt. This castle was the scene of such terror for her, and in truth, Charlotte had learned so much she was ready for her future. There was nothing left for Elizabeth to do here. The sensible solution was to send Charlotte to England with Elizabeth as her companion and protector.

He must have sighed out loud, for her eyes flew open and she started up in her bed. He would have fled, but she had seen him and he forced himself to stay. The fear in her eyes broke him utterly, and though he never had cried before, he caught a sob in his throat and choked it back.

"I am sorry," he whispered. "I just needed . . . I just needed to be sure you were . . . were well and sleeping. I will leave now. Please do not be frightened; I will never do this again, I promise you." And yet he stood, filling his heart and soul with the sight of her, hungry for her in ways he could not understand, starving for one kind word of understanding, one morsel of forgiveness.

She gazed at him and her eyes went to his bandaged shoulder. "Are you . . . are you in pain?"

He nodded and saw in her eyes compassion rising, like a warm tide.

"Did you succeed in the village?"

He nodded again.

"I knew you would," she said, a tinge of something like pride in her lovely voice.

Staring steadily at her, he felt the weariness overtake him and his knees buckled. With no strength left, with every bit of his stamina used, and with an unutterable pain in his heart that hurt so much more than the arrow in his shoulder, he sank to his knees at her bedside and bowed his head.

Elizabeth felt the tears stream down her cheeks as she watched the fierce and powerful count sink to his knees, his skin gray from weariness, his bandage bloody. "Nikolas," she whispered and slipped from the bed, swooping down on him and taking him in her arms. She rocked him against her and then tried to raise him. "Come, sit on the bed for a minute. You've worn yourself out."

"How can you bear to touch me?" he murmured, shivering under her arm around his bare shoulders.

She couldn't answer him because she didn't know. But as she helped him up and guided him to her bed, she began to understand herself and her feelings toward him. She made him lie down, pulled covers over him, and lay beside him, finding the courage to put her arms around his cold chest to try to warm him.

"Elizabeth," he whispered and pressed his lips into the hollow of her throat, where her pulse throbbed.

But she had no fear. Even in his wolf form, with fury burning in his silvery eyes, she had known herself to be safe. He was still Nikolas, and he had taken her into his circle of protection. As the leader of his family and guardian of his pack, he would defend them to the death, but he was no more mindlessly vicious than the animals he emulated. A wolf killed, from her understanding, for food and for protection, but never for revenge, nor wantonly . . . as Bartol Liebner had. Who was more the animal between the two men?

"Nikolas," she whispered, holding him close.

His lips sought hers and she allowed it, finding herself tasting him, wanting him, loving him still, with just as much fervor as before, just as much ardent desire and deep affection. And more . . . there were no secrets left between them, so their hearts were open to each other. But he was weak and a few kisses were all he could manage, his breathing ragged and his body shivering with weariness.

"Do you believe they will all recover?" he murmured. "They have been through so much."

"Your family," she whispered into his ear, "for all of its turmoil and trouble, has the most powerful bond of any family I have ever seen."

He told her that in his last conversation with Bartol Liebner the man had revealed his thwarted plans of wedding one of the sisters, Adele or Gerta. Together they postulated that he had, perhaps verging on madness himself, thought he could marry Charlotte and gain a measure of stature in the family. As mad as it sounded, it was all they could imagine. Never would anyone know the whole truth now, for gone forever was the fell presence of Bartol Liebner.

She talked for a while as he nestled close to her and told him about her conversation with Christoph and what she had discovered of the source of his conflict with his uncle, and his shame over it all now. She told him the sad tale of how easily Gerta had tricked Uta and Frau Liebner for the second time in one night; it had been as simple as her telling them she needed to relieve herself. They had thought her safe, but she had slipped away, still deluded by the powerful dose of the atropine concoction Bartol had stealthily administered in her tea that evening. The two old women were full of shame, but Elizabeth had tried to soothe their disgrace by telling them the truth—no one else would have done anything differently than they had.

He then told her that Count Delacroix had proposed to Adele, been accepted, and that they intended to use their wedding journey to Italy as a time for Gerta to recover, away from Wolfram Castle, and away from Christoph.

"I think that's wise," Elizabeth said quietly, staring into the dark, the moonlight gone from the room and silence a blanket over the whole castle. "He is deeply ashamed and scarred. It is best if they don't see each other for a long while, just so they can separately heal. He is mostly concerned for his younger sister now, and the effect of all this on her."

There was only the faintest vestige of light left in the room. Nikolas gazed up at her as she sheltered him and curtained him with her long hair, his eyes blazing with weary warmth. "I wish I had loved you one last time before . . ." he murmured, but then his eyes closed before he could even finish.

She held her breath in fear, but he merely fell into a deep sleep. She held him close. "I do too, Nikolas," she whispered. "I love you and I always will. I wish . . ." But she couldn't say it. She wished they could marry. She wished she could bear his children. She wished she could be with him always.

THE room was flooded with light and Fanny had already been there, Nikolas thought, as he awoke. He was better, stronger again; though the pain still throbbed in his shoulder and it itched fiercely, it was mending. One of the benefits of his wolf heritage was quick healing and a powerful constitution. He could smell the coffee on the table and his stomach growled in hunger. But he was not going to move, for Elizabeth lay in his arms, her face trustingly close to him, her lips softly pursed against the deep breath of sleep.

He ran one thumb down her cheek, relishing the soft texture of her skin, admiring the lush curve of her breast against his bare chest, and feeling every inch of her warm body stretched against his. In an instant he knew she was awakening; he felt the pulse of her heart rate quicken and the faint movement of her body. "Good morning," he murmured against her mouth, and then he kissed her deeply. With returning strength and the memory of her infinite kindness the night before came a faint hope.

She responded, curling her arms around his neck and stretching against him. His body pulsed with awareness. He ran one hand down the curve of her spine to her bottom, and her squirming pleasure as he caressed her bare skin encouraged the rapid swelling of his shaft as it swiftly burgeoned and found the curve of her thigh and the concave sweetness where her legs and torso met.

Her breathing was tremulous and rapid, and he felt the pulse at the base of her throat under his lips as it leaped and her heart hammered. His lips trailed down over her throat and to her breasts, pulling back the fabric with his teeth and nuzzling the sweet peak of her nipples budding in his mouth. She had released all fear of him; he could feel it in her acceptance of his advances and her readiness for loveplay. Her hand sought him under the covers and stroked him slowly as he found her dampness and spread the tender lips with his fingers.

Her rich scent reached his nostrils and he pulled her fragrance in; she was ripe and sweet as a plum, and . . . he stopped, quivering with need but knowing it was not to be satisfied.

"Nik?" In the silvery dawn light, Elizabeth opened her eyes as he stopped touching her. "What is it?" She touched him still and his rod thickened in her hand, pulsing with need just as she was aching for him. Even if she couldn't have him forever, even if he had no intention of ever marrying—and she could not stay with him in this role, this purgatory between mistress and wife—making love with him one last time, now knowing all he was . . . that would stay with her. But he had stopped and gazed at her with an aching intensity. Did he need to hear her to say it? "Nik," she murmured. "Make love to me, please. Once more, just once more."

He closed his eyes and his whole body quivered, shuddering with suppressed yearning; she could feel it in him, the desire and the need. He was sweating, his brow damp, as he restrained himself physically. "I can't," he groaned, clenching his teeth against a wave of desire.

"Why? You want me . . . I know you want me." She curled herself provocatively around him, rolling on top of him and straddling his body, feeling his erection nudge her, making her damp with passionate craving. His resistance to her seduction urged her on. She moved and pushed herself down on the thick knob, relishing his response, the jerk of his body as he pulled back, trying not to give in to temptation.

"I just . . . can't," he said through his teeth.

"Yes, you can," she said, brushing her hair over his chest and caressing the triangular muscle that capped his thick shoulder. The bloody bandage worried her, but as strong as he was he had defeated the poison; she felt it somehow, as if she was privy to his bodily sensations. She ran one hand down his arm, trailing her fingers over the contour of every steely muscle. She arched her back, moving, coating him with her wetness and feeling him spasm with suppressed passion. "You can. I know what you are now, Nik; I know *who* you are, and nothing has changed. I don't care; you're not an animal now, you're a man." She lay on his chest. "*My* man . . . for this one moment, at least. Make love to me," she said softly.

"Ah, Elizabeth," he groaned in her ear. "I can't. You don't understand. If I make love to you now, I will make you with child."

"You can't know that," she gasped.

"Oh, yes, but I do."

She reared up, straddling his thickly muscled waist. "How do you know?"

His eyes burned with fiercely restrained need. "I know. I can . . . I can smell it, taste it—it is like a flavor to me, a sweetness—the ripeness of you, the desire in your body to receive me and my own need to plant my seed. It is in you, the . . . the acknowledgment."

"Of what?" she whispered, gazing down into his eyes.

"You are mine and always will be, till the end of time." He stared up at her, tenderly pushing back one long strand of hair behind her ear. "And I am yours. Your life mate. The only one. Until I die, I am yours, and you . . . you belong to me, just as I belong to you."

"Until you die," she repeated, rubbing his scruffy chin, the thick beard dark against the pallor of his skin. She was aware of him, still throbbing, as just the tip entered into her. He did not push and in fact held himself resolutely still beneath her. "But . . . but you don't have a . . . a life mate. You don't intend to marry. You told me so."

He sighed. "And that is why I can't . . . we can't . . ."

"Make a child," she finished for him.

He nodded, his eyes gleaming with unshed tears. He framed her face with his hands. "I love you," he said, his voice a hoarse croak. "I will love you forever."

The words were like a balm, and the last vestiges of doubt fled. "Then marry me," she said, pushing down on him and watching his eyes roll back as he arched and thrust into her, his member throbbing, all control in her own grasp unless he was willing to toss her aside like a doll. "Marry me," she cried, surrendering to desire. "Plant your seed, make a son . . . or a daughter. *Marry* me." She sank down on him and kissed his lips, relishing the feel of him buried deep inside of her, their twined limbs pulling them so close not a quarter inch of space was left between them.

He groaned and rolled her over onto her back, drawing out but then thrusting back in, pushing deep, his muscles bunching; the sweet dance of male heat and female nectar, their sweat mingling, their mutual cries echoing up to the high ceiling, began. She felt the rising tide, tried to push it back, but gave herself over finally, feeling the ecstasy spiral in waves though her body, her skin shivering with delight, her muscles twitching, and her body reaching a delirium she had never thought possible. Waves of dizziness coursed through her until she no longer knew if she was on top, under him, or floating.

As he bucked and doubled above her, and she felt the heat of him bursting inside of her, her body drank him in as if she was long thirsty. She felt the welling of tears and they coursed down her cheeks. *I love you I love you I love you . . . forever!* Had she said it? Cried it out? Or only thought it?

She opened her eyes, her vision swimming with tears; he was gazing down at her, even as his thickness still filled her.

"Did you mean it?" he whispered, kissing her brow and the tears on her cheeks.

"Mean what?" she asked, kissing his lips.

"That you love me. That . . . that you'll marry me? Despite everything?" He pushed back the damp curls on her forehead.

There was so much hope in his gaze, so much tremulous fear and longing. She reached up and touched his lips with one fingertip. "Yes, oh yes, I'll marry you."

"Elizabeth," he sighed. "I think I will go mad from such happiness." He kissed her tenderly, even as he grew soft within her, his appetite satisfied for the moment.

No one came near the room all morning. They talked, and slept, and then made love again as the sun arched into the sky. As they lay together finally, passion again happily satisfied but both awake, curled together, she asked, "Why did you decide never to marry? Was it . . . was it the werewolfism?" She still felt foolish saying such an odd word, but she must accept fact.

"No . . . no, not really." He stroked her hair. "But for years now I have thought . . . been afraid, that madness was inherited among us children. I just didn't know. Gerta was so . . ." He stopped and shook his head.

"You thought she killed them, Anna and Hans, didn't you?"

"I was afraid it was so. I saw a figure that night, and I feared it was her. But it was Bartol. How could I have thought it of poor Gerta? But it was not really just the inherited madness I feared; I knew I would need to spend my whole life looking after her. I would never send her into exile, bar her from her family and her children. How could I devote my life to a wife and children, then, when I knew I would need to take care of her so carefully?" He paused, a thoughtful look on his face. "Uta told me I was a fool for taking the whole burden on myself and allowing no one to help me. I think I should have listened to her, for she tried to tell me that many times. Perhaps if I had, things would not have become so dangerous . . . Bartol would not have gained such a hold over this family."

"Perhaps. Or perhaps not. There is no going back, Nik, to do things differently. How . . . how did you truly come to know you were . . . were a werewolf? I know you told me it was the night of the fire, but . . ."

He sighed deeply. "I have never told anyone this. Adele knows, but she has never asked for details."

"But if I am to be your wife, I should know."

"Hmm. I think you will say that often in our lifetime." He kissed her forehead. "You will always know just what to say to me to make me do exactly what you wish. All right. In our family we are raised with a knowledge of werewolves, but no one told me I would become one. Although every von Wolfram male has the potential, it generally happens to only one male in every generation, most often to the eldest male, but sometimes just to . . . to the leader. To the man who will take care of his family."

She considered it. "That's why you and Christoph cannot get along; although you thought it was your own harshness in needing to subjugate him, it is more than that. It's not just his suspicions of you, and your frustration with him. In the normal course, he would have left the house, but he is—or has the potential to be—another dominant male . . . perhaps he will be a werewolf someday."

Nik appeared to consider it, and understanding flitted into his eyes. "You could be right. I feared he would have the potential, but I did not trust him to use it wisely, nor was I sure. But it would explain much, I suppose, of the tension between us, if that is his fate. In nature, when the wolves are growing, males, as they reach adulthood, are ejected from the pack by the lead wolf if they are dominant in nature. Some males stay, but they will likely never breed."

"Like Bartol," she said with a shiver.

"Hmm. True. And the females stay. The dominant male's mate—they choose one, you know, and stay together always—will be the dominant female and will protect the others." He gazed at her and touched her hair. "That is you. My life mate. You, who protected Charlotte and rescued Gerta so many times."

"You gave me courage; I knew you would be there when I needed you, and you always were. Do you know, even when you were in your wolf state, I knew you were near."

"Thank God you did not wait for me to ask for your help; you just thrust yourself into things."

"Even when you tried to tell me I had no stake in this family, I knew I did."

At long last they rose, and Nikolas ordered all who were able to gather in the drawing room. He and Elizabeth had agreed that his family needed to understand what had happened over the last few days. Melisande at first did not want to leave her father's side, but she was coaxed by Charlotte, who was regaining her strength and bossiness quickly. Even Uta had been carried down for this grand occasion and gazed around her in wonder at the room she had not entered for several years. Mina, who had sacrificed so much, was by her side in a chair, better, but still recovering from the massive dose of drug Gerta had, in her delusional state, delivered her. Gerta was the only one not present; her health was still too precarious, and her emotional state fragile. Fanny was sitting with her.

Nikolas stood before the fire and stared at his family, but Elizabeth had eyes only for him. Her husband; he would be her husband forever, and her lover and friend, protector and devoted slave, he had said. She smiled and then caught Frau Liebner's eyes on her, the intelligent blue eyes crinkled in thought.

"My family," he said, gazing at each one in turn. His gaze rested on the clutched hands of Adele and the Count Delacroix, and he winked, while his frosty sister flushed a brilliant cerise. He had a smile for Charlotte, a solemn nod for Christoph, who returned it with a respectful bow, and a wink for his aunt Katrina. For Uta he reserved a quick kiss on her lace-covered head. She smacked him away and a titter of nervous laughter broke out.

"My family," he said again, growing grave as he approached the subject of their terrible time. "We have come through a time of horror, and we have all suffered in some way. Most particularly has my sister Gerta suffered. Without our knowledge we had clutched to our breast a serpent, Bartol Liebner, his poison endangering every family member and every family relationship. He was a murderer, a man so foul I cannot believe I never saw what was in his black heart. For that, I feel I owe you all a profound apology. Perhaps if I had asked for help . . . perhaps if I had—"

"Nikolas," Count Delacroix said, interrupting, "do not blame yourself. We all had the opportunity to discover what he was, and even I, his . . . his closest friend—though I shudder to say those words—did not know what he was. His deception was masterful. It is over and he is gone."

Nikolas cleared his throat. "You're right, my old friend. It truly is over now, thanks to the courage of one woman." He held out his hand and gestured to Elizabeth. She joined him and he put his arm around her. Glances were exchanged, she could see, and she suffered an awful case of nerves as she realized what was about to be announced.

"It was not just me," she said, her voice ringing out, defying her nervousness. "Everyone here had a part in solving this terrible situation, and you should all have pride in your strength. And in your uncle and brother, who has been the might that has held you all together over the years."

His gaze was full of love; if anyone had been in doubt, she knew that his expression was revelatory, for love beamed from him, radiating in warm waves. She was already carrying their child; he had told her it was so, and she believed him utterly. She laid one hand over her flat belly.

"But soon," he said, "we will have much to celebrate." He looked down at her, and she knew he meant more than he would reveal to the others yet. He smiled but then looked up and around the room. "For at long last my good friend the Count Delacroix has seen the light and asked my dearest of sisters Adele to accept his hand in marriage."

It was no surprise to anyone, but congratulations were murmured, smiles exchanged, even as the countess ducked her head in embarrassment at being the center of attention.

"And our little Melisande . . ." he said. "Her father is safe and here at Wolfram Castle, where he can recover in peace."

Melisande smiled, tremulously. "Thank you, Count; you will never know . . . I can never thank you . . ." She broke off and looked down at her feet.

"There is nothing to thank. I did what anyone would do." He cleared his throat. "And I . . ." Nikolas paused, gazed down at Elizabeth, and caressed her cheek. "I have found love, and a wife. Elizabeth and I will be marrying within the month. Within the week, if she will allow me to hurry her so."

Joy burst out from all; even Uta sat quietly in her chair and wept, tears rolling down her wrinkled cheeks as the others hooted and shouted out their congratulations. After being toasted and applauded, Elizabeth found a moment for the old woman, crouching by the chair and whispering that she hoped she was happy for them.

"Happy! Oh, my little dear, 'happy' is not the word. It is joy so sharp, it hurts," she said, openly weeping as she pressed one hand to her breast. "You haf gifen back light to dis family."

Elizabeth enfolded her in her embrace and they hugged for long minutes as the noise around them grew quieter. When she looked up, she saw the eyes of all on them. She stood, meeting the smiling gazes with a bright smile of her own.

"But Nikolas, what is the rush?" Frau Liebner said. "Why do you not wait until June, when the flowers will be out and we can decorate the old chapel?"

"Oh, no," he said, holding his arms open for Elizabeth as she went to him. "Oh, no, I don't think we ought to wait," he said, folding her in his embrace and holding her close to his heart.

Elizabeth felt the rumbling of a chuckle deep in his chest as she was held to his heart. "No," she said gleefully, looking up into his eyes. "I don't think we will wait."

Frau Liebner stared at them for a long minute and then burst into guffaws of laughter so loud a servant poked his head in to see if anyone was ill. She winked at Nikolas and said, "Scoundrel! No, I don't think you should wait at all. Oh, yes, a baby," she crowed. "That is what we will have to celebrate this year, after all this time."

Nikolas dipped his head to kiss her lips, and Elizabeth met him halfway, standing on her tiptoes. Their two hearts, separate but with one rhythm, beat a steady pulse. But soon, very soon, there would be a third. Joy filled Elizabeth, and she felt an answering burst of delight from Nikolas. The future beckoned, shimmering with the promise of love and joy eternal.

Turn the page to see a special preview
of Donna Lea Simpson's new novel

Awaiting the Night

Coming soon from Berkley Sensation!

COUNT KAZIMIR Vasilov turned in a circle, eyes wide open but unseeing in the midnight darkness of the great hall, trying to feel Wolfram Castle and all its secrets. He felt known from the moment he approached it that it presented enigmas, dilemmas deeper and more far-reaching than those surrounding the people who inhabited it.

Some mysteries were clear enough to identify. Where in the castle was the chalice Mikhail Davidovich had stolen from the Romanian church in Constanta? How had he hidden it while imprisoned in Brandenburg, before he was released and bought here? Kazimir was sure he had it still. The man was afraid, and that was why he pretended friendship with Count Gavril Roschov, sworn in enmity to Kazimir. But why did Gavril, once long ago his friend, but now his nemesis, seek the chalice?

And the most puzzling question of all . . . was Melisande Davidovich a pawn of her father, or did she have more knowledge than she was revealing?

Melisande Davidovich, even her name was an enchanting combination of the French and Russian sides of her, the mystic and the stoic. Lovely and golden, a honey-colored lady of infinite attraction . . . her voice, speaking English, as was the way in Wolfram Castle, was golden and silky, faintly accented owing to her French birth. She had seemed somehow ground him, it had come to him in waves, that trembling awareness, a perfume of alarm that puzzled and yet attracted him. His immediate fascination with her only heightened, but when he looked into her eyes he saw revulsion mingled with perturbation.

COUNT KAZIMIR Vasilov turned in a circle, eyes wide open but unseeing in the midnight darkness of the great hall, trying to feel Wolfram Castle and all its secrets. He had known from the moment he approached it that it held puzzles, enigmas, dilemmas deeper and more far-reaching than just those surrounding the people who inhabited it.

Some mysteries were clear enough to identify. Where in the castle was the chalice Mikhail Davidovich had stolen from the Romanian church in Constanta? How had he hidden it while imprisoned in Brandenburg, before he was rescued and brought here? Kazimir was sure he had it still; the man was afraid, and that was why he pretended friendship with Count Gavril Roschkov, sworn in enmity to Kazimir. But why did Gavril, once long ago his friend, but now his nemesis, seek the chalice?

And the most puzzling question of all . . . was Melisande Davidovich a pawn of her father, or did she have more knowledge than she was revealing?

Melisande Davidovich; even her name was an entrancing combination of the French and Russian sides of her, the mystic and the stoic. Lovely and golden, a honey-colored lady of infinite attraction . . . her voice, speaking English as was the way in Wolfram Castle, was golden and silky, faintly accented owing to her French birth. She had seemed uneasy around him; it had come to him in waves, that trembling awareness, a perfume of alarm that puzzled and yet attracted him. His immediate fascination with her only heightened, but when he looked into her eyes he saw revulsion mingled with perturbation.

It would not do; he could not allow himself to lose concentration on his purpose, so he stood, emptying his mind of all the detritus of a long day and closed his eyes, spreading his arms wide. Deep in his mind's eye he saw the castle spread out before him like a web, passages and hallways and people scuttling to and fro, and at the heart of it was a woman. He stilled his heart rate, pulling in a long breath and holding it, then releasing it slowly, in a long, controlled sigh that echoed to the upper reaches of the great hall, beyond the gallery. That is where the enigma lay . . . an old woman was at the heart of it, an old woman who knew things that no one else knew.

He opened his eyes and began a slow ascent to the upper floors of the house, down silent corridors and passages, past doors where he could almost feel the inmates sleeping, some peaceful, some restless. Pausing, he put his hand to one door and felt a wave of longing. Ah . . . Melisande Davidovich. This, then, was her room. Her sweetness called to him even now. He could feel her beyond the door, beguiling in her provocative purity. How easy it would be to lose himself to such a lovely heart and mind, for a dark character like his own sought tempering, the ameliorating quality of untarnished virtue. But he had a purpose that was more important than the surge of sexual awareness that even now tingled in his body, the robust evidence of his manhood stirring with cravings not experienced for some time, since he had dedicated himself to another objective.

Besides, he thought, stroking the thick wood door, inserting himself into her innocent vessel would sully her but could not improve him. He was beyond the redemption that could be offered by a good woman.

He pulled himself away and found stairs at the end of the corridor. His objective was higher. Something about this castle puzzled him, but he couldn't put a name to it. It held its own mystery; he could not decide yet if that was his to discover, or whether it was immaterial to his purpose. Another floor up . . . he walked silently down the hall, narrower than the one below, and began to feel he was close. Here was his goal. On this uppermost floor he would find answers to some of his questions.

A room called to him and he put his hand on the handle, pushing down and letting the door swing open. The chamber was dark and silent, but the lone inmate was not sleeping, even in this, the middle of the darkest hour of night.

"You I have been awaiting," she said. "Enter, and shut the door."

"HELP! Help me!"

Melisande fought her way out of the deadly embrace, the hot animal breath fogging her frightened mind, and finally in the dark she sat straight up in her bed, panicked, great heaving breaths wrenching her slight frame. She put one hand over her breast, feeling her heart pound so hard it seemed it would shatter the confines of its cage. The darkness enclosed her, but it was blankets only that had her tangled and confined, and she pushed them aside, flinging her legs over the side of the bed and padding over to the window, throwing open the curtains and hopping up to sit on the thick ledge created by the stone walls of the ancient castle. Midnight, she guessed, had come and gone an hour or more ago.

"Wolves again," she said, into the darkness, encircling her knees with her arms. This time the wolves in her dreams had been fighting over her until both had leapt on her and battled each other over her body, their thick, writhing bodies bruising her with their combat, sharp teeth flashing above her, bloody foam flecking her skin from their snapping, snarling quarrel.

The moon emerged from behind the dark woods beyond the castle, and in the gleaming path of light she saw at first just a movement, and then more forms. Emerging from the shadows were wolves, and Melisande started back in fright, but then, knowing she was safe up in her room in the impregnable Wolfram Castle, she watched, her breath bated, her limbs trembling, her heart pounding.

Two separated themselves from the pack, one slightly smaller than the other, and moved toward the castle, seeking, it seemed, the dull gleaming path of platinum light cast by the full moon. They trotted toward the castle across the frost-encrusted green grass, up the knoll until they were about ten rods distant and then stood, staring up at the castle, directly at her window.

"What do you want?" she whispered, hands on the cold glass. The two turned and headed back to the forest, casting one long, lingering look back before reentering the dark shadows.

Wolves.

This was ridiculous! She leaped down from her perch. She was not going to sleep again, and knowing her father's habits from old, decided he was likely awake, so a visit would do them both good. They could talk uninterrupted. She had questions for him, and would stand no evasions this time.

The castle was dark and still around her, her flickering candle throwing just a pale wavering shimmer before her, but then a noise on the staircase from the fourth floor of the castle made her stop. Who was out this time of night? Who? She flattened herself against a wall and blew out her candle, irrationally afraid. Who could it be?

A bulky shadow slid ahead of its creator down the staircase. The flame in the lamp in the sconce that lit the stairs wavered with the motion of the form passing and threw the big shadow eerily across the wall, but even as the figure descended, emerging from the staircase, Melisande could not make out who it was. Then the man—for such a large figure could only belong to a man—paused.

Melisande held her breath, her back pressed to the wall, her fingers trembling around the warm but extinguished candle. This was idiotic, completely and utterly absurd, and yet she could not move, could not allow herself to just step forward and demand to know who was there.

"Miss Davidovich," a deep voice commanded. "Come out of the shadows, for there is, truly, nothing of which to be alarmed."

"Count Vasilov," she said, forcing herself to step away from the wall, trying to regain her dignity after such a foolish interlude. "What are you doing wandering the halls so late at night? And why were you up on the next floor? Those are family rooms only, you should know. Have you . . . lost your way?"

He was close, and he moved closer, his bulk a blot before the weak light of the lamp sconce, his features in shadow. "Yes, I fear that I have lost my way," he said.

But she was not sure it was truly an answer to her question.

"You had a candle," Vasilov said. "Why did you extinguish it?"

"I was afraid," she said, trying to make out his eyes in the darkness of the hall. Foolishly, she felt if she could just see his eyes she would rest easier. "I was afraid when I heard footsteps, for I wasn't sure who would be about at such an hour."

He reached out one big hand, and she thought for a moment he was going to seize hold of her, but instead he took the candle from her hand and went to the wall sconce, removing the glass—it must have been scorching hot, but he touched it as if it were as cool as ice—relit her candle and returned it to her, with a deep bow. Now she could see his eyes, the irises as black as obsidian but flecked with other colors. His black hair, swept back from his brow, framed a face of strong features that seemed perpetually drawn by some powerful inner torment, even though his expression appeared impassive. She felt his turmoil and though she could sympathize, the turbulence of her own life had been enough. She wanted no part of his suffering, whatever had caused it.

"Good night, Miss Davidovich," he said, and turned away.

"Why . . . what were you . . ." She had questions for him, but he was already gone, toward the guest chamber assigned to him by Christoph. She held the candle up until his dark form disappeared into shadow near the end of the hall, and then she heard the thud of his door closing behind him. Secretive man. What was he doing at the castle? He was an old school friend of Nikolas's, but that did not explain why he stayed, nor did it explain why Christoph allowed it.

Who was Count Kazimir Vasilov? And for that matter, who was Count Gavril Roschkov, whom her father now claimed as a friend? Two Russian counts arriving within hours of each other . . . that could not be mere coincidence, so what did they both want, and why could they not just be open about it? She would demand answers on the morrow, for there were too many secrets, and if there was one thing this family and this castle did not need, it was more secrets.

Also available from
BERKLEY SENSATION

Beloved Stranger
by Patricia Potter
In the second book of her Scottish trilogy, Potter tells
the story of a man who has lost his past and faces an
uncertain present of peril—and an impossible love.
0-425-20742-0

The Kiss
by Elda Minger
After she finds her fiance with another woman, Tess
Sommerville packs up and takes a road trip to Los
Vegas, ready to gamble—on love.
0-425-20681-5

Dead Heat
by Jacey Ford
Three beautiful ex-FBI agents, Aimee, Daphne, and
Raine, have founded a security firm—and their latest
job uncovers a fatal plot against America's top CEOs.
0-425-20461-8

Available wherever books are sold or at penguin.com

Also available from
BERKLEY SENSATION

The Star Witch
by Linda Winstead Jones
From the sultry *Sisters of the Sun* trilogy, the eldest of
three sisters and witches wonders how she can
remain chaste with a sensuous enemy tempting her.

0-425-20128-7

Flesh and Stone
by Vickie Taylor
Ancient garoyles take wing when a woman finds
sanctuary in the arms of a brooding guardian, who is
either the man of her dreams or her worst nightmare.

0-425-20805-9

Lion's Daughter
by Loretta Chase
A fiery noblewoman and arrogant rogue fall prey to
danger and their own desires on a perilous quest for
vengeance.

0-425-20950-9